CW00549862

HIDDEN DEFENDANT

A HARPER ROSS LEGAL THRILLER

RACHEL SINCLAIR

TOBANN PUBLICATIONS

Copyright © 2017 by Rachel Sinclair

All rights reserved.

No part of this book may be reproduced in any form or by any electronic or mechanical means, including information storage and retrieval systems, without written permission from the author, except for the use of brief quotations in a book review.

❀ Created with Vellum

CHAPTER
ONE

OH, God. My Uncle Jack was arrested for murder. *Out of the fire, into the frying pan.* But this one was personal.

Uncle Jack was my favorite of my mother's brothers. Unfortunately, it seemed that mental illness seemed to run in my mother's family, as my Uncle Patrick struggled with bi-polar disorder for many years, and Jack had always struggled with alcoholism and he recently was diagnosed with schizophrenia. The schizophrenia was latent, as he only started to show the signs of the disorder after he lost his beloved wife, Mary, five years before.

Just because Uncle Jack was accused of murder, however, didn't mean that he did it just because he was suffering from schizophrenia. Schizophrenics were generally no more violent than anybody else in society. I had always thought, and my therapists had confirmed this, that a mental disorder didn't make you violent, *per se.* You had to also have violent genes to go along with your mental illness, or have some other factor in your makeup that would make you violent. Just having bi-polar disorder or schizophrenia didn't necessarily make you a murderer.

I didn't know. What I did know was that I would have to race down to the county jail and see him. I just knew that he was feeling lost and alone and abandoned. I couldn't stand to think of somebody that I loved so much going through that.

I called Sophia. "Sophia," I said, "can you come and watch the girls? I have to get to the county jail as soon as possible. I, uh, have a new client who needs to see me."

"I'll be there as soon as I can," she said.

"Mom," Abby said, coming up to me. She was such a little empath. She could always tell what I was feeling and she usually had just the right things to say to comfort me. I didn't know how she was so wise at the tender age of 12, but I was grateful she was. "What's wrong?"

I tousled her hair and grimaced. "Nothing, Buttercup. I know it's late." I glanced at the clock, which read 9:30 PM. "But Sophia will come and watch the two of you. In the meantime, it's time for bed for the both of you."

Rina rolled her eyes. "I don't want to go to bed. It's Friday night, mom. All the other kids are staying up. Their parents let all my friends stay up past 11 on the weekends. I want to play some interactive video games with some of my friends on-line. Can I do that, please? Pretty please?"

I didn't have time to negotiate or argue with her. "Okay," I said, frantically looking for my car keys. "You can stay up until 11 playing games with your friends on-line. But no later than that." I felt my head start to swim as I went from one room to the next, looking for my elusive car keys. "Where are those damned things?"

A knot in my stomach was forming and I felt sick. Absolutely sick. I hadn't felt this sick since the days before Michael Reynolds' trial, when I constantly felt like throwing up. Making sure Michael fried for the murder of Judge Sanders was the most important thing in the world to me. I couldn't think of anything more important. Now that he was behind bars, where he would stay for the rest of his natural life, I was feeling slightly better about things.

Now this.

My mother called again. "Where are you, Harper? I'm down here at the jail, and they're not letting me see him. They've told me visiting hours are over. He needs to see you, Harper. He needs to see you now."

I sighed. "Mom, you've always hated what I do. You've always nagged me about representing criminals. Now do you see why everybody needs defending? Now do you understand?"

I could hear her crying hysterically on the phone. "Just get down here," she said. "Get down here as soon as you can."

I was being pulled in 20 different directions, none of them good. I had my mother crying hysterically, my girls looking at me like I had grown another head, my car keys were missing, and my beloved Uncle Jack was behind bars, waiting for his arraignment on a murder charge.

I closed my eyes, willing myself to concentrate. Just concentrate. Just think about something, focus on it, and let my brain calm itself. I stared at my umbrella stand, and then closed my eyes again. *Focus. Focus. Focus.*

I snapped my fingers and ran into my room, where I found my car keys sitting on my dresser. I kissed them and ran back downstairs. Sophia was waiting for me with a smile on her face.

"Thanks Sophia, you're a doll," I said. "You know the drill. Rina will be upstairs playing video games on-line with her friends. Abby will be in her room, reading a book, I think. Just make sure it's lights-out at 11. I'm really sorry for the late notice, but-"

Tears came to my eyes and I shook my head.

"What's wrong, Harper?" Sophia asked me as she put her arm around my shoulders.

I shook my head some more as I thought about my Uncle Jack. He was three years younger than my mother, and he and Patrick were her only brothers. Since Patrick had moved to Florida, however, Jack was her only close relative. And my mom and Jack were *very* close. He was also very close with me. He used to take me camping in the Smoky Mountains and I'd always get to go to the beach with him in South Carolina. My family never had a ton of money, and Uncle Jack was reasonably wealthy, so the only times I got to go on vacation was when I went with him.

"Nothing," I said. "I just need to see about a new case I picked up. I know it's late on a Friday night, but I need to see my new client. Thanks again for coming on such short notice."

She nodded, looking at me worriedly. "I'm always here when you need me," she said. "You know I have no life." She smiled.

I nodded back, unable to speak. I was afraid that if I opened my mouth, anything that came out would be an unintelligible mess. "Love you," I said, taking my jacket and walking out the door.

To my dismay, I felt the rain pelting down on my shoulders the second I walked off of my covered porch. I immediately went back in and grabbed an umbrella and hurried to my driveway to get into my car.

As I drove along, the sounds of my windshield wipers gave me a certain degree of comfort. There was something about the steady rhythm of the wipers that calmed me considerably. Even though I was about to be in the middle of an absolute horror, I knew that, no matter what, if I kept my wits about me, I could help Uncle Jack beat this. I could. I knew that. I could feel it.

I'd won impossible cases before. Not that Uncle Jack's case was impossible, exactly, but, even if the facts were bad, I could find a way around it. I could. I had to. That was the only answer. I had to figure this out. No matter the facts, I had to figure it out.

I saw on my console that my brother Brad was calling. "Hey Brad," I said, answering. "I'm on my way."

"Good."

"How's mom?"

"How do you think?" He said. "She's hysterical. She's been crying since she found out about Uncle Jack being arrested. She found out he'd been arrested about a half-hour ago when he called her from jail. I guess she was his one phone call."

I groaned. "Why didn't he call me first? Why call mom? I don't get that. He should've called me from the station. If he confessed to something without getting counsel, then I'm going to have to kill him myself." I shook my head. That was one thing that didn't make sense. He knew I was an attorney. I should have been the first person he called.

"Preaching to the choir, sis," Brad said. "That's what I told Mom. I asked her why Jack called her before he called you and she just said that she had no idea why."

I gripped the wheel as I sped down Main Street towards Down-town. Friday night was a night for party-goers, especially in the West-port District of town, which was right on my way to the County Jail. I saw the girls walking along the sidewalk in their micro-mini skirts and I felt slightly jealous. There was a time, before my Freshman year rape, when I was as carefree as those girls. That all ended that night in the Sigma Chi fraternity house. I never got to really enjoy college because of that.

That was finally okay, though, because Michael Reynolds, my rapist, was finally where he belonged – behind bars. I'd made sure he was convicted for murdering a Federal Court judge, Judge Robert Sanders, and that was the most satisfying thing I'd ever done. Seeing his face when that jury pronounced him guilty was my proudest moment. It was an even prouder moment than all the times I got a not guilty verdict for one of my clients, sad to say.

But I knew that if I could possibly get my Uncle Jack off of his murder charge, then *that* moment would be my new proudest moment. Of that, there was no doubt.

"Whatever," I said to Brad as I made my way downtown and saw the jail coming into view. "Listen, I gotta run. I see the jail, and I know Mom is there, sobbing hysterically, so I better get a move on getting in there. I'll see you in a bit when I get to the jail, so we can talk about what's going on. I need to get an assessment."

"Talk later," he said.

I stepped out of the car and put my umbrella up. The rain was now coming down harder than ever, each droplet seeming to land on me like an anvil. It was April, so I knew that this rain would be one of many. I felt the chill go along with it, so I wrapped my coat around me tighter.

I went into the jail where I saw my mother sitting in the waiting area. She had a cup of coffee in her hand, and she looked anxious.

She came up to me and gave me a big hug. "Thank God you're finally here," she said.

I nodded. "Where's Dad?"

She shrugged. "I didn't want to wake up him up," she said softly.

I furrowed my brows, thinking that was odd. "Okay," I said. "But don't you think he should be here?"

"He should be, but he's not."

That was weird, but I let it go. "Well, I better go up and see him," I said. "Let me find out what bloc he's in."

At that, I went up to the dispatcher and asked her where Uncle Jack was. "I need to see Jack Calhoun," I said to the lady, whose name was apparently Sheila.

She looked at her computer. "Bloc nine, pod three," she said, giving me my pass.

"Thanks."

I went over to Mom, who was sobbing. I then saw Brad coming out to the waiting room with some more coffee, one of which he handed to our hysterical mother. "Thanks for coming," he said.

"A great way to spend your Friday night, huh?" I asked him.

"Yeah. I got a sitter and everything for Haley, because it's a date night for Cecile and me. Best laid plans, I guess."

"As always." I gave him a quick hug and then went to the metal door that would lead me to the blocs of cells, one of which held my Uncle Jack.

As I got on the elevator, my mind wandered to the camping trip we took when I was nine. This was way before he started showing signs of schizophrenia. He was diagnosed relatively late in life, at age 51. His wife Mary was killed in a car accident that year, and, about a year after she died, Jack started to hear voices. He stopped showering and started to get very depressed, which worried all of us. He was never institutionalized like my Uncle Patrick was for his bi-polar disorder, but he got bad for awhile. He was trying to manage his symptoms the best he could, but I knew it was always a struggle.

My heart pounded as I got to Jack's bloc and then went into the waiting area for the inmates. I went through the metal doors, first one, which opened with a giant clang, and then the next.

"Who are you here to see?" one of the guards asked from behind the glass window.

"Jack Calhoun," I said.

The guard nodded. "He'll be out in a few minutes," she said. "You know the drill, of course. Just have a seat."

"Thanks."

I sighed and put my head on the metal table. *Jack, Jack, Jack, Jack.* I knew he was having a rough time lately. He was a partner in a large law firm, and he was fired and removed because he was causing problems there. At first, he showed the early signs of schizophrenia, but they were subtle. He would be extremely irritable and would shout and cuss out his secretary. He had never acted that way before. Everybody just assumed it was all a part of the grieving process, but, in fact, it proved to be early signs of what was to come.

As I waited for him to come out, I read the statement of information I picked up from my mother. Apparently Jack was arrested in a rectory. Father Kennedy, the pastor at a Catholic Church called Guardian Angels Parish in the Westport area, was the victim. When Officers Brown and Maddox arrived at the scene, acting on an anonymous tip that Father Kennedy might be in danger, they found my Uncle Jack laying on a couch in the living room, a bloody hunting knife in his hand. Father Kennedy was laying on the floor, having been stabbed in the heart. Uncle Jack was unconscious at the scene, but came to in the squad car on the way over to the station. He was disoriented in that squad car, but he didn't tell the officers much.

And he didn't confess. Thank God. That was one good thing. One less thing to overcome.

Nevertheless, the facts looked bad. I shook my head. Poor, poor Jack.

I looked up and saw him shuffling slowly out of the metal door that led to the pod. His wrists were shackled and he looked like an absolute mess. His grey hair, which was cut in a slightly hipsterish shaggy way, was going in every direction. He was always lean, but it looked as if he'd lost about twenty pounds since the last time I saw him, which was just last Thanksgiving. His head was drooping, and, when I looked into his eyes, I saw that his expression looked almost blank.

That said, when he saw me, he lit up. "June bug," he said softly. "Thank you for coming."

"Of course, Uncle Jack," I said. "Of course, I came. I'd come even if it was in the middle of the night."

"I know you would. You always were my little June bug."

I smiled. I loved that nickname, actually. He called me June bug because my birthday was June 20. "Tell me what happened."

He shook his head. "I don't know what happened, actually. I don't know." He sighed. "I might have killed him. I just don't know."

Then he started to cry. "Oh, June bug," he said. "I don't really know what happened. I don't know. All I know was that I was in that rectory. The rectory. They found me in there, in the confession booth and I was passed out. And apparently, I had a knife in my hand. A knife, June bug. A bloody knife. I really didn't know what happened. I didn't even know how I got there. I don't know, June bug. I don't know. I don't remember going into that rectory, and I woke up in the squad car on the way over to the police station, completely disoriented."

I got out my legal pad. I would have to figure this out, without putting too much emotion into it. I couldn't think of this as being my Uncle Jack. The man who took me camping and fishing and boating when I was growing up. He was just another client. He had to be.

He went on. "He was a priest. His name was Father Kennedy. He was a priest. He's not now. He's…dead now." He hung his head. "Dead. And I guess I killed him."

I stood up. "Uncle Jack, you'll have to be more clear than this. I know, I understand you've had your issues with…illness…but I need to get some straight answers from you. I need to do that, Uncle Jack, if we're going to beat this."

He shook his head, his grey hair hanging in his eyes. "Can we beat this? Do you think that we can?"

"Of course," I said, although I stated those words much more confidently than how I really felt. "We can beat this. I can beat almost anything. I've taken some really difficult cases and I've managed to pull a rabbit out of a hat almost every time. I can do this here, too, Uncle Jack. I can. But you have to be straight with me."

"I *am* being straight with you," he said. "I'm telling you I don't remember even going to that rectory. I don't remember it. All I know was that I was in that confessional, and then the police were there as well. They took me in and they booked me and I ended up here." He looked at his hands, which were clasped in front of him. "I'm here, June bug."

I decided to try a different tack. "Uncle Jack," I said. "Let me ask you this. Do you have blackouts?"

"I do," he said with a defeated sigh. "Ever since your Aunt Mary died, I've had blackouts. I haven't told anybody about this, though. My family. Your mother. Patrick. I've told nobody about the blackouts."

"Why haven't you told anyone?"

"Because. I mean, I've been hearing voices, so everybody in the family already thinks I'm completely crazy. I didn't want everybody to know I was also blacking out. I didn't want you guys to know. I've always been so together. I was a partner in one of the largest law firms in this city. I was making six figures a year. It's been so embarrassing. So embarrassing to go from having the world at my feet to barely functioning."

"But you've been functioning fine lately," I said. "Haven't you?"

He shook his head. "No. I haven't. Your mother has been wonderful. She's been the one who always took me to the doctor and tried to make sure I was taking my meds on time. I took my Stelazine just like the doctor ordered, but it didn't make the voices go away. And that med made me feel dull. Apathetic. I didn't have any kind of emotions, none at all, and that was…not living. That wasn't a life. So I stopped taking that medicine, even though I told your mother I continued on with it. I was hearing voices no matter what I did, so I figured I might as well not take the drugs that were supposed to stop them. I've felt much better after stopping that drug."

"But Uncle Jack, you seemed fine this Thanksgiving."

He looked at me, his brows furrowed. "I'm sorry?"

"This past Thanksgiving. You came over, we played a lot of games, you were cracking jokes just like old times. You seemed yourself."

He nodded his head. "June bug, I don't understand what you're telling me."

I tried to tamp down the impatience I was feeling right at that moment. I dealt with games from my clients all the time. I certainly didn't want to deal with games from my own uncle. "Uncle Jack, I don't know why you're questioning me. You were with us on Thanksgiving. Last Thanksgiving. You were back to the man I've always known and loved. You were. You were great. And now you're looking at me like I've magically grown another head, right in front of your eyes."

"That's because I don't know what you're talking about, June bug. I really don't."

I sighed. "Uncle Jack, you'll have to cooperate with me. You just have to. You'll have to stop making me feel like I'm going insane. If you don't, then we'll to lose. We'll lose, Uncle Jack."

He hung his head. "Please tell me what you're talking about."

I counted to 10. All at once, I wanted to leave. I needed to get out of there. I'd see Uncle Jack for his arraignment the next day. I could hopefully get him a bond reduction of some sort. I had no idea how much of a bond he had on him, but I was sure it was high. This was apparently a first-degree murder of a priest. I doubted his bond would be below a million dollars.

I sighed. I couldn't allow him to stay in jail for any period of time. After seeing him this way, I knew he couldn't survive much jail time. He was obviously having some kind of…break. A break, that was the only thing I could think of when I looked at him. A psychotic break.

"Uncle Jack, what is your current bond amount?"

He shrugged. "I think it's a million five. I'm not sure. You'll have to check and see about that."

"Okay." I took a deep breath. "I own my house outright. I'll take out a mortgage. I can probably get about $400,000 for that. Tomorrow, I'll try to convince the judge to reduce your bond to 10%, as opposed to you coming up with all that cash, which would mean you'd only need $150,000 cash to get out of jail. I can put that up for you. But if that judge won't reduce it, do you have assets you could liquidate? Anything at all?"

He had tears in his eyes. "You'd take out a mortgage on your home just to help me? Really June bug?"

"Yes, really. You're family. That isn't even a question. It shouldn't be a question, anyhow. Of course I'll help you. I can't just let you rot in jail."

"I'm going to rot in jail," he said. "Because I deserve it. I killed that man. I don't know why I killed him, but I did. I must have. I had to have killed him, Harper."

"Why do you believe you killed him? You just said you didn't remember killing him. That you blacked out and had no idea how you got to the rectory. You said that. Now you're saying you killed him. Why, Uncle Jack? Why are you changing your story?"

I had to admit, I was getting whiplash just talking to him. He was so incoherent and contradictory. I wondered if he was doped up. He certainly could've been. "Uncle Jack, are you on any kind of prescription drugs right now? Or any street drugs?"

He shook his head. "I've never taken street drugs, June Bug. And I'm not on any prescription drugs right now, either. I told you, I quit taking my schizophrenia drugs because I didn't like the way they made me feel. Why won't you believe me?"

"Well, you're not making a ton of sense. Maybe I should go home and come back when you're more coherent." I hated to leave him, but I felt like I was spinning my wheels, so I started to get really frustrated. I didn't want to take out my frustrations on my beloved Uncle, though, so I really wanted to leave.

He sighed. "I know I'm not making sense. I know that. I don't even make much sense to myself anymore." His voice went down to a whisper. "All I know is I still hear a voice. I don't know what he wants or why he wants it. I just don't know. But I know that it certainly looks like I killed Father Kennedy. It certainly looks that way."

I put my pen down and looked at my Uncle. He looked like the Uncle I had always known and loved, even though he was wearing an orange jumpsuit and his hands were shackled. He had grey hair, where before, when I was growing up, his hair was jet black. But his eyes were still as blue, his smile was just the same. I was looking at him and trying to figure out who he was, though. He looked the same, but he wasn't the man I grew up with at all.

I finally sighed. "Uncle Jack, I hate to do this, but I really have to leave. My head is throbbing, and, well, I need to get home. I feel like I'm not getting anywhere. I'm feeling really confused. I'm so sorry."

He said nothing, but just nodded his head. "I know. I know, Harper. I know. I haven't been right for a long time. Ever since Mary died, I haven't been right. I've tried, though. You know how I've tried. I want my life back. I've been wanting my life back ever since that accident. But I just can't seem to get it back. I can't. It seems like every time I try to get it back, something happens. Like at work, when I got fired from the law firm. That was humiliating, but I knew why they did it. I knew why. And now this."

He shook his head. "I just don't know what to think. Where to turn. All I know is that things were normal for a long time. I had it all. But things haven't been normal for at least the past five years. I wonder if they'll ever be normal again."

I looked at him, feeling my heart being ripped out as I thought about my beloved uncle having to go back to his tiny cell.

I stood up, and so did he, and he put his hand-cuffed arms around me and hugged me the best he could. I put my head on his chest and I felt the tears start to come. This wasn't the man I knew. It wasn't him. He was somebody else. A stranger.

I looked over at the guard's station, and they were watching us closely. I nodded to them to silently communicate that I was okay. I knew what they were thinking – this kind of close contact between an attorney and an inmate usually only meant one thing – the attorney was in trouble.

"Okay, Uncle Jack," I said. "I'll see you soon. Your arraignment is Monday morning. I'm sorry we can't get you out before then, but I need to see about getting your bond reduced. Do you have a place to stay? I can see if you can come and live with me. I can make that the conditions of your bond."

He shook his head. "I can't put you out like that. But thank you, though."

"Well, I guess that's probably for the best. I mean, you're not putting me out, but I have my girls at home. I don't know if the judge would take too kindly if I requested you stay with us."

Jack's face lit up when I mentioned my girls. "Oh, Harper, that's great. That's great. You have children now? I didn't know you adopted. I hope I have a chance to meet them soon."

I cocked my head and sat back down. "Uncle Jack, you met them. Thanksgiving. They were the twins. Rina pretty much talked the whole way through dinner, and Abby was the quiet one. Don't you remember?"

He shook his head. "I wasn't there with you on Thanksgiving, June Bug."

I felt tears come to my eyes and I realized my Uncle was suffering from some kind of major memory loss. Perhaps he was suffering from early-onset Alzheimer's? I knew something about that, and knew that early onset versions of diseases, such as Alzheimer's, tended to be much more aggressive than the latent versions.

I looked at him and saw him bow his head.

And then he looked up and smiled at me.

"He's gone," he said. "Just for now. But I wanted to tell you that he didn't kill that priest. I didn't, either. We're being framed, honey. I'm telling you, we're being framed. I don't know who killed him, but it wasn't us. Unless there's somebody else involved. That could be." He shook his head. "Anyhow, I wouldn't have killed Father Kennedy. I loved him. I was in love with him. He was going to leave the priesthood to be with me. He was."

I wrote down what he was telling me. "Uncle Jack, again, you're not making any sense."

He put his hand to his cheek and waved it. "Honey, I've been hiding this from you and from everybody. If people knew about me, Jack would have to go away somewhere and live behind closed doors. He wouldn't be able to get out of the nut house, and neither would I. You don't know how scared that makes me. So, I haven't told anybody about my existence. But you have to know about me now."

I shook my head, once again feeling completely confused.

"Uncle Jack, I don't understand."

Uncle Jack took a deep breath. "My name isn't Jack, doll. It's Mick."

CHAPTER
TWO

"JACK," I said. "I really am not understanding what you're saying. What do you mean your name is not Jack, it's Mick? I'm looking at you, and you look exactly like my Uncle Jack. In fact, just a few minutes ago, you were Jack. I don't understand."

Jack rolled his eyes. "Doll, let me tell you something. Jack hasn't been Jack, exactly, since your Aunt Mary died. You remember when she died, don't you?"

I nodded my head.

"Well, Mary represented something to him. She wasn't just his wife, you know. She was something else to him. She saved him when he was a young boy."

She saved him. I didn't quite know what Jack was talking about. I couldn't quite figure out why Jack kept referring to himself in the third person.

It was then that I noticed a few things. His posture was different than it was a second ago. He was leaning down on the table, and he had his right leg crossed over his left. I also noticed his voice was slightly different. It was higher pitched than it was previously.

He was also squinting.

He shook his head. "Oh, crap. My glasses. I forgot my glasses in my cell. I can barely see you, doll. But I remembered what you looked like at Thanksgiving. You really have blossomed into a beautiful young woman."

I started to feel even more gaslit. "Uncle Jack, you just said you don't remember coming to see us on Thanksgiving. Or don't you remember telling me that?"

He started to laugh. "You don't get it. Let me spell it out for you. My name is Mick. Jack doesn't know about me, so don't tell him I exist. Jack doesn't remember the murder, and I don't either, but I can tell you that I think that we didn't kill him."

I stood up. "Uncle Jack, you're scaring me. I really need to leave."

Jack rolled his eyes. "Fine, girly. Fine. You just go ahead and leave. But you won't be guaranteed to talk to me if you leave and come back. You might just be talking to him, and he's clueless, doll. Clueless. He doesn't know anything that I know about this. But go ahead. Go right ahead and leave. I wouldn't leave, though, if you want to know some hard truths about what happened to Father Kennedy." He waved his hand in the air. "I mean, he's called Father Kennedy, but I just called him Kelly. Or sweet buns, when I was in a really good mood."

I shook my head. "Guard, could you please let me out?" I turned and looked at my uncle, who was looking away and shaking his head. "Uncle Jack, I'll see you at your arraignment on Monday. Actually, it's an initial appearance. Nothing happens there, exactly, except that you're read your charges and given a new court date. I can reduce your bond there, though."

"Please do," Jack said. "The food they serve in this place is awful. I need a sushi fix like you wouldn't believe."

"Since when do you like sushi? We went to a sushi restaurant a few years ago, and you ordered Tempura. You said you couldn't stand uncooked fish. Or fish in general."

"I love sushi. It's my favorite thing in the world. And, trust me, they don't serve sushi in here. Oh, they serve things that are slimy and undercooked, and it might bear a passing resemblance to actual food, but sushi?" He shook his head. "Not a chance. So please try to get me out of here. If I don't get my hands on some unagi, I'm going to die."

"Um, okay, Uncle Jack. I'll…do what I can. I'll do what I can to make sure your bond is reduced."

"Ta ta," he said, saving his shackled hand in the air towards me. "I'll be seeing you Monday, I guess. Unless I don't. I can't always get out every time I want to. I hope you know that, doll. Of course, ever since Father Kennedy, I mean Kelly, was found dead, I've been allowed to come out much more, so chances are good I'll be seeing you on Monday after all."

I nodded my head and faced the double doors. One door opened, and then the next, and I was out in the hallway.

What the hell just happened in there? Jack had been strange these past few years, ever since he lost his wife. There was no denying that.

But he had never quite been this strange.

I got home, and the girls were already in bed. It was past midnight, and, after I changed into my pajamas, I crawled into my own bed and closed my eyes.

I thought about the night I had with Uncle Jack and my mother. My mother was still crying her eyes out in the waiting room. Brad had already gone home. I didn't know what to tell her, so I just said next to nothing.

"He has a court date on Monday," I said to her. "And we'll know more then."

"Monday. You mean he has to be in that place until Monday?"

"That's what I'm saying, Mom. He needs a bond reduction before he can get out of there, and only the judge can do that for him. I don't think he has a million five in cash. He might have that much in assets, but he would have to give us power of attorney to sell everything for him. That'll be a lot of rigamarole."

She started to wring her hands as she rapidly shook her head. "You have to do something, Harper. He can't be in there for too long. He's very sensitive. He's always been so sensitive."

"Uncle Jack, sensitive? I don't understand. I've never considered him to be sensitive."

"Oh, he has always been sensitive. You just never knew him when he was a young boy. He always cried whenever our daddy had to kill a bug in the house. He would bawl his eyes out when he would see dead animals on the road. He always talked about how the animal had a mommy and a daddy who were going to be very sad because their baby was killed. He just can't stand killing things or seeing things dead."

I sighed. "Well, I guess I can use that information when I try his case. 'Your honor, my Uncle could not have killed Father Kennedy. He literally would never hurt a fly.' Wasn't that what the crazy guy in that movie *Psycho* said? He wouldn't hurt a fly?"

"What's that supposed to mean?" mom asked. "Are you implying that Jack is crazy like the man in *Psycho*?"

"No, Mom, that's not what I'm saying. I'm just trying to make conversation, that's all." I was in the waiting room with her, getting ready to leave, and all I could think of was how I couldn't wait to get home. I loved my mother dearly, but she drove me up a tree most of the time. She and I just didn't relate that well. She didn't approve of my job, she was always bugging me to get married and give her grand-children, yet she didn't consider Rina and Abby to be her grand-children.

I guessed she only wanted biologically related grandchildren.

We both got to our cars and I gave her a quick hug goodbye. "I'll see you Sunday," I said. I had dinner with her every Sunday, as did Emma and Brad and Albany. My other brother, Jason, lived in New York City, so I saw him only rarely.

"Sunday. And then on Monday, you get Jack's bond reduced and you get him out of that cell. He can't survive in there, Harper. I don't think you know how sensitive he is."

"I know, mom. You just told me about his sensitivity." I gave her another hug. "I love you, mom. I'll see you Sunday."

CHAPTER
THREE

I TOSSED and turned in bed, hoping I wasn't in yet another manic phase. The medicine they used on me, Geodon, was working, so far, to even out my mood swings. I was grateful for that, but I also knew taking meds for mental illness was hit and miss.

What was up with all that nonsense he was spouting? Pretending he was somebody else and referring to himself in the third person? And he suddenly acted so weird. I mean, he needed glasses? Since when did he wear glasses? And his voice changed suddenly. He said he didn't remember coming for Thanksgiving, and then he turned around and told me he saw me on Thanksgiving. I mean, what the hell is going on?

Since I couldn't sleep, I went into the kitchen, made hot milk, and watched a movie.

I made some hot cocoa, sat in my big leather recliner, and turned on the television. One of my favorite channels was TCM – Turner Classic Movies. That was the channel that showed old movies. Some movies were from the 1930s and 1940s, others were more recent, but none seemed to be made any more recently than the 1970s. I was partial to any movies starring Katharine Hepburn or Cary Grant, and if a movie starred both, like *The Philadelphia Story,* I would definitely watch it.

I chuckled as I saw the movie playing, right at that moment, was *Psycho.* Speak of the Devil. I was just talking about that show to my mother. I clicked it on and saw the movie was part of a theme that night. *The Three Faces of Eve* was the movie that came after *Psycho,* and I knew both movies involved some kind of mental illness.

I popped some popcorn and sat down to watch the movie. I knew the ending, and, in the back of my mind, I knew I was watching this movie for a purpose.

As I watched the movie, I thought about Uncle Jack. About how he was acting. Not that Norman Bates was acting like Uncle Jack, or, rather, that Uncle Jack was acting like Norman Bates. But...

The ending came, and the twist was that Norman Bates was also his mother. That his mother was dead and had been dead for many years. Norman's " arguments " with his mother weren't arguments between two people. They were simply arguments between Norman and Norman playing his mother.

It wasn't until 3 AM, when the next movie, *The Three Faces of Eve,* came on, that I got the picture. This movie dealt with a young Southern housewife with multiple personalities. There was Eve White, the main person; Eve Black, Eve White's alternative personality; and Jane, another of Eve White's alternative personalities. They were all distinct. Eve White was meek, mousy, and insecure. Eve Black was fun-loving, sexy and free-spirited. Jane was calm, confident, and assured. Eve White had a disturbing break when she was a small child and was forced to kiss her dead grandmother in her coffin.

I thought about that movie and how it contradicted what I knew about people with alternative personalities. I knew something about dissociative identity disorder, which was what Eve White suffered from, and DID was caused by repetitive abuse and torture, usually suffered in childhood. As I understood, the main person would create alters because the alters would have the strength to take the abuse, whereas the main person didn't. I, therefore, thought it was silly that Eve White would suffer from DID just because she kissed her dead grandmother.

I closed my eyes, seeing, yet not wanting to see, the connection between Eve White and Jack. It was inescapable. Jack seemed to suffer from some kind of dissociative identity disorder. I never even considered that to be a possibility. I mean, Jack...

Jack, what? What? I'd known him my entire life, but then again, perhaps there were things I didn't know about him. My grandparents were loving but flaky. My mother would always say that about them. My grandfather was eccentric – he never knew how to fix a car or anything around the house, but he knew about every sci-fi movie ever made, and he knew his way around classical musicians and composers. My grandmother was loving, kind, and hilarious.

I couldn't imagine either of them repeatedly abusing Jack or anybody else. Then again, sometimes abuse is well-hidden. Perhaps Mom would know what, if anything, happened to Jack when he was a kid. She would know if anything happened to him that would cause him to dissociate.

I also wondered if DID could be latent. Aside from what I'd learned about the disorder from the movies and books I read, I knew little about it. *Sybil* was a great example of a book I'd read as a kid. She had about 30 different personalities, which were brought on by years of severe physical abuse at the hands of her insane mother.

Since I still wasn't tired, I logged onto the computer and quickly read what I could about the disorder. The web page about DID showed it could be latent. Sometimes the disorder doesn't manifest until a major event in the person's life caused so much stress that the alters would make themselves known for the first time in the person's life.

That made sense to me. Jack said he hadn't felt normal for the past five years. His wife, Mary, was killed in a car accident five years ago. That was when he showed the symptoms of what everybody assumed was schizophrenia, but might've actually been the cracks of DID peeking through.

As I read further, I realized hearing voices was one of the main symptoms of DID. The voices the person heard were those of the alternative personalities struggling to communicate. Jack had been hearing voices ever since Mary died. He was still hearing them. Perhaps it wasn't an auditory hallucination, at least not a classic one that is a hallmark of schizophrenia. Perhaps it was simply Jack's alternative personality coming through. His alternative personality talking to him.

Mick. That was the name of his alternative personality. Mick. Mick was homosexual and in love with Father Kennedy. Mick had poor eyesight. Mick was with us on Thanksgiving, leaving Jack behind.

Was Mick murderous? Was Jack? Were there other alters inside of Jack who were? And what happened to Jack that he would dissociate like this?

I looked at the clock, realizing it was presently 6 AM. I had stayed up all night watching these movies and obsessing about Jack. This worried me because I needed to take better care of myself. Besides taking my meds, I needed to ensure I ate and slept properly. Staying up all night could make my brain chemicals go haywire again, and I couldn't have that.

I went to bed and tried to sleep. I tried very hard but tossed and turned and tried to get comfortable, but I just couldn't. My mind was too wired. Too many questions were bouncing around in my brain about Jack, and I hadn't even thought about his case. I was just thinking about him. About whether he really had alters, or perhaps he was faking it because he wanted me to get a "not guilty by reason of insanity" or "NGRI" plea. Or maybe he thought I could have him declared incompetent to stand trial.

Surely he wouldn't do that to me. But then again, people do drastic things when staring at the possibility of spending the rest of their lives behind bars. Either way, you're going to end up confined. But I had to admit that being in a psychiatric facility had to be infinitely better than prison. So maybe Jack was faking a mental illness to end up in a psychiatric facility and not prison.

My mind wandered as I tapped my pencil on the desk and stared at my computer screen. It wandered to Jack and Mick, and it wandered to Father Kennedy. I would have to start my investigatory process on this case sooner rather than later. I had to at least entertain the possibility that Jack had a mental illness at the time of the murder, such that he didn't know the nature of his acts and didn't know it was wrong. Therefore, I'd have to get a psychiatrist for Jack immediately. Maybe the psychiatrist could explain if Jack was legally insane at the time of the killing and if Jack could even stand trial.

But first things first.

I would have to talk to my mother.

CHAPTER
FOUR

"OKAY, HARPER," my mother said when I barged over to her house that morning. "I'll tell you what you need to know about my brother."

Rina and Abby were home with Sophia because I needed to speak with my mother alone. This was bound to be a heavy topic that would shed light on Uncle Jack and what I needed to do with his case. If anybody knew whether Jack had such strong and glaring issues that he needed to plead not guilty by reason of insanity, it would be my mother.

"Thanks for letting me come over and ask you these questions," I said. "They're going to be hard for me to ask and probably harder for you to answer, I'd imagine."

She nodded. "I wish you'd do something with that hair," she said. "Harper, you look like a fright right now. Have you tried that Brazilian blowout? It costs a lot of money, but it's worth it. It's such a shame you got the really curly hair."

I bit my lower lip and counted to ten. "Mom, I told you, I like my curly hair. It's very me. It's who I am. I have hair that frizzes in the humidity. Hair that never wants to behave. But that's not why I'm here, Mom. I'm not here for a lecture about my hair. I'm here because I need you to tell me about Uncle Jack."

She looked away, towards the front porch, and then back at me. She had a necklace on, and her right hand went to it. She stroked it while she looked down at the ground. "What, what, what..." She got up and went into the kitchen. "Would you like a cup of tea, dear?"

"No, Mom. No cup of tea. I need you to talk to me about Uncle Jack."

"What would you like to know?" Her voice sounded forced, like she was consciously trying to sound cheerful when, in reality, she was feeling anything but. "What would you like to know?"

Mom was acting strangely, too. I wondered if she had gone outer limits. *Was everybody in this family crazy?* "Uncle Jack was acting weird the other night when I saw him in jail."

"Weird?" Mom's voice shot up several octaves. "What do you mean, weird? I guess I don't know what you're talking about. You know he's been struggling with schizophrenia, and he's been taking medicine for it. You know that."

"I know that," I said. "I realize that. Or maybe I don't realize that. Maybe I don't realize much of anything anymore. What I do realize, however, is that you're stalling and hiding. You're nagging me about my hair. You're making yourself some tea. It won't be long before you tell me about how I need to eat more and how I need to marry Axel soon and bring you grandchildren. I'll never know why Rina and Abby won't suffice for grandchildren, but I'll tell you this – Rina and Abby will be my *only* children, so you might as well know that right now."

Now *I* was the one who was getting off-topic. Mom had a way of keeping me off-balance. At the moment, she was hiding, just as much as Jack hid that he had a Mick inside of him, just dying to get out.

"Dear," Mom said. "I don't want to talk about Jack right now."

"You can't do this," I said. "You can't just declare Uncle Jack off-limits. He's been arrested for murder, or did you already forget about that? He's been arrested for murder, Mom, and he could die with a needle in his arm if we don't figure this out together. And if he doesn't die with a needle in his arm, he could spend the rest of his life in prison. I don't think that he could survive that. Maybe Mick could, though."

"Who's Mick?" Mom asked, a slight smile splashing across her face.

I raised my eyebrow. "Why do I think you know exactly who Mick is?"

She shook her head and said nothing.

I could tell she was lying. She was a terrible liar, just terrible. She was even worse than me, and I could never lie about anything. My face and body language would always betray me. "Mom, you need to come clean with me. You know who Mick is. I think you know why Mick is around. Somehow, you know everything, and you've kept it from me all this time. Well, Mom, the time is now for you to tell me everything. I'm Jack's lawyer, so I need to know everything. Everything, Mom. Everything."

She shook her head. "You shouldn't put this kind of pressure on me, Harper. You know how my angina flares up when I'm under pressure." She fingered her necklace some more as she stared off into space. Her eyes didn't meet mine.

"Mom, I know you don't want to talk about this. I know you don't. I realize that. But this is Jack's life on the line here. I can't properly give him a good defense if I don't have all the information I need."

She sighed. "The Calhouns never talk about these things. We don't. We don't talk about…family issues. Family tragedies. We pretend they didn't happen, and everybody just goes their way. That's how we do it, Harper. That's how our family stayed together after…"

I was finally getting somewhere. "After what, Mom? After what?"

She shook her head. "I need to make us some lunch," she said, her voice getting high-pitched again. "I bought that wonderful prime rib roast. Very tender and juicy. Let me make you a sandwich, dear."

"Mom, I don't want a sandwich." I actually wanted a sandwich, but I wanted her to focus on what I was trying to ask her. I had to get her to quit stalling, somehow, someway.

"Well, I can't talk about serious issues on an empty stomach. That prime rib is calling my name. Don't you hear it, Harper? It's calling my name. 'Claire. Claire.'" She nodded her head and smiled. "You can't deny the prime rib roast. When it calls out to you, answer it."

I sighed as I saw my mother enter the kitchen to pull out the roast. She tossed it on the counter, on top of a cutting board, and cut into it. I saw the meat was slightly bloody, very pink on the inside, and brown on the outside. My mouth watered as I watched my mother carve up the meat. "Mom," I said weakly. "Oh, okay, make me a sandwich. How can I argue with prime rib? But we need to talk about Jack. We need to discuss him as soon as lunch is over. Or maybe talk about him over lunch. Either way, we need to talk about him. I need to know about his mental health."

Mom continued to cut into the meat. She sliced it thin, piled it on a plate, then got out four slices of rye bread and carefully put the roast rib meat on the plate. "How do you like your sandwich?" she asked gaily.

"I would like my sandwich with pickles and red cabbage with a dab of horseradish sauce."

I watched her as she piled the roast beef up on my two slices of bread, then put the pickles and red cabbage on it. She slathered an enormous amount of horseradish sauce on the meat, and I cringed. "I know you said you wanted just a little of the horseradish sauce, but Harper, I think you need to live a little. Indulge yourself just a little. You're too skinny. I think you need more horseradish sauce in your life."

"Mom, it's not that I'm watching my weight. It's just that..." I shook my head. Mom had a point. I only requested minimal sauce on my sandwich because I didn't want the extra calories. She always had a way of seeing right through my ulterior motives.

"It's just that what?"

"Nothing. Keep on slathering on the horsey sauce, Mom."

She made the two sandwiches, and we ate on her covered porch. "Now, Mom," I said, "you're not getting out of this. You need to talk to me about Uncle Jack. He's acting very peculiarly, Mom. Very peculiarly." I didn't want to tell her my suspicions that Uncle Jack had Dissociative Identity Disorder. If I knew my mother, she wouldn't believe me even if I told her about that. I didn't even believe it, really.

She sighed. "Some iced tea, dear?" she asked me, picking up her pitcher.

"Sure." I didn't like to drink a lot of caffeine – it weirded me out. But I wanted to be polite. I figured that the more polite I was with my mother, the more likely I could get *something* out of her. And that was all I wanted – for her to tell me something to chew on.

She swallowed and looked down at her sandwich and iced tea. Then she sighed. "Okay. You think Jack is acting peculiarly. I know he is. I know it." She shook her head. "He was only 11 when it happened. Only 11." Then she started to cry. "And he couldn't have survived all those years after without the protection and care of Eli."

I nodded. "Who is Eli?"

She sighed. "Let me just back up a little. Jack, while he was walking to school one day, vanished. Just vanished." She started to cry. "My mother was frantic, my dad was beside himself, everyone was going crazy. Just crazy. Everyone in the neighborhood teamed up to look for him. There were posters everywhere. His face was everywhere on those little weeklies, like they do. Even now, I cry when I look at those weeklies and see the missing people. You know those bios they put in the little newspapers you get – date missing, date of birth, picture, age regression. You know what I'm talking about."

I nodded, feeling stunned my mom was telling me this. Uncle Jack was abducted? And who was Eli?

"Well," Mom said. "He was gone for two years. For two years, Harper. For two years, my mother cried every single day. She would go into his room, pick up his little shirts, baseball hat, and uniform, and bawl. My father just withdrew. He was a hands-on father before this all happened. He took us camping, fishing, boating, and all of that. He played baseball with Jack and took us to games. He was just a typical father, but after Jack was taken, he was…void. Lost. He came home from work and went into the den to watch television every evening, and he never said a word to any of us."

I felt my own tears as my mother told her story about Jack and how he went missing.

"Then, one day, he was back. Just back on our doorstep. Only it wasn't him. It was somebody else. He called himself Eli. He told us Jack was gone for good and that we needed to get used to the name Eli because that would be the only name Jack would answer to from then on."

I tried to muffle a sob, but I couldn't. The tears came, and I hung my head while my mother put her arm around me and put my head on her shoulder. Just like when I was a little girl. "Who was Eli?"

"Oh, Eli was tough. Really tough. He went out and got tattoos the second he got home. He demanded our mother take him to get tattoos, and she did. She did anything he asked. She was that happy to have him home. Eli was a chain smoker who smoked marijuana and even did harder drugs. Cocaine. Heroine. Meth. My mother knew about it all and let him do whatever he wanted, just as long as he stayed home. She was terrified about letting him out of her sight. She said she would rather he did drugs at home than go out on the street to do them."

I raised an eyebrow. Uncle Jack, a druggie? And who was Eli? Was that yet another alter?

"So, what happened? And how did Eli get free from wherever he was?"

She shook her head. "A child rapist held him hostage. A pervert who lived on our street before moving a few miles away. I got the story from Eli. Eli acted like he didn't even care he was with this guy. The pervert's name was Steven Heaney. He kidnapped little boys and girls, raped them and murdered them. The only way that Jack could get out of there, the only way that Jack could survive this guy, was that he agreed to help this Steven Heaney find the victims. Eli explained he would wear a disguise and find these young girls and boys for Steven." She shook her head. "He was used as bait for others."

"Why didn't he just leave? Find a police officer and tell him what was going on? I mean, this Steven Heaney guy let him leave the house, right?"

"Yes. I asked Eli this. Why didn't you just leave? And Eli said Steven told him if he left and found a police officer that..." She shook her head. "I don't know. It made little sense to me, but Eli told me he wanted to protect Steven. He thought of Steven as a friend and didn't want to see him go to prison. I knew then that Jack had some serious issues. He was Eli, not Jack, and he only showed up at our house because Steven had died in the house of a heart attack. If not for that, Jack would never have come home."

I nodded my head. Sounded like a classic case of "Stockholm Syndrome," where the kidnapping victim bonds with the kidnapper for various reasons. I would have to look into that more. "Who was Mary? I know Mary was Uncle Jack's wife, but she was somebody to him during this time. Who was she to Jack? What did she do for him?"

"Mary literally saved him. She was the one who brought Jack back." Mom hung her head and sighed. "Mary was Steven's last victim. Steven would have killed her if he didn't die first. At least, that was what Eli told me. She was in the hospital for a year after she got out of that hellhole. A psychiatric hospital. She refused to speak. The doctors said she was catatonic. She was somewhere inside of herself, but she was having problems coming out. She was that traumatized."

"Okay. So how did Jack get in touch with her?"

"Eli was in the hospital at the same time. He was in there because he broke his leg when a car hit him while he crossed the street. After he was up and walking, he walked around the hospital grounds for exercise and saw her. She came up to him and spoke her first words in over a year, and somehow, she brought Jack back. Eli was gone. Jack was back."

"How did that happen?"

"Jack's therapist told me Jack was suffering from Dissociative Identity Disorder and that Eli was Jack's protector when he was with Steven. Eli was tough and strong and could withstand the abuse, whereas Jack was just a young boy. Eli was much older, much tougher, had been through it all, and could take anything that Steven dished out. At least that's what Jack's therapist, Dr. Tom, told me about Jack when he finally returned. I don't know. I don't understand that. I still don't understand it. And somehow, someway, when he saw Mary, Jack came out. Only later did I find out exactly what it was about Mary that brought Jack back out and made Eli disappear."

I was piecing everything together. Why Jack was normal all those years, and why he "relapsed." I didn't know Jack had dissociated years ago. I knew nothing about Eli. I certainly knew nothing about this Steven Heaney incident.

"What was it about Mary that brought Jack back?"

"Well, apparently, Mary and Jack bonded while Steven held them. Mary was there for a month, and they stayed in the same room. He was Jack when he was with her in that room because Mary made him feel safe. He didn't feel safe otherwise while being held by Steven, so that was why Eli was around and not Jack. But Mary made Jack feel safe, so he was Jack when he was with her, and when Mary wasn't around him, he became Eli again."

I nodded my head and drank some of my tea. I didn't know how any of this was significant to Jack's murder case or if it even was. But my mother gave me a road map on why Uncle Jack suffered from DID. It was apparently necessary to create a tough older alter to take the abuse the kidnapper dished out, and since Mary was tender and loving with Uncle Jack, he could push Eli aside to be with her.

"So, Jack went into remission? Eli disappeared when Mary came back into the picture?"

"Yes. That's what happened. He had a spontaneous remission, and Eli went dormant. At least, that was what Jack's therapist told me. And Jack could live a normal life. He didn't even remember being held hostage by Steven and what Steven did to him. He couldn't remember any of that. He didn't even remember meeting Mary and staying with Mary in that bedroom. He didn't know who Mary was when he saw her in the hospital, but he told me later that she gave him a strong feeling that he knew her and was in love with her. And Mary was the same. She didn't remember him, either, but she had the same strong feeling for him."

"Okay. So, what happened, then? I mean, he got therapy, of course. Did the psychologist bring any of that out for him? What had happened to him? Did Dr. Tom hypnotize him or anything to bring out what had happened?"

"No. Dr. Tom said doing that would be more damaging to Jack. You have to understand that Jack lived a normal life. He really did. He wasn't haunted or depressed or anxious or any of that. Eli was the one who had the memories of being held by Steven, not Jack. Jack was slightly bothered because he had lost all that time – he couldn't remember at all two years of his life. But that was the only thing wrong with him. He finished school, played football, and was popular with all the girls. He and Mary married right out of high school, went to the same college, and lived their lives. Everything was just fine for Jack."

"Until Mary was killed."

"Right. When Mary was killed, Jack relapsed. Eli was back, and so was this guy named Mick. Mick is a homosexual, I guess." She shook her head. "To each his own, but I'm surprised Jack would create somebody who was gay."

"I don't think Jack has a choice in that, Mom. I don't think Jack said, 'I think I'll create a gay alter today.' It probably just happens."

"Well, I guess. Jack started seeing his therapist again after having blackouts and hearing voices. He gave me permission to talk to his therapist. His therapist told me that Jack created Mick, and Mick was probably always with Jack during the abuse. It made sense to have an alter who enjoyed gay sex because that was what Steven did to him. He was raping him, but by creating this Mick character, a promiscuous gay man, Jack could endure what Steven was doing to him."

I nodded. "That makes sense, Mom." I was stunned, absolutely stunned, to hear all of this about my uncle. I had no clue about any of it. I was a little upset that my mom had lied to me about Jack's condition by telling me that Jack had schizophrenia, which was why he was hearing voices and suffering from depression and the other symptoms he showed. I knew why she lied, though. She obviously didn't want to tell me everything she just told me.

She nodded her head and put her hand on mine. "So, Harper, that's why I'm so protective of him. Why I've always been so protective of him. He's my baby brother. And he's in trouble. You have to save him, Harper. You have to. If you don't, then Jack will be gone forever. Eli will probably just come out and be out for good if Jack ends up in prison and-" She sobbed and rapidly shook her head. "And if that happens, Harper, then I'll have lost him again. Nobody ever thought Jack would come back after Eli appeared. We despaired he would come back. His therapist told us that Eli might be the person we might always have and that we were to call him Eli, not Jack, and realize that Eli was a completely different person than Jack. When Jack came back, it was like a miracle."

Mom put her hands up towards the ceiling and smiled. "A miracle, Harper. And now he's in trouble. I can't lose him, Harper. Not again. Not this way. You have to figure out something to save him."

I closed my eyes, wondering how to figure any of this out. Of course, I still needed to dig into the case itself. I'd just seen Jack and talked to him. Now my mother had cleared up what was going on with him. Yet, I hadn't had the chance to really look at the police report, go to the crime scene, interview the witnesses, or any of that. The case was just beginning.

There was one thing I was fairly certain of, though – I'd have to find a way to acquit my uncle. Not try to get a plea for Not Guilty by Reason of Insanity. No. I'd have to go balls to the wall and try for a full acquittal. An NGRI plea would just result in my Uncle Jack going to a criminal facility for the mentally insane for the rest of his life. As Mom said, this would no doubt bring Eli out for good, as Eli was apparently the alter that protected Jack from bad things. Going to a mental institution for the rest of his life, with no chance at all to come out, would certainly be a "bad thing."

I realized then that I was crying. The tears were streaming down my face, and I let out a sob. "Poor Uncle Jack. I didn't know any of this. I mean, he was so normal when we were growing up. So normal. I didn't think there was anything wrong at all."

She nodded. "That's because only Eli has the memories of that house of horrors. Only Eli knew what was going on during that time. Jack had no clue and still doesn't know what happened." She sighed. "I know, Harper, that I've gotten on you over the years about what you do for a living."

She shook her head. "But I've never told you why your chosen profession has always upset me. Now you know. You defend people like that scum Steven. I know you do. If he was your client, you would do all you could for him, even though you would know what he did to young girls and boys. Sickos like him need to just be locked up and have the key thrown away, or, better yet, they should be treated like criminals were treated in Russia – after the trial was over, if the person got the death penalty, they would just take the prisoner out back and shoot them right then and there. No years of appeals. Just a guilty finding and bang!"

She had a sick point. At least for guys like Steven, a sicko who would always be a sicko and a pervert and a murderer, there shouldn't be any plea bargaining. Guys like him deserve the death penalty. In my mind, they were the only ones that really did, however. And that was because guys like Steven were unredeemable. They couldn't possibly live amongst us in society. They were predators, and that's all they were.

"I don't defend guys like Steven," I said. "I don't defend serial killers."

"You defend all kinds of scum just like him," Mom said accusingly. "You defend drug dealers and murderers and rapists."

"I don't defend rapists," I said. "Nor anybody even accused of rape." Mom didn't know my story about my rape, and I wasn't planning to tell her. That was finished, anyhow. Michael was behind bars, where he would remain for the rest of his life. That was all that mattered. "But I defend drug dealers and killers. I do. I also defend the innocent. Like Heather. Like Uncle Jack. Those are the cases that keep me going. Those are the cases that make everything else worthwhile. I'm going to get Uncle Jack off of this murder. I'm going to do it if I have to die trying."

She smiled, perhaps for the first time in the day. "Don't die trying, Harper. Just please, please, please help him. Make sure he doesn't spend a day in prison. Get him out of that jail, please, Harper. His bond is a million-five. We don't have that. Please figure out a way that he can have a bond reduction. Do this for him. He's gone through so much in his life. He can't go through much more. It's not fair."

No, it wasn't fair. It wasn't fair for him to spend two years of his life in the clutches of a sicko perverted serial killer. It certainly wasn't fair for him to spend the rest of his life behind bars.

I would have to figure out this case.

And I would have to figure it out soon.

CHAPTER
FIVE

THE FIRST THING I would have to do, of course, was to find out all I could about this disorder, and that would start with speaking with Jack's therapist who treated him right after he got out of Steven Heaney's house of horrors. I had Jack sign a waiver to speak with him and made an appointment that day. He said he could slot me between his therapy sessions, which he ordinarily wouldn't do, but he knew how urgent my request was, so he made an exception.

Dr. Wheeler's office was in the Menorah Hospital on the edge of Leawood, right by the Town Center on 119th Street. It was a typical doctor's office suite, with a receptionist behind a window and soft music in the waiting room.

"Dr. Wheeler will be right with you," Hannah, the receptionist, said.

And, sure enough, he was. He was tall, about 6'3", with a bald head and glasses. He had a kindly smile, and his grip was strong when he shook my hand. I immediately felt comfortable.

"Ms. Ross," he said. "Come right on in. I'll be glad to answer any questions."

"Thank you," I said, following him back to his office. I went in and sat on his red plush couch and put my hands in front of me. "Thank you for seeing me on such short notice."

"Well, of course," he said. "I knew I wanted to help when you explained what you needed. I saw the news about the murder of Father Kennedy in the paper and saw that Jack Calhoun was arrested, and I..." He shook his head. "It's a tragic situation." He cleared his throat. "But I assume you have a waiver signed by Mr. Calhoun so we can speak freely?"

"I do." I gave Dr. Wheeler the waiver that Jack signed before a notary. "Here it is."

Dr. Wheeler examined the waiver and handed it back to me. "Thank you," he said. "That's all I need from you. Now, where would you like to begin?"

"How did Jack come to you?"

"Well, I know you know I wasn't speaking with Jack. His name was legally Jack Calhoun, but he was going by Eli. Eli was the person I met and the person I treated."

"Right," I said. "I guess I need to back up. Was this the first case of Dissociative Identity Disorder you've seen and treated?"

"No," he said. "I admit, though, that DID is an extremely rare phenomenon. Extremely rare. I have worked with three other patients with this disorder, but two came after I saw Mr. Calhoun. Understand, I was only 30 years old when Jack came to me. I've been practicing for 43 years since I first saw Jack, and I've only come across two other cases in all that time."

"How did you know Jack wasn't faking his having DID, or how did you do a differential diagnosis?"

"Well, I ruled out schizophrenia or mania based on the symptoms. With other disorders of the mind, no distinct personalities present themselves. We must observe a very strict protocol with DID to determine whether the patient has the disorder. We must observe several criteria before we can make a proper diagnosis. Mr. Calhoun presented with every one of those criteria."

"What are the criteria?"

"Well, the first criterion is self-evident - two or more distinct personalities must exist. And by distinct, I mean that each personality has a separate and distinct way of looking at the world and will have different behaviors. Each personality perceives the world differently and relates to their environment and self differently. Many times, the different personalities have different names. Sometimes, they have different speech patterns and dialects. Sometimes a personality is a different gender from the individual – a man might present with a female personality, for instance. But they all have different consciousness and might have different memories."

I nodded my head. "And the next criterion you must use to assess this disorder?"

"The patient must have experienced amnesia. Gaps in their recall of everyday events and traumatic events. I spoke with Eli most of the time, but occasionally, I could speak with Jack. And he told me he had experienced prolonged periods he could not recall. He told me he couldn't recall the prior two years of his life. I understood this was because Eli and Mick had taken up that time."

"The third criterion was that the amnesia must distress the person, which was certainly true with Jack. He was panicked that he couldn't remember the prior two years of his life, and as he recounted this, he changed back into Eli immediately. So, I gathered Eli was formed to protect Jack from extreme psychological torment."

"Okay," I said. "And what are some of the other elements of this diagnosis?"

"The fourth criterion is that the disturbance is not a part of a normal cultural or religious practices. For instance, a child might have an imaginary friend, which is not evidence of this disorder, and there are some cultural and religious practices where multiplicity is a common phenomenon. So, we must rule this factor out."

"The fifth criterion is that the disorder is not because of something physiological like substance abuse or seizures."

I nodded my head. "And Jack met all these criteria."

"Yes," Dr. Wheeler said. "He did."

"What did Eli tell you about why Jack dissociated?"

"Good question," Dr. Wheeler said. "He explained how Jack was abducted by Steven Heaney and suffered through profound abuse for two years. He told me that Jack was an extremely weak child who would never have survived the trauma he endured if Eli hadn't taken over. That's commonly how DID occurs – through trauma. Severe abuse is typically the root cause of this disorder because the alters in the patient's psyche are formed to protect the patient. These alters might be tough and strong, whereas the patient is weak and vulnerable. That's why the psyche fractures in this way. The mind cannot tolerate abuse, so it creates personalities that can tolerate it. Personalities are formed that will protect the patient. That is what happened with Mr. Calhoun."

"How long did you treat him?"

"I treated him for two years. He went into spontaneous remission when he broke his leg and met up with a girl he met at Steven Heaney's home. Her name was Mary, from what I understand, and the alters went dormant from the moment he met up with Mary. I treated him for another year after he and Mary were reunited, but I soon concluded that, while Jack's personalities were not integrated, so he was not cured, the alters were in dormancy. I also concluded that Jack had no memories of being abducted and held by Steven Heaney. Because of this, I determined Jack could most likely live a normal life."

I nodded my head. "He did, you know. He lived a normal life. Until now."

"Yes, until now." Dr. Wheeler shook his head. "It broke my heart to see that he was arrested for the murder of Father Kennedy. I hope this isn't true. I would hate to see Mr. Calhoun suffer behind bars after all he went through in that house with Mr. Heaney."

"Is it unusual for there to be a spontaneous remission from DID like Jack had?"

"Unusual, yes, but not unheard of. And, as I noted, this was not a remission in that the personalities were integrated. It was a remission in that the other personalities were dormant for many years. A true remission would result in integration, where the alters are not dormant but are integrated with the patient's personality. With true remission, there would not be any alternative personalities but just one personality. Just one self. That occurring – the spontaneous integration – is exceedingly rare. But what happened to Mr. Calhoun, where the other personalities went dormant spontaneously, is less rare."

We spoke for another hour, and I felt satisfied I'd found out as much as possible about Jack's disorder.

Now that I had this knowledge, I would have to figure out what to do with it.

CHAPTER
SIX

I GOT HOME that night and saw Axel with the girls. They had dinner ready and waiting for me – takeout Chinese. I smiled when I saw them. "You guys," I said. "You didn't have to do all this."

"Oh, we have to do this, Mom, we do," Rina said.

Axel put his arm around me and kissed me on the cheek. "We're a little worried about you. We know this case with your Uncle Jack is very personal. So, we did something nice for you – make it so you don't have to worry about cooking dinner. We got this."

"Thanks," I said to him as Abby and Rina came up and wrapped their skinny little arms around my waist. "I don't know what I would do without you guys. Probably curl into a ball and die."

We ate our Chinese while Rina did her usual gabbing, and Abby sat quietly eating. I was worried about my little Buttercup. She never had the gift of the gab like her sister did, but she usually said a few things at the dinner table. Tonight, however, she just quietly picked at her food, stabbing it with a chopstick slowly. The orange chicken went into her mouth one by one while she stared blankly into space.

I sighed. I would have to figure out what was wrong with Abby. There clearly was something amiss with her. I made a mental note to spend some alone time with her and find out what was happening.

It turned out I didn't have to worry about that. Rina already announced what was going on with Abby. "Abby's really quiet, Mom, tonight because she's sad." Then she lowered her voice into a whisper as if Abby couldn't hear what she was saying. "James broke up with her. He's already moved on to another girl named Emmaline. Abby didn't know about it until she got to school, and he was there with Emmaline. He apparently went out with Emmaline this past weekend when Abby was trying to call him and find out if he wanted to hang out." Rina shook her head. "The scum."

At that, Abby got up from the table without a word, tears in her eyes. She ran upstairs to her room and slammed the door.

Axel nodded. "You need to talk to her, mate," he said. "She needs her mother right now."

"Yes," I said. "I guess she does."

I went up to Abby's room and knocked gently on the door. "Abby, Buttercup," I said. "Can I come in?"

"No, go away. I don't want to talk about it."

"Okay. I'll just be downstairs, then. You know where to find me."

I turned to walk away, but Abby opened her door and lay on her bed. I heard loud sobbing, and it broke my heart.

"Abby," I said, going over to the bed and putting my arm around her. "Do you want to talk about it?"

"No." She shook her head. "I want my mom."

"I *am* your mom."

"No. My real mom. I want to talk to her and I can't. I can't tell her about this. She never got to see me get my first boyfriend. She should've been the one who took me and James around. She should be the one who I can cry to. I love you and think of you as my current mom, but I should have her around. I should. It's not fair."

My heart was breaking as I listened to her. She was right, of course. I was her adoptive mom but would never be her biological mom. I could never be that for her. That was just something I would have to face. Abby would have to come to terms with that. Rina too. Rina, thus far, had said nothing like this – that she wanted her real mom there instead of me. But I knew that was coming. A girl needs her mother during periods like this – when you get your first broken heart. When you have your first kiss. First date. When you go away to college.

When you get married. There were just milestones that a girl needed her mother for.

"I know, Buttercup. I know." I continued to stroke her back while she cried. "You'll get through this. You will. It will get better. I promise you this. There will come a day when you forget all about James. James will be a distant memory when you fall in love for real one day. It hurts like the dickens right now, though. I know that."

She nodded her head into her pillow. "Thanks, Mom, for coming in here. And I hope you're not sad that I talked like that. That I talked about how I needed my birth mom."

"Not at all. I don't know how you feel, but I can imagine it. I love you, Buttercup. Never forget that."

"I love you, too."

I went downstairs and saw Rina and Axel playing a board game on the floor. I sat down next to them. "Is she okay?" Rina asked me.

"Yes. I mean, no. But she will be."

"What about Uncle Jack?" she asked. "Will he be okay?"

I bit my lower lip. I didn't want to talk to Rina about that. I knew she was just too young to hear about such things. She wouldn't understand that Jack wasn't really Jack anymore. That Jack wasn't actually Jack at Thanksgiving, which was the day Rina met him. How could I explain to her the concept of Dissociative Identity Disorder? How could she possibly understand such things? I knew Axel would understand. He was a detective. He knew everything and had seen it all.

"He's going to be okay," I said. "At least, I think he is."

Later on, after Rina went to bed, I went into the sunroom and joined Axel on the couch. He put his arm around me. "So, what's going on, mate?" he asked me. "What's going on with your Uncle Jack?"

I pulled a blanket over us and leaned against his chest. I heard his heart beating, and I felt the warmth of his skin. Feeling his love radiate was comforting. There was nowhere else I'd rather have been than right there with him.

"He has issues," I said. "To say the very least. Poor Jack. He's gone through so much." I shook my head. "So much."

"What has he gone through?"

"I can't even tell you about that. But I need to win this case. Full stop. I need to win it. If I don't win it, then Uncle Jack will literally disappear. As it is, he's hidden behind somebody else. Behind several somebody elses maybe."

Axel furrowed his brow. "I don't understand? What do you mean by that?"

"Jack has Dissociative Identity Disorder."

Axel nodded his head. "I've heard of that. I haven't encountered it, though. That's very rare, isn't it?"

"I think so. I need to do much more research on it."

"So, what you're saying is that your Uncle Jack might have been somebody else when he killed that priest? Assuming he killed that priest?"

"Yes. I think so. But I would like to think that Jack didn't kill that priest. If he didn't kill that priest, there is a chance for a full acquittal. But if he killed that priest, even if he was somebody else at that moment, he'll end up either in prison or in a psychiatric institute for the rest of his life. I can't stand that happening. I love my Uncle Jack."

He kissed my forehead, and I kissed him on the lips. "I love you," he said. "And I'll always be here for you. I hope you know that."

"I do. I know that."

We went upstairs, with him carrying me to my room. Being with Axel made me feel normal for the first time in a long time.

And being normal, at this point, was the best thing in the entire world.

CHAPTER
SEVEN

MONDAY MORNING, I showed up in court. I had seen Uncle Jack in jail on Sunday, and he was the same way he was before. That is, he was apparently Mick, not Jack. He had the same posture, the same cadence of how he spoke. I found out more about Mick, including the fact that he didn't wear glasses on Thanksgiving because he had on contact lenses.

"Love," he said. "Of course, I won't wear glasses. I look nerdy in them. But I'm surprised you didn't realize I wasn't Jack at Thanksgiving. I guess you're not very observant."

"I guess I'm not."

When I got to court, I saw the prosecutor there. Her name was Sarah Pitts, and I knew she wouldn't be the permanent prosecutor on the case. In the Jackson County courts, one prosecutor showed up for all the initial appearances on that docket, but that prosecutor rarely saw the case through trial.

I went over to her. "What offer do you have for Jack Calhoun?" I asked her.

She went through her files and shook her head. "I don't have an offer for you yet," she said. "I know he's your uncle, but you must understand. This was a violent, violent murder. It looks like he did it, too." She put her hand on my shoulder. "I'm so sorry, Harper. I know how you must feel."

No, she didn't know how I felt. She couldn't possibly know how I felt. Unless she had an uncle who she looked up to, who never appeared to have a thing wrong, only to find out that said uncle was suffering from Dissociative Identity Disorder that was brought on by being kidnapped by a serial killer in his youth and then finding out said uncle was accused of a brutal murder of which he had no recollection – then, maybe, she would understand how I felt.

"Well, I need to ask for a bond reduction."

"Of course you do. But I doubt that you'll get it. A million-five is standard for these kinds of first-degree murder cases."

"I know that. I realize that. But he's hardly a flight risk. I'll keep an eye out for him. He can live with my mother. She's right over there," I said, pointing to Mom in the audience. She smiled and waved at Sarah and me. "She'll tell the judge he can stay with her. All I want is a 10% bond. That's all I'm asking for."

"I know what you're asking for," she said. "But I'm telling you, you won't get it."

"All rise," the bailiff said as everybody in the courtroom stood up. "Court for the 32nd Division of Jackson County is now in session. God save the State of Missouri and this Honorable Court."

The judge came on the bench. Judge McFarland was white-haired and was probably 90 by now. Yet, he still played tennis almost every day and took long walks. He insisted he was fit as a fiddle, and even though people had been trying to get him to retire for the past decade, he always insisted he never would. He would say he would die on that bench, and nobody would convince him otherwise.

I admired him greatly.

He started calling the cases, one by one, and then he got to Uncle Jack's case. "The State of Missouri calls Jack Calhoun," he said.

My uncle came up to the bench, his wrists shackled. I looked into his eyes and realized that he was probably Mick right at that moment. His expression was one of levity. His blue eyes twinkled, his lips curled in a slight smirk, and he winked at me when he came up to the bench. "Don't worry, love," he whispered. "I got this taken care of. Daddy will be alright."

I groaned, but for some odd reason, I was happy. Mick seemed happy-go-lucky, whereas Jack, my uncle, seemed depressed and down. If Jack had to spend the time before his trial in jail, he might as well do it with an alter who could actually take the punishment.

"Mr. Calhoun, you have been charged by the State of Missouri with one count of murder in the first degree. How do you plead?"

"Not guilty, your honor." Jack's voice was high-pitched, and his posture was ramrod straight. He raised an eyebrow and smiled at me.

"Your honor," I said to Judge McFarland. "I would like to request a bond reduction. I would request that Mr. Calhoun's bond be reduced to 10%."

"On what grounds are you requesting this?" Judge McFarland asked me.

"He has no priors. He's not a flight risk. He can stay with his sister, who is my mother. She's right over there if you want to speak with her, your honor." I pointed into the audience, where my mother was sitting, smiling and waving.

"Oh, I see. This gentleman is your uncle. Do I have that straight, Ms. Ross?"

"You do, your honor. He is my uncle."

He nodded his head. "Do you have any objections, Ms. Pitts?" Judge McFarland asked Sarah.

"I do, your honor. This was an especially heinous crime, and there is no reason for the bond reduction."

Judge McFarland looked over at my mother. "Ms. Ross, please ask your mother to approach the bench."

I felt my heart soar as I went over to my mother. This judge would at least entertain the possibility that my uncle could post a 10% bond so he could get out of jail for the duration of his pre-trial. "Mom, the judge wants to speak with you."

Mom stood up, gathered her purse, and eagerly walked through the little door that led to the restricted area, and she went right up to the bench. "Yes, your honor?" she asked. "My daughter, Ms. Ross, said you wanted to speak with me."

Judge McFarland nodded to her as he continued reading the State-ment of Information in front of him. "Yes. As I understand, you're the sister of this defendant. Is that correct?"

"Well, yes, he's my brother. Yes, he is."

"And you're willing to take custody of him as he awaits trial?"

"Yes. I am your honor. He's my little brother. I've always looked out for him, no matter what. Always. And I'm not about to stop now."

Judge McFarland smiled broadly. "That's a good spirit you have there. Now, is there any reason you would believe that you would be a proper custodian of Mr. Calhoun? You understand that Mr. Calhoun will have special conditions for his bond, which you must meet. I hope you understand that."

"What conditions?"

"He will have on an ankle monitor, so his movements will be restricted. He won't be able to leave your house for any period except if he needs to get to court or any special court-ordered visits. And, of course, he cannot have any contact with known felons or Guardian Angels church. He cannot contact anyone who is a part of that church. Do you go to that church, Ms.-"

Judge McFarland looked at me. "I'm so sorry, Ms. Ross, I didn't get your mother's name."

"It's Claire Ross," she said with a little giggle.

I rolled my eyes. What was it with Mom? She was looking at the judge with her eyes batting. Almost like she was flirting with him. A 90-year-old man. And what was up with her and Dad?

"Ms. Ross, do you attend that church regularly?"

"No, your honor, I don't. I don't attend any church regularly. My brother doesn't, either. I don't know what he was doing in that church when he was apprehended. I don't think even he knows."

I stepped on her foot. She was saying way too much. I hadn't yet decided if I wanted Uncle Jack to have a mental examination because I didn't know if I wanted to go the NGRI route. I knew I didn't want my uncle to be examined and have it determined he wasn't competent to stand trial. If that happened, he'd have to spend his time in a mental institution until he would be competent for trial, and who knew when that would be? He might never be competent for trial. Ever.

I didn't know if I was doing the right thing. I knew my affection for my uncle clouded my decisions. I hoped I was doing the right thing, though. That was all I could hope for.

The judge shook his head. "Ms. Ross, do you plan on mounting any special defense for this gentleman? Do I need to order a mental examination?"

"No, your honor," I said. "I do not plan on introducing a special defense. I do not plan to ask for a mental examination to determine if my client is competent for trial. No, your honor, I don't."

"Then why did Ms. Ross say that Mr. Calhoun didn't know what he was doing in that church when apprehended? It sounds like a mental examination is necessary to me."

I silently cursed my mother. "She simply means that the defendant, Mr. Calhoun, rarely attends church, so he didn't know why he would be in there. She didn't mean he doesn't remember going in there or anything like that."

"But Ms. Ross, the police report states he told the police he had no recollection of going into that church," Judge McFarland said, looking carefully at the police report. "I think I should order a mental examination, just to be safe."

I groaned. That was the last thing I wanted. The last thing. The only thing I could've hoped for was that my uncle could fake being sane enough to go to trial. But I wondered if I would be pressured to try for an NGRI plea, even if I didn't want that.

"Thank you, your honor," was all I thought to say.

"Okay. Here's what I'll do. I'll order the defendant's bond to be one million five hundred thousand, 10%. The conditions of the bond will be that the defendant remains in custody with Mrs. Claire Ross, that he is fitted with an ankle monitor, that he not leave the premises of Mrs. Ross' home, except for court-ordered appearances, that he not have any contact with any known felons, and that he submit to a mental examination as soon as possible. It is so ordered." He banged the gavel and called his next case.

"That's good, right?" Uncle Jack whispered. "That's good."

"I guess," I said as we walked back to the jury box, where my uncle sat back down. "I guess it's good. I don't know yet. I don't know if it's good that you've been ordered to have a mental examination. We'll have to see if that turns out good."

"Oh, I'm not even talking about that, doll. Don't worry. I'll act as sane as rain. I'll make sure I'm talking to the doc, not Jack, and we'll all get through that with flying colors. But I'm talking about my staying with your mother before trial. That's a good thing, isn't it?"

"Yes. It *is* a good thing. That means you don't have to stay behind bars."

"Oh, good. Good. I can't stand this hideous uniform they make us wear, and the food in jail isn't fit for a dog. I didn't even feed my dog, Toby, food like that. But I met a cute guy in there." He smiled and winked. "So there's that."

"Well, that's lovely," I said, not thinking about anything else I could say. "Um, okay, then."

He smiled and laughed as the guard led him out. "I'll be seeing you later, doll. I guess you'll pick me up, won't you?"

"I will."

I shook my head as he was led away, and then I turned and saw my mother. She was looking bright and happy. She waved her fist in the air as if saying, "Good going," and then she turned and walked out of the courtroom. I closely followed her.

"You did a remarkable job in there, Harper," she said. "Just remarkable."

I sighed. "I guess. I don't know how we'll get around this, though, Mother. I don't know. Neither Jack nor Mick seem to know what happened to Father Kennedy. Neither personality seems to know how Jack got there in the first place. That means there must've been some other alter who walked into that church. Some other alter who knows what happened in there. Do you think Eli came back into the picture? If so, how do we bring him out?"

She shrugged. "I don't know, I guess. But wouldn't Mick know about it, even if it was a different alter? I don't know. I've spoken with therapists about this through the years, and sometimes the alters all know what the other alters are up to, even if the person himself doesn't know."

"Sometimes. Not always."

I would soon get a good education on all of this.

CHAPTER
EIGHT

"AXEL," I said as we dried dishes after dinner that night. "Have you ever known anybody who led a double life?"

He shrugged. "In what way, mate?"

"Well, not somebody with different personalities, *per se.* You already told me you've never come across that. But maybe somebody who just has two different lives. The family man who visits prostitutes, maybe, or the church-goer who kills people. That sort of thing."

"All the time," he said. "Most people I apprehend are perfectly normal, upstanding people in their daily lives. But they have a nasty side to them. A brutal, nasty side to them."

"I wonder about that," I said. "How can they do that? How can they, say, look their spouse in the eye, tell them they love them, and then go out and sleep with someone else? Or, worse, how can they have a family, go to church, play with their children, and then go and brutally murder somebody? What causes people to do things like that?"

"People are broken inside," he said. "Things have happened to them, and they compartmentalize those tragedies and hurts they experience in their earlier days. They have a hidden side to them, but it comes to light when they're triggered. That's why Ted Bundy could seem so normal to many people yet become a wild animal when nobody looks. Did you know that Ted Bundy worked at a suicide hotline? People there thought he was caring, affable, and concerned about their lives. And he probably was. That was one aspect of who he was – the nice, concerned guy. The other aspect was the brutal killer. And I, for one, think both aspects were him. He was a really nice guy, but he had a side that was…not so nice. To say the least."

"So, what are you saying?"

"I'm saying that nobody is all one or the other. When Ted Bundy was talking to people in crisis, talking them off the ledge, he wasn't hiding that brutal monster inside during those times. He really was the caring person he showed to the world. That brutal monster was a distinct other facet of his personality, and, while he was the brutal monster, no part of him was the kind Ted his co-workers encountered."

"I wonder if he had DID."

"No." Axel shook his head. "I've read books about him. There was no sign that he told anybody about different personalities or that he came out and said he was somebody else. He just had two very distinct facets of his personality. There are people like that. Lots of people like that. You can be a good church-goer bloke and a lover of prostitutes and not be a hypocrite. You have two distinct facets of your personality; never the twain shall meet. So the church-goer bloke who visits the prostitutes probably doesn't feel guilty when he visits these prostitutes because that facet of his personality doesn't have those guilty feelings. And when that same man is in church, he doesn't necessarily feel like lusting after every woman he sees – that part of him is only reserved for those nights he visits the prostitutes. At least, that's the theory that I have for people."

"Interesting. That's one way of looking at it. It's an interesting theory. I'll give you that."

"Why do you ask?"

I sighed and put the glasses back in the cupboard, one by one. "I ask because, well, my uncle. I don't know what to think about him. I don't know if there was maybe a personality who killed that priest. I wouldn't think so. From what I understand, Mick, my uncle's homosexual alter, was having a love affair with Father Kennedy. I need to speak with him more about it, which I can because he's staying with my mother. But he was having a love affair with the priest, so why would Mick kill him? As for Jack, I don't think Jack even knew that priest. I don't think he did. So, which one of Jack's personalities would have motive to kill Father Kennedy? It makes little sense to me."

"Who are his other personalities?"

"I only know of one other one. His name was Eli. As far as I know, though, Eli hasn't been around since Jack was a young boy. Eli came out to protect Jack when he was suffering from the after-effects of something brutal that he endured as a young boy. Eli was a tough guy with tattoos who drank, smoked and took drugs. He talked tough. He *was* tough. Jack was a sensitive young boy. Actually, the Jack I'd always known was sensitive and kind. Not a rough and tumble bone in his body. He never had a bad word for anybody, ever. That was who he was. Eli was very different from that."

As I put the dishes away, one by one, my mind wandered to Jack, Eli and Mick. I wondered if there was anybody else in there. Perhaps Eli killed the priest? If so, why? What kind of beef would Eli have with the priest? Or maybe it was Mick. Maybe they had a lover's quarrel? That would make sense to me, really. Perhaps Father Kennedy did something that sent Mick into a rage? I couldn't imagine that Jack would've killed the priest. I didn't see the connection between Jack and the priest. Jack had never been religious. I didn't think he'd ever been inside a church in his life.

"What are you thinking, lass?" Axel asked me as he came up behind me and put his arms around my waist.

"I don't know. I'm just…thinking. It's all so weird what happened." I turned around, put my arms around his neck, and kissed him. His lips were soft, and so were his cheeks. He kissed me back, kissed my forehead, and leaned into me on the sink.

"Get a room," Rina said, coming into the kitchen.

"Don't you have homework to do?" I asked her.

"I guess. Abby does. Plus, she has to practice her flute. Tell her she can't quit band just because James is a tool. You bought her that instrument, Mom, and she can't quit. You just go in there and tell her."

"What? Abby is thinking about quitting band?"

"Of course. I don't want to say I told you so, but I told you so. She only wanted in band because James is in band. And now that James has shown his full tool colors, she wants out of band. She doesn't want to face him every day."

I sighed. Looks like there was another crisis for me to face. As crises go, though, this one seemed rather minor. Of course, I wouldn't let Abby quit band. She'd been practicing her flute every day and was getting better and better. She was no longer last chair but was now third chair. Considering there were nine flute players, all girls, that was remarkable. She'd made a lot of progress in a short period. I wouldn't let her stop that progress by quitting.

I went into the living room, where Abby was watching television. She was on the colorful throw rug, her little hands on her cheeks, and, from time to time, she kept lowering her face to the ground, and I could hear little sobs coming from her.

"Abby," I said softly. I sat next to her on the floor and stroked her back. "Buttercup, talk to me. Rina says you're thinking about quitting band."

She said nothing, but just nodded.

"You can't quit. You love it. You're really good, Buttercup. You really are. I've listened to you and heard that you've been getting better and better. You've made a lot of progress. You can't quit."

She got up, put her arms around my neck, and sobbed. I put my arms around her and felt her little body shake while I held her. I stroked her hair while she cried.

"I can't go back to that band room, Mom. She's there. James' new girlfriend, Emmaline. I walk into the band room and they're sitting together, holding hands. You don't know how it feels, Mom. I don't have any friends in the band yet. There's nobody I can talk to about it. It's the end of the world, Mom. I just can't watch them anymore."

That was a tough one. I'd been there. Who hadn't been there before? Seeing the person who you loved and cared about with somebody else? There have been many songs sung about just this kind of situation. No matter what age you are, heartbreak was the same. Whether you were 12, like Abby, or 82, seeing the person you love with somebody else is the ultimate heartbreak.

Yet, I couldn't just let her quit. She could regret that for the rest of her life. She'd miss out on playing football games. She'd miss out on local, regional and national competitions. She'd miss out on taking band trips overseas. Being in the band was an experience I never forgot. I played the flute for several years myself, and I always had the memories that stayed with me. It was important to be a part of something; that was what Abby was – she was a part of something.

"Abby, I'm so sorry, Buttercup, but I can't let you quit. I spent a lot of money on that instrument, and you love doing it. You're getting great at it. You might be first chair sometime soon, so you'll get solos. You have potential, little girl. I know how tough it is to see James with another girlfriend, but you must look at the big picture. One day James will be a distant memory, but the memories you build with some of your other bandmates will be memories you'll have forever."

"Okay," she said. "I need to go to bed, Mom. Is that okay?"

"Of course."

She trudged upstairs and shut the door. I went over to Axel, who was sitting on the couch. "Poor little Abby," I said. "I know how hard it is to like somebody so much and have them not like you back. I really thought she and James were good together. I can't believe he's such a damned heel."

Axel grinned. "Ah, young love. Young heartbreak. Who hasn't been there? But Abby will get through this. You can't let her quit band. She needs to know that just quitting something isn't an option. You need to always stick it through."

Rina came up to me. "Give me the clicker," she said. "The shows Abby watches are so lame. I need to see what's on the DVR."

I threw her the clicker, and she sat on the leather recliner and flipped through the channels. I smiled at Axel, and we went upstairs to my room. "Rina, I'll check on you in about an hour. You better be ready for bed by then."

"Whatever." She rolled her eyes.

At that, Axel and I went upstairs to my room.

CHAPTER NINE

I KNEW I'd have to do a stringent investigation of my Uncle Jack's case. An investigation that would be more thorough than anything I'd ever done before. I was determined to see my Uncle Jack acquitted.

But first, I'd have to figure out a way around him passing his psychological exam. The last thing I wanted was for him to be declared unfit for trial or be forced by the trial judge to try for an NGRI finding. I wanted this trial to go to ensure Uncle Jack went completely free. I had the feeling he didn't do it. I also wondered if there was another hidden personality who knew exactly what happened in that rectory.

I went over to see him at my mother's house. Albany would meet me there. She told me she had some news about Jack. She also told me she had some news about Steven. News she thought I should know.

Knowing Albany, that could've meant anything. It could've meant she had concrete evidence about Steven, Uncle Jack's abductor. It could've also meant she'd claim to have been in touch with Steven's ghost. Albany was known for doing things like this. She was forever claiming to have been in touch with spirits, angels, and things that go bump at night. She had her own personal psychic. She gave me crystals her psychic blessed, and she wanted me to carry these crystals with me always.

I even went to a psychic with her one time. It was pretty much as I expected – they even had a crystal ball. The psychic, Lady Starlight, or something of the sort, tried to sell me two special candles. They were red, and, according to Lady Starlight, they were blessed. They were also $1,500. She told me that if I burned these candles every night, I'd get an acquittal in the case I worked on back then. She guaranteed it. "Your guardian angel has chains around her," she said. "She needs to be released. If you release her by burning these candles, then everything your heart desires will be yours."

I didn't part with that money. Albany, however, did, and she insisted that burning these candles helped her find the job of her dreams. It also helped her relationship with the man she was seeing then. They broke up two weeks later, but for one brief shining moment, they were together again. Albany said it was because she burned her candles.

I had no idea how much money Albany spent on candles, crystals, tarot readings, and magic stones. I imagined it was quite a lot. Not that I would get on her about that. It was really none of my business. She made decent money as a therapy masseuse and acupuncturist, so I had no cause to criticize her. To each her own.

I got to my mother's house, and Jack greeted me. "Doll," he said, his voice in the same high-pitched cadence he'd affected since that day in jail when he insisted I call him Mick. "Come here, you."

I went over to him and gave him a big hug. "It's so good to see you, uh, Mick."

"And you. I'm not in that hideous jumpsuit because of you. I can't tell you how happy that makes me."

Mick was dressed in khaki slacks and a long-sleeved white golf shirt. His grey hair was newly cut, slightly shaggy in the front and longer in the back. He looked like my Uncle Jack, but he wasn't. I knew this.

"I need to talk to you."

"Oh, I know. I know. I need to talk to you, too."

We went into my mother's house, and I followed him into the sunroom. "Where's Albany?" I asked him, looking around.

"She's around. She's been looking for you. She told me she has some information about Steven." He raised his eyebrow. "I'm interested in finding out about that."

I cocked my head. "Do you remember Steven?"

"Of course. He was my lover. I know I know – people said nasty things about him. They said he was a child rapist and a murderer and all that. And he was. He was. All those things. But I saw a different side to him. He was very loving with me. Very tender. I saw him for who he really was. He was my first. My first sexual experience and my first real love." He nodded. "He was my first." He looked sad. His eyes turned down to the floor as if he was thinking back to that time.

I bit my lip, not wanting to show judgment on what he was saying. I'd have to approach this entire thing as a scientist. I had much to learn about DID, but I was determined to learn as much as possible. "Mick," I said. "Are you saying Steven was your boyfriend? Is that why you stayed with him? Is that why you found boys and girls for him?"

He shuddered. "Oh, I didn't do that. Finding those young girls and boys. I wouldn't take part in such sick practices. That was all Eli." He shook his head. "I can't stand Eli. He's a worm. A druggie bastard. A worthless piece of shit. I didn't want to share Steven, so why would I bring in more boys and girls for him to fuck? Eli got rid of the bodies, too." He shuddered again. "No way would I do something like that."

I wondered about that. Why wouldn't Eli have escaped if he was getting the boys and girls for Steven? "How did Eli think about Steven?"

"He hated him. Hated him. I always took over for the fucking, though. But Eli was there for the rest of it." He looked out the window. "Eli was the one Steven hung up by his wrists for an entire weekend. Eli was the one who took the beatings with the belt. He took the burnings with the hot branding iron. Eli was forced to watch while Steven had sex with the young boys and girls. He was forced to be in the room when Steven had sex with these kids, and if he closed his eyes, he was forced to take a scalding shower, so, of course, he watched. He watched when Steven gutted those kids like pigs. He dumped the bodies. He did all that."

I then knew exactly how Eli and Mick split their duties and why Mick was homosexual. Mick was apparently created because Jack needed an alter who loved gay sex. That way, the raping of Mick seemed like love-making. Tender love-making. On the other hand, Eli was tough enough to take the torture and abuse. He was tough enough to watch children being raped and murdered.

I wondered if Eli was violent. And if he was violent, would he be violent enough to murder Father Kennedy? What would Father Kennedy have done to bring Eli out, though? Mick and Father Kennedy were apparently in love, but then again, Mick was also in love with Steven. I wondered if the relationship between Father Kennedy and Mick had the same dynamic. Maybe Father Kennedy was actually raping Mick, and Eli came out and killed him?

That was an inescapable thought. If that were the case, I'd have no choice but to try for an NGRI plea for Jack. As much as that would kill me, that would be the only way to try this case. Not that I would give up, though. I still had hope that somebody else did this and framed Jack.

"Mick," I said. "Can I talk to Eli?"

"No," he shook his head. "Eli can't come out. Not now, and not ever." He shook his head again for emphasis. "No. He can't come out. Sorry."

"Why not? Does Eli know what happened with Father Kennedy?"

Mick screwed up his face, his nose scrunching and his eyes twitching. His reactions disturbed me, to say the very least. "Mick, I'm asking you a question. Does Eli know what happened to Father Kennedy? Was he there when Father Kennedy was killed?"

Mick opened his mouth, but at that moment, Albany entered the room. "Harper," she said. "I'm glad you came."

I groaned. Albany came in right when I was possibly about to find out what happened to Father Kennedy. Mick seemed to know about Eli and appeared to know about Eli's movements and Eli's activities. Mick seemed to know what Eli knew and what Eli saw. He knew, but he was trying to hide Eli. He was ensuring Eli didn't come out and tell me exactly what happened.

Then again, maybe I didn't really want to know what happened. I didn't want to know that maybe Eli killed Father Kennedy. If I knew that, there would be an issue. I couldn't possibly go for a full acquittal if Eli killed Father Kennedy because it was Jack killing the priest. I needed Jack to be absolutely innocent. I didn't want to hear anything else.

Albany and I quickly hugged, and then she sat down. "I wanted you to know what I've been finding out from Lady Starlight," Albany said.

I nodded my head, trying hard to humor her. She meant well. I knew she did. But I just couldn't get into her ramblings about her psychic and her tarot cards and all that. It was just such hokum to me.

"What did you find out from her?" I asked Albany.

"She told me Steven Heaney isn't dead."

CHAPTER
TEN

I ROLLED MY EYES. "He isn't dead? What the hell is that supposed to mean? If he's not dead, then who's in Steven Heaney's grave? Who were the newspapers talking about when they announced Steven Heaney had been found dead in his home? Tell me that, Albany?"

She shrugged. "I don't know the answers to all those questions, Harper. I only know what she told me. I only know that she told me Steven Heaney wasn't deceased. See, I tried to contact Steven myself the other night. I thought he might have some answers about who killed Father Kennedy." Her voice turned to a whisper, and Mick and I leaned forward. Mick was watching Albany with interest, but he wasn't saying anything. It looked like he was thinking about what she was saying – his hand was on his chin, and his blue eyes were trained on her like a laser.

I leaned back in my chair. "Okay. You tried to get in touch with a dead man. I see. What did you do – light candles and chant? Get a Ouji Board out to ask him questions? How did you try to contact him?"

She raised her right eyebrow. "Go ahead and make fun. Just go ahead. You know I don't mess around with Ouji Boards. Prominent Demonologists have written books about how those things bring demons into people's houses."

"Demonologists? There are people who try to track down demons, things which don't exist?" I was ready to get up and leave, but I didn't want to insult Albany, so I stayed. But that was the *only* reason I stayed.

"Listen, Harper, I don't insult you and what you do. Why do you have to insult me? Don't you go to a Catholic church every Sunday? Don't you?"

"Well, yes," I said. "I do. It's something I believe in. Why do you ask?"

"I believe in spirits, demons, tarot, and angels and my ability to speak with the dead. You believe in the crucifixion and resurrection of Christ. Neither of us can have concrete proof of what we believe in, at least not enough to satisfy each other. So, why don't you respect my belief, I'll respect yours, and we can both call it good. How's that?"

I was chastised, so I nodded. "Okay. I'm sorry. Now, please, Albany, please tell me about your trying to contact Steven Heaney."

"Well, that was just it. I thought for sure Steven Heaney would be around. I thought he would've attached himself to Uncle Jack, I mean Uncle Mick, because Eli allegedly killed him. And, since Eli is a part of Uncle Jack, Steven Heaney would be attached to Jack's body."

I was slow on the uptake because I just let her ramble on. But two seconds later, my head almost spun around. "Wait, what? What are you talking about, Eli killed Steven Heaney? Steven Heaney died of a heart attack. Didn't he?"

Albany shook her head. "Harper, you really need to research this whole case more. I know you haven't started getting into your defense of Uncle Jack yet, but you need to get up to speed. No, Steven Heaney didn't die of a heart attack. He's not dead at all, but the story was never that he died of a heart attack. The story was that Eli killed Steven Heaney when Steven told Eli that he, Steven, would have to kill Mary. Eli killed him. However, he was never charged in the case because the police figured that Eli, or Jack, had suffered enough, and they didn't want to drag him through a trial. They didn't want to traumatize him further, so they simply believed his story that he killed Steven Heaney when Steven was in the middle of strangling Mary, and no charges were ever filed. But that's what happened."

"Now, why didn't Mom tell me that little tidbit of information? I really should've known about that. She told me Steven Heaney died of a heart attack."

Albany shook her head. "Mom has always wanted to protect Jack, so she will tell nobody the truth about what happened. She won't tell the truth, even though everyone knows the truth, because it was all in the papers when Jack escaped from that house of horrors. But you need to know everything because only if you know everything can you defend Uncle Jack on these murder charges."

I sighed. "Okay. Go ahead. Tell me what else I need to know. What's this about Steven Heaney not actually being dead? If Eli killed Steven Heaney, then he's dead. What am I missing here?"

"I don't know yet. I don't know. All I know was that I did a ritual to try communicating with Steven, and I couldn't. So I saw Lady Starlight. She's one of the top psychics in the Western Hemisphere. I know you think she's a crock, but trust me, she's always been right on the money. She did her own ritual and informed me she couldn't contact him either. So, she told me Steven wasn't dead after all."

"Oh, I see. I see. Just because Lady Starlight couldn't contact him, he's not dead. Well, that settles it, then. Steven Heaney is still alive."

"Again, I hear the sarcasm in your voice," Albany said. "And I don't appreciate it. You need to have an open mind about this. You need to figure out if what I'm saying is true. If it is true, you can crack the case."

"How will that crack the case? I mean, really. How will it crack the case? I don't understand what you're getting at."

"I don't know, but the Steven Heaney angle is significant. You can find out if there was a connection between Father Kennedy and Steven Heaney and go from there. Maybe Steven Heaney was behind it all."

"Or maybe his ghost came in and killed Father Kennedy. Did you ever think about that?"

At that, Albany got up. "Come back and speak with me when you have an open mind. Okay? At the moment, I'm going to find people who might listen to me about all of this."

"I'm sorry, Albany. I'm really sorry. But you have to understand – I deal with facts. Cold, hard facts. Facts are the only things that matter in a court of law. Not hunches. Not emotion, although you must produce an emotional response in juries if you ever want to succeed in court. But facts win cases. This entire thing sounds like hokum to me."

"Whatever. Listen, I gotta go. I'll see ya later, sis."

At that, she went out the French doors, which led into the kitchen.

I turned to face Mick. "Mick," I said. "Can you do anything about Eli? Can you try to talk to him and bring him around?" I knew that of Jack's personalities, Eli would be the most likely to know what happened to Steven Heaney. He would be the one I'd need to speak with to understand all of it.

It was then that I saw the subtle changes in Jack. He no longer had his legs crossed. Mick sat like a woman, one leg crossed completely over the other. However, Jack was no longer sitting like that. Rather, he was sitting with his feet firmly planted on the floor. He took off his glasses and looked at them with wonder – as if he was trying to figure out why he would wear a pair of glasses in the first place. He then looked at me with a quizzical look on his face. "June Bug," he said. "Where am I?" He looked around. "I see I'm at Claire's house. Why am I here? How did I get here?"

My heart broke as I saw Uncle Jack hang his head and put his face in his hands. His head was shaking back and forth, back and forth, and I could hear tiny sobs coming out of him. "Oh my God, I'm losing so much time again. So much time. I last remember talking to you in jail. Now I'm here. I don't know what happened. What's happening to me? What's happening to me?"

I put my arm around him and gently stroked the back of his neck while he cried. "Uncle Jack," I said softly. "I got you out of jail. I convinced the judge to reduce your bond to a 10% bond. Mom and I got together and got the money for you to get out of jail. You have to stay here, Uncle Jack, while you await trial. Mom has custody over you. You also have an ankle monitor on."

Jack looked down at his ankle, saw the monitor, and then looked up at me. "You got me out of jail. Thank you, June Bug. Thank you. I just wish I could remember any of it. I was talking to you, and then I'm here. Out of nowhere, I'm here."

It disappointed me that Jack was back. I knew Jack was clueless about everything. He didn't know Father Kennedy. Mick knew the Father. Mick apparently was in love with the Father – at least, that's what he told me. However, I had a feeling Eli was the one who really knew what had happened, and Mick was protecting Eli. Mick was making sure Eli couldn't come out. I didn't know what that game was, but I somehow knew Eli knew exactly what had happened in that rectory.

But Jack? Jack knew nothing. He, therefore, couldn't be much use to me. I didn't think he could help me pursue the truth of what had happened in this case.

"Uncle Jack, I'm so sorry. I need to go. I need to figure a few things out."

"What do you need to figure out?"

"I just need to do some thinking and some investigating. I love you, and I'll be back to visit you soon. Probably tomorrow. But I have to follow up on a few things right now."

Jack just nodded. He looked so sad…my heart went out to him.

I got up and went through the house. Mom and Albany were sitting in the living room, talking. "I have to go," I told them both. "Albany, I'm sorry about earlier. Really. I need to find out more about what you were telling me. I won't discount it. I promise you this."

"Thanks," she said. "I hope you don't. I don't know if it's significant, but I hope it is. I hope it's something you can use. Something that will put you on the right track." She nodded her head. "I think it will. You just have to keep an open mind."

"I will."

As I left, I knew Albany might be right. I didn't know how it could've happened, though.

I had the feeling Steven Heaney was really alive somewhere.

I got to my office and first wanted to learn all I could about Steven Heaney. To my surprise, this was a huge story back in the day. The early 1970s, when Jack was 11 years old, were a different time from today. This was before the huge case of Adam Walsh had blown up, which put child abductions on the front page and at the forefront of people's consciousness. It was before Ted Bundy, Jeffrey Dahmer, and other guys who made worldwide news and convinced people that dangerous monsters were walking amongst us.

So, when Jack escaped Steven Heaney's home, and the police went into that home and found the bones of missing children, that was a huge deal. It was front-page news for months after the fact.

I read through the news articles and found Albany was correct. Jack apparently killed Steven Heaney. However, he was never charged because of his youth, and the police apparently figured he'd suffered enough. Besides, the police no doubt felt that by killing a monster like Steven Heaney, Jack was doing the world a tremendous favor.

There also wasn't a mention of Eli in any of these articles. That was because Eli probably didn't reveal himself. He probably "played along" and pretended to be Jack so the police officers wouldn't be suspicious. Also, the early 1970s was a time when DID wasn't generally known. It was a rare disorder now, but was really rare back then. Well, maybe it wasn't more rare back then, but people didn't hear about it. After all, the story of Sybil entered the pop culture consciousness around 1976, when the television mini-series hit starring a young Sally Field. Eli probably rightly thought the media attention would've been even more intense if he made himself known.

I sighed. How did I not know about any of this? How could my family keep something like this under wraps? Every family had skeletons in their closets, but this one was a doozy. My Uncle Jack was not only kept by a monster, but he apparently killed that monster, or Eli killed him. I didn't even know if Uncle Jack recalled any of this. My mom indicated he didn't, but I couldn't understand how that was possible. The alters were out the entire time Jack was in this house of horrors, but I still figured there would be some kind of memory somewhere in Jack's consciousness.

I wrote on a piece of paper. *Find out if Steven Heaney really was still alive. Speak with the other priests at the church. Do an independent DNA analysis on the knife found at the scene. Try to talk to Eli.* That last one would be difficult. I might've been able to speak with Eli if I could've convinced Mick to let him out. But Jack didn't seem to control any of them. Jack didn't know those other alters existed. I mean, he probably had some kind of knowledge that they were there, mainly because he was told they were, but from the literature I'd been reading on the DID disorder, the main person wasn't always aware the alters existed, but the alters usually knew about one another.

Eli held the key.

But so, possibly, did Steven Heaney, assuming Steven Heaney was still alive.

I called Anna. "Anna," I said. "I need you to do a background check. On Steven Heaney."

"Steven Heaney, the serial killer?" Anna sounded excited over the phone. "Rad, dude."

I had to smile. *Was I the only person in the world who had never heard of this case?* "How do you know about Steven Heaney?"

"Oh, God, I know all my serial killers. If there's a book about a serial killer, I've read it. Sorry, I know that makes me sound so fucking warped, and you're right. I'm warped as shit. But yeah, I love reading stories about serial killers. They're so fascinating. The psychology and all that."

"Well, okay then. I guess this is your dream assignment. Anyhow, I need you to find out all you can about him. Find out about his family. Find out if he had any siblings." I snapped my fingers. "Find out if he had an identical twin."

"I'll do it," she said. "I'll have that report by the end of the day."

"Thanks."

I'd have to figure this one out.

But first, I would have to go to the church. Go to the scene. Talk to the cops on the scene and the priests in the parish. Maybe somebody saw something and was afraid to come forth. The police report said that nobody but Jack was around in the rectory when Father Kennedy was found. But maybe somebody was actually there.

It was certainly worth a shot.

CHAPTER
ELEVEN

I WENT to the church after making an appointment to see the Associate Pastor, who was serving as an assistant to Father Kennedy. Guardian Angels was a gorgeous church in the heart of Westport. As I entered the church, I closed my eyes, feeling the peace I always felt when I entered places like this. There was just something reverential about this place. I didn't always believe in God – I always questioned why a deity would allow such evil to happen. Why a deity would allow people like Steven Heaney to exist. Men who preyed on innocent children. Men who tortured boys like my Uncle Jack. How could men like Steven Heaney exist if God was always looking out for all of us?

Those were always the questions that I had. Where was God when my uncle was suffering? When those kids were being murdered? Where was He when bad things happened? I didn't know. That was the only reason I often had problems believing in God, even though I tried to go to Our Lady of Sorrows, a Catholic Church by the Crown Center, every Sunday.

I swallowed hard. I didn't want to prejudge this case. I didn't know if Father Kennedy was having an affair with Mick. It concerned me greatly that Mick said he was in love with Father Kennedy. It worried me because Mick also told me that Steven Heaney was his lover. He said Steven Heaney made tender love to him when, in reality, Jack was

11 years old, and Steven Heaney was raping him. Mick was created so the raping seemed like love-making. That was the only way Uncle Jack could get through it. That was what alters did for the "host" body – they took abuse so the "host" person didn't have to. Mick was a homosexual who loved gay sex, so he somehow converted Steven Heaney's raping into something else.

Now Mick said he was in love with Father Kennedy. Did that mean Father Kennedy was raping my uncle, too? That would make sense, actually. Mick was apparently the alter Jack had created when there was raping involved.

If that were the case, would Eli have come out to kill Father Kennedy? That apparently was what happened with Steven Heaney, assuming Steven Heaney wasn't alive, as Albany seemed to believe. If Eli killed the priest, Jack would be in prison for the rest of his life. Or, maybe, best-case scenario, Jack would be in a psychiatric facility for the rest of his life.

I didn't want either scenario to happen. I needed Jack to be factually innocent.

I went to the offices, which were on the west side of the church. There was a secretary back there, young, blonde, and pretty. She looked up at me. "Can I help you?" she asked me.

"Yes. I have an appointment today with Father Mathews. My name is Harper Ross."

"Oh, yes. Yes. Right this way."

She led me to a suite of offices, and she opened the door of one. "Father Mathews, this is Harper Ross," she said.

He nodded and stood up, giving me his hand to shake. "Ms. Ross, hello," he said. "It's very good to meet with you."

Father Mathews was relatively young – he looked not much older than 30. He was dark-headed, dark-eyed and fit. His hands were soft, as if he hadn't done a day of manual labor in his life, which he probably hadn't. He had a ready, easy smile, and I immediately felt comfortable around him. I smiled as I thought about how many young girls and women probably had a crush on this man. People tended to have crushes on priests, but priests who were young and handsome, as this one was, would be a target more than most.

I knew why Father Mathews was young. He was an Associate Pastor until the day Father Kennedy was found dead. He probably never dreamed he'd become the main priest so soon. He probably thought he'd be an Associate Pastor for another 10 years. Yet, here he was, thrust into this position. I hoped he wasn't overwhelmed.

"Have a seat," he said. "I was just working on my Sunday sermon." He shook his head. "We've been working on the problem of attracting more youth into the pews on Sunday mornings and afternoons. It's an age-old problem, really. People have been straying from church attendance for far too long. I didn't think I would take the main position so quickly, and there's always a lot of work to be done."

I nodded my head. "It seems that way, doesn't it?"

"Yes. So, enough about me and my problems. What can I do for you?"

"I wanted to ask you about my client, Jack Calhoun. What do you know about the relationship between Mr. Calhoun and Father Kennedy?"

"Jack Calhoun." He grimaced. "That's the guy arrested for murdering Kelly?" He shook his head and just stared at me. "What do you need to know about the relationship between Kelly and Mr. Calhoun?"

"How close were they?"

"Not very. Not that I could see. I knew Kelly was always attending to troubled parishioners, and he often told me Mr. Calhoun was one of his most troubled. But it was strange, though. He never referred to him as Jack. He usually called him Mr. Calhoun, but sometimes, he used his first name, and he called him Mick. I never heard the name Jack, so it surprised me when I read in the papers that a Jack Calhoun was arrested." He shrugged. "I figured maybe Mick was his middle name, and he was being called by his middle name, as people sometimes do."

"So you met Mr. Calhoun in person, then?"

"No, I didn't. I never met him. I knew Kelly was having issues with him, but he wanted to help. Mr. Calhoun was coming to him, asking him for help. He said he was new in town, didn't know anybody and was having problems coming to terms with something that happened when he was a kid. I don't really know exactly why Mr. Calhoun had latched onto Kelly because, as far as I knew, Mr. Calhoun wasn't even a part of this church. As far as I knew, Mr. Calhoun wasn't religious. He was questioning and was more agnostic than anything. I don't know how he came to know Kelly in the first place. All I knew was that Kelly was counseling him, for what, I don't know, but he was counseling him. And he was afraid of him."

"He was afraid of him? Why was he afraid of him?" My heart sank when Father Mathews said Father Kennedy was afraid of Jack.

"Kelly was afraid of Mick because Mick kept making sexual advances. Now, I know what you must think. With so many priest scandals over the years, you probably think we priests are all going about, breaking our vows and having sex with adults and young boys. That's an unfortunate stereotype we're forced to live down."

I shook my head. "No. I don't believe that about all priests." I had seen the movie *Spotlight*, which told the story of the journalists who had uncovered the scandals involving the diocese in Boston, where many priests were molesting young boys. But I never thought this was a systemic problem affecting every parish. I thought, however, that there was a chance that Father Kennedy and Mick were having an affair. However slight of a chance. I also thought there was a chance that Father Kennedy raped Jack, which was why Mick appeared.

"So, Mick made sexual advances on Father Kennedy?"

"Yes. Apparently, he did. Kelly didn't want to be alone with Mick for just that reason. Yet, he was counseling Mick on some pretty awful things. I didn't know what they were, but I knew Kelly had indicated they were serious issues. The only thing Kelly told me was that what happened to Mick involved another parishioner we had in our church long ago."

"Another parishioner? Who was that? Did Father Kennedy give you any names?" I wondered if Steven Heaney was the other parishioner who Father Mathews was talking about.

He shrugged. "No. Kelly was bound by the ethical rules governing our counseling services. We cannot divulge names, details or any of that. He shouldn't have told me as much about Mick's case as he did. Kelly told me he had to keep counseling Mick because Mick was going through something extremely serious and what Mick was talking about involved a former parishioner. I'm very sorry. I can't tell you anything more than that."

I sighed. "Okay. Did Father Kennedy have any enemies you know about?"

"Enemies?" Father Mathews looked at me curiously. "No. He didn't. None that I knew about, anyhow. Nobody threatened his life, if that was what you were trying to ask. Kelly was somebody who walked the straight and narrow his whole life. He wasn't like me. I came from the streets. I'm not ashamed to say it. I grew up on the West Side and got along just like everybody else did in my neighborhood. I dealt drugs, got into fights, and went to prison for twenty years. I was on the path poor kids go on until I found God. I found a Bible in prison, and I read it every single day. I got out of prison five years ago, when I was 45, and immediately went into the seminary. I lived that rough life, Ms. Ross. I lived it. Kelly didn't. He had a very different path than I did."

I nodded, but I was stunned. Father Mathews was 50? Seriously? He looked so young. *Good genes.*

I liked that Father Mathews was so open. I wondered if he had tattoos underneath his robe. He probably did. "What was his path? Do you know?"

"Yes. He had a religious upbringing. Catholic schools his whole life. He had been a part of this church since he was young and an altar boy. Ever since he was a young boy, he always knew what he wanted to do with his life. At least, that was what he told me. I admired him because he didn't have to go through the experiences I did to get here. He didn't have to live knowing he hurt people." Father Mathews face looked sad and pensive suddenly. "He didn't have to look in the mirror and know he was responsible for the death of a 13-year-old boy. I didn't have that luxury."

I put my hand on his arm, responding to Father Mathews' sudden sad facial expression. "What happened to that 13-year-old boy?"

"I sold drugs to him. He overdosed that day. I didn't know he was a first-timer. I tried not to sell drugs to the neophytes. But I needed the money. He had the money, so I sold them to him." Father Mathews shook his head. "That was why I went to prison for manslaughter. But I was lucky to get out in one piece. I was very lucky, so I knew I'd have to turn it around when I got out. And I did. I did. Considering how I was brought up, you might not think a guy like me is lucky. But I am." He took his rosary beads out from under his robe and kissed them lightly. "I am."

"You're very open about all that happened."

"Yes. I am. I'm open about it to everyone. Especially people who come in here seeking my help. I have parishioners here just like me. They come from poor areas, too. I see kids just like me. Kids growing up just like I did. And I do outreach to them. I go to their homes, play basketball with them, and take them out to eat. I bond with them. I let them know there's an entire world out there and try to help them overcome their problems. This is my life's work, Ms. Ross. I've spent the past five years trying to make up for my responsibility for the death of that 13-year-old boy. This is my penance."

"Are you sure," I began. "That Father Kennedy doesn't have a similar story to yours? Maybe he hurt somebody when he was younger, and that person showed up to take revenge."

Father Mathews shrugged. "I don't think so. I mean, you never quite know somebody, do you? I've been very open about my past. I tell anybody about it who wants to know. I feel being open sets me apart from other priests. It tells my parishioners they can feel comfortable telling me anything. But Kelly wasn't like that. He didn't go into detail about his past at all. He only said that he went to Catholic Schools his entire life, was a part of this church his whole life, was an altar boy and that his parents were normal, middle-class parents who raised him in the Loose Park area of town. I feel his parents are fairly well-to-do."

He sighed. "I miss Kelly. He was like a father to me. He was my mentor. I was still sorting through things when I first arrived at this church. Sorting through my life. I didn't know if I made the right decision to go into the priesthood. Kelly helped me see this was not only the right decision, but the only one. He guided me through transitioning from being a wild street punk to the priest I am today. I will always be grateful for that."

"So you really can't think of any enemies he might have had?"

He shook his head. "If there was anybody in this diocese who would have enemies gunning for them, it would be me. I know that. That was why I thought what happened to Kelly was so unjust. I didn't think I'd die at the hands of somebody irate, but I deserved it more than he did. That's for sure."

That was odd that he said he deserved to die more than Father Kennedy did. I wondered why he would go there.

"Well," he finally said. "I'd love to chat with you some more, but I have a service that I need to prepare for and a basketball game I need to attend. I don't mean to brag, but I play a mean game of hoops. You should come and see our games sometimes. We play at the Sacred Heart gym on 25th and Madison."

"I'll try to catch it," I said. "Thank you for taking the time to speak with me, Father Mathews."

"Of course. If I can do anything to help, I will."

I left the offices and the church, feeling out of sorts. The only thing I found out in there was that Father Mathews was a thug, and Father Kennedy was somebody who apparently was a good guy his whole life.

Or was he? Father Mathews had a story to tell. A past. He said he got into the priesthood because it was that or going back to prison. He knew that path he was going down and didn't want to travel down it further. He found his life's calling in the priesthood.

Might Father Kennedy have done the same? Maybe he, too, had a past where he hurt people. Maybe one of those people came in and killed him. Maybe that was what happened, and Jack was there. He witnessed it and freaked out so much that Mick came out. Or Eli. Or maybe he had still more alters inside of him.

I would have to find out more.

I walked along the tree-lined streets to my car and got in.

I didn't know if I knew anything more about Father Kennedy than I did this morning. But I hoped that I would soon be getting closer to the truth.

CHAPTER
TWELVE
JACK (MICK)

"OKAY, MISSY," I said to Harper. "I'll see your court-appointed therapist, and I promise you, he'll tell you I'm sober as a damned judge and just as sane. Oh, wait. That means judges are sober and sane, and we all know they're not."

I knew Harper meant well. However, it was a struggle for me to come out before the date with the shrink. I would have to be the one the shrink would talk to because I knew Jack would never get through it.

Jack was weak. I could always take over any time I wanted, especially now. He wasn't weak for many years, though, many years. He kept us hidden, gone for all those years. I didn't like being pushed down and forgotten about. I didn't like that I couldn't come out anymore. I tried to get Jack to let me out, but he wouldn't. He was just too strong.

Then Mary died, and we all got to come out to play once again. After she died, it was easy for us. I could come out much more often, and so could Eli. And so could Sam. Sam was somebody nobody even knew about. He was likely to pass himself off as Jack, but he wasn't Jack. He wasn't. He was somebody else entirely. Unpredictable. Violent. He wasn't good for Jack, so I tried to keep him from coming out. Once I found out about him, I tried to take control and ensure he always stayed hidden.

That was the role I'd taken. It was the role Eli had before, but I became, over the years, more dominant and powerful than Eli ever was. Eli used to be the keeper, the one who managed us. He was the one who allowed me to come out. If Eli didn't allow it, I couldn't come out. In fact, when we were living at Steven's house, I could only come out when Steven was fucking Jack. Other than that, it was all Eli.

But Jack got rid of us for all those years. All those years when he was strong, because of Mary, we were dormant. Dormant, but never gone. Then Mary died, and I was in control. I got to tell the others what to do. And I did. I told Eli that he wouldn't come out anymore. I didn't want Jack to get into trouble. I knew Eli would get him into trouble, too, because Eli was nothing but trouble. He dealt drugs; he fucked a lot of women; he did way too many drugs himself. He gambled, too. He came out a few times after Mary's accident, but I saw what he did, and I didn't like it. I made him go back and stay back. I wouldn't have that bullshit.

I ran a tight ship, and Eli wasn't part of that. He still got out occasionally, but I immediately controlled him and reined him back in.

Sam wasn't a part of my tight ship, either. I didn't even know about Sam until he came out a few times, and then, when I found out about him, he was toast. I tried to make sure that he could never come out at all. The last thing that I needed was a violent alter.

Like Eli, though, he got out from time to time. I couldn't stop him from coming out twice since the accident. Like Eli, I reined him in immediately.

"Are you sure, Mick, you can pass this psychological exam?" Harper asked me. "Remember, pretend you're Jack. You can't slip up and call yourself Mick. And remember the story you need to tell Dr. Jansing. You need to tell Dr. Jansing that you blacked out in that church because you had a fainting spell. You had really low blood sugar. Having low blood sugar was always a problem for you. Can you do that, Mick? Can you convince him you passed out at the rectory because of a physical issue, not a mental one?"

Harper was anxious. She wanted to make sure we all went to trial.

She wanted to ensure Dr. Jansing didn't find out we were loony tunes. After I came out, she explained that if Dr. Jansing found we weren't fit for trial, we would have to go into a nuthouse until the judge found we were fit for trial. And she also explained that if Dr. Jansing found we were insane at the time of the murder, the judge might order her to ask for a plea of not guilty by reason of insanity and we'd be locked up indefinitely in a different nut house.

Harper wanted to try this case. That was important to her. She felt that if she could try it, we could get off completely. She was working on finding out if somebody else killed that priest and framed us. She was looking for somebody who possibly knew Jack had mental problems and knew he would be the perfect person to be in that rectory when the other person, whoever that might be, actually murdered Father Kennedy.

I didn't know. I didn't know if any of us killed Father Kennedy. I didn't know if Eli did it or Sam. I was in the dark about all of that for whatever reason. I wanted to know what the others were up to. I didn't like not knowing things. For all I know, Jack himself could have been at that rectory. If that was the case – if it was Jack and not Eli or Sam - then I wouldn't have known what had happened. I never knew what Jack was up to. I could only keep tabs on Eli and Sam.

"I will, doll, I will. I promise you. I'll tell Dr. Headshrinker that I passed out from low blood sugar. I hope you know what you're doing, though. I hope you know."

"I know. If the doctor knows the truth, that trial will never go through, and they will lock Jack, you and everyone else up, possibly for the rest of your natural lives. I don't want that to happen. I think I can prove Jack is innocent, and I need that chance."

"Well, honey, I certainly don't want to be locked up in a nuthouse for the rest of my life, so I'm gonna do my best to convince Dr. Head-shrinker that Jack is not insane in the membrane."

We got to the doctor's office, the doctor that Harper had arranged for us to see.

We went into the suite, and there he was. As cute as a button, really. He didn't look very old at all. Maybe 35. Or maybe he just looked younger than he was. I never could really tell. What I knew was that he was cute. Sandy blonde hair, big dimples, big blue eyes. I could feel myself batting my eyelashes, but I had to stop. I had to act like Jack, and Jack didn't have a queer bone in his fucking body.

"Dr. Jansing," Harper was saying. "This is my Uncle Jack. Uncle Jack, this is Dr. Jansing. He'll be the person who will examine you for the court."

I had to remember to act perfectly straight. That would mean trying to speak like Jack, sit like Jack, and have the same speech cadence as Jack. That wouldn't be too hard to do. This guy didn't know Jack from Adam, so I assumed he probably wouldn't know the difference between me and Jack.

Harper had explained she didn't want Jack's therapist from back in the day to examine us. That was all a part of her plan to ensure we weren't found incompetent. That other therapist would probably report to the court that we were crazy. If I could only fool him for a half hour, this therapist might not.

"Hello, Jack," Dr. Jansing said. Dr. Cutie, I thought to myself. "Come into my office."

I followed him in, watching his slight wiggle while he walked.

I sat on the couch while he sat behind his enormous desk. "Jack," he said. "Is it okay if I address you as Jack?"

"Of course," I said. I was afraid that I'd come off as wooden because I was trying so hard not to act like the queen I was. *Jack is masculine. Jack is a man. Jack isn't queer. You remember that.*

"Jack," he said. "Do you understand why you're here?"

"Yes. I'm here because the judge in this murder case, the murder of that poor priest, Father Kennedy, ordered I be here."

He nodded. "Yes. That's true. Do you know why that judge ordered you be here?"

"Yes. I do."

"And what do you understand about that? Why did Judge McFarland order you to see me today?"

"Because of how that murder happened. I blacked out when I got into that rectory. I didn't eat that day. I have a terrible problem with blood sugar. I felt light-headed before getting there, but I just ignored it. I ignored my need to have food, and I got in there and seemed to have passed out."

He cocked his head. I was afraid he'd see right through my excuse. "I see. Did you see anything before you blacked out? Did you see anybody in there before you blacked out?"

I shifted uncomfortably in my seat. The timing of when I blacked out would be important in this. Did I black out after the priest was killed or before? From what I understood, Father Kennedy had been dead in this rectory for two hours before they found Jack with the dead Father Kennedy. I didn't even know who was present when that body was found. It wasn't me. I don't think it was Eli. It might have been Sam. Sam was a wily one.

"I don't remember," I finally said.

"I see." He nodded his head. "Why did you tell the police that you did not know how you got there and didn't remember going into that rectory?"

"Well, sometimes I get memory loss when I black out like that." I looked down at my shoes, knowing I'd have to change course if I didn't want to blow the psych examination. "Oh, okay, I'll tell you the truth. I got stinking drunk that day. I didn't have low blood sugar at all. I got really drunk, and I don't know what happened. I don't remember any of it. I remember nothing about going to the rectory at all. That's why I told the police I didn't know how I got there."

"I see. And why did you lie to me just now?"

"I'm embarrassed about my drinking problem. But I figured I might as well come clean."

He made some notes, and I felt slightly panicky. I hoped he wouldn't write that I was loony tunes. That was the last thing I wanted.

"Jack," he said. "Do you know what day it is?"

"No. I don't know the date. I never know that."

"Do you know what day of the week it is?"

"It's Wednesday."

"Do you know what year it is?"

"2023."

He made some more notes. "Do you understand it would be a crime if you killed somebody?"

"Of course."

"Do you believe it is wrong to kill somebody?"

"Of course." What kinds of questions were these? Then I remembered – Harper told me that if I were to be found not guilty by reason of insanity, I would have to not know the nature of my act and not know it was wrong. So, assuming I killed Father Kennedy, if I didn't know I was murdering him, and I didn't think it was wrong, and that could be proved, I could be found not guilty by reason of insanity. Harper didn't want that.

"Do you understand that the State of Missouri has charged you with First Degree Murder?"

"Yes."

"Do you understand what that means?"

"I do."

"What do you understand that to mean?"

"It means the State of Missouri believes I committed a murder. It also means there will be a trial on the matter. My lawyer wants to take it to trial. She doesn't want to plead me guilty." I was talking like a robot. I knew it. I hoped the shrink didn't figure that out, though.

"Do you understand what it means when you say your lawyer wants to take your case to trial?"

"Yes. That means she'll gather evidence and witnesses, and the prosecutor will do the same. Then we'll go before a judge and jury and present our evidence after the prosecutor presents her evidence, and, hopefully, the jury will return a verdict of not guilty, and I'll go free."

"Do you believe you can participate in your trial?"

"Do you mean I can tell my story on the stand and help my attorney gather evidence and all that?"

"Yes."

"Of course. I can do all that. That's not a problem at all."

"Okay." He nodded his head. "This examination is cursory and preliminary. The judge might order a more thorough examination, but for now, you are deemed competent to stand trial. I'm also going to make a preliminary finding that you appear to know the nature and wrongfulness of murder, so I don't see a basis for a not guilty by reason of insanity plea. But this is just preliminary, you understand. I believe, however, you're definitely competent to stand trial. That finding will be definitive. The other finding, about whether you met the legal definition of insanity at the time of the murder, will have to come later if the judge orders such an exam."

"Thank you," I said, standing up. "Dr. Jansing. I appreciate your time."

"Of course. Let me show you out."

At that, he opened up the door of his office, and I went into the waiting room. Harper was sitting there, looking anxious. I smiled at her, and her face relaxed. She nodded.

"I'm ready, Harper," I said, turning around and smiling at Dr. Cuty-Cute. "Thank you, Dr. Jansing," I said.

"You're very welcome."

We left the office, and Harper linked her arm through mine. "How did it go?" she asked me after we got on the elevator.

"Oh, it was awful. Just awful. He made me go through all these tests. I didn't know what end was up. Why didn't you tell me he'd show me a porno in there and ask me if it got me hot?"

She furrowed her brow at me, and I laughed. Then she looked at me for a few seconds more, and she also laughed. "You got me there, Uncle Jack," she said. She called me "Jack," just in case somebody was around to hear her. She told me beforehand why this was important. "Really, how was it?"

"It was a pretty lame exam. He wanted to know if I knew that murder was wrong." I rolled my eyes. "As if I would say 'no, I didn't know killing somebody in cold blood was wrong.' Really, Harper, where do they find these shady doctors?"

We got into her car, and she shut the doors and put the windows up. We needed to speak freely, with no prying eyes and ears around.

"He's not a shady doctor. He's simply asking you questions to determine if you were legally insane at the time of the murder. What else did he ask you?"

"He asked me what day it was, if I knew why I was talking to him, if I knew I was being charged with murder, if I could participate in the trial. Things like that."

"Again, he was just trying to determine if you're competent to stand trial."

"I am. I don't know if Jack is, though. I don't think he is. He can help you with the trial, but I don't think he can withstand it. He better not come back out, at least not until all this is through. Sometimes he has a will, though, Harper, and he comes back out, whether or not I want him to. The little bastard."

"Why do you call him a little bastard? It's his life, you know. You've just hijacked it."

"Yes, I did. He can't handle reality right now. He hasn't been able to handle reality since Mary died. Do you know he almost killed himself? Bastard went into the bathroom, and I knew what he was thinking. He had this huge razor and had it on his wrists, and if I didn't come out right at that moment, we all would've been pushing daisies. Little girl, I know you think I hijacked him, but trust me, I didn't. I saved him. Never forget that. I saved him."

Harper shook her head. "Oh, Mick, I didn't know that."

"He almost killed himself." I hesitated. "Harper, I'm very sorry we have to be around. I'm sorry Jack had to go through what he endured when he was a little boy. You have to know, though, a part of him knows everything. Part of him knows about the burnings, the beatings, and the torture Steven put him through. A part of him knows about the fucking Steven did to him. A part of him knows he helped Steven get rid of those bodies and that he helped find young boys and girls for Steven. Jack, deep down, knows all this. That's why I have to be out, Harper. I have to save Jack from all that knowledge. Mary was the one who had helped him before. She's gone now, Harper, and right now, I'm the only one who can protect him from himself."

Harper nodded. "I know, Mick. I know. I appreciate what you've done for him. I really do." She gave me a quick hug and started the car. "Now, let's get you to Mom's house."

I rolled my eyes. "Oh, yes, your mother. Yay! I can't wait to stay with her. By the way, where is your father?"

"I don't know. He works a lot." She looked sad when she said that, and I wondered why. "Let's go."

We headed to Claire's house, where I knew I would stay.

I would try to keep Jack away.

I hoped I could.

CHAPTER
THIRTEEN
HARPER

"MOM," I said when I brought Mick back to the house. "I need to speak with you."

"Oh?" she said as she greeted us both at the door. "Hello, Harper, hello, Mick," she said.

"Yes," I said. "Mick, I'm so sorry, but I must speak to my mom alone."

Mick rolled his eyes. "I'll be in my room if you need me." Then he lowered his voice. "Don't kill each other. I know you want to, but try to refrain until I'm out of the house. K?"

"Sure." I looked at Mom. I suddenly knew I had to have a few answers.

Mick went to his room, and Mom played with her necklace, not looking at me.

"Where is Dad?" I asked. "He hasn't been here the last few times I've visited. And Mick asked me in the car where he was. That made me realize he must not be around, period, because Mick has been staying here, and he would know, of all people, if Dad were around. So, where is he?"

My mom sighed. "He's not around, Harper. He left." She looked nervous. "Harper, there's something you should know. Something your father, I guess, hasn't wanted to tell you. And I swear, I just found this out myself."

"What? What's the big secret?"

She sighed again. "Your father is gay."

I sat down on the couch. "Stop. Stop, Mom. I don't know if you're playing a joke, but it's not funny."

"I'm not laughing." She bit her lower lip. "I swear, Harper, I had no idea. No clue. I never thought your father liked men. But he came out to me about two months ago. He sat me down and told me he met somebody."

What the hell? My mother was talking about Dad coming out as gay like she was talking about making a chicken pot pie for dinner. She had that much emotion as she spoke. "Mom, I don't understand."

"Understand this. I guess Arthur was always attracted to men and never talked about it. And then he met this guy at his golf club, and his name is Sergei – he's Russian, if you can't figure that out from his name – and I guess Sergei and Arthur started seeing each other behind my back. Sergei was married, too. Of course, he's not married anymore. Or he won't be for long. But Sergei and Arthur are living together. They found a place together about a month ago. And that's why Arthur hasn't been around for family dinners and isn't living here anymore. And, really, it's all just fine. The passion died long ago, so he was like a roommate anyhow. We're friends, too, Harper. Your dad and I are good friends."

I felt like I was falling through the looking glass again. It was true; Dad hadn't been around for a few months. He wasn't even in the hospital when I went to the psychiatric facility for those 72 hours when I became manic. But I never imagined…this. My dad was gay. Gay. What did that even mean? He and Mom had been married for, what, 40 years? 40 years and Mom never suspected a thing? My mom? My mom had always been so nosy and micromanaging my life, and she never even suspected her husband was gay?

I looked at my hands. "Well, okay. Why didn't you tell me?"

"You've had so much on your plate; the time never seemed right. You've been so busy with those two girls, your cases, and your boyfriend. And now you'll see that my baby brother doesn't serve time in prison for murder. You *are* going to see to that, aren't you, Harper? Well, I just never saw the right time."

I sighed. "You're just full of secrets, aren't you, Mom? You kept what happened to Jack as a kid from me all these years. And you kept that my father has fallen in love with a Russian guy from me, too."

I suddenly felt sympathy for her. "And all that must've been very hard on you." I went over and hugged her, and she hugged me back. "Please, Mom, please don't keep secrets from me anymore. I'm a big girl. I have big girl panties and everything. I can take it. I promise you, I can take it."

"I know, dear. I know. But I worry so much about you. You take on too much. And you're so fragile."

I let go of holding her when she said that. "I'm not fragile," I said. "I had a problem with my brain chemistry a few months ago. That's better now. Since I've been on Geodon, that problem seems to have resolved itself. I'm lucky, I guess, because I know how difficult it is to find the right meds and the right dosage. But I seem to have hit on just that. So, Mom, please never say I'm fragile because I'm not. I can kick anybody's butt in the courtroom, too."

"Oh, I didn't mean to say that to be insulting. I wanted to show that I know you don't always have it all together, as much as you try to pretend otherwise. There's nothing wrong with that, Harper. Nothing wrong with that at all. Let people help you, though. You can't always be shutting all of us out. And Albany means well. I know you think she's as nutty as a fruitcake, and I do, too, but she means well. Let her help you."

"Mom, her way of helping me is to contact Miss Cleo to give me a tarot reading. I don't think that's helping."

"See, you're insulting her by calling her psychic 'Miss Cleo.' Her psychic is Lady Starlight, and Albany insists she's the best in the business."

"Oh? Isn't she in one of those shacks with a huge sign right out front, where the word psychic is spelled P-S-Y-C-I-C?"

Mom shook her head. "Harper, you've always been so arrogant about things. You've always been such a know-it-all. If you don't believe in it, it doesn't exist. Your way of thinking is much scarier than

Albany's. Albany has much more flexible thinking. You're just way too dogmatic."

I sat down on the couch and hung my head. Mom was right. Mom was always right. She always understood my insecurities. Truth be told, I was dismissing Albany and her psychic because I didn't want to believe what that psychic said about Steven Heaney still being alive. I didn't want to think that. I wanted to think that the psychic was an absolute quack and that Steven Heaney wasn't alive. I couldn't handle knowing that such a heinous monster still walked among us. I couldn't ever think that Jack might run into him again. That would put him right over the edge, for sure.

"Well, Mom, okay. You're right. So, where can I find Dad? Where is he?"

"He and Sergei will be back from Russia in a few months. You can talk to him then."

"Russia? Russia, Mom? Dad's in Russia?"

"Yes. Sergei wanted to go home to see his family. His mother's very sick. Arthur went with him. Arthur was very excited about going to Russia. He's never been, you see, and he has always wanted to see the Kremlin. I admit, the Kremlin looks like a beautiful building. I've always wondered why they don't have those temples in Kansas City. I know Russian Orthodox people live here in town; I wonder why they don't have those beautiful temples?"

I sighed. Mom was rambling on like she did whenever she was nervous. "It's okay, Mom. Just tell me when Dad gets back. I'd like to talk to him about...Sergei. But I'm trying to figure out why you're not more upset about this."

"Because, dear. Your father and I have been living like roommates for years. It's time for him to move on and for me to move on, too. Not that I'm dating again. I can only think about that once Jack's case is over, and I know he's not going to prison. I have to ensure he gets a good therapist who can help him, too, but I'll worry about that after the trial. But I have to ensure that Jack is safe and secure, and then I'll worry about finding my next act in life, whatever that may be. I'll figure it out, Harper. But right now, all I can think about is Jack."

I nodded. "Mom, what if Jack did it? I don't think Jack did it, exactly, but what if Eli did it? We'll have to face the reality that Jack might end up in a mental institution for the rest of his life, whether or not we want to admit it."

Mom rapidly shook her head. "No. I won't accept that, Harper. I just won't. You'll figure out who did this, and you'll make sure Jack wins his trial. And after you do all that, I'll ensure Jack gets the therapy he needs to integrate again. I thought he had integrated before, but it turned out that the other alters simply went dormant. They didn't disappear. Jack needs to integrate completely."

"What if he can't integrate?" The integration process meant that all the personalities fused into the main self so that every one of the personalities became facets of the main personality, as opposed to separate and distinct alters. Jack would become Jack and never again have blackouts because Eli and Mick would never again take over. That would be a painful process because Mick and Eli protected Jack, but I knew it would be necessary for Jack to live a normal life.

"He *will* integrate. He will. I'll find the best therapist in the world to ensure he integrates. But that's not the problem right now. The problem is that he's facing life in prison for a murder he didn't commit. You figure that out, Harper. Find out who really did it."

I scratched my head and rolled my eyes. "I hope I can do that, Mom. It won't be easy. I'm talking to the cops on the scene on Monday, and hopefully, they can illuminate more about what happened. Hopefully, they can tell me something I can go on. I hope they're doing an active investigation on this as well. I know it's easy for them to settle on Jack because Jack was found by the body with the knife in his hand. It looks bad, but it also looks like a total setup. I'll figure it out, though, Mom."

"I hope you can, Harper," she said. "Please don't give up."

"Oh, I won't give up, Mom. I can assure you of that. Whether or not I can prevail, though, is an open question. I'll have to try my best, put my best effort in, and see what happens."

Mom gave me a quick hug as I left, and I went upstairs to Jack's bedroom to say goodbye.

"Bye, doll," he said. He was sitting on his bed, typing on his computer propped up on a little makeshift stand. "Don't worry about Claire. She'll be okay."

"You obviously don't know about my father."

"Oh, I know now. I overheard. So, he's queer. So what? That doesn't mean he's any less your father than before you found that out about him. And Claire seems fine with it. I know it'll be tough to see your father with this Sergei fella, whoever he is, but try not to be judgmental. I know that's tough for you, Harper, but try."

"Okay. Well, Uncle Mick, I'll see you soon. I'm doing all kinds of investigations. I'll find out who did this. I promise you."

"I know you will. Well, ta ta. I'll see you soon."

I kissed his cheek and went down the stairs.

As I left, I knew I'd put my heart and soul into this case.

I prayed it would be enough.

CHAPTER
FOURTEEN

THE NEXT DAY, it was time to talk to the cops on the scene. Officer Brown and Officer Maddox were the ones who got to the scene first. I had a copy of the police report, which told me what happened. But I needed to actually interrogate the cops to see if they could provide any other tidbits for me. I'd subpoena them for a deposition if they told me something good. That was a Jackson County rule for criminal proceedings - I could conduct depositions as part of discovery. This wasn't the case in many local jurisdictions, but it was in Jackson County, so I'd run with it.

"Hey, Harper," Officer Brown greeted me when I entered his office. "How are things on the other side?" He grinned and offered me a donut. "I know, I'm such a stereotype with these donuts, but I'm kinda addicted to Lamar's."

I took a jelly donut out of the box and noted that Officer Larry Brown, despite his professed donut habit, seemed to be in amazing shape. "Thanks, Larry," I said, biting into the middle. The raspberry filling oozed out, and Larry handed me a napkin, a smile on his face.

"So, you're here to talk about Jack Calhoun," he said. "I got the file right here."

"Yes. Jack Calhoun. I wanted to ensure I got the details right and if there was anything else you could tell me about it."

"Go ahead. Ask away. I'll tell you whatever you need to know. As usual, I'm an open book."

I cleared my throat. "Okay. Here's what I understand happened. You and Officer Maddox got to the rectory early in the evening on a Wednesday this April 12. And why were you called? That part wasn't on the police report."

Larry got out the file and looked at his notes. "Yeah, sorry about that. Sorry, I didn't put that into the report. I do so many of these goddamn things a day; sometimes, I leave out details. But according to my notes, we received an anonymous call about a welfare check. This person was worried about the Father. He wanted me to check on him and ensure he was doing okay."

I furrowed my brows. This seemed significant to me. It annoyed me that Office Brown had left it out. "He was worried about the Father? Why was he worried about him? Did he say?"

"Yeah. He said the Father had been in the rectory with a known harasser. I guess that your Uncle Jack was known around the church for being somebody who was stalking the Father. Father Kennedy had told his Associate Pastor, Father Mathews, that he was worried about Jack. He thought Jack was just a bit unhinged. And, when Jack was in that rectory for such a long time with Father Kennedy, this person got concerned."

I made notes carefully. Something about this story wasn't adding up. Father Mathews indicated that Father Kennedy had repeatedly told him that Jack was making sexual advances on Father Kennedy. But I didn't recall him telling me that Father Kennedy had found Jack dangerous. He certainly didn't use the word "unhinged."

"So," I said. "You got to the rectory because this person called you, and what happened? What did you find?"

"We knocked and announced. Nobody answered. We then got a locksmith to break into the rectory. When we entered the door, your Uncle Jack was lying on the couch, passed out, with a knife in his hand. Father Kennedy was lying on the floor, covered in blood, and recently deceased. I arrested Mr. Calhoun." Larry bit into a lemon-filled donut that was covered in powdered sugar. "Damn, Lamar's knows how to make donuts."

"Yes, they do." I took another bite of my raspberry-filled donut and rubbed my stomach. "What did Mr. Calhoun say to you when you arrested him?"

"Well, he was unconscious, so he didn't say much. With his hands behind his back, we handcuffed him and carried him into the squad car. On the way over to the station, he woke up."

"What did he say?" This wasn't in the police report, either. I wanted to know if he announced he was Jack, said his name was Mick, or claimed not to know what was happening. Either way, I didn't know why Jack would've been unconscious. When he flipped over to Mick, he didn't lose consciousness. He simply changed over. It was almost seamless. I was suspicious about this, to say the very least.

"Not much. He asked where he was. We told him he was in the back of a squad car. He asked why he was in the back of the squad car. We told him he was in custody for the murder of Father Kennedy. He then looked out the window and refused to say anything more. It was rather odd how he acted. He had no clue what was happening, but once he figured out he was in the squad car, he clammed up. He apparently knew enough to not say anything more. Then we got him into the station for questioning, and he refused to speak. He said nothing at all. So, yeah, we got little out of him. To say the very least."

"Did anybody bother examining him? Physically? Did anybody stop to consider why he was passed out in the rectory?"

"Well, yes. Of course." Larry looked down at the table. "I mean, we checked to see if anybody hit him on the head. Apparently, nobody did."

"No other examination?"

"No. We took him into custody. We didn't take him to the hospital because he woke up and seemed fine. He was talking, and he was coherent." Larry screwed up his face. "And that was that."

After talking with Larry, I thought I had some fruitful avenues to explore. It sounded like there was the possibility that somebody came in and killed Father Kennedy and maybe overpowered Uncle Jack and made him pass out. Then again, maybe he passed out because of the trauma of what happened. Uncle Jack was so fragile and broken, that was a definite possibility, too. Losing consciousness after doing something like that wasn't unheard of.

"Is there anything else you can tell me?" I looked at the police report. It indicated that the knife found in Uncle Jack's hand was sent for DNA analysis immediately after Uncle Jack was taken into custody. The addendum to the report showed the DNA analysis matched Father Kennedy's blood and Uncle Jack's fingerprints. I wanted to have a glove analysis done, and I would, but without figuring out who could've done this, getting a glove analysis done would be pointless. I needed a solid suspect to pin this on. Thus far, I wasn't getting any closer to that.

"No. That's really all I can say. There wasn't a sign of a struggle. Nothing was out of place in the rectory. We checked, and there wasn't so much as a book that had fallen off the shelf. And Mr. Calhoun was a mute man." He shrugged. "We're still investigating, mind you. But, for now, it looks like your Uncle Jack is our guy. Sorry about that."

"Don't be sorry. You're just doing your job." I wanted to acknowledge that everything looked bad, but I didn't want to admit that.

Jack was no help, of course. That was because he wasn't Jack when this happened. He apparently wasn't Mick, either.

I needed to talk to Eli. I didn't know why Mick was hiding him, but Eli held the key. I knew he did.

Why didn't Mick let me speak to him, though?

CHAPTER
FIFTEEN

I WENT to see Jack again after talking to the cops. I wanted to coax Mick into giving up Eli. I wanted to ask him why he was hiding him. I was determined to get answers, and I didn't have any answers thus far.

Unfortunately, however, when I got to my mother's house, I realized Jack was out. I didn't know why. From what I knew about Mick and what I had been reading about DID, I thought Mick would be out until the trial. Mick was the strongest of Jack's current alters, and Mick would be the one who would keep the others in line. And, because Jack was going through a great deal of stress, I didn't think he would be "allowed" out by Mick. But, apparently, he was.

"Hi, Uncle Jack," I said to him. I noted he wasn't wearing glasses, his feet were firmly on the floor, and I knew he was Jack and not Mick before he opened his mouth.

"Hi, June Bug," he said. He was sitting on my mother's front porch swing, drinking a glass of lemonade. He seemed relaxed and calm. "How are things going in my case?"

"Not too good." I felt irritated that I was talking to Jack, not Mick, because Jack knew nothing.

"Why? What's going on?"

"Well, I've been trying to find who might've done this. I have very little to go on right now." I sighed, not really knowing what to ask Uncle Jack. "And you're sure you never knew Father Kennedy, right?"

"No, June Bug. No. I never knew him. I don't go to church. I haven't been religious ever since Mary died. I prayed while she was in the hospital after that accident. She was in a coma, you know. And she was on a ventilator to help her breathe. I prayed to God every night for Him to save her. And then I prayed some more. I even told God that I would gladly take her place if only He would spare her. And He didn't listen to me. He wasn't there. So, I just gave up on ever believing in Him again."

Uncle Jack looked into the distance. "And, you know, June Bug, it seems that something else in my life happened to me. There was another time when I prayed a lot to save myself and others, and nothing happened. I just don't know, though. I just can't seem to get those memories back. I've tried. There's something there, June Bug. Something there." He shook his head. "But something happens every time I try to bring back those memories. I…"

"You, what?"

"I black out again. Every time I get close to finding out what those memories are, I totally black out and lose time. But there's something. Sometimes I can smell something, and it trips something in me. A certain smell. A certain song. A certain house. I keep going to this house on the East Side of town. It's a large house. A shirt-waist, one of those homes built around 1910. A big old house with a fenced-in yard that looks abandoned. Tall weeds growing up in the yard. It looks almost haunted. And there's something about that house that trips me up, June Bug. Something about it. But it gets frustrating because I get so close to finding out what that house means to me – so close I could touch it. And…nothing. I black out. Like I blacked out in that rectory."

"Do you remember blacking out in the rectory?"

"Oh, heaven's sake, no. I don't even remember going into the rectory, June Bug. I would have no cause to go there."

I bit my tongue. I wanted so much to make him remember going in there. Maybe he saw somebody in there. Perhaps he walked in on the real killer, and he fainted from seeing the sight of the blood. Or maybe the real killer forced him to drink some kind of powerful sedative that caused him to black out. There could be any number of scenarios that could help me out, but thus far, I wasn't getting anywhere. Unless I could speak with the alter who actually walked into that rectory, or Jack himself could remember, I wouldn't get anywhere.

I could put him under hypnosis, but I was afraid of that. I was afraid Jack couldn't handle the memories that would come flooding into him if he were put under hypnosis. I was afraid for his mental health. He was on the precipice as it was. Jack was so vulnerable that Mick might take over for good because Jack simply couldn't handle what was in his psyche. That was clear – the moment he remembered, even just a little, what happened in Steven Heaney's home, Mick took over. Or Eli.

Just then, I looked at my phone. It was Anna calling.

"Excuse me, Uncle Jack," I said. I had forgotten I asked Anna several days ago for more information about Steven Heaney. I hadn't followed up with her. I wondered if she was calling about what she found out.

My heart started pounding for some odd reason. "Hey, Anna," I said. "I'm so sorry. I forgot to call you back. What did you find out?"

"No," she said. "I'm sorry. I should've called you earlier. But I've been finding out some amazing things about Steven Heaney. I think you and I need to meet. And talk about this. You just won't believe what's going on."

My heart was pounding even more. "Okay, where do you want to meet?"

"I'll come to your office," she said. "When can you be there?"

"Half an hour."

"See you then."

I got off the phone. "Uncle Jack," I said. "I need to go. I'm so sorry."

"It's okay, June Bug," he said. "I'll be here. I'm not going anywhere. Mainly because I can't go anywhere, but I don't have anywhere to go, even if I weren't on restriction."

I kissed him on the cheek, and he smiled.

"Bye, Uncle Jack."

As I left him, I wondered if he would be Jack when I got back to him. Or Mick. Or Eli.

Or maybe even somebody else.

CHAPTER
SIXTEEN

ANNA MET me at my office. She was already there when I got there, talking to Pearl. She stood up and smiled when I walked through the door. "Seriously, hemp oil," she said to Pearl. "It does the most amazing things for your skin."

"I'll try that, girl," Pearl said with a smile.

I nodded. "Hemp oil, huh? That's what makes your face so amazingly smooth?" I always admired Anna. She was so gorgeous without even trying. Effortlessly gorgeous. I had to wear makeup all the time to cover up my freckles and make my eyelashes visible. I looked like a freckled ghost if I didn't wear mascara and foundation. But Anna, with her long dark eyelashes and olive skin, was beautiful without an ounce of makeup.

"You got it," she said. "Let's go into your office. I need to show you what I learned about this guy."

We walked into the office, and I sat down. "Okay, girl, what you got?"

She nodded. "Well, your sister was right. Steven Heaney is still alive."

I knew that. On some level, I knew that to be true. I didn't want to admit that psychic hack was onto something, though.

I had to grudgingly admit that Lady Starlight was on the level, at least with this. I certainly wouldn't go to her and ask her for insight on Jack's case, though. I wouldn't have her look into a crystal ball and tell me who did it. But, on this one thing, Lady Starlight seemed to have it all figured out.

"How is that possible?"

"Well, that's what I was trying to find out. I finally tracked down the birth records for Steven Heaney, and he has an identical twin. Had an identical twin, I mean. That identical twin was the one in that house. That serial killer that everybody knew as Steven Heaney wasn't Steven Heaney. It was his twin, whose name was Robert Heaney."

"The serial killer wasn't ever Steven Heaney?"

"Now, I'm not saying that at all. I'm simply saying that Robert Heaney was killed in that house. The house of Steven Heaney. But I won't tell you that the serial killer wasn't Steven. It still might have been."

"But how did you figure all of this out? How did you figure out that Robert was killed and not Steven?"

She smiled. "Well, I must admit, I'm not all that sure about it. All I know is that I spoke with a guy going by the name of Robert Heaney. I found him, and I went to his house. I'm telling you, this assignment has been the highlight of my life." She shook her head. "You just can't imagine the rush I got from being in this dude's presence." She shuddered. "It was the most rad thing in the entire fucking world, man. The most rad thing."

"Wait, wait, wait. Back up. You talked to a guy going by the name Robert Heaney. How did you know this was Steven Heaney and not Robert Heaney?"

"Because, dude, it's like this. I'm like this geek when it comes to serial killers. I already told you all about that, but it bears repeating. And I got this shit memorized. The pictures they have in those books about this Steven Heaney guy, I have them memorized. And those pictures of Steven growing up showed this birthmark on his right arm." She pointed to her right forearm. "Here. It's a pretty distinct birthmark. It looks like a teeny, tiny Florida. Complete with the panhandle."

I furrowed my brow. "Okay. So this Robert Heaney guy had that birthmark?"

"Yeah, dude. He did. He had it on his forearm. So, I knew it was him. But this dude was on the level. I don't know, but I'm fascinated by evil. Sometimes I wish I could do what you do, be a prosecutor or something. I would work with this shit all the time. That would be my dream job."

I wrote while listening to Anna but was trying to make sense of it. First, why didn't the cops figure out that the dead guy in that house was Robert Heaney and not Steven Heaney? And who was to say that the guy who killed the kids wasn't Robert all along, taking the identity of Steven? Maybe Steven was innocent of any wrongdoing, and his identical twin brother was the one doing all that killing?

Or there might have been a much more sinister solution. Maybe Steven was the actual killer, and he somehow, someway, got his identical twin brother to go into that house, and Uncle Jack killed him. Uncle Jack killed Robert, not Steven, and Steven, no fool, decided to high-tail it out of there.

No doubt about it; I would have to speak with Eli. Only Eli had the details of the "death" of Steven Heaney. There might've been something that led to "Steven's" death. There had to be some triggering incident that would have made Eli want to kill "Steven." Might Steven have put Robert in his place, knowing Eli was on the verge of murdering Steven? That would've been the perfect way of getting out of what he did. Lure his brother into that house, make sure his brother was killed, and then skate out of there with nobody being the wiser.

Back in the 1970s, they didn't have DNA testing; at least, it wasn't as widely used as it is today. The cops wouldn't do a DNA analysis on Robert's corpse, even if they knew there was an identical twin, which wasn't a sure thing. It probably wasn't even known they were twins. As for the birthmark...I doubted if the cops figured out that the corpse in that house didn't have that distinguishing birthmark. According to the stories that I'd read about Steven Heaney's death, the cops interviewed Eli, who was the only coherent survivor, as Mary was in a catatonic state at that point.

I tapped my pen against my desk repeatedly. There was something about this. Something about the fact that Steven Heaney was alive was significant. I wondered if Steven Heaney was somehow, someway, behind the murder of Father Kennedy.

"Harper," Anna was saying. "What are you thinking about?"

"I just need to speak with somebody. And goddamnit, I can't figure out how to reach him." I shook my head. "I just don't know how to reach this person. I don't know."

"Who is it?"

"Nobody important." I didn't want to tell Anna about Jack's issues. I was still so protective of him. "I mean, it is. But-"

"But what?" Anna was looking at me suspiciously. "You want to talk to somebody important, but you won't tell me who it is?"

I sighed. "You probably wouldn't believe me if I told you."

"Try me."

"Well, it's like this." I took a deep breath as I got up to shut the door to my office. "My Uncle Jack has Dissociative Identity Disorder, or DID for short. He was Steven Heaney's last victim. He developed alternative personalities to protect him while living at Steven's house. He has Mick, who is gay, and apparently in love with Steven, and Eli, a tough druggie dude who took the torture and severe abuse. Those are the only ones I know about, but I think there might be more. Mick, the dominant personality, won't let me speak to Eli. I think Eli not only knows the truth about Steven Heaney and his death, but he also might know the truth about the death of Father Kennedy."

Anna was nodding, her beautiful face lighting up when I spoke about Uncle Jack's problems. "Oh my God, you've been hiding this from me all along? You bitch." She smiled when she said that, so I knew she was joking. "Fascinating. I've never known anybody with that disorder, and trust me, I've known some freaky people."

Then she looked embarrassed after she said that. "I mean. I don't mean that your Uncle Jack is freaky. I just meant..." She shook her head. "Open mouth, insert foot. I have to stop my diarrhea of the mouth. Sorry."

"Oh, it's okay. But, you know, I have a mental illness, too. Many people would label me crazy because, before I got my bipolar diagnosis, I occasionally heard voices, and I would go into an alternative reality. You had to call 911 because I was having a mental breakdown."

I raised an eyebrow. "So, my uncle has a mental illness, but who wouldn't under those circumstances? His DID allowed him to live normally for much of his life. His alters went dormant, and because his alters were the ones who remembered what happened in that house, Jack himself doesn't have those memories. Those memories are in there, however. Buried. Before his wife died, though, he lived normally. He was a partner in a large law firm. He had no children but spent time with his nieces and nephews, doing normal things like camping and fishing. He was a wonderful uncle, and if his wife never died, his alters would probably still be dormant, and he still would have no clue about what had happened to him."

"Yeah, I know. I'm sorry, Harper. I shouldn't be so condescending. I didn't mean disrespect."

"I know you didn't." I sighed. "So, here's the practical question for you. How do I get in touch with Eli? Mick, the dominant personality, told me I couldn't talk to Eli. How do I break through? I need to speak with him. He has the answers. He has the keys. Without speaking with Eli, I'll be crawling around in the dark."

Anna screwed up her face. "Hypnosis?"

"I thought of that. I'm afraid hypnosis will do permanent damage to Uncle Jack. He might start remembering what happened to him in that house and be permanently scarred by that. I think I might have to have that done after I speak with the therapist he had back in the day – the therapist who treated him after he got out of that house. But I just don't know. I think that should be a last resort."

Anna drummed her fingers on my desk, and she stared at me. She had a question in her eyes. She stared at me, shook her head, and then stared at me again. I knew she was thinking something she was maybe afraid to say out loud. Something she thought was inappropriate or silly or something that I would just say "hell no" to.

Finally, in a small voice, she said, "Doesn't your sister know a psychic?" She winced like she thought I would slap her across the face for even saying such a thing.

"Yes. She does. Her name is Lady Starlight. She has an office on Blue Parkway. Why do you ask?"

"Well, maybe this Lady Starlight can communicate with Jack's alters. It's worth a shot."

I raised an eyebrow, thinking this wasn't a bad idea. But, then again, maybe it was. I doubted I could drag Mick over to that office. Mick was the one who controlled everything. I doubted he would allow me to drive him to a psychic, knowing that the psychic would try to speak with Eli.

"I don't think that would work. Unless..."

Would Lady Starlight make a house call? I couldn't take Jack to her premises on Blue Parkway because Jack was restricted and couldn't really leave my mother's house unless it was court-ordered, and seeing a psychic wouldn't qualify as something I could get a court order for. But if she could come to the house...

Oh, what are you thinking? Seriously, you're thinking about calling a psychic to come to your mother's house and speak with Eli? "No, that won't work. I'll have to figure something else out."

"Okay," Anna said. "Well, I hope you figure it out. I need to sort this out, too. I'm intrigued."

Intrigued. That was a good word. Intrigued.

I, too, was intrigued. I now had another path to go down.

I had no idea if the fact that Steven Heaney was alive was significant.

I had a feeling that it was, though.

CHAPTER
SEVENTEEN

WHEN I GOT HOME, I found a pleasant surprise. Abby seemed better. Much better. She was smiling. I hadn't seen her smile for so long; I almost forgot what it looked like.

"Mom," she said. "I made dinner for you. Rina helped."

I had a light chuckle as I saw that her dinner comprised scrambled eggs and fried tortillas. She also apparently opened a can of pinto beans and boiled them up. "That looks amazing, Buttercup," I said. "What's the occasion?"

She shrugged. "I feel bad for what I said to you before. When I said I wanted my birth mother. That wasn't a very nice thing for me to say. And I didn't really mean it. Anyway, I'm feeling better."

I entered the dining room, where Rina was busy setting the table. "Mom," she said. "Abby is trying to say that she got all crazy over that loser James when the real problem was that she got her period for the first time." Rina rolled her eyes. "She didn't even tell me about it, Mom. Like it's some big secret."

"Abby, honey," I said, entering the kitchen to find her. "Why didn't you tell me you got your period?"

She shrugged. "I was embarrassed, I guess."

"Embarrassed? Why would you be embarrassed?"

"I don't know, it's just embarrassing."

I had bought Abby and Rina some tampons and pads earlier in the year in anticipation of this happening, but I figured they would come and tell me. I was slightly hurt that Abby wanted to keep it all a secret. "There's nothing to be embarrassed about. You're becoming a woman." I said and immediately regretted saying it. Becoming a woman. That was such a cliché and not at all helpful. Besides, I didn't want her to grow up too soon. I wanted her to be my little girl. I felt selfish as I realized how much I needed her to stay just as she was for a little while. Soon enough, she would date, drive, and cuss me out. Right now, though, she was sweet as pie Abby. I didn't want her to change.

"And," she whispered. "Rina hasn't gotten her period yet. I don't want her to feel bad."

"Buttercup," I said. "Why would she feel bad?"

She shrugged. "Maybe she would. Maybe she wouldn't. But I don't want her to feel I'm passing her up. I don't know." She looked down at the beans, which were boiling on the stove. "I don't know, Mom. But I'm feeling better. Last week, I was crying every day. I thought it was because of James, but I told my counselor at school and told her I had my period, and she said that I could expect to get emotional a lot. I felt better after speaking with her."

"Good," I said. "I'm so happy to hear it." I tousled her hair. "And how are things with James? You're not still thinking of quitting band, are you?"

She shook her head. "No, Mom. I challenged the first chair today, and I won." She beamed. "I won, Mom. I'm the first chair. I know it's not that big of a deal to be first chair in the eighth grade because this is just eighth-grade band, but…."

I hugged her. "Stop trying to minimize this, Buttercup. That's huge. First chair is amazing. You started later than all those other flute play-ers, and you're already better than all of them. You should be proud of yourself. All your hard work has paid off. And you'll get into the regular band next year, and I know that when you do, you'll work your way up there, too. This calls for a celebration."

Rina came into the kitchen. "Okay, is your mother-daughter talk over? I'm hungry."

"Yes, it is. Abby made first chair."

"Yay. That's great." Rina's voice was bored, and she rolled her eyes. "Now, let's eat."

We sat down to eat, with Rina chatting about all the latest gossip at her school. "James and his new girl are already broken up," Rina announced. "And James is trying for Abby again. But Abby has told him no way, José." She and Abby high-fived, and Abby giggled.

"Oh, so that's the reason you're feeling better, huh, Abs?" I asked her with a smile. "Good girl. You just keep telling him you're not interested. Show him he can't come crawling back when he gets dumped by his new girl."

"Yeah, that's right, Abby," Rina said. "You just stand strong. James is such a douche."

"He is," Abby said, giggling. "He is."

The girls and I ate the rest of our meal while laughing and giggling about James being such a douche, and we joked around about many other things as well. It occurred to me that these girls kept me sane. They kept me out of the psychiatric facility. I knew I'd be devastated if something happened to either of them.

I suddenly had a great deal of sympathy for my mother. I couldn't imagine what it was like for her as a child, not knowing if she'd ever see her brother again. I couldn't imagine what it would be like to live under that roof, with everyone devastated and depressed. I couldn't even imagine what it would be like to have Jack back, only to find he wasn't Jack anymore. How it would be to go through the roller-coaster of trying to get used to a drug dealer and drug user who insists on being called Eli when he was clearly Jack. I didn't even want to think about all of that.

No doubt about it, if any monster came and tried to hurt Abby and Rina, they would have to deal with an angry Mama Grizzly coming after him. I would kill anybody who even thought about hurting my girls.

CHAPTER
EIGHTEEN

THE NEXT DAY, I summoned Axel. "I need to do something," I said. "And I think I might need some kind of protection. I definitely need a search warrant. I hope you can arrange that for me."

"What do you need a search warrant for, lass?" he asked. "And what kind of protection do you need?"

"There's a house I need to go to. It's abandoned. I need to go there and see if I can find anything. It's the house Steven Heaney used to live in. I am still trying to figure out what I'm looking for. I only know I need to turn over every stone to figure out what's going on with Jack's case."

"Sure, mate," he said. "Give me the address, and I'll get a search warrant for you. I'll come with you, too."

"It's on the East Side," I said. "On Agnes." I gave him the address. "I'll meet you there in an hour. Okay?"

"Okay. I'll see you then."

I didn't really know what I'd find in this house. Maybe nothing. It was abandoned and had been for years. Nobody had lived in that house ever since Steven Heaney was found dead there, and they'd found the bones of all those children. That made me feel sick to my stomach. How could a monster like that walk among us?

And was he still walking among us? I didn't know. There were two theories I was working on. The first theory was that Steven Heaney was never Steven Heaney at all. Rather, the killer was Robert Heaney the entire time, taking the identity of Steven Heaney. Robert Heaney was killed in that house and did the killing. In this scenario, Steven Heaney was the innocent and wronged party.

The other scenario was that Steven Heaney was doing the killing the entire time. He lured his identical twin brother into the house and had Eli kill him while he slipped out the back door. Under this theory, he would do that because the authorities were closing in, or maybe Eli threatened to kill him. He put his brother into his place, his brother was killed, and Eli had no idea he wasn't killing Steven.

The third scenario was that maybe the two brothers were inter-changeable. They both were crazy killers, and they both took turns doing horrible things in that house. I remembered reading a book about this once, where there were two killers, but everybody assumed there was only one. The other one was the twin, and he got away.

What are you hoping to find, Harper? What would I find in that house that would clue me into what happened? I really needed to speak with Steven Heaney. Anna had his address. I'd do that, too, but only after I got my ducks in a row. I didn't even know how to approach him. What could I do? Just go in there and say, "I'm Harper Ross, and you're Steven Heaney, and I need to ask you some questions?" I simply had to find out some answers before I approached him. He might be a totally innocent victim.

Then again, he might be a psychotic killer.

I obviously had to know who he was before I approached him.

CHAPTER
NINETEEN

WE GOT to that house on Agnes, a neighborhood East of Troost, commonly known as the dividing line in Kansas City between poor and middle-class neighborhoods. I didn't think this was necessarily true, as there were some nice neighborhoods East of Troost, too. Unfortunately, this street wasn't in the middle of these nicer east-side neighborhoods.

My heart was pounding as I approached this house. Axel was holding my hand, but I was freaking out. I'd also called Albany, and she would also meet us here.

Why did I call Albany? I didn't really know. I didn't want to admit that Albany could get some kind of vibe from the house. That she might sense a presence. I didn't believe any of that hokum. But, in the back of my mind, I really did. The whole thing about Steven Heaney being alive made me a believer. As much as I hated to admit to that fact.

"Your sister will be here, right?" Axel asked me.

"Right." I swallowed hard. The house looked just like any other house on this block. It was a three-story house with a tiny window at the top of the house. The porch in front was old and badly needed a paint job. The house was white with green trim, and the windows were boarded up. The door was solid wood with a screen door that wasn't locked because it banged in the wind. The weeds were a good four feet tall, but I was surprised they weren't even taller. After all, this house had been abandoned since Steven or Robert Heaney was found dead there. Jack was only 11 years old at that time. The State of Missouri currently owned the house, as it took possession when the property taxes went unpaid.

Nobody had been in this house since 1972. The last time anybody had been in this house, the Vietnam War raged, and Nixon was still in office. Nobody even knew the term "serial killer." An FBI agent and profiler named Robert Ressler coined that term in 1974. So, really, the last time anybody had been in this house, the term "serial killer" had not yet been coined.

I wondered if there would be restless spirits in that house. Maybe it was haunted. Lots of children died there. My Uncle Jack probably would've died in there if he didn't have that badass Eli protecting him. Probably Mary would've died there as well. I shuddered as I thought about all those innocent children playing on the streets like kids did in the early 1970s. They were abducted as they played stickball, rode their bikes, and walked home from school. Then they suffered unspeakable horror at this sick man's hands.

Or men? I still didn't know if perhaps Robert and Steven both were sickos who killed kids. Perhaps it was one or the other. They might have alternated. I didn't really know.

I knew Anna had tracked down Steven Heaney in Oregon. My new assignment for her was to find out if there were missing kids in Eugene, where Steven lived. That would tell me if Steven was one of the active serial killers because that would mean he was still doing it. He was still evil.

But if there weren't missing kids, a spate of them, in Eugene, then what did that mean? That probably meant Steven Heaney wasn't ever the serial killer. It was Robert Heaney, taking Steven's identification and posing as him. And if that was the case, then was Steven Heaney even relevant to Jack's case? Was he even relevant to Jack's case, even if he was one of the serial killers who lived in this house? If so, what was his relevance?

I heard a car pull up, and Albany got out of it. Even though it was

May, and the weather was already 80 degrees, she had sweaters in her arms – three of them, one for each of us.

"Here," she said, giving a sweater to Axel and me. "Trust me, you two will need these sweaters. You probably don't believe me when I say that, but you'll know why once you get into that house."

I furrowed my brow. "Albany, it's like a million degrees out here."

"Why do you question me?" She shook her head. "Seriously, sis, wasn't it enough that I told you Steven Heaney was alive, and then you found out from Anna this was true? Come to terms with the fact that this world has another dimension. It co-exists with this one. It's a dimension that people like you don't know about or don't want to know about, but sensitive people like myself are very in touch with this other world. And when I tell you that you'll be freezing your ass off in that house, you can take that to the bank."

I reluctantly took the sweater she gave to me. Axel already had his sweater on. "This fits well, Albany," Axel said with a smile.

"I thought it might. That sweater belongs to our father. He's about the same size as you."

"Thanks." Axel grinned, his dimples showing, and, as usual, I melted just a little. I wondered when I would stop feeling like I was melting whenever I was around him. I hoped I never would.

I took Axel's hand and gripped it tight. I felt a keen sense of anxiety, and I didn't know why. This was a house. That was all it was. A house just like any other. There wouldn't be any lingering spirits in this house. There was no such thing.

So why did I feel so apprehensive?

We walked up to the door and unlocked it. Axel had arranged for a locksmith to come in and change the door lock so we could get in.

I stood there on the porch, my feet rooted to the ground. I didn't want to take another step. "Axel," I whispered. "I'm kinda freaking out here."

"It's okay, lass," he said. "I am, too."

For her part, Albany had a big smile as she opened the door and walked on in. Axel and I stood on the porch while Albany walked into the living room and beckoned us with her hand. "Come on in," she said. "This is kinda amazing in here. I guess they didn't do the usual thing when a killer is found in a house, which is to hold a massive estate sale and then raze the damned place. It looks like they came in, did their thing, found those bones, arrested that man, and got the hell out. They've left everything in here completely intact."

I tentatively took a step into the house, and Albany was right. I was glad I had my sweater on because it was cold inside that house. Really cold. She was also right about something else – the house was left intact inside.

"Albany," I said. "Why is it so cold in here?"

"Because there are restless spirits in this house. Can't you feel them? That sense of foreboding you feel - that's them. That's why you feel like that. That's why you're freezing. Their spirits are a part of the energy in this house, and they have so much energy that they're literally taking all the heat out. They have to draw on the energy in this house, and the heat is the energy they draw on."

Albany was all smiles, just like Anna when I asked her to research Steven Heaney. I couldn't understand either of them. I didn't like the idea that possibly otherworldly spirits were trapped in this house. That these spirits were somehow doomed to stay here. I didn't believe in them to begin with, although this case changed my mind about the matter.

"This is so cool," she said as she sat on the dusty couch right in front of an old-school fireplace. She banged her feet on the equally dusty throw rug underneath the coffee table. "I just can't believe nobody has been in this house for 50 years."

There was so much dust in the air that I felt I couldn't breathe. Cobwebs were everywhere – in every corner, underneath the formal dining room table and chairs, all over every piece of furniture. I half expected to see a horde of bugs, but thankfully, I didn't. If I did, I probably would've run screaming from that house.

I hate bugs.

I took one of the flashlights Axel had in his hand and clicked it on. Even though it was broad daylight outside, this house was quite dark. "I don't know what I'm looking for," I said. "I need to find evidence that will tell me that Steven Heaney is the guy alive in Oregon and Robert Heaney died in this home."

What evidence would that be, though? Seriously? The cops had been here in 1972 and took every piece of evidence they could find. Or had they? I didn't know. The cops, back in the day, didn't do as thorough of a job on crime scenes as the cops of today. Did they miss something? Perhaps they went through the house and found the bones of the missing children and didn't do a better search of the entire house?

"Let's start in the attic," I said to Axel. "I think the attic would be where we might find something helpful. Don't you think?"

"I do, lass," he said. "If there'll be any helpful evidence, it'll be in the attic."

Axel and I creaked up the three flights of stairs, which were narrow, winding, and bounded by walls. The steps were wooden, and we heard a creaking noise with every step we took. Creak, creak, creak, went our feet as we made our way to the top floor of the house. The attic was not a liveable part of the house, even though it was in many of these houses. The gateway to the attic was a small trap door with a handle. Axel was tall enough to just reach that handle, and he gripped it and brought it down.

An attic ladder attached to the trap door came down with the door. I took a deep breath, not wanting to go up there. This house was creeping me out. This attic would *really* creep me out.

"Albany," I said. "You come up here with me."

"I will," she said. "Oh my God, I really should have a séance here. That would be amazing. Then again, I probably don't want to hear all those horror stories that those poor children will tell me. You just don't know, Harper. You probably can't feel the spirits, but I can. They're restless, angry, and hurt. Very hurt. They can't move on because of the violence done to them." She nodded her head. "I think we need a proper medium in this house. Only then can the spirits be released to where they're supposed to go. They need to move on to the next world, and right now, they can't."

"Okay," I said, not wanting to pay attention to Albany's rambling. "I know what you're saying, Albany, but we must focus on this world. Only in this world can we find evidence that will hopefully clear our Uncle Jack."

Axel looked at the stairs, and I knew he wanted to enter the attic. I would have to ask him not to do that, though. "Axel," I said. "I hate to do this to you, but can I ask you to stay down here and wait for me to come out? I'm terrified something might happen if we all three go up there – like this attic door shutting on its own and maybe locking us in. I need somebody to stay down here in case something weird happens and the police need to be called. You don't mind, do you?"

"Of course not, lass," he said. "Although I'm the detective. I can probably find little clues better than anybody here."

"I know that," I said. "You can go up there and explore after I get back."

I carefully went up the stairs that led into the attic while Axel stayed behind. Albany followed me, trailing behind me as closely as possible. "Don't get out of my sight," I told her. "Seriously."

"I won't, sis," she said.

My heart pounded as I crouched and looked around this dusty attic with my flashlight. I coughed from all the dust, and my flashlight landed on a little doll in the corner. The doll was one of those turn-of-the-century dolls with a porcelain face and pouty mouth. The hair was painted on, and she was dressed in a pink onesie-looking number. Her tiny little feet had on a pair of black shoes.

"Damn, that's a creepy doll," Albany said as she looked at the porcelain face eyeing both of us disinterestedly. "I wonder who it belonged to?"

"I don't know," I said. "But I think I need to snag it." On the search warrant Axel had obtained, we were given permission to take anything from this house that we could find that would likely lead us to evidence helpful in Jack's case. This doll fit the bill, maybe. I thought about possibly showing Jack this doll and seeing how he reacted. I hated to say that seeing the doll would trigger Mick to come back or, even better, Eli.

Why did I believe that? Maybe the doll belonged to Mary. I thought Mary, and her death, was the weak spot in Jack's psyche. There was a spot in his psyche that harbored the memories I needed from him. The memory, specifically, of what happened when Jack entered that rectory. I was desperate to find that out. There was some part of Jack that knew. I'd look for anything that might trip that memory out of him.

And, if all else failed, I would have him undergo hypnosis. But I wanted this memory to come out of him spontaneously because anything he remembered under hypnosis would never be allowed in court. Any statement he made while under hypnosis wouldn't be allowed.

On the other hand, if I could trip Jack's memory without hypnosis, he could testify in court on his own behalf. That was very important to me – to have Jack testify to the jury and tell them what he saw.

I walked further around the attic and saw little more in there. I didn't see anything I thought might be significant. There were some old record albums in a box and a record player with about six inches of dust. More furniture was up here – another couch and a fully intact bed.

There was a chest of drawers in the corner, and when I opened up the chest of drawers, I saw it was filled with men's clothing. There were blue jeans, work shirts and T-shirts in these drawers. There were also socks and underwear.

Some female clothes were hanging up on a makeshift rack, like the kind you find in a thrift store. Those were curious, so I went over to them and looked through them. There were dresses and women's slacks and shirts. Most of them were floral.

I took them off the rack, wondering why these would be significant, too. I knew they would be, though – why would a man have these female clothes? They were small clothes, too, almost like a child's clothing, but just slightly larger than that. Whoever it was who wore these clothes was tiny – extremely short and extremely thin. Bony.

"What are those, sis?" Albany said, looking at the clothes lying in my arms.

"Clothes," I said. "Here, take a heap. If we work together, we can bring all these clothes downstairs."

"I know these are clothes. I can see that. But I wonder who they belonged to?"

"Who knows? Maybe Jack knows, though. I'm determined that he'll remember something about that murder of Father Kennedy. He will. I promise you that."

Then I went over the record albums and saw it. I saw the main reason why I went into this house.

Written clearly, on every record album, on a piece of masking tape, were the words "Property of Robert Heaney."

I got excited as I went further into the attic and discovered a bookcase filled with books on one wall. I opened up each book, and each book said the same thing. "Property of Robert Heaney." There was never a mention of Steven Heaney.

"What does that mean?" Albany said as I handed her a load of books, and I took some of these books myself. "What does it mean that these books and albums belonged to Robert and not Steven?"

"I think this whole thing is door number 2. Steven Heaney might've been an innocent party all along. Maybe Robert lived here while taking Steven Heaney's identification, and Steven Heaney himself was his identical twin but maybe never had a thing to do with any of these murders." I shook my head. "I wonder why the cops never thought to look in this attic? If they did, they would've seen evidence that Steven Heaney had nothing to do with these murders."

Albany was shaking her head. "No. You're wrong about this." She shivered. "You're wrong, sis. You're wrong. Steven Heaney isn't innocent. He lived here, too. He did." She pointed at me. "Think about it, Harper. If Robert was living here, taking Steven's identity, why would he label the record albums as his property? That makes zero sense. And..." She shook her head. "I can sense Steven's presence in here. Like the furniture and the walls and everything are infected with his energy. And Robert's as well. No, Harper, I think you're wrong."

"I think Steven and Robert both were living here," Albany said. "One lived in the attic, and the other lived downstairs."

I shuddered as I thought about this house. What if Albany was right? She was sensitive to spirits. I really wasn't. She might have sensed the energy that both Steven and Robert had left behind. I couldn't feel any kind of leftover energy. She also had the sense there were spirits around.

"So, your theory is that Steven and Robert lived here and killed these kids? Yet Steven got out."

"I don't know. It's just a theory. I don't know how Steven got out, and I don't know if the people who lived here with the two twins – Uncle Jack and Mary – knew what the game was, but my theory is that both twins were equally guilty of heinous crimes. I wish I could talk to Jack about this."

"You can talk to Jack, but he doesn't remember this house. And you can't talk to Eli, who knows the most about what happened in this house," I said. "Eli is being protected by Mick. Dammit." I shook my head. "There has to be a way to reach Eli."

I thought about the scenario in that house. Eli killed Robert, and perhaps people had no idea identical twins lived in this house. Maybe society didn't know about the twins. That would certainly be possible – Robert and Steven could've easily lived in this house together, and as long as only one of them was seen around the neighborhood at a time, nobody would ever know there were two of them living in this house.

That was even assuming one of them left the house regularly. But surely one of them did. After all, they had to have food in the house. Either Robert or Steven, maybe both, alternating, had to leave the house to get groceries. As far as I knew, Eli didn't help bring groceries home.

But would the people in this house realize that two men were living there? Assuming one man actually lived in this attic. One man at a *time* lived in the attic.

I could only assume that Jack and Mary, the only survivors of this house of horrors, probably didn't know two different men lived there. If so, Eli, the alter who killed Steven, or Robert, as it were, would've known he had to kill a second man. But, then again, he was only 11 years old. And he might really have killed Robert in defense of Mary. He probably didn't even mean to kill him. If that was the case, he might not have bothered the second twin or told the cops about him.

This was all confusing for me. Even more confusing was how any of this fit into the overall scheme of things with Jack and the priest. Was it even significant, or was I completely being flummoxed? What did any of this mean?

I gathered all the evidence I found in this house and put it into an empty box in the corner. Then I opened up the attic door and climbed down. Albany followed shortly after me.

"Okay, Axel," I said to Axel, who was standing right at the base of the attic steps. "Your turn. Go on up there and see if you can find anything else to help us in this case."

"I will mate," he said, climbing into the attic.

"So," Albany said. "What do you think all this means for Jack? How might you help him with the things we found in this attic?"

"I'm not sure," I said. "Maybe I can show this stuff to Jack, and it might trip his memory. I'm nervous about doing that because I don't want to spin him out. He might have a mental breakdown if he faces these things. His psyche is so fragile, anyhow." I sighed. "But I might have no choice. I need to speak with Eli, and showing Jack these things might bring Eli out. That's so dangerous, though. What if Eli comes out and stays? What if Jack faces the reality of what happened to him and disappears forever? He told me the other day that he felt something terrible had happened to him and was trying to access those memories. He said he would black out whenever he got closer to the memory of what happened. That tells me that another alter took over whenever Jack himself accessed these memories."

I would have to go easy with the evidence I found. It might be something that would bring out Eli, who could tell me what happened to Father Kennedy, but it might be something that would completely destroy Jack in the process. In that case, I couldn't win, period. Eli would be out and Jack would be gone. That would be the devastating result of this strategy.

I could use this information to see Steven in Oregon. He was living there, according to Anna, in a secluded house far away from civilization. Anna said he was living off the land - he raised his own vegetables and hunted rabbits, squirrels and deer. He didn't have running water or electricity – he had gas lamps for his lights and a fireplace to heat his home. Everything in that home, according to Anna, looked like he had hand made it. An individual crafted all the furniture, and the house was a log cabin that looked homemade. She said Steven was living like a pioneer.

She also told me Steven was very welcoming to her. He treated her like an old friend. She got the sense that Steven was lonely living alone in the woods. I knew why he was there, too, living by himself. It was obvious to me, really – he couldn't make himself known to society. Steven Heaney's face was known to many people. The people like Anna, who were obsessed with serial killers, would recognize him. Granted, he wasn't as famous as Ted Bundy, Jeffrey Dahmer, or John Wayne Gacy. Those were the faces people knew because they were the most famous serial killers of them all. Steven Heaney's face wasn't widely known like these other killers were. He was, however, known by the really dedicated serial killer buffs, and he probably knew this. He couldn't live in society.

Axel came down. "I didn't find anything else," he said, "that would be significant. I assume you and Albany found the record albums, right?"

"Right."

"Well, here are some," he said. "I just took a few."

Gordon Lightfoot, The Beatles, and Carole King were the albums he had in his hands.

"Thanks, Axel," I said. "Well, I think it's time to get out of here."

The three of us left the house, and I was struck by how much warmer it was outside than in the house. I was getting used to the chill in that house, but it contrasted with the 80-degree weather outside and was striking.

I gave Albany a quick hug. "I love you, girl," I said to her.

"Right back atcha," she said, air-kissing me. "I'll head over to Mom's tonight," she said. "I can see if Jack is back to Mick. I'll call you if he is. I've been there three times this week, though, and he's been Jack every time."

"It's just as well," I said. "That he's Jack. Mick isn't much help in this case, either. He keeps saying he was in love with Father Kennedy. I don't even know what that means. I talked to Father Mathews, and he indicated that Jack was stalking Father Kennedy." None of that added up to me, either – if Jack wasn't religious, and Mick certainly didn't seem religious, how did they end up going to that church and meeting Father Kennedy? I'd have to look into Father Kennedy's outreach activities to the community. Perhaps that would lead me to where Mick and Father Kennedy met. And maybe that would also lead me to more evidence.

I got in the car with Axel, and he reached for my hand and kissed it. "Lass," he said, "what did you think about that house?"

"Creepy. It felt like a haunted house and not one of those manufactured haunted houses in the West Bottoms." As a kid, I used to go to those haunted houses – they were enormous buildings in the bottoms area of Kansas City, transformed into houses where people would come after you with chainsaws and mannequins played eerie music on organs. They even had rooms that made you feel you were in heaven and hell. They had names like "Main Street Morgue," "Edge of Hell," "Catacombs," and "The Beast," and they involved slides from the top of the building to the bottom. They were always a lot of fun to go to when I was a kid because I knew they weren't real. They were manufactured and constructed for one reason – to make money. Lots of money.

These haunted houses differed greatly from houses like this one. This house, where the Heaneys lived, was a real haunted house. I knew it. I could feel it. I could feel it in the chill of the house. I could feel it in the oppressive air. The entire house seemed like it was depressed and anxious if that made any sense at all. The entire house felt foreboding. I was glad to be getting out of there.

"So, what's next?" Axel asked me. "What are you going to do next?"

"I'm going to look and see what activities Father Kennedy engaged in," I said. "Father Mathews does community outreach. He plays basketball with troubled youth, and he goes to community events to meet people out in the world. I think Father Kennedy probably did the same thing." I nodded my head. "I just wonder...."

"What do you wonder?"

"I just wonder if Father Kennedy ever came in contact with one of the Heaneys." I cocked my head. It certainly could've been possible. Father Kennedy was 71 when he was murdered, which meant that, in the early 1970s, when the Heaneys were killing children, he would've been in his early 20s. I needed to learn much more about him, to find out if he ever came in contact with the Heaneys.

From there, I would have to work out a motive.

Steven Heaney was connected to this murder. I just knew it. I had a feeling. My hunches were rarely wrong.

I would have to figure out exactly how.

CHAPTER
TWENTY

WHEN I GOT to my office, I first wanted to track Steven Heaney in Oregon and try to pick his brain. No way I would tell Axel what was I was planning, though. He probably would've killed me if he knew. After all, it wasn't the safest thing to do – going alone to visit a possible serial killer at his home in the woods. I felt this was the only way to get the necessary answers to help my uncle.

But I was stopped in my tracks when I got to my office suite.

There was Heather, sitting on my couch, waiting for me. She was flipping through a magazine, looking bored and restless. Her nails were back to black, her hair was growing, and she was in full makeup again. She was also back to wearing her high-heeled shit-kicking boots.

I had to smile. To tell the truth, I missed that girl. I hadn't had the chance to talk with her these past few months because I was so occupied with everything in my life.

She stood up as I walked through the door. "Hey, Harper," she said, her eyes fluttering just a bit. "How's tricks?"

I grinned. "Same old, same old. I-"

I then looked at Pearl, who gave me a strange look. I had no idea what that look was about. Did that look have to do with Heather or something else?

She then handed me a huge document. I groaned as I saw what it was. Michael Reynolds filed an appeal for ineffective assistance of counsel. I sighed. I was expecting that. I was hoping that, somehow, someway, it wouldn't happen, but it did.

I faced the reality that Michael Reynolds could get out of prison and soon have a new trial. I prayed his appellate attorney was just as incompetent as I was on his case.

A bar complaint was bound to be next.

My "victory" with Michael Reynolds would probably be short-lived.

"I'm so sorry," I said to Heather as I read the document. "Why don't you come to my office? We can catch up a bit." I read more of the appeal while walking slowly into my office.

Heather followed me in. "Harper, I didn't want to bother you. Charlie and I aren't together anymore, and I need a job."

"A job." I was distracted, and I needed not to be. Heather was trying to talk to me, and I swore I wouldn't dump her by the side of the road. So, I reluctantly threw the appeal brief aside and looked right at Heather. "A job. Okay. What can you do? What skills do you have?"

She shook her head. "Not many, I'm afraid. But I'm willing to learn whatever you can teach me. I can answer phones or do whatever you need. I can even dress professionally. I went thrift-store shopping and picked up many suits, dresses, slacks and all that. I can do whatever, Harper. I just need something right now." She hung her head.

"How are things going with you and Louisa?" Louisa was never prosecuted for taking the butcher knife in Heather's case, mainly because I begged the prosecutor to lay off her. And, on the issue of her assisting the reverend in his murderous ways, she turned state's evidence against him for full immunity. So Louisa, legally, was free and clear. That made me happy. I really wanted Heather to know her birth mother. That was the only family she had.

Heather smiled. "They're great, actually. I love her and we get along great. So, what can I do for you? I can train for anything you need. Really."

I sighed. Pearl was really my assistant, but I could use another one. Maybe somebody who could learn how to type up petitions and motions and things like that. Most petitions were standard. Motions were more complicated because they generally weren't boilerplate, and you had to put thought and case law behind them. Then again, Heather showed she could do legal research – after all, she found my *Law Review* article. Perhaps she was smart enough to be trained.

I had the budget to hire somebody else, too. What I didn't have, however, was the patience or time to train her. "Okay, Heather, here's what I'd like you to do." I handed her the appellate brief Pearl had given me. "Read this appellate brief and find case law possibly refuting the allegations. Bear in mind I'm not involved in this appeal. I only got a courtesy copy of the brief, so whatever you find won't be something I can use. I'd like to find out who the other attorney is on this thing. It'll be somebody working for the State of Missouri. Find out who that is, and if I find you come up with some novel cases and ideas, I'll send that other attorney the cases. But, really, I just want to see how good you are with legal research."

Her face brightened. "Oh, I love that idea! Believe it or not, I love doing research like this. I'm good at it, too – I found your *Law Review* article, didn't I?" She rubbed her hands together. "I just need your Lexis or Westlaw password, and I'll get to work."

I nodded. "I'll see how you do. I probably could use a research assistant. I'm working on some heavy appeals." Doing appellate work was a small part of my business but quite lucrative – one appellate brief paid $30,000, and they were easy enough to write. I'd always considered research and writing my strong suits and had won a good percentage of the appeals that I'd taken. If Heather could find case law and statutes I could use in these appeals, half the battle would be won.

I scribbled down my Westlaw password and looked at the clock. My heart started to pound as I saw it read 1:45. I'd booked a flight to Eugene that morning, and it was due to leave at 3:30. I was losing track of time getting distracted with Heather and this damned appellate brief. "Heather, I'm so sorry, but I have to run. I, uh..." I didn't want to tell Heather what I was doing. I didn't want anybody to know what I was doing. If anybody knew, they'd talk me out of it. I didn't want that. I wanted to just interrogate Steven Heaney the best I could. I didn't even know what I was looking for. I knew Stephen

Heaney could provide clues on where to look for Father Kennedy's killer.

Maybe. But, then again, maybe Stephen Heaney might give me better insight into my uncle's psyche. That would also be helpful.

Or, there was always the possibility Steven Heaney would make me his next victim. I didn't think so, though – I didn't fit the profile of somebody he'd prey upon. If he was a serial killer working with his brother, he evidently was a child predator, and I was far from a child.

"That's okay, Harper. When do you need this research project finished?"

"Well, I'll be back in town tomorrow. I have some important pre-trial conferences." One of the pre-trial conferences wasn't Jack's, though. His case had not yet gone through the Grand Jury, so the trial judge hadn't been assigned. As soon as that judge was assigned, I'd have to get my head together about my defense. I still didn't want to try for an NGRI plea. I didn't want Jack in a mental institution for the rest of his life. I wanted him to be free.

"In town? Where are you going?"

"I'm going to Oregon," I said. "Just for the evening. I have to be back here by tomorrow afternoon."

"And who's watching your girls?"

"Sophia, of course. She always watches them when I have things I have to do. When I go out of town for whatever reason, she watches them. I don't know how I'd get along without her."

Heather nodded. "I'll have to meet her sometime. We probably would have something to talk about." She smiled. "I never, uh, told you how much you mean to me. What you did..." She looked at her shoes. "Going to jail like that to buy some time to get Louisa on that stand...No other attorney would do that. I don't know how you thought up that scheme, but I'm so glad you did. If you didn't, I'd be in prison right now."

"I know," I said. She was right, really. Heather would be in prison if Louisa didn't take the stand at the 11th hour. No doubt about it. Everything in that case worked against her. Everything. Louisa was the key, and I was forever grateful for her taking the stand when I needed her the most. "But let's not think about that. You have your whole life ahead of you. And, if you do well on this research project, you'll have a job here. I really could use a research assistant. I love doing appeals, and the key to winning appeals is finding the right case law and statutes. I'll look forward to what you come up with."

At that, I got my overnight bag underneath my desk and headed to my SUV. "Pearl," I said as I made my way out of my office suite. "I have to go out of town this evening. I'll be back tomorrow, though. There's a witness that I need to see in Oregon."

Pearl raised her eyebrow. "Girl, I hope you won't meet a creeper by yourself or something like that." She shook her head. "You take way too many chances. I hope you know that."

I nodded and made a snap decision. I'd email Pearl when I got on the plane to tell her where I'd be. I didn't think anything would happen when I saw Steven Heaney, but I couldn't be too careful. Pearl knew I'd be back in the office the next day, so if I didn't show up, she'd know where to send the police after me.

"I know I do," I said. "But it hasn't caught up with me yet." I went over to the desk, which was made of wood, and knocked on it. "I'll see you tomorrow."

I ran out to my SUV and drove off towards the airport. I didn't know what answers I'd get from him. I didn't even know exactly what answers I was seeking. I only knew he had some answers for me, and I needed to speak with him.

Jack's life depended upon it.

The plane touched down several hours later in Eugene. I had the coordinates Anna had sent me for Steven's cabin. I felt nervous, however, as I went into the Avis Rent-a-Car place, where I gave the guy my credit card and found my rental car. It was a small car, a Nissan Versa hatchback in cherry red.

I would arrive at this place at dusk. The flight was about 5 and a half hours long, so I was arriving at 7 PM. Since it was May, this was just about when it was getting dark.

I shook my head. This was a spur-of-the-moment trip. I'd struggled my entire life with my impulsive nature. I was forever doing ill-advised and stupid things without considering the consequences. Sometimes those things worked out, as when I went to jail during Heather's trial to buy time to get Louisa to testify. If I didn't do that, Heather would've gone to prison. There was no doubt about that.

But other times, those impulsive moves didn't work out so well. I hoped this wouldn't be an ill-advised and stupid, impulsive move. It might've been. I didn't know yet. If it worked out, maybe things would go well with Jack's trial. Maybe I could figure out how to speak with Eli – maybe this guy could tell me how to get around Mick's protective nature and get to the elusive Eli. That is if Steven was aware of the other personalities. I didn't know if he was.

My greatest hope was to get some important answers that might help figure out who killed Father Kennedy. If that were the case, this trip would be well worth it.

I tried to quell my racing heart as I turned off the main road and onto a dirt one. The dirt road ran through a heavily-wooded area. It was totally dark by this point. I opened my window and heard the sounds of birds, frogs and crickets. Those sounds were the only sounds I heard, however.

A cabin in the woods. Far from the beaten path. I hoped the coordinates Anna gave me were correct. Another thing was running through my head - what if I couldn't find this guy? It was amazing Anna could find him. She could find anybody, it seemed. The woman really should be a PI.

About a half hour after I left the main road, I came up on it. It was literally a log cabin, just like Anna had described it. It was made with fat logs piled up, one on top of another. It was well constructed, however. It looked like Steven built this place with his hands, but he was talented because the house looked like it could withstand an earthquake.

I saw a man on a porch swing. He had white hair and wore a button-down shirt and blue jeans. On his lap was a dog he was busy petting. The dog was a mid-sized pooch and looked like a cross between a blood-hound and a Golden Retriever. She had the coat of a Golden Retriever and the long, floppy ears and droopy eyes of a blood-hound.

He looked up at me. "Anna sent you?" he asked.

I nodded. "She did. How did you know about that?" I didn't tell Anna I was coming here. I wondered how this guy knew to expect me.

"I figured." He swung on the swing while he continued to pet the dog. "I don't know how that girl found me, but I can't say I was upset to see her. I haven't had company in over 50 years, and it was nice to have another person to talk to for once."

I studied him. His hair was white, and his face was wrinkled, but his eyes were steely-blue and very clear. He looked like he had gotten too much sun in his life, which was why his skin had the consistency of leather. However, if it weren't for that, it was possible he wouldn't look old. But he was older – he was almost 75 years old. I read in the paper he was 25 at the time all those killings happened, and that was 50 years ago. "Are you upset to see me?"

He shrugged. "I can't say I know who you are or why you're here. I only figured you knew Anna because she's literally the only person who's been here since I built this place." His blue eyes looked sad. "It's been almost 50 years since I've banished myself from civilization because of my brother. He cursed me to this life. I may never forgive him for that."

I stood there because he hadn't yet invited me to sit down. It felt incredibly awkward, but I no longer felt frightened. This man wasn't intimidating. He was old – I would hazard that his years on this earth were much shorter than those he felt. In other words, he seemed much older than his chronological age. And I was genuinely curious about what he said about his brother cursing him to this life. What did that mean? I was sure it meant his brother was the serial killer and had taken his name and identity. That's what it sounded like to me.

"Well," he said, standing up. "You might as well come in the cabin. I have some bathtub whiskey in there. Don't worry. It tastes better than it sounds. I think I've perfected it over the years if I must say so myself."

I followed him into the cabin. He motioned me to sit in a chair before an enormous stone fireplace. I sat down, and he went into the kitchen, which consisted of a cast-iron cauldron and a stone stove heated by flames. The stove looked like he probably made it out of rocks around the property.

He came back in with a bottle in his hand. I took a deep breath. I couldn't take a drink, of course. As much as I was dying to taste the fascinating concept of "bathtub whiskey," I couldn't risk my sobriety. Besides, I needed my wits about me to figure out any clues Steven might give me.

"I'm so sorry," I said politely. "But I really can't share this liquor with you. I'm a recovering alcoholic and haven't been on the wagon all that long. It's not even been a year since I last fell off the wagon."

He nodded. "I get it. Well, I wanted to offer it up. I didn't want to be a terrible host. I also have stew cooking on the stove. Or the cauldron or whatever you want to call it. Rabbit stew. It's pretty good. I grow all my own vegetables, of course, and I've even learned how to bake bread out of the wheat I've managed to grow around here. You'd be surprised what skills you can learn if you need them."

"Actually, that would be nice. I haven't had dinner." I wasn't actually hungry but wanted to be polite. I knew the best way to bond with somebody was to literally break bread. Especially if that person prepared a home-cooked meal, which Steven evidently had done.

"Good," he said. "Let's go into the dining room, and I'll give you a bowl of my rabbit stew. It's not dinner at The Ritz, but it works. Nutritious, too." He chuckled. "Anna told me organic vegetables are all the rage, so I guess I'm on trend."

I sat at the table, and Steven brought out a bowl of stew. "It's pretty hot," he said, giving me a piece of bread. "Dunk this bread in the stew. That's how I do it."

He sat down and took a sip of his whiskey.

I took a bite of the stew, and, I had to admit, it was delicious. It was pungent with fresh herbs, just the right amount of salt and an extremely tender rabbit. It was chock full of carrots, potatoes, green beans and peas. The broth was rich and flavorful. I eagerly ate my bowl while I noticed Steven watching me carefully as he ate a bowl of stew.

"Do you like it?" he asked anxiously.

"Oh, my, yes. Yes, I do."

He beamed proudly. "I hoped you would. You have to understand that, in almost 50 years, I've had just two dinner guests here. You and Anna. I'd forgotten how much I craved company. I'd gotten used to being completely alone here, except for Stella and my paperbacks I've read a million times." He motioned to a little bookshelf with about 60 paperbacks on it. He tended towards the classics - Dickens, Dostoevsky, Dumas, Hugo, Fitzgerald and Hemingway. He also had everything Hunter S. Thompson ever wrote. I was impressed.

He shrugged as I looked at his book collection. "When you've nothing else to do, you can concentrate on what these writers are getting at. Every time I read *The Count of Monte Cristo*, I get something else out of it. Same with every other book I've read again and again."

Stella came up and whined softly. Steven reached into his stew and, with his fingers, brought out a piece of meat and fed her. She eagerly ate the meat and begged for more.

"She's so spoiled," Steven said, stroking her ears and neck. "Stella. I found it in the woods, believe it or not. I don't know how she managed to get this far in. When I found her, she was starving, mangy and on her last legs. I didn't care. She was beautiful because I needed somebody to keep me company. I was damned near ready to commit suicide when she arrived at my doorstep and saved me from myself."

He took a deep breath. "Animals are so much more valuable to this world than anybody appreciates. They bond with you and know your emotions better than anyone could understand. There's a reason for therapy dogs and why dogs are brought into hospitals to visit people. They save people's lives in more ways than one."

I nodded, thinking that even Hitler loved animals, especially his dog, Blondie. But I wasn't quite sure this guy was evil like Hitler. He might've been a patsy. His brother could've been the killer, not him. I had a feeling this was the case.

"Well, this stew certainly is delicious," I said. "If you don't mind, I'd like seconds."

He smiled big. "Music to my ears. I should've been born Italian because I always ensured my guests were well-fed. Plus, I've always liked to cook. When I was younger..." His voice trailed off. "Well, that's neither here nor there. My life has been nothing but a waste. But when I was younger, I wanted to be a chef in a five-star restaurant. That was my dream. I never thought I'd end up in the woods, far from civilization. I never dreamed this would be my fate. But after my brother was found dead, and everybody thought I died in that home, I didn't know what else to do. I feared the police thought I had something to do with what happened in that house. I had nothing to do with what happened. Nothing."

He sighed as he stared at his glass of whiskey. "You ever make bathtub whiskey, Ms. Ross?" he asked.

"No, I never have."

"It's easier than you might think. You just have to get some corn and mash it, add yeast and water. Then just let it sit a few weeks to ferment. The first time I made this, it was the most wretched thing in the world. It was rank. It smelled disgusting and tasted even worse. But it did the job. I've refined my techniques over the years. I've learned how to make it smooth as butter. I had nothing else to do but figure out how to make better moonshine. It's been a challenge, but I've risen to it."

I looked at the bottle of whiskey and felt my mouth water. I wondered if I could ever be around alcohol, especially alcohol that piqued my curiosity, as this moonshine did – I couldn't get my mind off of how much I wanted to taste it and see if Steven was right about his whiskey-making skills – and not even have a taste. Not even a taste.

I swallowed hard and bit down on my lip. *You won't try that alcohol. You won't try that alcohol.*

"You sure you don't even want a taste?"

"No. I'm not sure. I'm never sure. Recovering from alcoholism has been white-knuckle all the way. It always has been. But I'm stronger than the drink. I just have to keep telling myself that."

"Okay." He looked disappointed. "You're only the second person I've seen in almost 50 years, and I've been anxious to see if my whiskey is as good as I think. I guess I'll never know. I mean, Anna loved it, but I wanted a second opinion."

I focused on the fire because I didn't want to look at that glass of booze as I asked my questions. "So, Steven, tell me again why you felt you had to drop out of society. I guess I don't understand."

Out of the corner of my eye, I saw him bring that glass of whiskey to his mouth and take a sip. "You see, it's like this, Ms. Ross. My brother, whose name was Robert, stole my identity. And he was evil to the core. He was determined I'd pay for his sins. Bound and determined." He shook his head. "Robert was a bad seed. To say the least."

I finally felt brave enough to look in his direction. I saw he had tears in his eyes. "I don't even want to go into the things he did when we were kids." He pet his beautiful dog, who was staring at him with love in her big brown eyes trained on him. "But he..." Steven shook his head. "Poor Sadie, our golden retriever. I don't want to talk about that."

I didn't want to talk about that, either. No matter how much I saw, heard, and found about in my job, I couldn't hear about animal abuse.

Steven had a lump in his throat. "He lived in that house, but it was in my name. The utilities too. He kept me prisoner in that house in the attic." He shook his head. "The bastard. He made that poor kid who stayed with him, who sometimes went by the name Eli and Mick other times, dress up in girl's clothing and parade around before he did unspeakable acts to him. Robert found clothes at the thrift store like the clothes our mother wore. He then made Eli wear these clothes while he beat him, burned him and hung him up by his wrists for days. He called Eli Margaret. Our mother's name."

This was a different story. I was getting another wrinkle in this entire tale – Robert hated his mother so much that he made Uncle Jack dress like her while doing horrible things.

"Tell me about Eli," I said to Steven. "You said he sometimes went by the name Mick as well. Is that right? Did he ever call himself something different? Were those the only two names you heard him call himself?"

He stared at the fire while he sipped his whiskey. "No, actually. There was one time I heard him call himself a different name. I heard this different name on the day he killed my brother."

CHAPTER
TWENTY-ONE

MY EARS PERKED UP. "What does that mean? You heard him call himself something different on the day he killed your brother?"

He sighed. "Let me start from the beginning. When this skinny kid was brought to this house, my brother decided to keep him as a house boy. That was what he told me – the kid would be a houseboy. Run errands, get food and things like that. I didn't really know what Robert was doing at that time. As I said, I was kept prisoner in that attic for years. He locked me in."

"Why did he lock you in?"

"Robert was posing as me. Nobody even knew there were two of us – our parents had died, and we moved to Kansas City from Omaha, where nobody knew us. Robert decided he didn't want people to know there were two of us, so he knocked me out. When I came to, I was locked in the attic. I soon found out Robert had been posing as me, using my name, around town. He had my identification and used that to open utilities, put the house in my name and all that."

I knew why Robert did that. It was obvious. If the police found the house of horrors and the bones of all those children, Steven would be implicated, not Robert. Steven's name was on the deed and the utilities. And Robert ensured people in Kansas City didn't know there were twins. Robert could just skate away and leave Steven holding the bag for his crimes. It was perfect, really.

He went on. "Eli called himself Jack when he first got to the house. He was a scared kid, frightened of his own shadow. Cried all the time. But he called himself Eli within a day or so of his being there. I…"

He shook his head. "I understood what was going on. I saw it in my mother before she killed herself. She had multiple personalities. It was something Robert and I lived with our entire lives. My mother was named Sheila, but she'd sometimes go by Nanette and sometimes be called Summer. Sheila was frightened of her shadow, just like Jack was, but Nanette was a wise-cracking, hard-drinking, loud woman who hosted large poker games in our home and flirted with every man in the place. As a kid, I liked Nanette a lot because she was fun. Our mother was the very opposite of fun. Our mother was quiet and meek, locked all the doors and windows and always talked about danger in the world. Nanette was the opposite and was hilarious."

It was fascinating discovering Steven's mother apparently had DID. "What about Summer?"

"Well, even though the third personality called herself Summer, she was unbelievably cruel. She beat us every day and put hot wax on us. She kicked us and forced one of us at a time to go into the cellar and stay there." He shivered. "That was horrible. It was dark down there, and the bugs. The bugs. As a kid, I was terrified of bugs, and they were down there by the millions. I think Summer is why my brother got so messed up. I hated what he did to all those children, but I knew why he was messed up. It was because of Summer."

I saw into the psyche of Steven and, to a certain extent, Robert and saw why they were screwed up. Steven might've just been screwed up because of what his brother did. But it had to be horrible growing up with an insane mother. I felt for this poor guy – first, his mother abused him, and then his brother did too.

Now he was banished to the cabin in the woods. Isolated, alone, and fearful of the world. All because of what other people did to him.

"Our mother hanged herself one day when she returned to being our mother. Robert found her, and, believe it or not, he tried to protect me from seeing what he saw. I think that was why he went off the deep end. He was never the same after that."

With every word Steven spoke, I better understood what happened to Robert. Why he had that break with reality. I didn't think it excused his heinous acts by any stretch of the imagination. His acts were the very definition of evil. But I saw what tripped him into doing what he did.

"So," I said. "You saw Uncle Jack come in. He called himself Jack, and then he called himself Eli. You knew what was happening?"

He looked at me strangely. "He was your Uncle Jack? I mean, is your Uncle Jack. I'm assuming he's still alive."

"He *is* my Uncle Jack. Yes, he's still alive." I would tell Steven about my Uncle Jack's murder charge, but I wanted to hear his story first. I didn't want to interrupt him, so I shut my mouth about why I was there.

He nodded. "That's good he's still alive. That's very good." He paused. "I worried about that poor kid after he killed my brother. I knew he'd be permanently scarred. I wanted to check in on him occasionally but couldn't. After my brother was found dead and everybody knew what he did, I knew I couldn't live in society. I was afraid everybody would assume I was in on that, too. I figured the best thing I could do would be to escape out here to escape my brother's notoriety."

"I guess I don't understand. In your previous life in Omaha, people knew there were two of you. Once the stories about your brother got out into the newspaper, the teachers and others who knew both of you probably told the cops there was a twin. Right?"

"No." He shook his head. "Summer was the dominant personality. Summer decided she wanted only one of us known. Only one of us could be seen at any given time. She imprisoned one of us at a time in the attic of our Omaha home. Some weeks I was lucky enough to go to school, but the next week, I'd have to stay in the attic, and Robert would go. I don't know why she did that, to this day, except that she was insane. Literally insane. And, for some reason, the alternate personality, Nanette, did the same thing. They didn't want it known there were two of us. God knows why."

"What about Sheila? Didn't she let both of you out at the same time?"

He shook his head. "No. That's just the thing. Our mother, in general, didn't want there to be twins around. I think her feelings bled out into the alternate personalities, so all three of the personalities refused to let us out at the same time. I wish I knew the reasoning behind it. Then again, when you're crazy, you don't have very good reasoning, do you? For all that anybody ever knew, there was only one of us, and his name was Steven. My name was the name people knew both of us by."

It all suddenly made more sense to me – why Steven would drop out of society and come to live in the woods. There was only one Heaney boy known or seen in society, walking around, and that boy was named Steven. Robert took Steven's identity his entire life, so he took his identity again when they became adults.

"So, yeah," he continued. "Since nobody knew there were two of us, I decided it would be dangerous to be seen. I didn't want people to think I was also guilty of killing those kids. That's why I'm here. I don't know how your assistant Anna figured that out, but I'm glad she did."

I nodded, but I wanted to get back to my earlier thread. I needed to get the story on Eli, Mick and Jack. And the mysterious other personality who was around when Steven's brother Robert was killed. "Let's return to what you said about Eli and Mick earlier. When did you realize there was a Mick?"

He shrugged. "I never saw Mick. My brother told me Jack became Mick whenever they were…" He sighed. "I don't know what to call it. When they were intimate, Robert said Jack called himself Mick. That was the only time, though. The rest of the time, he called himself Eli."

"Raping," I said softly. "The word you were searching for was rape. Your brother and my uncle weren't 'intimate.' There was no intimacy. There was only violence, humiliation and degradation. My Uncle Jack was raped." I shuddered as I thought about my own rape and how Michael Reynolds was still trying to torment me by appealing his conviction based on my admitted ineffective assistance of counsel.

"Yes," he said. "I know. I'm sorry; I shouldn't have used a word like 'intimate.' I should have called it like it was – a rape."

"It's okay. I'm very sensitive about...labeling rape as anything other than what it is. I shouldn't have interrupted you, though. Please go on."

"Well, on the day my brother died, Jack came up after he killed him. He said he would free me and told me to leave the house. Which I did. But he called himself something different that day. A name I'd never heard him call himself before."

I felt excited. This was the key. I had the feeling there was another personality buried in my Uncle Jack's psyche. I just had that hunch. There was another personality I'd have to try to talk to to get to the bottom of who killed Father Kennedy. This was the personality who would know who did that.

"What was the other personality's name?"

"Sam."

CHAPTER
TWENTY-TWO

AS EXCITED as I was to find out there was another personality, I was terrified as well. This Sam apparently was the violent personality in Uncle Jack's psyche. It wasn't Eli after all. But what did that mean? Sam killed Robert. Eli didn't. Eli might've hated Robert, but I felt Eli also feared his captor. After all, if Eli didn't fear Robert, he probably would've gone to the police and told them what was happening in that house. Eli was let out of the house regularly.

As for Mick, he felt he was in love with Robert. That would be why he never wanted to turn in his captor.

But Sam...Sam was apparently only "allowed" out once, and that was to kill Robert. Sam was violent. Did he kill Father Kennedy?

"Tell me about Sam," I said. "Did you only see Sam one time?"

Steven nodded. "Yes. Only one time. I saw Eli the rest of the time. I bonded with Eli. Eli was the only personality that knew I existed until Sam. Sam knew me. Sam knew I was around because Sam freed me and told me to high-tail it out of there because he would call the cops and tell them what had happened. Sam told me he killed Robert to protect Jack because Jack was in love with Mary, who was also staying at that house, and Robert wanted to kill Mary. Sam said he couldn't let that happen, so he killed my brother."

"No other time? Sam didn't come out any other time?"

"No. I only saw Eli. Full stop." He raised his eyebrows. "Why are you having a tough time believing this?"

"I'm not." I stroked my chin. "But I want to make sure I have all this straight. It's very confusing, even for me."

Steven shook his head. "The poor kid. He took so much torture, so much abuse. I don't know about Sam, but I feel he protected all of them. Eli was a tough character, but he wasn't violent. From what I understand, although I never met him, Mick was a homosexual. I don't think he was violent, either. At least, that's how Robert described Mick to me. But Sam was violent. He was the only personality that was, I think."

My heart sank. At first, I was excited to know the name of this fourth personality. But when Steven told me Sam was violent, I knew there was a real downside to knowing about Sam. I could try to bring him out of Jack's psyche, but what if I did, and he told me he killed Father Kennedy? What then? At that point, I'd have no choice but try for NGRI, but insanity defenses weren't always granted based on DID. Jack might go to prison, and, best-case scenario, he would be incarcerated in a psychiatric facility for the criminally insane until the day he died.

I prayed Sam didn't kill Father Kennedy. I prayed none of Jack's personalities killed Father Kennedy.

"What's wrong?" Steven asked as he studied my face. "You suddenly looked extremely depressed."

I shook my head. "I don't know. I'm defending Jack on this murder charge, and I now know Jack has a violent personality. I'm faced with the knowledge that Sam is capable of violence. I…" I shook my head. "I'm afraid Sam might've murdered that priest. That thought makes me want to vomit."

Steven bit his lip as he examined me carefully. "I wouldn't be worried about that. You have to understand, this was a special thing. To say the least. My brother needed to be killed. He was going to kill that sweet young Mary. Sam came out to protect Mary. Sam knew Jack was in love with Mary, and he knew Jack would never come out again if Mary was killed in that house. Sam had the best knowledge about Jack's state of mind out of any of them. He knew Jack's long-term sanity was at risk. That was the only reason he killed my brother. Just because he killed Robert doesn't mean he is generally a violent personality. He only did it to protect Mary and Jack."

Steven's theory made a lot of sense. Still, I couldn't escape that out of all the personalities struggling in Jack's psyche, there was one personality capable of violence. Granted, the violence only came out when lives were on the line. But that personality was still violent.

"I know what you're saying," I said. "But I don't know. It's concerning."

"Well, tell me the facts on this murder that Jack is being accused of. Tell me those facts, and I can advise you on what I think might have happened."

I cleared my throat and straightened up in my chair. "There was a priest, his name was-"

"Father Kennedy." Steven nodded his head. "Go on."

"Yes." I furrowed my brow. "Father Kennedy. How did you know about that?"

He shrugged. "I figured. The second you said there was a murdered priest, I knew what name you would throw at me. I just knew it."

I narrowed my eyes. "But how? Why? How did you know this name?"

He shrugged. "My brother was obsessed with that man. Father Kennedy. See, Robert actually went to church. He went to church every Sunday."

Steven shook his head. "Ironic, isn't it? That a guy like my brother, an evil guy like my brother, who was raping and murdering children, would go to church? But here's the thing. My brother fell in love with Father Kennedy. He only attended church for the first time because of Mick. My mother wasn't religious and never took us."

My ears perked up. "Mick wanted your brother to go to church? Why would that be?"

He sighed. "I think Mick was in love with that priest, too. That's the only thing I could think of."

I bit my lower lip as I tried to think about what Steven told me. Mick was in love with Father Kennedy all those years ago? Yet, Mick only appeared once he got into that house. For Mick to be in love with

Father Kennedy, it presupposed he had met Father Kennedy *before* he was kidnapped. Otherwise, how would Mick know to take Robert into that church in the first place? How would he have *already* been in love with Father Kennedy?

And Jack was only 11 when he was kidnapped. Only 11.

The darkness started to descend upon my brain. I concluded that maybe something happened between Father Kennedy and Jack when Jack was only 11 or younger.

I didn't want to believe that. Didn't want to think that way. I didn't want to ever believe Father Kennedy might've molested Jack when Jack was a young boy. Because if that were the case, Jack would have had reason to kill him.

If Jack had a reason to kill Father Kennedy, and he actually killed him...

I swallowed hard. "So, your brother was obsessed with Father Kennedy?"

"Yes. He was. Very obsessed with him. He talked about him all the time and went to church every Sunday so he could see him. I guess that, in his day, he was quite the handsome man."

I nodded, thinking of Father Mathews. Father Mathews was young, handsome and fit. I wondered if Father Kennedy was much the same back in the day. "He was a handsome guy, then. Was there any other reason why Robert was obsessed with Father Kennedy?"

"Yes." Robert nodded his head. "He said Father Kennedy reminded him of a teacher he had in the fifth grade. Obviously, I had the same teacher – we traded off going to school. But that teacher's name was..." He furrowed his brow as if trying to remember the name of this teacher. "Dean was his first name." He nodded his head. "It was weird; he wanted the kids to call him by his first name. But his last name was...."

He sat in his chair, his hand on his chin, thinking about it. "I don't know. I don't remember his last name. But he was our teacher in the fifth grade. Our homeroom teacher. He was good and kind, and Robert saw him as a mentor. I think Robert saw him as the father we never had. We never had a father around because our mother, I guess, got pregnant by a one-night stand or something. So, Robert latched onto

Dean. He was the first male teacher we had. The first male person of authority. Robert needed guidance, obviously."

To say the least. I wondered about all that. Two boys go through the same kind of torture day to day. One turned out to be a serial killer. The other turned out to be somebody screwed up but not a bad guy at all. The two boys also literally had the same genetics. In the nature vs. nurture controversy, where did the Heaney brothers fall? They had the same nature and the same nurture. Why did one go so wrong, and the other didn't?

"Robert needed guidance," Steven continued. "And Dean provided that to him. Then Father Kennedy apparently provided that to him. Guidance. Mentoring. I guess Robert told me all that Father Kennedy told him because Robert often went to see him at his rectory." He shook his head. "Now, I know what you're thinking, but Father Kennedy wasn't doing anything wrong with Robert. Robert would've told me if he were. He just said he went to see Father Kennedy in his rectory because he could talk to him. Father Kennedy tried to put Robert on the straight and narrow, but obviously, he couldn't. Robert was just too far gone by the time he met him." He paused. "I'm so sorry. I'm going off on a damned tangent. I just am so happy to see somebody, talk with somebody. You don't know what total isolation can do to a person, Ms. Ross. You just don't know."

I nodded my head. "I can only imagine." I put my hand on him, and he smiled wanly.

"Thank you for understanding," Steven said. "Now, please, continue with your story about how Father Kennedy was killed and what happened."

I took a deep breath as I thought about the statement from the police and the pictures I received from the prosecutor's office. In these pictures, Father Kennedy was covered in blood and lying across a white throw rug in his rectory. He had been stabbed in his heart. He was dressed almost completely in black, as he wore his robes, so the effect of seeing all that blood could've definitely been worse. I didn't want to imagine what it would've looked like if he wore all white. The blood pooled on his chest, but it didn't spread much further, as Father

Kennedy died as soon as he was stabbed, so the blood didn't pulse for very long.

"Well, my Uncle Jack was there in the rectory. He doesn't know quite what happened. He was unconscious and didn't regain consciousness until he was put in the squad car. He tells me he doesn't remember going into that rectory, let alone recollect what happened to the priest. The cops don't know, either, I guess. They only knew Jack had a knife in his hand, which was the murder knife. And, of course, there was a body lying on the rug. The body of Father Kennedy. There are other details in there I just can't seem to fill in because Jack doesn't remember what happened. There was another personality that came out in that rectory. Another personality took over and brought Jack into that rectory in the first place. That's what I'm trying to figure out. One of Jack's personalities holds the key to this whole thing, but the frustrating thing is Mick is the one out. Mick is the only one that comes out. Mick took over the gatekeeping role somewhere along the line, so the others can only come out if Mick lets them. And, so far, Mick isn't letting them."

Steven nodded his head. "I see. And the knife, you've done forensic analysis on it?"

"Of course. I've had it done independently. No prints on it except Jack's, which looks bad. There's not even a glove print I can link to anyone, not that a glove print does any damned good unless you find a pair of matching gloves." I smiled as I thought about how the glove print sunk Michael. That only worked because I had his gloves. If there was a glove print, I'd have to figure out who owned that pair of gloves and hope to get my hands on them.

"I see. You know there wouldn't be a print if the killer used a pair of latex gloves. Right?"

I smiled. "Of course I know that." I cocked my head. "How do you know so much about all this?"

Steven looked sad. "When I escaped, I knew I'd do very little for the rest of my life. I knew I wouldn't be in society. I'd have to entertain myself, so I took as many books from our house as possible. I could fit about 200 books in my car; those have been my lifeline. I think I'd have gone crazy a long time ago if I didn't have these books to escape into.

Some of my favorite books are thrillers and mysteries, so I know quite a lot about evidence, although I'm quite sure forensic evidence has come a long way since 1972."

I thought about his bookshelf with the classics on it. Somehow, many more books were in the cabin, and they kept him sane. Good thing something did.

I nodded. "So, I guess you know there's the possibility that somebody else killed Father Kennedy and put that knife in my uncle's hand. I don't know exactly when he passed out, though. That's the other thing vexing me. I have several working theories. One is that my uncle walked in while somebody else was killing Father Kennedy, got freaked out and went unconscious at the sight. The other theory is that my uncle was in the rectory with Father Kennedy, minding his own business, when the killer came in, knocked out my uncle with some kind of a sedative, killed Father Kennedy, and then put that knife in my uncle's hand."

I took a deep breath as I contemplated the last scenario. The one I didn't want to even think about. "The third scenario, possibly my last scenario, is that my uncle killed Father Kennedy. Rather, one of his personalities did, and the stress of doing this caused my uncle to black out. But that can't be true. If it were, my uncle would be in prison or a psychiatric facility for the rest of his life."

Steven looked sad. "I know you don't want to consider it, but you might have to. I don't pretend to know what could've prompted your uncle, or any of his personalities, to kill Father Kennedy. As far as I have ever known about the Father, he was a good, kind, upstanding man with infinite patience. Those are the conclusions I got from Robert and how he talked about his encounters with Father Kennedy. I really don't know if your uncle had a different impression of him or had different encounters with him. It stands to reason your uncle knew Father Kennedy before my brother abducted him, as Mick introduced my brother to him. So there's some history there."

I put my hand on Steven's again. "Thank you for your help and all your knowledge. I would like to help you in return."

He cocked his head. "How could you help me?"

"I'd like to help you return to society. I know you're frightened you might be implicated for all your brother did. And you're right. You probably will be investigated. But if anything comes of it, if the police try to charge you with anything, like being an accomplice or, God forbid, actively helping your brother murder those children..." I shook my head as I thought about the innocent life taken by Robert Heaney. It made me sick.

I cleared my throat. "If they try to charge you with anything, I'll take your case *pro bono*. That means I won't charge you a dime. You've helped me more than you'll ever know."

He smiled. "You would do that for me? For a man you just met?"

"Yes." I nodded. I felt a bond with this older man. I felt an affinity for him. He was wasting away, but he was a good, kind man. There wasn't a reason for him to be resigned to living in isolation for the rest of his years. However, many years there were for him anymore.

He looked at the ground. "I don't know if I would fit in with society anymore. Everything has just passed me on. The last President I've known about was Nixon. As far as I know, the Vietnam War is still raging. I'm in a time capsule here, and I wonder if I'd be overwhelmed if I left this place."

I had to smile. "Maybe, but I'm sure you'll adjust. And you seem to like to do a lot of reading. You'll have all the reading material you need on the internet."

His eyebrows furrowed. "The internet? What is that?"

"Well, you get on your computer and can access anything you want worldwide. Anything you want to read, you can. Any information you want is right at your fingertips. I think you'd like that very much."

"Computers?" He looked mystified. "How does anybody have a computer? I know large companies had computers, and so did the government, but they were enormous. Behemoths. And they were worth thousands and thousands of dollars. Are you telling me people actually have those monsters in their homes?"

I smiled. "Oh, you wouldn't imagine all the technology that has happened since the 1970s. Yes, just about everybody has their own computer. In fact," I said, bringing out my phone, "this is a computer, too. It does everything that a bigger computer does. It has the internet, e-mail and everything I need."

"E-mail?"

"Electronic mail. People send messages over your computer, and you can answer them immediately."

He took my phone and looked at it. "This is a computer?" His eyes got wide, and then he started to laugh. "And you say I can read anything I want on here?"

"Yes. It's also a phone."

"A phone? Really?"

"Yes. Really. Unfortunately, right now, it's neither a phone nor a computer. I don't have service for either thing out here."

He looked perplexed. "What do you mean you don't have service?"

"Well, see, there's these towers. Cell phone towers. And if you're out of range, you can't make phone calls or get on the internet. You only have data if you're in range. Which we are at the moment."

He raised an eyebrow. "Oh, my." He shook his head. "Oh, my. I wonder if I can cope with all this. I never imagined anybody could have a telephone outside their home, let alone a computer in their home. Let alone having a computer the size of a phone."

"Yes. And, by the way, the Vietnam War ended in 1975. We lost. President Nixon resigned in 1973 because he was about to be impeached for breaking into the Democratic National Headquarters to get information about his upcoming opponent. We've been in several wars since Vietnam, all in the Middle East. And the World Trade Center was destroyed by terrorists over 20 years ago. Those are the biggest stories since you dropped out of society."

He shook his head rapidly. "Wait, hold on. I'm glad to know the Vietnam War ended. I'm not surprised we lost because our military leaders seemed incompetent. And I'm not surprised to hear about Nixon, either. I always knew he was crooked as a dog's hind leg. But the World Trade Center is gone? How did that happen? How could a building as large as those two buildings be destroyed?"

"Terrorists from the Middle East took over two commercial airplanes and flew them into those two buildings. It didn't take long for them to collapse."

He looked stunned. "Wow. Just wow. I guess the world is quite different than the one I left. Who is the President now?"

I raised my eyebrow. "Joe Biden, but it was Donald Trump." I strained to remember if Steven would even know who Donald Trump was. He'd been a part of the nation's consciousness for many years, but I didn't think people back in 1972 would've heard of him.

I could see in Steven's face he had no recognition of that name. "I see. Who is Donald Trump? And are you talking about Senator Biden? He was a new senator when I dropped out in 1972."

"Yes, Senator Biden. As for Trump, he was a businessman. A billionaire."

"He any good?"

I sighed. "Didn't like him, but lots of people did. And do."

He nodded. "You really can help me? If I get arrested for the murder of those kids, you can help?"

"I will help you. I promise."

He smiled. "Okay, then. I'd like to fly back with you. And start establishing my existence again. However I need to do that. I'm pretty excited, actually, to be getting into that world again. It sounds like a lot has happened. I never thought we'd be in another war after Vietnam. Sounds like this nation never learns its lesson, does it?"

"No, it never does." Truer words were never spoken. "But you can't fly back with me. You need a picture ID."

He looked strange. "Picture ID? To fly? Why?"

"Well, after those terrorists brought down those towers with those planes, everybody has to go through security to get on a plane, and everyone has to show an ID."

He nodded his head. "Makes sense. So, how will I return to Kansas City if I can't fly? I can't drive, as you can see. There's no car left. When I moved out here, I figured I wouldn't need my car, so I chopped it up and used it to gird this house. I guess I'm stuck after all."

I had to think about this one. I wanted Steven to come to Kansas City and get re-acquainted with society. He deserved to live his golden years in peace and around people.

"I'll send somebody to come get you and drive you back," I said, thinking Heather might be the best candidate for that job. I could pay her to come and get Steven and Stella, which would help her with her financial issues and enable Steven and Stella to come to Kansas City.

Two birds, one stone. "And I'll help you figure out how to get an ID, an apartment and all that. It'll be complicated because you have no history, but I'll figure something out. I'll pull some strings and make sure you can get the ball rolling."

I looked at Steven, and he had large tears in his eyes. "I guess humanity isn't such a bad thing after all. There are people like you in the world who will go out of their way to help a sad old man. You don't know what that means to me."

I stood up and gave him a hug. "You helped me. I was a stranger, and you embraced me like an old friend. And you've given me some invaluable information about my uncle." I drew a breath as I realized something. If Steven came to Kansas City, how would my uncle react? Steven was the identical twin to Robert, the man who tormented him for two years. Yet, Steven had aged 50 years, so maybe Jack wouldn't even recognize him.

I could only hope. The last thing I wanted was to spin Jack back into those years. Jack was as fragile as it was. I didn't think Jack's psyche could handle seeing the man who tortured him.

He nodded his head. "When do you have to be back in town?"

"Tomorrow. I have an early flight."

"Well, then, you'll sleep here, of course."

"No need. I have a hotel room."

He looked disappointed. "Okay." He looked down at the ground, and I felt sorry I had to leave. I could imagine being in his shoes – not seeing a living soul for over fifty years, and then somebody shows up, and you never want that person to leave.

"I'll have somebody come and get you, though, so don't despair. Okay?"

"Sure, sure." He looked skeptical. "I mean, you don't have to do that. I won't expect anybody to show up, but if somebody does, I'll be grateful."

I smiled. "I'm as good as my word. I wouldn't tell you something like that if I didn't plan to do it."

He sighed. "You have to understand, the only people I've known in my life have been pretty terrible. My mother and my brother. I went to school when I was younger, trading off with Robert, so I kinda knew people in my youth. But in my adult years, I only knew my brother and he...." He shook his head. "He was evil. I'll have a hard time trusting."

"Of course you are. But I'll help you assimilate. You'll see."

I hugged him again and then went to my rental car, which was right outside the door. I looked out the window and saw Steven on the porch, sadly waving, his left hand stuck in his pocket, Stella by his side. And then he went back into the house, his head hanging.

My heart went out to him. I could just imagine how he was feeling right at that moment. He probably thought I wouldn't do what I said. He probably thought he'd be alone for the rest of his life.

I'd show him I was a woman of my word.

CHAPTER
TWENTY-THREE

AS I SAT on the plane on the way home, I doodled mindlessly. I appreciated Steven's candor and hospitality. But I was bothered by what I learned from him. I'd have to figure out what Jack's initial encounter was with Father Kennedy. Maybe something happened to Jack and Father Kennedy that nested in Jack's psyche and finally caused him to go off the deep end and kill him.

I had to acknowledge the facts were pointing to that scenario. Everything I learned about this case pointed to it. Father Mathews indicated Father Kennedy was "afraid" of Jack. Steven told me Jack had a violent alter, one I didn't know about, and Jack knew Father Kennedy before Robert took him captive.

I lay back in my seat and closed my eyes. I wouldn't give up. No way I'd give up. But the facts weren't looking good.

I got into the office and prepared for the pre-trial conferences lined up for some of the other criminal cases I had in my pipeline. One was a drug case, the other was armed robbery. The drug case would be simple enough – it was a first-time offense, and Drug Court was the offer. Drug Court meant my client would complete the requirements the judge set for him – go to drug rehabilitation, give periodic urine tests, and stay away from criminals for two years, among other requirements – and the case would be dismissed. If something happened and my client messed up, he must take the conviction.

The armed robbery would be trickier, of course. My client faced 10 years in prison. He was good for the crime, so I'd have to find some avenue to get the sentence reduced. That was really all I could do for him.

My mind, however, was on my Uncle Jack. I hoped and prayed something else would pop up. Somebody else I could focus on for this murder. Thus far, I didn't have anybody to look at. Nobody else would have it in for Father Kennedy.

Tammy came into my office. "What's going on?" she asked me. "How are things with your uncle?"

I sighed. "Terrifying. I've reached a dead end and will be at this dead end until I can break through it. I have to figure out who else would have a motive to kill him. And I have to somehow reach some of Uncle Jack's other personalities. I must reach the alter that knows what happened in that damned rectory. I have to figure that out."

Tammy sat down. "I think you'll have to resort to hypnosis. That might be the only way."

"I know. I know. I don't want to put him through that if I don't have to, though. It'll certainly be the last resort."

Pearl poked her head through the door. "The Grand Jury came back on your uncle. He was indicted. The case has been assigned to Division 15."

I nodded. Division 15 was Judge Greene. He was an African-American man who was kind, patient and fair. He was anything but an impatient hothead, and he always judged each case by merit, never pre-judging anything. I was lucky. If I had to be in front of any judge in Jackson County for a case like this, I wanted it to be a guy like Judge Greene. I might actually have a chance in front of him.

A chance for what? The jury would decide if my uncle was guilty or not guilty. The judge would decide if my uncle was not guilty by reason of insanity. At this point, that was the best I could hope for.

My heart was breaking as I thought about that possibility. I pictured Uncle Jack locked up in a psychiatric facility, being poked, prodded and drugged for the rest of his life. He wouldn't have anybody around him who he loved and cared for. He would be as lonely and isolated as Steven but wouldn't have a reprieve. He would be in that facility for the rest of his life. There would be literally no hope for him.

That was the best-case scenario. The other scenario was that Jack would spend the rest of his life in prison. I heard horror stories every day about how prisoners were treated inside. One prisoner I heard about died because he didn't have water for an entire week. Another prisoner was scalded to death in a shower. Both of those prisoners were mentally ill, as Jack clearly was. And what if the alter that came out in prison was Sam, whoever he was? What then? Sam would be violent and start trouble, and then Jack would end up in isolation or worse. Maybe Sam would kill a guard, and Jack would end up on death row.

I put my head down on my desk as I thought of my beloved uncle going into an isolated cell after Sam came out to start a prison riot, and I felt his despair. He wouldn't understand. He wouldn't begin to comprehend what had happened to him.

I had tears in my eyes. It was so unfair. It was unfair Jack came upon the serial killer, Robert, all those years ago, which permanently scarred him and tripped him into mental illness. It was unfair he lost his beloved wife so tragically. And now this. If one of his alters killed that priest, he'd be locked up forever.

He would never recover.

Neither would my mom.

There were just no easy answers.

Tammy was still staring at me on the other side of my desk. "Harper, earth to Harper. What's going on? I keep losing you."

I shook my head and realized I was sobbing. "Tammy, I don't know where to turn on my uncle's case. I just don't know. The signs aren't good. Maybe my uncle had a beef with that priest. He knew that priest when he was a child. I don't know. What if Father Kennedy molested Uncle Jack when he was a child, and somehow Uncle Jack repressed it, but this memory came out, so he went over and killed the priest? Uncle Jack has a violent alter whose name is Sam. It's all fitting together, although I don't want it to. I need it not to. I need some alternative suspect for this, and I just don't know where to start."

Tammy had a worried expression on her face. "Harper, I think you're taking this case too personally. I know he's your uncle. I know that. I know he's gone through hell in his life. I know that, too. But you have to somehow detach and see this as just another case. Maybe that will help you see things more clearly, and that will help lead you to the real suspect. Or, maybe, if you lose..."

"I lose, what? What then? My uncle will be locked up in a psychiatric facility or prison for the rest of his goddamned life. It's not fair. It's just not fair."

Tammy stood up. "You'll figure it out, Harper. I have faith in you. I know the knife had your uncle's fingerprints on it and only your uncle's fingerprints. I know your uncle has a violent alter. I know your uncle knew Father Kennedy when your uncle was a kid. I admit, those facts don't look good. But you have to think outside the box on this one. You have to. I have faith you can."

I finally felt composed. "I'm glad you have faith in me because I certainly don't. I don't believe I can find the real person who did this because I think my Uncle Jack did it. I think he did." I shook my head and put my face on the desk. "I think he did."

CHAPTER
TWENTY-FOUR

I GOT HOME, exhausted from my day in court. Nothing went right. My Drug Court client said he didn't want Drug Court after all. When I got into court, he informed me that he had talked to his buddies and didn't want to "deal with the bullshit."

"I don't want no random piss tests," he said. "And I don't want no classes. Just plead this shit, give me whatever they want, and it'll be cool."

I sighed, not wanting to deal with that crap. "Okay, then, you'll have a felony record. Good luck renting an apartment or finding a job. You'll still be on probation, too, so you'll have to check in with your probation officer periodically and do random drops. And if you drop dirty, you'll serve prison time. A felony plea won't give you a better deal, it'll be worse, but it's your call."

At that point, my client, Alton Gallagher, got up and left in a fury. I didn't chase after him. I was tired of chasing down my clients when they decided they didn't like what they heard and stormed out of the courtroom.

The judge called his case, but he wasn't there, and a warrant was placed for his arrest.

That was strike one.

The armed robbery case didn't go much better. I tried to work out a plea agreement where my client could have his sentence reduced to five years and the actual charge reduced from a Robbery 1 to a Robbery 2. That was important because, in the State of Missouri, felons convicted of Robbery 1 had to serve 85% of their sentence as a mandatory minimum. For Robbery 2, however, they could get out of prison if they were good and didn't catch any more cases while behind bars after they served just one-third of their sentence. Plus, his sentence would be less for the robbery in the second degree, or "Rob 2," because that was a B Felony, whereas the robbery in the first degree, or "Rob 1," was an A felony.

That was the plea agreement I was shooting for. I figured I could get it.

But no. The prosecutor, Vince Malloy, my nemesis in my Heather Morrison case, wanted to be a hard-ass. He informed me he wouldn't reduce the charges and we'd have to try the case.

My robbery client was Ty Pennings, an overweight African-American man with a bald head. He insisted he didn't want to participate in that armed robbery but did it as part of a gang initiation. This fact didn't make the crime any better, but I felt sorry for him. He was so young – only 18 – and his life was ruined.

I had to break the bad news that my promised plea agreement to Rob 2, in which I hoped my client would be out in a few years, wouldn't materialize yet. If at all.

At this point, he started to cry. His wrists were shackled, and he was in his orange jumpsuit. My heart just went out to him.

So, I felt out of sorts when I got home. To say the very least. I was getting too emotionally involved with my clients, including my Uncle Jack, and all I wanted was to go home, kick off my shoes, make a glass of Glenfiddich Scotch Whiskey, turn on a playlist of classical music or put on one of my many Cary Grant DVDs, and drown my sorrows. That's what I used to do when everything got overwhelming. That was my usual routine when I was under stress – go home, get hammered while watching Cary Grant pratfalls or Audrey Hepburn high jinks, and then pass out into sweet, sweet oblivion.

Instead, I had to deal with Rina, who was pulling Abby's hair for some ungodly reason while Abby screeched like a banshee. That was the scene I was treated to when I got home after the day I had, and I was at my wit's end.

"What's going on here?" I asked them. Sophia had left a half hour before, as she had to be home early, and I figured two 12-year-old girls would be okay in the house alone for less than an hour without adult supervision.

Apparently, I was wrong about that.

Rina stopped pulling Abby's hair, but that didn't stop Abby from wailing. She came over to me and wrapped her arms around my waist, and bawled.

"Rina Marie," I said. "Do you mind telling me what you were doing just now? Why were you pulling your sister's hair?"

She shrugged, which made me angry. That was such a passive-aggressive move, that shoulder-shrugging business. She knew damned well what she did to Abby, but she wouldn't tell me.

"Okay, fine, I'll have to ask the source." I looked at Abby's big brown eyes. "Abby, Buttercup, what happened? Why were you and Rina fighting like that?"

Her little lips were quivering, and her eyes were filled with tears. *More crying.* I couldn't handle crying. I couldn't handle it when I saw my gang-member client crying, and I couldn't handle it from my little 12-year-old daughter.

She pointed at Rina. "She's mad because the teacher caught her cheating. She caught her looking at her phone in class while taking a test. She was looking up the answers to the test. She's mad because the teacher asked me about it, and I didn't know what to say. Rina said I should've stuck up for her."

I sighed. This was the last thing I needed. The very last thing. "Rina, is that true? Were you cheating on that test?"

She shrugged again, and I almost blew a gasket.

"Well, this is great. Just great. I suppose you were expelled, too? Or suspended?"

She stuck out her tongue. "No. It was only a pop quiz, and I looked up some answers on my phone. The teacher took my phone away, gave me an F for the quiz and sent me to see the headmistress, who chewed me out. But Abby was such a little weasel. She could've stuck up for me. She could've, but she didn't."

I took a deep breath. "Rina, you were caught doing something wrong, and you're mad at Abby about it? How does that make sense? I think you're just mad at yourself that you weren't prepared and taking it out on your sister, which isn't quite fair. It's not fair at all, as a matter of fact."

She sneered. "If I can't get my sister to take my side, who will?"

"Rina, you have to take responsibility for yourself. When you do something wrong, you can't expect Abby to tell your teacher you weren't wrong. You must take your punishment, realize there's only one person to blame - the person in your mirror - and move on. Take your licks. Abby will stick up for you when you're in the right, as she should, but if you do something wrong, you can't expect her to stay behind you."

Rina sneered again and ran upstairs to her room, slamming the door behind her.

Abby was still wrapping her arms around me and crying. "Buttercup," I said, "let's get something to eat. I have a rotisserie chicken in the fridge and some baked potatoes from last night. Let's eat and not think about Rina's behavior for now."

She nodded without a word, and we got some plates down and set the table.

"Other than that little bit of drama, how was your day?" I asked her.

She shrugged. "Okay, I guess. James wants to go out again, but I don't want to anymore. Not after the way that he dumped me for that Emmaline. So, he's spreading lies about me." She whispered. "He's telling people we slept together. Isn't that gross?"

I shook my head. "Slept together? You guys are both twelve years old. How is that even possible?"

"Oh, it's possible. Mom, I know some girls who have done it. Gone all the way. Girls in my class. Now everybody thinks I'm one of those girls. It's horrible."

I sighed. "Abby, honey, did you ever think maybe those stories about those other girls who have gone all the way, as you put it, aren't true, either? Rumors have been around since the beginning of time. And they're just that – rumors. It doesn't take much to get a good story going around, a story that grows taller down the line. Now, you have to stop this rumor as soon as you can, and, in the meantime, I'll have a talk with James' mother."

James' mother, whose name was Ann-Marie, was a friend. She was about my age, and we got along well when we took Abby and James around on their little dates. I was appalled at his behavior, though. Spreading rumors about little Abby just because she wouldn't go out with him again?

Oh, to be 12 years old again. I wouldn't wish that on my worst enemy.

And when I was 12…I didn't know anybody who went all the way or even claimed to. That wasn't a rumor around the school when I was in the seventh grade. I was shocked this was something said about 12-year-olds, but I probably shouldn't have been shocked at all. It was a different time than the era I grew up in. I had to accept that fact.

I felt like an old fuddy-duddy.

Rina came out of her room and stomped down the stairs. "Weren't you going to call me for dinner?" she demanded.

"No," I said calmly. "If you want to throw a tantrum, you can but don't expect me to go chasing after you. You're a big girl. You know when to come downstairs. You know we eat dinner right at 6 PM every night."

Rina rolled her eyes. "Every night you're home this early. Which isn't a lot."

I opened my mouth and shut it. She wasn't wrong about that. My job was demanding, and there were days when I didn't get home until 8. On those days, the girls ate dinner with Sophia. I was cutting those long days short, more and more, even though I knew that I had to make up that time someplace else. I hadn't shortened my workload when I got the girls. I couldn't. They were added expenses, and I had to work more than ever to give them what they needed. Their private school, cell phones and internet plans, clothes, bags and school supplies – it all added up. I was also furiously saving for their college tuition, which would be a bear, to say the least. They were both very bright and my dream, simultaneously my nightmare, was that they could attend an Ivy League school.

It was my dream because that was what I wanted for them – the very best.

It was my nightmare because I couldn't imagine footing simultaneous $100,000-a-year schooling for each girl. It was $60,000 a year for Harvard now for room, board and tuition. It might be $100,000 or more a year when they were ready for school. That kind of price tag kept me awake at night.

So, yeah, I had to work my tail off to make sure the girls had the best of everything. I didn't want them to want anything. But that necessarily meant I'd be working nights, either at the office or late at night, after they went to bed. That was my life – I was on the hamster wheel and would never get off it.

I dished a baked potato, a cupful of corn and a chicken leg on Rina's plate. "Rina, now, I know I have to work late some nights, but I'm doing it for you and Abby. I have to make sure the two of you get the best education you can, and that's expensive."

Rina rolled her eyes. "Mom, you won't bring back our other mom, no matter how much money you spend on us." She bit into her chicken leg as she glared at me.

"Where did that come from?" I was perplexed. Rina hit a nerve, for sure – there was a part of me that was still assuaging my guilt over their mother being killed by my client, John Robinson. But how did she work that out in her head?

She shrugged. "I talked to my guidance counselor today. I told her about how you work all the time because you want to make sure we go to fancy schools, and she told me you feel guilty, and that's why you're doing it. She also knows about what John Robinson did to our other mom."

Oh, great. Great. Now I have a 12-year-old who has my number. "Rina, that's not why I'm spending all this money on private schools and saving up for your possible Ivy League education. I'm doing it because-"

"You love us. I know." Rina rolled her eyes again and wolfed down the rest of her meal. "Can I go now? Can I be excused?"

I closed my eyes and counted to ten. "Yes," I said. "You may be excused." I didn't usually like it when Rina went upstairs right after dinner. I wanted her to hang out so I could talk with her about her day. But, right at that moment, I was at my wit's end. It was all too much – the cases going crappy today, Jack's case, and now Abby having to endure scandalous rumors at school. I just wanted to take a bubble bath, crawl into bed and not have to think about much more.

It was either that or take about six shots and pass out, but that wasn't an option.

That would never be an option again.

Abby came over and put her hand on my shoulder. "Don't worry," she said softly. "Rina's having problems in school, but she'll get through it. She misses our birth mother, though. I know she does. I hear her crying out at night in her sleep."

The girls' rooms were side by side, separated only by a door. They liked it that way, but I knew they heard each other when they would snore or talk in their sleep. My room was a bit down the hallway, so I was insulated from these things.

I sighed. It sounded like I'd have to talk more with Rina. Try to reassure her and get her to explain why she was acting out in school and crying at night. I knew why, though. I knew why. Her mother was violently murdered. That had to affect her deeply.

As much as I yearned for the days when I didn't have the responsibility of two traumatized girls under my roof, I knew those days were long gone. The reality was that I would never get a break from my stress. There would never be a time when I could just come home, flip on a DVD, drink, and laugh myself silly after a rough day.

This was the life I chose, and this was the life that I'd live.

CHAPTER
TWENTY-FIVE

"SO, HOW DID IT GO, MATE?" Axel asked me the next time I saw him. We met for lunch, and, as usual, lunch wasn't relaxing. I was always on and couldn't get away from any of it.

"I'm sorry. How did what go?"

"Your pretrial conferences. Did you get those deals to send those two blokes on their way?"

I shook my head. "No. I didn't." I sighed. "There might be even more trials in my near future. I have to think about that on top of what's going on with Uncle Jack. Sometimes I don't know how I'll do it all."

I didn't even tell Axel about the Rina thing. That was just one more stressful thing to think about on top of everything else. My talk with her could have gone better. She clammed up and refused to tell me much of anything. I tried to get to the root of why she was so upset, but I couldn't. I would have to make an appointment for her to speak with a therapist, another expense I'd have to meet.

Axel put his hand on mine. "You're strong. You'll get through this. You've gotten through everything else. This is child's play, mate. Child's play."

I had to smile. "Child's play." I stared down at my half-eaten sandwich. I didn't have the appetite to think about taking another bite. "Child's play." I sighed. "Why does life have to be so difficult?"

I was whining, and I knew it. I hated not having answers or when the answers I had were horrible. As they presently were.

Axel paused and took a sip of water. "This restaurant is nice," he said, looking around the open-aired space of the Italian restaurant where we met. Then he looked at me. "But I can tell you aren't in the mood to discuss the décor."

I buttered a piece of bread and didn't meet his eyes. "No, I guess I'm not. My mother has always told me, and so has Albany, and my sister Emma, that I get too involved with my cases. Too emotionally attached to my clients. They have a point. I sometimes wonder if I'm in the wrong profession. I mean, what other profession has as a feature that you lose a good 80% of your clients? That's how many of my clients end up going to prison for something because I plead most of them out. It's heartbreaking."

"Why is it heartbreaking, mate? If your clients did the crime, they need to pay their debts, right? What am I missing here?"

I sighed. "It's just not as simple as all that. My clients, by and large, come from horrible circumstances. Many were abused all their lives, most of their fathers are in prison, and most of their mothers have too little time and money for them. They go to schools that don't teach them and grow up in environments without opportunity. Who can blame them for turning to gangs or dealing drugs? Who can blame them for holding up a 7-11 to afford diapers and formula for their babies? It has never seemed fair that some people grow up with so little and others grow up with so much, and the ones that grow up with little end up in the prison system where they're abused further and not given the skills they need to assimilate into society."

Back on my soapbox. I had to smile just a little as I saw Axel's dumbfounded face, looking increasingly perplexed with every word I said.

"Lass, I love that you have such a big heart. Don't get me wrong. But if somebody is hurting people by robbing them or dealing drugs to children, they need to go away. They need to be taken out of society."

"Oh? That sounds well and good, but what happens when they come back into society? The prisons aren't exactly known for trying to rehabilitate their prisoners. They go into prison one way and come out much worse. Now they have a felony conviction, so nobody will hire them. What options do they have when they get out? Most of them don't even have a high school education. What can they do? There has to be a better way, other than locking these people up in for-profit prisons without helping them get their GEDs and learn a trade so that, when they get out, they have no options other than turning back to the streets."

Axel's face was now looking amused. "Oh, my God. I'm in love with a liberal." He shook his head. "Well, the wedding is off, mate." He grinned and shook his head. "Just kidding. I love somebody I can spar with."

"I hope this is the only issue we'll spar about. Because if you take conservative positions across the board, I'm afraid this won't work." I was dead serious about this.

He smiled. "Don't worry. I'm sure we'll have many areas of agreement along the way. It's just that you and I approach the criminal justice system from two very different positions. I investigate these criminals and speak with the victims. But I agree prisons should do more to rehabilitate criminals. You have a good point there."

I sighed with relief. "Thank God." I took a sip of water and buttered my bread some more. "Let's change the subject. I need to brainstorm some on Uncle Jack. That's the main thing worrying me, other than the fact that Abby's little ex-boyfriend has been spreading rumors around school that he and Abby had sex."

Axel raised his eyebrows. "Wait, wait, wait. Abby is 12. What am I missing here?"

I shook my head. "Oh, you're missing a lot. I said the same damned thing, and then I looked on the internet, and sure enough, kids are having sex at her age today. I'm trying to figure out how to deal with this. I'm torn. On the one hand, I want to tell James' mother that if he doesn't take back what he said about Abby, I'll see him prosecuted for statutory rape. Put the fear of God into the little shit. But I also think this would only make things worse for her. I'm hoping the rumor will die on its own. After all, from what Abby says, many girls get gossiped about that way."

I shook my head. "Sometimes I forget what a jungle middle school is. I'm surprised any of us went to middle school and lived to tell the tale."

"And that's the truth, mate. Doesn't sound like any good options there, although I like the one about threatening to turn James in for statutory rape if he doesn't tell the truth. That would put fear into him."

"Yes, but here's the rub with that one. If I turn him in for statutory rape, she goes down too. The statute doesn't discriminate, although I think the girl would get more leniency than the boy. So, threatening that ultimately wouldn't have any teeth. His mother would probably see right through that threat. Plus, I don't want to make Abby's life harder than it is. Seventh grade is a disgusting time. I remember it well. Kids are vicious and can be such sneaks. I'd hoped I could insulate the girls from that by sending them to that fancy private school, but lo and behold, the kids in that school are like kids everywhere at that age."

I fiddled with the bread, and the waitress came around and brought us our entrees. Mine was Fettuccine Alfredo with shrimp, while Axel got steak. I dug into it with gusto. Fettuccine Alfredo was my favorite pasta, even though I could feel my arteries clogging up with every bite.

"Well, we'll come back to that mess later, lass. Tell me what's going on with your Uncle Jack. You said you needed to brainstorm it with me."

"Yes, I do. You were an enormous help to Heather. You gave me the idea about who to look for tampering with the crime scene. Maybe you can give me an idea of who to look at for this thing."

"I'll do what I can."

I took a deep breath. "I went to see Steven Heaney yesterday at his home in Oregon," I said quietly. I hunched down, waiting for the inevitable lecture I'd get from Axel for going off and seeing a guy who might've been a serial killer. I had to admit, as gambles go, this one wasn't the brightest and most informed.

"I see." He glared at me. "Lass, what were you thinking? That bloke could've killed you." He shook his head. "Why didn't you ask me to go with you? Did you even bring a gun or anything to protect you?"

"I have pepper spray in my purse," I said. "I always carry that with me because I can never be sure when one of my clients will stalk me because he's unhappy about something I did." I dug into my fettuccine some more and started to feel attacked. I knew he was only looking out for me, but I didn't like being talked to like I was five.

"That didn't answer my question. Why didn't you have me go with you?"

I sighed. "I needed to see him on my own. I didn't know what to expect, but it was safe to assume that one woman coming to visit wouldn't upset him, but two people, a man and a woman, just popping by might make him freak out. I needed to be on good terms with him because I would ask him some important and sensitive questions." I crossed my arms in front of me and glared at him.

Axel seemed to back down. "Well, I guess you came out of it in one piece, but don't do that again. Seriously, Harper, I need to know when you will do something like that. You have a detective on your side. You might think about using him once in a while. And I'll have to teach you how to fire a gun. I'm sorry, I know you're against them on principle, but if you're going to go and do stupid stunts like seeing a possible serial killer who lives out in the woods, all by yourself, I'd feel better if you carried. Okay, I said my piece; now tell me what you learned from this bloke."

"Well, he told me quite a lot. But the things he told me make me think, more than ever, that Uncle Jack is guilty. That's why I need to bounce this off you. You can help me see an angle I never thought about.

He nodded and cut into his steak, putting a tiny piece on my plate. I put that tiny piece in my mouth and closed my eyes. *Just like butter.* "Well, he told me things I knew," I said. "But also things I didn't. There apparently was a third alter in Jack's psyche named Sam. Sam killed Robert Heaney. So, Eli didn't kill Robert, like I had thought, but Sam. Sam apparently is Uncle Jack's violent side."

"Okay, that's an interesting wrinkle, but we knew Jack killed Robert, so that's not necessarily new. We just didn't know he had yet another alter. Did Steven think Sam was a violent alter, or did he think Sam killed Robert to protect Jack?"

"The latter, but it worries me all the same. I don't know this, Sam. It's the first I've ever heard of him. My mother was familiar with Eli, who didn't seem violent. What if Sam is? What if that's the only reason he exists - to kill people who hurt Jack?"

Axel dug into his baked potato, took a sip of water and paused. Apparently, he was thinking about my question because he had a look on his face that told me that he was deep in thought. "Okay, that's interesting. Go on, though. Tell me your theory on why Jack would kill Father Kennedy if this alter, Sam, only comes out to kill people who hurt Jack? That would mean Father Kennedy hurt Jack somehow, right? Yet Jack claims that he never met Father Kennedy. That doesn't make much sense, does it?"

"Oh, but Jack knew him. That's the other piece of important information I got from Steven – he told me Jack apparently knew Father Kennedy before he was abducted by Robert Heaney. I know this because Jack, who was Mick at the time, introduced Robert Heaney to Father Kennedy, and Robert fell in love with the Father. So, Jack must've known Father Kennedy before the age of 11. Otherwise, he wouldn't have introduced Robert to the Father in the first place."

I took another sip of my water. "And you make a good point - Jack says he never met Father Kennedy, yet he did. That must mean he blocked out memories of Father Kennedy. That looks bad, too - why would he block out those memories?"

"The plot thickens." He nodded. "But don't jump to conclusions. Just because there've been so many priest scandals through the years doesn't mean something happened between Jack and Father Kennedy. That makes the most sense, but I wouldn't make that conclusion. You need to do more background research on Father Kennedy and see if anybody has accused him of anything before you think Father Kennedy molested Jack, which would cause him to lose it and kill him." He cut into his steak. "And don't worry about Jack blocking memories of Father Kennedy. He probably didn't block the memories so much as it was so long ago, and those memories have faded. Do you remember everyone you knew at the age of 11?"

"Good point."

I didn't have to explain to Axel what I was thinking. He already knew. He was smart enough to connect the dots in my mind, and I loved that about him. "You're right. I need to find out if any accusations have been made against him over the years. I admit that theory popped into my head when I found out Jack knew Father Kennedy before he was abducted. I'm almost embarrassed to fall for that stereotype."

Axel nodded his head. "The pedophilia scandal only implicated a tiny minority of priests, but since the media focused so much on it, it seemed every priest in the country was molesting children. That's unfair, so I'm glad you won't jump to conclusions and wait for the facts to reveal themselves. Which they will."

"I know." I nodded my head. "I know they will."

"Okay. Now that I've hopefully gotten you off that track, you can focus on trying to find the alternative suspect for this murder. Now let's try to figure this out. Who do you know who knows about Jack's other personalities? About Jack's alters? That's a good place to start."

I nodded my head. "In what way?"

"Well, now, let's see. You have three theories on this case, right?"

"Right. One is that Jack did it and then passed out in shock. The second is that Jack walks in on the person killing the priest, making him pass out from shock. The third is that Jack was sitting in the rectory, minding his own business, when the killer came in, killed the Father and drugged Jack before Jack could see who it was. In other words, the killer was stealthy, drugged Jack and killed the Father." I sighed. "Unfortunately, no tox screening was done on Jack when he was arrested. I wish Jack would've called me earlier because I would've demanded one be done on him."

"Okay," Axel said. "Let's try to game out a fourth scenario. There's somebody out there who knows about Jack's disorder. Knows Jack loses memory and time because he has DID. That person knew they could take advantage of that. That person knew that pinning the murder on Jack would be easy *because* Jack had gaps in memory. That person also knew Jack would go into an alternative personality because of the stress of seeing Father Kennedy killed in such a way.

That person knew Jack's precise vulnerabilities, and he or she elaborately planned this murder to make it look like Jack was guilty."

He continued on. "In other words, this person had been planning this murder for the past five years. They had their patsy all along, and it was just a matter of making that patsy unstable enough to pin this murder on him."

"Well, in your scenario, that person also had to have it in for Jack," I said. "This murder was brutal, and Jack was framed. That would mean this person also wanted to specifically make sure Jack fried for the murder. That makes sense, right?"

Axel nodded. "That's what I would get at next. But, yes, my theory presupposes the criminal also wanted to get revenge on Jack. You're absolutely right about that."

"Well, that makes your theory much more complicated than any of mine. Under my theories, the person who killed Father Kennedy didn't have something against Jack. It was just that Jack was in the wrong place at the wrong time. Under your theory, the culprit absolutely had something against Jack."

"Right. The person not only had something against Jack, but he or she also knew about Jack's DID. If you can find that person – the person who hates Jack and knows he is vulnerable – you might find your man. Or woman."

I tapped my fingers on the table and took another sip of water. Axel did one thing – he focused my mind on a different angle. The person who killed Father Kennedy might've wanted the Father dead and Jack, specifically Jack, to pay for it. It was an interesting theory and better than my other theories because it made me realize I would have to look for the intersection. Before, when I thought the person who killed Father Kennedy didn't even know Jack, but Jack was in the wrong place at the wrong time, it would be extremely difficult to find the real culprit. A needle in a haystack. But now that there was possibly an intersection, I could narrow it down.

I narrowed my eyes. "Well, this is interesting. Very interesting. I'll have to think about that." I put my hands on Axel's. "Thank you. You can always help me see outside the box. It'll still be tough to figure this out, but less tough than before. Much less tough than before."

"I'm glad I could help," he said with a smile. "Now, if we could only figure out Abby's situation with that sleazy bloke James." He shook his head. "Who would have thought. I liked that kid. Now he does something like this, and I want to smash his little punk face in."

"Me too. Me too."

We talked for the rest of the meal about other things. The entire time, though, my mind was focused on what Axel had said before. *Look for somebody who had it in for Jack and for Father Kennedy. Look for that intersection. That will be your murderer. And then, the hard part – trying to sell a jury on your theory. Trying to sell a judge on it, so he lets you introduce evidence about it.*

It was still an uphill battle, to be sure. But there might be a light at the end of the tunnel.

I only hoped that light wasn't an oncoming train.

CHAPTER
TWENTY-SIX

THAT MONDAY MORNING was my first pre-trial conference on Jack's case. I went to pick him up at my mom's house, wondering who I would be talking to. I had to hope it was Mick because Jack, more and more, acted bewildered and depressed. I didn't want the trial judge, Judge Greene, to even suspect there was something mentally off about my uncle. Mick managed to ace the psychological examination about whether Jack was fit for trial. I didn't know if Jack could do the same.

I felt relieved when I saw him sitting on a chair on the front porch. He was wearing glasses, his leg was crossed like a woman's, and his right hand was dangling while he drank a glass of water with his left. Mick was left-handed. Jack was right-handed. "Hey, doll," he said with a wave. "It's showtime, huh?"

I smiled. "Hi, Mick. Yep, showtime. You ready for this?"

"As ready as I'll ever be. Let's get the show on the road. I'm dying for a cocktail, and it wouldn't do to get stinking drunk before my big court date." He rolled his eyes. "If you had to stay here with Claire, you'd know why I'm dying for a cocktail, love. That woman is standing on my last nerve."

"Oh, I know. But she means well. Never forget that."

"I won't." He stood up, put on a sweater and called through the open screen door. "Claire, I'm going to court now with Harper. I'll see you when I get back."

"Okay," Mom called from inside the house. She appeared at the open door and wagged her finger at me. "You be careful in court today. We don't want Jack locked up, so we don't want that judge to find he's not fit to stand trial."

"I know the drill, Mom."

She nodded. "I know you do, honey. I just…" She shook her head. "I have faith in you."

"I know."

At that, Mick and I walked to my SUV parked on the street.

I loved the neighborhood where Mom lived. It was an older neighborhood, but not as old as mine – the houses here were built in the 1940s, judging by the architecture, which meant the trees were all mature and the houses were small with wooden floors and porches. Mom's house was built bungalow style – one level of living area, with an attic with pitched ceilings. Jack was staying in the attic, which Mom fixed up because he wanted his privacy and living in the bedroom next door to Mom wasn't working out.

"So, what's with the sweater?" I asked him. Mick had linked arms with me as we walked to my SUV, and he started to skip.

"Oh, honey, you don't know how cold it'll be in that courtroom. Sometimes they turn the AC up so high, I absolutely freeze."

"Good point. I never think about it because I'm always in a suit."

"About that, doll. Don't you have a personal stylist or a personal shopper or something? Because, I hate to tell you, you need it. You must have a bit of flair when addressing those juries. A pop of color certainly wouldn't hurt. We must go down to The Plaza after court and find you a nice canary yellow bag. That would certainly brighten up those grey and navy suits you love to wear so much. Or, better yet, let's find you a pair of red pumps. That would look divine with what you're wearing."

I rolled my eyes. First Heather, now Mick. What was it with them criticizing my clothes? Yes, I wore grey and navy a lot. For this court appearance, I wore my grey pantsuit. It wasn't out of style–I just bought it at Nordstrom. The legs were slightly flared, and the jacket was fitted. I wore a sleeveless turtleneck underneath it in taupe. My shoes were also taupe, as was my bag. I always went for classic, and it never steered me wrong.

"Tell you what, Mick, I'll buy some colorful scarves," I said. "But I'd feel like a hooker in high-heeled red stilettos."

"Whatever, love. Trust me, you could use some color. But I'll shut up now. After all, the only color I might wear for the rest of my life will be hideous orange." He shuddered. "Yuck."

I opened the door, and he sat down, and I went over to the driver's side. "Now, Mick, you won't be wearing hideous orange. Not if I have anything to say about it. Which I do, of course. I have everything to say about whether or not you end up in an orange jumpsuit."

He sighed. "Well, I can tell you one thing, doll. If we end up in prison, I've decided to stay out and not let Jack leave anymore. He's pretty strong right now. He has a strong will, even if you don't see it so much. But if he gets sentenced to prison...." Mick made a slashing motion with his hand across his neck. "He'll be so messed up there won't be a problem with my getting out. It'll be tough for me to live that way, but trust me, love, I can handle such a thing much better than Jack."

I nodded as I focused my eyes on the road. "That's what I'm afraid of. That's what I'm afraid of."

Mick looked at his hands and frowned. "Don't be afraid of that, doll. Don't be. We'll be okay, no matter what. Who knows, I might have some fun with those burly prison boys. I've always liked a tattooed man, you know. Always." He sighed. "Like that Father Mathews. God, what a dream that man is."

I heard the name "Father Mathews," but it didn't register. I was too busy concentrating on the road because, for some odd reason, there was a traffic tie-up, and I was anxious about getting to the courthouse on time. "Dammit," I said. "Why is there always a tie-up when you're running late?"

"We're running late?" Mick asked mildly. "What time are we supposed to be there?"

"1:30." I looked at the clock and saw it read 1:10. I shouldn't have cut this so fine. That was always an issue with me – running late to court. Ordinarily, if there was a docket situation, it would be fine. I would just call the clerk and explain, and they'd put my case at the end of the docket. But for a pre-trial conference, you had to be on time.

Finally, the cars started to move, but I didn't relax. It would be tight trying to get to court on time. That was the last thing I wanted. I wanted to be on a good footing with Judge Greene. It was bad enough that I drew Vince again as the opposing prosecutor. Granted, he helped me with my Heather case, which meant he wasn't a bad guy, but I hated his show-boating. He was also super-aggressive with cross-examining witnesses, and I was afraid he'd break down Jack so much that he would turn into somebody else right before our eyes. I could imagine what would happen if he cross-examined Mick, assuming Mick took the stand, and freaked him out so much that violent Sam came out. It would be even worse if Jack was on the stand because Jack was sure to go into one of his alters, which might not be a nice one.

"Relax, Harper. The judge will wait."

"No, he won't. Pre-trial conferences are slotted in. If we're late, we lose our slot, and the judge will be pissed."

"Let him be. He can cool his jets." Mick shook his head. "Everybody's always in such a hurry these days. Go, go, go, go, go. That's all anybody ever thinks about."

"Well, that's what we must think about right now." I saw the courthouse come into sight and prayed I could find a parking spot fairly close.

When I got to the parking lot closest to the courthouse, I knew my prayers were answered. I found a spot right away and parked. "Come on," I said to Mick as I looked at my watch. "Let's move."

"Okay, okay. I'm dancing as fast as I can here."

I was galloping towards the courthouse as fast as I could in my three-inch heels, and Mick was close behind me. We got to the entrance, and I showed my ID while Mick went through the metal detector after taking off his watch and depositing his phone in the white tub that went through the machine.

"I don't know why we have to do all that," he whispered after he got through the metal detector. "What do they think my phone is, some kind of tiny bomb?"

"Don't say the word bomb," I whispered. "Not even in jest."

"Whatever."

The elevator arrived, and we got on it with about twenty other people. I rapidly walked towards the courtroom and went through the massive wooden doors. I felt slightly winded as I saw I arrived at 1:30 on the dot.

"Hey, Harper," Vince said. He was standing right in front of the bench, chatting with Judge Greene before I arrived. "Glad you could make it. You haven't been returning my calls about this case. I suggest that you start taking my future calls."

"I'm sorry," I said. "I've been busy. I haven't received any offers or discovery, so I didn't want to entertain anything until I get something from you."

"Hello, Ms. Ross," Judge Greene said kindly. "Are you ready for this pre-trial conference?"

"Yes," I said, trying to compose myself. I hated running late because it usually put me in a bad frame of mind for the court appearance. It started it out on a bad foot.

"I see you have your client here," Judge Greene said, gesturing towards Mick. "Mr. Calhoun, please approach."

Mick walked slowly through the small wooden doors that separated the restricted area from the audience area and took his place next to me. "Thank you, your honor."

I noticed his voice was weird. It didn't sound like Mick, and it didn't sound like Jack. My heart stopped briefly as I wondered if somebody else had taken over, but then I saw Mick wink and smile at me, and I let out my breath.

I wanted Sam or Eli to come out, but not like this. Not when I wasn't ready for it. I'd prepared Mick for this court appearance. The other two alters would be too much of a wild card.

I suddenly realized why Mick's voice sounded weird, though. It was as if he was trying hard to sound masculine and straight. It sounded like somebody was purposely trying to affect a different intonation in their voice – like when a woman imitates a man or vice-versa.

It sounded unnatural, in other words.

I inwardly groaned and hoped that neither Judge Greene nor Vince would pick up on the weird tone of Mick's voice and question me about it. I looked at their faces and saw that neither man thought anything was amiss, so I was relieved.

"Mr. Calhoun," Judge Greene said. "I've read the statement of information and reviewed the psychological notes on this case. Dr. Jansing is of the opinion that you are mentally fit to stand trial. I wanted to ask you a few questions before I decide the same."

Mick looked at me, and I swallowed hard. "Okay, your honor."

Judge Greene nodded. "Do you understand, Mr. Calhoun, why you are here?"

"Of course. Father Kennedy of Guardian Angels Catholic Church was murdered when I was in the rectory with the murder weapon in my hand. I was arrested and charged with his murder."

Judge Greene nodded. "Do you understand the charges that have been leveled against you?"

"Yes. I know what murder in the first degree is. I understand that if a jury convicts me, I will serve life in prison without the possibility of parole. My lawyer, Ms. Ross, explained all this to me."

"Do you feel you could assist your attorney in preparing your case? I assume Ms. Ross has explained the discovery process with you and depositions and what they mean. Could you assist her all the way with these steps?"

"Of course."

Judge Greene nodded, satisfied my client was lucid and sane. At least he was sane enough to stand trial. I considered that my first hurdle and thanked my lucky stars for having Mick there talking to the judge, not Jack. I wasn't sure that Jack, with his incoherent thinking and meek affect, would've passed this test as well as Mick did.

"Well, then," Judge Greene said. "Let's begin our pre-trial conference. Where are we on this case? Is it close to a resolution?"

"No," Vince said. "Both sides need to do depositions and exchange discovery. At the moment, I don't have an offer to give Ms. Ross, and I don't anticipate I will before trial. Because of the brutal nature of the crime, my office has only authorized me to offer life in prison without the possibility of parole."

"Does the defendant plan to introduce an affirmative defense to the charges?"

"No, your honor, I don't," I said.

"Do you plan on introducing any expert witnesses?"

"No, your honor, I don't."

"Okay." He nodded. "So, you are telling me, Ms. Ross, that you do not plan on introducing a witness that would testify about whether or not your client meets the legal definition of insanity. Is that true? You will not try to introduce the possibility that I might find your client not guilty by reason of insanity?"

Judge Greene looked over at my client. "I'm very sorry, Mr. Calhoun. I don't mean to imply anything by that question. I must admit, it concerns me that, according to this statement of information, you stated you don't remember what happened in that rectory."

I shifted uncomfortably. I hoped and prayed my strategy was the right one. If I didn't appoint an expert witness to testify to Jack's sanity at the time of the murder, the NGRI defense wouldn't be available.

Was I willing to roll the dice?

There was a part of me that didn't. I couldn't simultaneously try for NGRI and SODDI – Some Other Dude Did It. I had to pick a lane and stay in it because I couldn't try to convince the jury both that Jack did it, but he was legally insane at the time and that he didn't do it at all. Those two theories of the case were incongruent to one another, and I would have to pick one.

Go big or go home. "Not at this time, your honor."

"Okay." He looked at his calendar. "Let's see, today is May 5. I'll set this case for trial on Monday, September 18. Both sides must have written discovery into one another by August 18 and must have a witness list by July 18. That should give both sides plenty of time to depose one another's witnesses. As for expert witnesses, Ms. Ross, you shall have until July 1 to name an expert witness in your case, should you decide to call one. If you do not have an expert named by July 1, then I shall assume that you will not ask for a not guilty by reason of insanity defense, which means this option will be foreclosed at that time."

I felt my heart racing. I'd have just under two months to try to figure this out. If I couldn't figure out an alternative suspect by July 1, I might try for an NGRI defense.

I almost cried when I thought about that possibility. It was just something I never would've dreamed would be possible when I was a young child, floating lazily on the river while Uncle Jack clapped his hands every time I would pull a tiny fish out with my pole. When I was 10 years old and so excited over seeing palm trees for the first time and then squealing with glee as I approached the ocean, I never would've imagine ending up here with my uncle.

All those nights around the campfire, telling ghost stories and roasting marshmallows and wieners on a stick...all those days hiking up a mountain, my Uncle Jack carrying a huge pack, while Albany and I carried our smaller packs, with Uncle Jack banging two sticks together to scare off any wild animals...all those evenings where Uncle Jack came over to play penny poker and let me win...I shook my head and tried to hold back my tears. I wouldn't cry in court.

"Is there anything else?" Judge Greene asked. "If there will be any affirmative defenses, I need to know about it now."

"No, your honor." I hung my head. "We don't have any affirmative defenses."

"Okay." He smiled kindly. "Then I'll see both parties back here on September 18 unless there is a disposition of this case before that. I would suspect, however, that if the prosecutor persists in offering life in prison without the possibility of parole, this case will not be disposed of before trial."

"That's correct, your honor."

He nodded his head. "Okay, I'll see the parties back here on September 18 for trial."

I turned around and saw the next group heading into the courtroom.

I walked towards the door, and Vince was walking next to me. We got outside the courtroom, and Vince put his hand on my shoulder.

"Let me talk to you alone," he said, gesturing down the hall.

I nodded. "Uncle Jack, you don't mind, do you?"

"Of course not." His voice still had that odd intonation and stiff cadence. He was definitely trying too hard to sound like somebody different. I hoped he wouldn't have that same tone of voice when I put him on the stand.

Vince and I walked toward the end of the hall, and I sat down on one of the benches. Vince sat down next to me.

"Defending your uncle's a tough break," he said.

I looked into his eyes and saw his sincerity, so I nodded. "You don't know how hard."

"I know. Listen, I'll see what I can do to reduce that sentence. I don't know if I can, though. Killing a priest is a big deal. When I learned Jack Calhoun was your uncle, I talked my boss out of the death penalty."

I smiled. "Thanks, Vince."

"Not a problem, Harper, not a problem. Hey, I don't hate you. I hate most of your clients, but you're pretty cool."

I nodded. "Well, see what offer you can come up with. Not that I'll take anything on this."

"You trying for SODDI?" he asked me.

"Yeah."

He shook his head. "Even though your uncle was found at the rectory with the body and the murder weapon in his hand?"

"Even though."

"You're a braver person than I. I just hope you're doing your client justice. You can't let your emotional ties cloud your judgment here. It looks bad for Mr. Calhoun."

"I know how bad it looks. I know that. You don't have to tell me." I glared at him. "I'm not stupid."

"No," he said. "You're far from stupid. But you might be too emotionally attached to this case. You might not see it clearly. That's all I'm saying. If I were you, I'd appoint an expert to evaluate your client. Judge Greene is a decent, fair judge. He's not a hard-ass. If your client is mentally ill, and he didn't know what he was doing when he killed that priest-"

"Allegedly killed that priest."

Vince nodded, acknowledging my point. "*Allegedly* killed that priest, okay, but if he met the legal definition of insanity at that time, Judge Greene will be more likely than most judges in this circuit to sentence your uncle to a mental institution instead of prison. I know you don't want that because he's your uncle, and you love him, but you have to think of this case as if Mr. Calhoun is just another one of your clients."

I took a deep breath. I knew Vince was right but didn't want to acknowledge it. "I have until July to figure that out," I said. "In the meantime, I'm going with SODDI."

"Your call, of course," he said. "I won't tell you how to do your job." He shoved his hands in his pockets and rocked back and forth on his heels. "Well, then, we have our marching orders. Let's try to get our discovery to each other even earlier than the dates Judge Greene gave us, okay?"

I nodded and said nothing. I turned around and saw Mick staring at me, his hand on his chin. "I'll see you later, Vince."

"See ya, Harper," Vince said, motioning back to the courtroom. "I have to get back in there. I'm on the next case, too."

We walked back down the hall, and I linked arms with Mick. Mick put his head on my shoulder, and we went to the elevator.

"What was that all about?" Mick asked me once we were safely on the elevator. We were the only ones in that space, so I knew he felt confident enough to talk openly with me.

"Oh, Vince is trying to get me to hire an expert, so you might be judged legally insane. That's all."

Mick laughed. "Oh, honey. Honey. We are insane, of course. Jack himself had no idea what happened in that rectory. I can't tell you what happened in that rectory because somebody else took over before we got into that place, but I can tell you one thing – the person who walked into that rectory wasn't Jack. It wasn't me, either, but it wasn't him. So, yes, Jack meets the legal definition of insanity. Jack literally didn't know what he was doing at that time."

I sighed. "And you have no idea if Jack killed that priest, right? I know that's what you've been telling me, but I just wanted to ask again."

"That's right, doll. I am also trying to figure out what happened in that rectory. Usually, I know what those other alters are up to, but only sometimes. Only sometimes. In this case, nobody told me what was about to happen, and nobody's told me since what happened. Sorry."

"Mick, you need to let me talk to the others. I need to speak with the alter who knows what happened. Why are you not letting me talk to him?"

"How do you know it's a him?"

I rolled my eyes. "What is that supposed to mean? There are only three of you, right? Right? You, Eli and Sam?"

"Doll, those are the only two I know about. And how did you find out about Sam?"

I opened my mouth and shut it. I didn't think Mick should know about my visit to Steven. That piece of knowledge would freak him out for sure. "You told me about Sam. Remember?"

I was lying, but I hoped Mick didn't figure that out.

He shrugged. "I don't remember telling you about Sam, but I guess I did. But, yes, there is me, Eli and Sam. But there might be others. I don't know about them."

I groaned. "How many others?"

"How am I supposed to know? Listen, I'm not Jack's secretary. I'm not the appointed scheduler of all the alters. I've only come in contact with Sam and Eli. They're the only ones who talk to me. But that doesn't mean there are no others. There might be. I just don't know."

"Well, let me speak with Eli and Sam and ask them. Surely one of them knows what the hell happened in that rectory."

Mick raised an eyebrow. "I wouldn't be so sure about that."

We walked to my SUV, and I let Mick in the passenger side. "Let me be the judge. You're being stubborn, Mick. Jack's life is on the line here. Do you get that? His life is on the line. All of you will end up in a psychiatric facility if I don't get to the bottom of this, so I need to speak with both Sam and Eli to see if either of them can give me some goddamned answers."

Mick rolled his eyes and looked at his nails. "Doll, you don't under-stand. I don't want to let either of them out. I had a hard time making them leave before. Not Sam, though. Sam was just a one-time thing. But Eli..." He shook his head. "Eli is tough. He wants out, but he wants to stay out. And if he's out, I can't control him."

Mick continued on. "Eli's trouble, lady. I don't think you want Eli running around, screwing women, taking drugs and running away.

Yes, I said running away. If Eli comes out, he'll run. And what happens if he runs? He gets picked up by the lovely bounty hunter, his ass is hauled into jail and the suckers who put that $150,000 up for Jack lose all of it. That's what happens. You and Claire lose your money, and we must go to jail to await trial. As much as I hate staying with Claire, it sure beats the hell out of having to stay in jail before trial."

I groaned. I didn't want to hear that. Yet, I knew he had a point. I didn't need a wild, untamed alter who would run. That was the last thing I needed. I also didn't need an alter who would take drugs. Jack had to do random drug tests as a condition of his bail, so if Eli came out and started taking meth again, I couldn't keep Jack out of jail.

Yet, I *needed* Eli to come out. Even if Sam was out at the time of the murder, Eli might still know something. "Okay," I finally said. "I won't make you let Eli out."

"Thank you." Mick looked at his nails again. "And I'm dying for a cocktail. Did I mention that earlier?"

"Yes, several times." *I'm dying for a cocktail, too, but I can't have one. Ever.*

"So, let's go and get one." He clapped his hands together. "I'm feeling so cooped up at Claire's. She's like a warden, you know. No cocktails, no men, no fun. No men for me and none for her, either. She's like a nun, you know. A nun."

"Mick, I think you know that-"

"I know, I know." He affected an even higher-pitched voice than his usual Mick voice, which told me he was probably imitating me. "The conditions of your bail are that you can only leave your prison, I mean Claire's house, to go to court and any court-ordered classes." He switched back to his usual Mick voice. "Which there have been none. *You* try to stay in one house for months, only being let out to go to boring court. It's maddening."

"It might be maddening, but Mick, it's a helluva lot better than spending your pre-trial period in jail. And that's where you'll be if that ankle bracelet detects you're going anywhere but home and to court." I wagged my finger at him. "Staying at Mom's house might be boring, but you get three squares a day, a warm bed to sleep in, television to watch and books to read. And you can wear whatever you want. Plus, you don't have to shower with a bunch of guys. Be grateful for what you have."

"Doll, at least in jail, I get a chance for some action. At Claire's, there's no chance of that happening at all. I'm like a cat in heat over there."

That was the last thing I wanted to hear my uncle say. I finally sighed. "Listen, Mick, I can't take you out for a cocktail. I can't take you anywhere but back to Mom's house. I'm sorry about that, but when I get all of you off for murder, you can do anything you want. Okay?"

Mick crossed his arms in front of him, pouting. "I guess. But you know, doll, I have the feeling if you get us off for murder, Jack might want to come back again. I don't want that. I like being out. I like living."

That worried me. Mick was strong, and Jack was weak. I knew Jack had really been weak since Mary was killed. I wondered if Mick would try to take control once everybody was free. I knew that, no matter what, Jack would have to get intensive counseling from the best psychologist in the country after he was freed.

If he was freed. I still didn't know how to manage that, and that thought terrified me.

Mick looked out the window. "Well, I guess we're here. Back to jail."

I followed him into Mom's house. Mom was standing in the kitchen, taking a casserole out of the oven. "I'm so happy you two are back," she said. "I was worried."

"What were you worried about?"

She shrugged. "I've just been worried, dear. I lay awake, night after night, tossing and turning. I just can't sleep."

"I sleep like a baby," Mick said. "I don't know what you're so worried about, Claire."

"How can you sleep like a baby when I don't sleep at all?" My mother was apparently getting into hysterical mode, the only mode she had been in since Jack was arrested. "I just don't understand you, Mick. I don't know how you can be so relaxed about this when Jack's life and existence are on the line."

Mick shrugged. "What is there to be uptight about? Listen, Claire, you don't have to worry your silly little head about us. If we go to prison, we go to prison. You don't have to worry about Jack suffering in prison because he'll never come out again. It will be me, and I'll be just fine."

At that, my mom started to cry. I went over to her and put my arm around her. "I know, Mom, I know. What Mick said just now is the last thing you want to hear – Jack will disappear if he goes to prison. I know. That's why it's so important that none of them go to prison." I pulled her tighter, my arms enfolding her while she bawled. "I'll figure this out, Mom. I will. I promise you that. I will figure this out."

"And what if you can't? What happens then?"

"I will. There's just no other choice."

I got up to leave. I had to get to my office. I would call Heather to see if she could meet me there. I hoped she was okay with getting Steven. I also wanted to see what kind of case law she got for me for Michael Reynolds' appeal.

I kissed my mother on the cheek and gave Mick a hug. "Love you guys," I said.

"We love you too." Mom gave me a hug. "Please find a way to help Jack."

"I will."

As I got into my SUV, though, I started to cry.

Did I just make a promise that I could never keep?

CHAPTER
TWENTY-SEVEN

I GOT to the office after calling Heather from the car. She was waiting for me in the lobby of my suite. She was dressed in a grey pantsuit with a colorful shirt underneath. Her hair was held back by her trademark red headband. I had to smile because she looked nervous – as if she was coming in for a job interview.

She'd come a long way from the young girl with the big attitude I met almost a year ago. She had been humbled, but more than that, she'd found a family who accepted her. She and Louisa were getting along; that was all I ever wanted for her.

Because of all that happened, she no longer had to hide behind a façade. I had the feeling I'd get to know the real Heather. And if I could help her in the world find her place, I'd know I did my job.

She stood up when I walked in the door. "Hey, Harper," she said. She had a briefcase with her. It was tattered, and the locks didn't look like they worked, but it was a briefcase. I had to assume she found it in a thrift store. "I have your legal research here."

"Thanks. Come on in the office. I have another assignment for you that I hope you can help me with." I drew my breath. This was an unconventional assignment, for sure. I hoped she'd do it for me.

We walked in, and she sat down on the other side of the desk.

"Here," she said uncertainly. "I read through that legal brief three times. I must admit, when I read their arguments, I was scared I couldn't find anything to argue with. But when I started to find case law on West-law, I realized something. There really isn't any law, is there?"

I touched my nose, impressed she figured that out so quickly. "No. I mean, there is law, in a sense, because our legal system is based upon statutes. But these statutes are so open to interpretation that you can make any argument and still be right. It all depends on which argu-ment is more persuasive to the judge. It's all very complicated, but you have to start with the statute, then find the case law and possibly the legislative history. You can usually find case law to fit any argument you want. I like to think of the law as malleable – living and breathing, as opposed to simple words on a page."

Heather nodded. "That's what I found, too. Their arguments are good, but I found others just as good."

I opened up her file folder, which was filled to the brim with printed-out decisions. I was impressed, really. Heather apparently did her homework. She pointed out cases from the 8th Circuit, but she also found cases from the Missouri Supreme Court, the Western District of Missouri and the United States Supreme Court. She included some *Law Review* articles and statutes. In all, she did an admirably thorough job.

"How long did this take you?"

She shrugged. "I pretty much worked around the clock for the past three days. I was intimidated at first, but I got the hang of it."

"You're a natural researcher. I'm impressed." I nodded as I skimmed over the cases she found. "I think I found my research assistant."

Her face lit up. "Really? Seriously? Harper, you're the shit."

"No," I said. "You are. Really. I took an entire class devoted to legal research, and that was how I learned all this. Of course, I had to do everything from the books in the library, which was a pain in the rear. Learning about the doctrine of *Stare Decisis, En Banc* versus full court decisions, and which case law is binding versus just persuasive takes a while. Things like that. I don't expect you to know any of that, but I think you have a real future. If you like, I can send you to a paralegal school, and you can work for me part-time. That would teach you everything you'll need to know to become a paralegal anywhere you want."

She eagerly nodded. "Actually, Harper, I think that would be hella cool if you could do that. Hella cool." She looked at her nails. "I was scared, Harper. Scared my life would be a waste. I dumped Charlie. After I beat that murder charge, I knew I didn't want to blow my second chance, which I would've if I stayed with him. He's such a waste. He's mad because he paid your legal fee, and he feels I owe him." She took a deep breath. "I had to do a few things to pay off my debt. Things I'm not proud of. But I'm free and clear now and ready to walk the straight path."

I groaned. I didn't want to hear what kinds of things Heather had to do to pay off her drug-dealing ex-boyfriend. But I felt I had to. I didn't want to be caught unaware if the cops came and arrested her again for something. "And what did you do to pay off your debt to Charlie? I almost hate to ask."

She looked out the window and then looked at her nails again. "I went down to Mexico three different times. The first time, I brought back a drug shipment. The other two times, I brought illegals into the country. So, I guess I was both a coyote and a mule."

I bit my lower lip. "Oh, Heather. Heather, Heather, Heather. You better hope Charlie doesn't get arrested and rat you out. I wish you would've come to me. I would've given you the money to pay off your debt."

"I'm not an Indian giver. I gave you that money for your fee, and that was worth every goddamned dime. I won't come to you and ask for that back. No way. I'm not like that."

"But Heather, you-"I sighed. "Well, let's just hold our breath that the authorities don't get wind of what you did for Charlie. In the meantime, let's look at some schools where you can enroll for your paralegal certificate. But, before we do all that, I need you to do something."

"What's that?"

"A lonely old man is living in the woods. I need you to drive out, pick him up and bring him to the city. I have an apartment for him, ready to go." I rented out a studio apartment close by where I lived. It wasn't much, but I knew it would be fine with him, plus I made sure it was pet-friendly. I wouldn't ask him to give up his dog, not for the whole world.

She furrowed her brow. "I don't understand. You need me to pick up a random dude?"

"Well, yes, that's what I'm asking. It's a long story, but he's a man who dropped out of society back in 1972. He's been living isolated in a log cabin ever since. I know this is an unconventional request. I can rent a car for you if you like."

"Nah, that won't be necessary. I picked up a beater 1993 Honda Civic. It runs fine. I just need gas money."

"Yes. Gas money, and I'll pay you $3,000. How does that sound?"

Heather whistled. "Fuck yeah. I'll take that deal. Just tell me how to get to where he is, and I'll be there."

I wrote down the coordinates of where he was. "Put this into your Google Maps. It'll get you there. In the meantime, I owe you for this research project you did for me. I'll pay you $25 an hour when you're my assistant. How many hours did you put into this?"

She shook her head rapidly. "About 50, but you don't have to pay me for all those hours. It took me a long time to find simple things."

I got out my checkbook and calculator. "Let's see, 50 times $25 is $1,250." I made out the check for that amount. "Here. With this money and the money I'll pay you for getting Steven, that should get you on your way to getting an apartment and whatever else you need to get started in life again."

Heather looked at the check, and I saw tears come to her eyes. "Harper," she said after a long hesitation. "Thank you. Thank you for believing in me. Thank you for accepting me. I just don't know..." She started to cry. "How to repay you."

I smiled and put my hand on hers. "You repay me by getting your life together. You repay me by staying away from the wrong people, like Charlie. That's how you repay me."

I stood up. "Come here," I said, spreading my arms.

She came up to me and hugged me hard.

And then she abruptly broke away and smiled. "I'll go and get your friend and be back in a few days."

"I'll see you then."

I watched Heather leave, and then I sat down at my desk. I swiveled my chair to face the window and looked down. At the ground level was the Country Club Plaza, and I could see people walking around with large shopping bags in their hands. They seemed not to have a care in the world.

Oh, how I envied them.

CHAPTER
TWENTY-EIGHT

THE NEXT DAY, I went to the Sacred Heart gym to catch Father Mathews again. I found out he would be playing basketball with the team that evening, and my plan was to catch the game and hopefully speak with him afterward.

I didn't quite know what I hoped to find out. However, I thought there was something I'd know after the game. Something I didn't know before.

Albany came with me. She enjoyed watching basketball games. I really didn't, but Albany was a fan. She got into March madness – she filled out her bracket every year and sometimes even won money online. Her favorite team was the Kansas Jayhawks, which made me want to puke. I was a Mizzou fan all the way, as that was my alma mater, and, as a Mizzou fan, I was destined to hate the Kansas Jayhawks. They were our rivals. Unfortunately for me, though, Mizzou always sucked in basketball and football, where the Jayhawks usually did pretty well. They routinely won national championships, which I don't think my team ever did.

This dynamic led to much teasing by Albany, but I tried to let it all slide off my back.

"Now, why are we here again?" she asked as we sat in the stands.

She had nachos and a bag of popcorn, while I had a hot dog and some cotton candy.

"Father Mathews down there," I said, pointing to the Father dressed in the basketball uniform. "Is playing. I want to talk to him again."

"I see. And why didn't you just return to his office and speak with him? Why come here?"

I sighed. "I'm not sure. I have a hunch."

She nodded. "A hunch." She munched on her popcorn and took a sip of her Coke. "You know, you're always getting on me about not believing in psychic powers. Yet, you're always getting hunches, and they almost always turn out right. Explain that."

"I believe in the power of the subconscious mind. The subconscious mind picks up on cues the conscious mind doesn't. That's where my hunches come from. I don't believe that some guardian angel taps me on the shoulder and tells me what I need to know."

"Okay." She looked skeptical. "I just wish you weren't so close-minded. You went into that house where the Heaneys lived. You felt the presence there. You felt how cold it was. You felt the oppression, the fear. Yet you still refuse to believe."

I raised my eyebrow at her. "I believe in what I can see, touch and feel. I also believe in the power of the mind. I don't believe in spirits."

She sighed and decided to change the subject. She wouldn't change my mind, and I wouldn't change hers. "Father Mathews is hot."

"Yes, he is." I smiled. "Do you remember that book *The Thornbirds*?"

She nudged me and laughed. "Oh, yes. Of course. Meggie and Ralph. Richard Chamberlain played Ralph in the mini-series. Man, he was smoking in that."

"Right?" I looked down at the gym, where Father Mathews was warming up with lay-ups. I was amazed at how agile he was and how well he could dunk the ball. "I'll bet that more than a few women dream about Father Mathews like Meggie dreamed about Ralph."

"Uh-huh. But just remember, Ralph fathered her child in that one."

"Yep." I took a bite of my hot dog. "Not that I think Father Mathews breaks his vow of chastity, but to look at him, you wonder how he doesn't. And he had a life before the priesthood, too. He dealt drugs and went to prison for dealing to a minor who died of an overdose. That was why he decided to enter the priesthood – he knew he was heading down the wrong path and wanted to change it all around. That's why he does outreach now. He really walks the walk – he goes to soup kitchens and plays basketball with these underprivileged kids. He doesn't always stay in the rectory and write his sermons – he's really out there."

Albany looked stunned. "Wow. I never thought a priest would have that kind of background. I can see how some of them might have come from a hardscrabble life, but I guess I never pictured a drug dealer turning into a priest."

"Well, good for him." I took another bite of my hot dog. "I hope Heather can turn it around, too. I think she can. I have faith in her. I'll do all I can to help her, too. She really deserves a second chance. If anybody deserves a second chance, it's her."

"I agree. She may act tough, but she's really not."

The game began with a jump ball, which went to Father Mathews' team, the Grizzlies. Father Mathew dribbled the ball, evading defenders along the way, and passed it to one of the kids, who easily dunked it.

As the game went along, I was impressed. Father Mathew had mad skills. He seemed a born athlete – agile, in control and strategic. I also noticed, as I couldn't help but notice, that both of his arms were covered in tattoos. He fit right in with the other guys on the court, most of whom also had tattoos.

The buzzer was called, signaling half-time, and Father Mathews looked around and caught my eye. He looked perplexed and shook his head. I didn't know what that meant.

It was then that I noticed the coach of this team looked very much like Father Mathews. He was slightly older but had the same bone structure as Father Mathews. He had the same dark, wavy hair and height and build. He put his arm around Father Mathews and patted him, and the two of them were laughing at a private joke.

He almost looked like he was Father Mathews' twin, but not quite.

He had to be a relation. Probably a brother. I watched the two of them as I finished off my Coke.

"What are you looking at?" Albany said.

"Father Mathews. Do you see that other guy down there? The coach?"

She nodded. "Yeah. That guy looks just like him."

"Right." I narrowed my eyes. "He does."

I went down to the edge of the court, and Father Mathews saw me, so he came over to where I was standing. "Hey, Harper," he said. "I'm glad you could make it."

"Yes," I said. "You mentioned you play basketball here, so I had to come down and see for myself. I've never known priests have such athletic skills."

"Well, priests generally don't, but I do." He nodded. "I know I'm a good basketball player. These guys know it, too. The other team also has a priest. He's a priest at Our Lady of Lourdes, but, between you and me, I think he sucks." Father Mathews laughed. "But don't tell him I said that, though. Of course."

"I won't," I said with a laugh. "Is this your brother?"

"It is." He put his arm around the coach. "He's my Irish twin. Do you know what that is?"

"Of course. It's two kids born within twelve months, but they're not twins." I personally could never imagine doing that – giving birth and then getting pregnant again right away. I didn't know why anybody would want to do that, but I knew some women did.

"You got it." He motioned to the guy who looked like him but didn't quite. "This is my brother, Raymond. Raymond, this is Harper Ross."

"Hello," he said politely. He smiled and then walked away.

I saw Father Mathews look at his brother, who was now talking to some of the other players in a huddle and look back at me. "He's not the most sociable guy in the universe, but he's my brother. It's a wonder he can even coach a team."

I narrowed my eyes as I watched him huddle with the other guys. "Oh, that's not a big deal. He's pretty busy, I can see."

"Yeah." Father Mathews took a towel and wiped his face with it.

"Well, the game is about to start again." He put his hand on my shoulder. "I'll chat with you after the game, huh?"

"Sure, sure. After the game."

I returned to the stands, where Albany was sitting, having gotten another batch of nachos and Coke. Next to her, on my seat, was a hot dog. "Here," she said. "I got you another hot dog. I hope you don't mind."

I laughed and bit into the dog. "I know. Something about sporting events makes me want to chow down on crap." I usually ate well - grass-fed beef, free-range chicken and eggs. My vegetables and fruits were organic, and I was a decent cook. Passable, anyhow – I enjoyed buying celebrity chef cookbooks and making things out of these books. But every time I went to a sporting event, I would gorge on hot dogs, nachos, candy bars and Coke. From the looks of things, Albany was the same way.

"What did you say to Father Hottie down there?"

"Not much. He introduced me to his brother, Raymond. He looks just like him close-up, too. They're Irish twins."

Albany sat back on the bleacher, putting her elbows on the bleacher behind her. "Maybe that was why your subconscious mind led you here. You needed to meet that brother of his."

"Maybe. But why would the brother be significant?"

"You tell me. You tell me."

I scratched my forehead, remembering what Mick had said in the car. Something I blew off but stuck with me.

I studied his arms as I watched Father Mathews dribble down the court, fake out his defender, and pass the ball. The tattoos. Aside from the fact that it was strange to see a priest with so much ink, I knew there was another reason why I was examining them.

I felt increasingly frustrated as I tried and failed to access why those damned tattoos were so significant. I leaned back so that I was sitting right next to Albany, who was also leaning back against the bleacher behind us, and swung my legs.

I studied Raymond. I narrowed my eyes and saw he had a stiff posture and almost looked like a coiled snake. He was very intense – he studied the players and the refs, and, more than once, he went over to the refs to chew them out for one thing or another. I saw him as being somebody with a bad temper. I could tell that. Something about his pacing around the floor and shouting at the players and refs led me to believe he didn't take much crap from anyone.

Father Mathews was much the same, really. I could tell he had a temper on him as well. But his brother seemed to be a piece of work.

"What are you looking at, Harper? You really seemed focused on something."

"I *am* focused on something." I took a deep breath. "But I'm not sure exactly what I'm focused on."

I shook my head, trying to clear out the cobwebs. "Hey, Albany, I'm going to get up and stretch my legs. You can come with me or not."

"I'll hang out here," she said.

I nodded and then headed out the gym door.

I decided to call Heather. "How are things?" I asked her.

"Good. We're on the road. Steven is excited, to say the least. Do you want to talk with him? I got here, and he was all ready to go. He seems anxious to get back."

"No, that's okay. When do you think you'll be getting back?"

Just then, though, I heard Steven's voice. "Ms. Ross, this is Steven. I can't thank you enough for doing this. I didn't think you'd come through. I hoped you would, but I never thought you would. Heather tells me you have an apartment for me to move into. Is that right?"

"Yes. I rented one out for you. It's in Mid-Town. It's not much, just a studio, but I think you'll like it."

"I can bring Stella, right?"

"Right." I grinned. "Hey, and call me Harper, okay?"

"Harper. Thanks so much, Harper. Here's Heather again."

She got back on the line. "Harper? You there?"

"Yes, I'm here. You'll be back when?"

"In a couple of days. It takes a while to cross the mountains, of course. I've never driven cross-country like that before. It was fun."

"I'll see you then."

I hung up the phone and contemplated my next move. Would I introduce Steven to Mick? Would that freak him out to see him, considering Steven was Robert's identical twin? Would that freak him out so much that perhaps Jack would come back, or a different alter?

I needed to be careful. Mick was right – if the other alters were unpredictable, it would be too risky to try to summon them. Somehow, I knew that if I introduced Steven to them, it would probably cause a break. That was the last thing I wanted at that point.

I went back to the stand. "The game's over," Albany said. "Father Mathews' team, The Grizzlies, won. He's an amazing player, really."

"Yeah." I stared at him. He was standing next to his brother, his hand on his shoulder. He was laughing, but his brother was standing perfectly straight. He didn't appear to have the same easy gait as Father Mathews.

A coiled snake. That image kept coming into my head.

"Let's go," I told Albany. "I think I need to do some research when I get home."

Albany and I got up and walked out of the gym. I waved to Father Mathews, who waved back and smiled.

There was something weird about this whole scenario.

My subconscious mind knew what it was.

I wished my conscious mind did as well.

CHAPTER
TWENTY-NINE

I WENT HOME, saw my two kids and paid Sophia as she left. "Abby," I said as she came up and hugged me. "I need to talk to you. I need to run a few things by you."

I went in, sat down on the couch and patted the spot next to me. Abby came and sat down. Rina, for her part, was sitting in the chair in front of the television and made no move to greet me as I came in the door. She was sitting with a TV tray in front of her and eating a bowl of cereal.

I felt guilty. I was at the basketball game while I left the girls at home with Sophia. I knew Sophia fed them, but Rina was increasingly annoyed that I was not home for dinner.

As much as I thought, in my head, that I would someday make it up to her and start coming home before 6, I didn't want to lie to myself. This was my life. It was a life of chasing witnesses, doing legal research, and seeing people in jail. It was a crazy life of constantly juggling the demands of clients, opposing counsel and judges. It was anything but an 8-5 job, as much as I wished to work fewer hours and focus more on the girls.

"What did you want to talk about, Mom?"

"Yeah, Mom, what did you want to talk to Abby about?" Rina asked from her position on the leather chair. "I hope you want to talk to her about that scumbag, James, because the whole school now thinks Abby is a slut."

I groaned. That was the last thing I wanted to hear. "Abs, is this true? Is that rumor getting out of control?"

"Yes," she said, little tears forming in her eyes. "It is."

I bit my lower lip. "Well, I'll have to call his mother. She needs to hear about this. And I think she'll have to come over tonight. This is getting out of hand."

Abby didn't try to stop me, and I saw Rina was looking at me with interest but didn't say a word. I took their acquiescence to mean they both were on board with my doing things this way, and I was heartened.

I didn't know what I was doing with these girls. I was fumbling around in the dark, really, trying to do the right thing but never quite knowing what that right thing was. This whole Abby situation had been in the back of my mind. I'd hoped it would resolve itself and the rumor would die down. I guess I was naïve about that.

"Anne-Marie," I said when I called James' mother. "This is Harper Ross. I need to speak with you. I was hoping you were free tonight. I need to nip something in the bud."

"Oh, hey, Harper," she said. "I can come over tonight. I'll just ask Brett to babysit James."

Brett was her husband. I couldn't, for the life of me, understand why Anne-Marie had to have Brett "babysit" James whenever she wanted to go somewhere. Why wasn't it his responsibility to watch that kid, the same as hers? Why was it that when Brett was watching James for Anne-Marie, it was some special thing, where Anne-Marie was just expected to watch their son?

I shook my head. I could never understand why the woman was always stuck with the "second shift," which referred to all the child-care and house-care women had to do once they got home from their jobs, while men were still expected to come home, crack open a beer and watch television. Anne-Marie was a dentist, her husband Brett was a software engineer, and both worked as many hours as the other. Yet, whenever I called her, she was making dinner or helping James with his homework while speaking quietly because she didn't want to interrupt Brett's program on TV.

"Good," I said. "I'll see you about 8?"

"See you then."

I got off the phone. "Okay, Buttercup, Anne-Marie is on her way here." I hesitated. "I hope Anne-Marie can get James to do the right thing without threatening him. But I also think that kid needs to have the fear of God put into him. I mean, not the fear of God so much as the fear of the State of Missouri slapping him hard with a..." I shut my mouth. Abby was too young to understand what I was prepared to do.

"With a what?" Abby asked.

"Nothing, Buttercup. Nothing."

Anne-Marie arrived right at 8. I had a glass of wine ready for her and made myself an iced tea. I usually always had wine for guests, and I knew she'd appreciate the gesture. She worked just as hard as I did, so I knew her time with her friends was her time to relax.

She hugged me, and I gave her a glass of wine. "Oh, thanks," she said. "Where do you want to talk?"

"Let's go into my sunroom," I said. "Away from prying ears."

Rina heard me say that, and she rolled her eyes. "Okay, Mom, go and gossip about Abby behind closed doors. Way to have open communication."

Rina was forever throwing shrinky terms like "open communication" at me, a product of our counseling sessions before she officially came to live with me. She remembered bits and phrases from those sessions, and once in a while, she parroted them back to me.

"I know, Rina, but I need to speak with Anne-Marie alone. I'll invite you guys in when we're ready."

Anne-Marie and I went into the sunroom, and she sat down, pulling the crocheted blanket that hung over the leather chair over her legs. "This is such a cozy room," she said, admiring the fireplace and the large windows that looked out into the backyard. "You're so lucky to be living here."

Anne-Marie and her husband lived in a newer area of town, where the trees were small and spindly, and the houses were enormous and expensive. It was a new development on the edge of town, which wasn't far from where I lived, but much pricier. "Yeah, I love this area. It's so close to everything but far away enough."

She took a sip of her wine. "So, what did you want to talk to me about?"

"It's about your son."

She rolled her eyes. "Oh, yes, my son. Egads, I wish we could have a conversation that didn't involve him, but I know that's impossible. To say I've been having problems with him would be an understatement, unfortunately."

"What kind of problems?"

"Oh, he's been acting out in school. Getting in trouble with the principal, slipping grades, and getting into fights. I have no idea why he's been acting this way. I'm at my wit's end."

I felt for her, and I didn't want to pile on. But I knew I had to. "Oh, well, I'm sorry to have to tell you this, but I need to because James needs to make things right." I took a sip of my iced tea. "There's no way to tell you this except to come out with it. But James has been spreading rumors about Abby. He told his friends he and Abby slept together. Obviously, that's caused a great deal of stress for her. Rina just told me kids are calling her a slut behind her back. I need James to make this right and tell everyone he lied."

I didn't know if having James tell people the truth would make things right, but it had to help. In a way, I knew the damage was done. Whoever said, "A lie travels around the world before the truth gets its pants on," was right.

"Oh, no," she said. "No." She shook her head and sighed. "That's all I need to hear." She took a sip of her wine. "Did you ever think your life would come to this? I mean, I'm not saying anything about you. I guess I'm talking more about me. I never thought my life would come to this."

"What do you mean?"

"Well, you know, you get married and have a kid. You think everything will always go great. You have a decent job and education, and your husband has a master's degree and a fantastic job. You have the kid, and you just imagine you have it all. The kid breastfeeds, eats and poops, and you never think about what'll happen when he hits puberty and starts acting like a spoiled brat. You never think about those things as you're staring at your little angel in his crib, sleeping peacefully. Then one day, boom, you wake up and don't recognize yourself anymore. You don't recognize your husband anymore, and you certainly don't recognize your angel anymore because your angel is suddenly causing all these headaches and issues."

She looked sad, so I put my hand on her arm sympathetically. "Believe me, I know where you're coming from. I have a demanding job and two tweens under my roof, one of whom seems to hate me every other day and love me every other day. But my Abby really has been a little doll. She hasn't given me a lick of trouble. Now she's suffering at school, and I need it to stop. What James has done to her is one of the worst forms of bullying. Again, I'm sorry for having to pile on when you already have so many issues with him."

She shook her head. "No, no. You need to pile on. If James says those things about Abby, he must make it right. I just don't know how to find out if he actually does the right thing. Who is to say he won't tell me he told everyone the truth but didn't?"

"Abby will tell me. So will Rina. Rina is more connected in that school than Abby. She's a part of all the gossip. She'll know in one day if the rumor dies down and the kids at school start talking about how James lied instead of how Abby is a slut." I furrowed my brow. "And by the way, why aren't the kids talking about James behind his back? If he and Abby had sex, like he's saying happened, why is only Abby getting hammered for it and not James?"

Anne-Marie chuckled. "Good question, but it's the age-old one, right? Girls who sleep around get called a slut, while the boys who sleep around are called a stud. Not that anybody is calling James a stud, that I know about, but you're right. It's such a double standard. It's 2023, for the love of all that's holy. It's time for people to treat girls and boys equally, but they won't."

At that, Rina knocked on the door. "Mom," she said, "can we come in?"

"Sure. Come on in."

The two girls walked in. "So," Rina said, looking at Anne-Marie. "Is James going to stop spreading that lie about my sister and tell everyone the truth, or isn't he?"

Anne-Marie smiled and then smiled at me. "Yes, Rina, I'll straighten him out when I get home."

I bit my lower lip. "Rina, Abby, I just need to speak with Anne-Marie privately for a few more minutes. We'll come out in a few minutes, I promise."

Rina mumbled and grumbled, but she returned to the living room and closed the doors behind her.

I took another sip of my tea, and Anne-Marie sipped her wine. "Listen, Anne-Marie," I said. "I wanted to just give you a heads-up. But the State of Missouri has a very specific statute regarding statutory rape. Any sexual contact with a child under 14 is considered first-degree statutory rape, no matter the age of the other child. I'm only telling you this if James gets defiant about doing the right thing. There's nothing like threatening a child with the fear of prosecution to get him to do the right thing."

She looked at me strangely. "Really? That's the law? I thought one of the kids had to be over 21 for that to be against the law."

"No, that's something different. If one of the children is under 17, and an adult over 21 has sex with that person, that's second-degree statutory rape. But first-degree statutory rape involves a child under 14, and it doesn't matter how old the perpetrator is in that case."

"Oh, wow. You mean that if my son and your daughter did it, they'd be committing a felony?"

"Yeah. That's exactly what that means. It's not usually prosecuted like that unless one of the parents is motivated to punish the other kid."

She nodded her head. "Good to know. Maybe I'll use that threat to make him do the right thing." She sighed. "Oh, Harper, I just don't know. Parenting is hard, you know? You try to do the right thing by your kid. You try to give them every bit of guidance, every bit of wisdom. But a kid will do what he's going to do. If that's his will, he'll act like a little shit, and it's hard to figure out how to stop it."

"Don't I know that."

"Yeah, I guess you do. Not as much as I do, though." She looked at the clock. "Well, it's getting late. Thanks for the glass of wine, Harper. I'll give you a call when I speak with James. And get that little Rina to report to you what the kids are saying. We'll figure this out, one way or another."

"I know," I said. "And we need to quick. The sooner we nip this in the bud, the better off Abby will be."

I only hoped it wasn't too late. Abby's reputation would be irreparable if it went on much longer.

CHAPTER
THIRTY

STEVEN AND HEATHER made it back to my office two days later, safe and sound, and I gave Heather a check for $3,000, which she gratefully accepted. "Harper," she said, "I found an apartment, too, in the art gallery area. I'll be having a housewarming party, and we'll do it right. Kicking up our heels. Don't worry; there won't be too many freaks there. Just Steven." She nudged him, and he grinned.

"Thank you for bringing Steven here," I said, touching her shoulder. "Now, Steven, let me drive you to your apartment." I hesitated. "I have to say, though, I'm concerned about how well you can assimilate. It's been a long time since you've been in a city."

"Yeah," he said. "But it's almost like riding a bike. I returned to the city with Heather, and it felt like coming home. I'll have to learn everything. Heather was explaining more to me about the internet and cable television. This HBO sounds like a pretty groovy thing. And she told me about VCRs, DVD players, CD players, YouTube, Tik Tok and streaming services." He shook his head. "Wow. It's amazing how much the world moves in a short period."

"Don't I know it? Anyhow, let's go to your apartment. I hope you don't mind, but I furnished it, too. I just wanted you to move in and not worry about much."

Steven nodded. "I really don't know how to thank you, Harper," he said.

"Well, you've been a real help to me. And I think I need to ask you some more questions, too. I have a feeling you might help me crack my uncle's case. So, I know you'll feel you owe me, but I might end up owing you a lot more."

Heather left my office, and Steven and I drove to his new apartment in the Hyde Park area of town. Hyde Park was a stratified area, to say the very least – some parts of Hyde Park were older and a bit run-down, but just down the street a bit, there were veritable mansions. These were mansions built around the turn of the century for the barons of the day - they weren't the "McMansions" that popped up post-1980, but actual mansions.

Steven's studio was in a quiet tree-lined neighborhood and part of a four-plex – two apartments downstairs, two upstairs, all of which had a balcony or a front porch. This building was built in stone and brick and was probably at least 100 years old. The hallway had a musty smell, and as we stood outside the apartment, waiting to get in, a twenty-something guy with a man-bun and a bicycle walked out of the apartment next to us and wheeled his bicycle out the door.

Steven looked at the man-bunned guy and smiled. "Is that the style?" he asked.

"Yeah, unfortunately," I said. "The man-bun style is the worst thing since mullets."

"Mullet?"

"Yeah. Short in the front and side and long in the back. We call it business up front and party in the back." I shook my head. "That was all the rage in the 1980s. Be glad you missed that particular era. The Reagan era."

"Reagan?"

"Ronald Reagan."

He looked confused. "The movie actor? Win one for the Gipper and *Bedtime for Bonzo*? That guy?"

"One and the same. Considering his background, he was a surprisingly serious President, but I don't think he was very good. I didn't like his policies, but I was just a kid when he was in office."

Steven shook his head. "Wow."

"Well, our last President was a reality-TV star."

"Reality TV?"

"Yes." I shook my head. "Don't ask. I'll tell you all about that in a bit, but I need to ask you some more questions. Some things have been nagging me since I saw you in Oregon."

"Okay." He looked around his little apartment. I furnished it with a futon, which I showed him how to work, a flat-screen television, and a coffee table. On the hardwood floor was a colorful throw rug, and on the balcony, I put some flowers in a pot and some tomato plants. There was also a small dining area, and I bought a wooden table and chairs.

Stella, for her part, was sniffing around the place and whining softly.

I showed Steven the microwave oven, and he looked at it with wonder. "You mean you can cook something in there?"

"Yeah, and it doesn't take very long, either. I try to heat stuff up instead of cooking things from scratch, though."

"How much will this apartment going to cost?"

"Well," I said. "It's $1,200 a month," I said. "But don't worry about that for now. I'll help you apply for social security benefits." I was worried about that, though – Steven dropped out of society 50 years ago. I doubted he'd be entitled to many benefits. I knew he'd have to find a job. I'd have to speak with him about that. He had skills – he knew a lot about horticulture and seemed to be a decent carpenter. I'd have to help him find something that would put these skills to use.

But first, though, I needed to ask him some follow-up questions.

We sat down on his futon. "Okay," he said. "Go ahead and ask your questions."

"Thanks." I hesitated. "Did you ever remember the name of that teacher who Robert idolized? You said that his name was Dean. Do you remember Dean's last name?"

"No." He shook his head. "That memory is hazy. To say the very least."

"I guess I also wanted to know another thing. You might know the answer to this question because you were there. But Robert used Eli to find the little boys and girls for him. This was in the papers. Do you know, specifically, if he found all the boys and girls or just some of them?"

Steven looked into the distance and squinted his eyes. "That was so long ago," he said softly. "But I think Robert found most of them himself. He had a van and told me he'd go around and ask kids if they found his lost puppy. The kid would approach his van, and he'd snatch them. He also took them from playgrounds."

I was following a hunch. "But Eli found some of the kids, too. Right?"

He nodded his head. "Right."

"How did he find these kids?"

Steven put his hand on his chin, lost in thought. "Robert would take Eli to different neighborhoods and drop him off. He would make him approach kids playing in the street and tell them the ice cream man was coming. The kids would follow Eli to the van, and then my brother would get out and force them in." He nodded his head. "That was how Robert said he used Eli."

I nodded. That would explain why Eli never ran off. It sounded like he didn't get that chance if Robert was just around the corner.

"Did Robert threaten Eli? Did he threaten him to make him come back to the van? I mean, how did he know Eli wouldn't just go and tell the kids what was going on? How did he know that?"

"Yes." Steven nodded his head. "Robert told Eli that he would kill him if he talked. That's what Eli told me. Eli also told me about the ice cream ruse. I asked him those questions, too. I wanted out of that prison, and I wanted Eli to help. But Eli wouldn't do it because he was terrified of Robert and what he would do. He always told me he didn't want to die." Steven shook his head. "That poor kid. That poor, poor kid."

I took a deep breath. There was one more question that I needed to ask Steven. It was a question that might lead me in a concrete direction on finding Father Kennedy's killer.

"Steven," I began. "I'd like to ask you another question. I hope you can answer it for me."

He nodded. "Sure. I'll answer it if I can. If I can remember, that is."

"Okay. Now, you said Robert was obsessed with Father Kennedy. Do you know if he confessed to him about what he did?"

Steven nodded his head slowly. "Yes. He did."

Steven and Heather made it back to my office two days later, safe and sound, and I gave Heather a check for $3,000, which she gratefully accepted. "Harper," she said, "I found an apartment, too, in the art gallery area. I'll be having a housewarming party, and we'll do it right. Kicking up our heels. Don't worry; there won't be too many freaks there. Just Steven." She nudged him, and he grinned.

"Thank you for bringing Steven here," I said, touching her shoulder. "Now, Steven, let me drive you to your apartment." I hesitated. "I have to say, though, I'm concerned about how well you can assimilate. It's been a long time since you've been in a city."

"Yeah," he said. "But it's almost like riding a bike. I returned to the city with Heather, and it felt like coming home. I'll have to learn everything. Heather was explaining more to me about the internet and cable television. This HBO sounds like a pretty groovy thing. And she told me about VCRs, DVD players, CD players, YouTube, Tik Tok and streaming services." He shook his head. "Wow. It's amazing how much the world moves in a short period."

"Don't I know it? Anyhow, let's go to your apartment. I hope you don't mind, but I furnished it, too. I just wanted you to move in and not worry about much."

Steven nodded. "I really don't know how to thank you, Harper," he said.

"Well, you've been a real help to me. And I think I need to ask you some more questions, too. I have a feeling you might help me crack my uncle's case. So, I know you'll feel you owe me, but I might end up owing you a lot more."

Heather left my office, and Steven and I drove to his new apartment in the Hyde Park area of town. Hyde Park was a stratified area, to say the very least – some parts of Hyde Park were older and a bit run-down, but just down the street a bit, there were veritable mansions. These were mansions built around the turn of the century for the barons of the day - they weren't the "McMansions" that popped up post-1980, but actual mansions.

Steven's studio was in a quiet tree-lined neighborhood and part of a four-plex – two apartments downstairs, two upstairs, all of which had a balcony or a front porch. This building was built in stone and brick and was probably at least 100 years old. The hallway had a musty smell, and as we stood outside the apartment, waiting to get in, a twenty-something guy with a man-bun and a bicycle walked out of the apartment next to us and wheeled his bicycle out the door.

Steven looked at the man-bunned guy and smiled. "Is that the style?" he asked.

"Yeah, unfortunately," I said. "The man-bun style is the worst thing since mullets."

"Mullet?"

"Yeah. Short in the front and side and long in the back. We call it business up front and party in the back." I shook my head. "That was all the rage in the 1980s. Be glad you missed that particular era. The Reagan era."

"Reagan?"

"Ronald Reagan."

He looked confused. "The movie actor? Win one for the Gipper and *Bedtime for Bonzo*? That guy?"

"One and the same. Considering his background, he was a surprisingly serious President, but I don't think he was very good. I didn't like his policies, but I was just a kid when he was in office."

Steven shook his head. "Wow."

"Well, our last President was a reality-TV star."

"Reality TV?"

"Yes." I shook my head. "Don't ask. I'll tell you all about that in a bit, but I need to ask you some more questions. Some things have been nagging me since I saw you in Oregon."

"Okay." He looked around his little apartment. I furnished it with a futon, which I showed him how to work, a flat-screen television, and a coffee table. On the hardwood floor was a colorful throw rug, and on the balcony, I put some flowers in a pot and some tomato plants. There was also a small dining area, and I bought a wooden table and chairs.

Stella, for her part, was sniffing around the place and whining softly.

I showed Steven the microwave oven, and he looked at it with wonder. "You mean you can cook something in there?"

"Yeah, and it doesn't take very long, either. I try to heat stuff up instead of cooking things from scratch, though."

"How much will this apartment going to cost?"

"Well," I said. "It's $1,200 a month," I said. "But don't worry about that for now. I'll help you apply for social security benefits." I was worried about that, though – Steven dropped out of society 50 years ago. I doubted he'd be entitled to many benefits. I knew he'd have to find a job. I'd have to speak with him about that. He had skills – he knew a lot about horticulture and seemed to be a decent carpenter. I'd have to help him find something that would put these skills to use.

But first, though, I needed to ask him some follow-up questions.

We sat down on his futon. "Okay," he said. "Go ahead and ask your questions."

"Thanks." I hesitated. "Did you ever remember the name of that teacher who Robert idolized? You said that his name was Dean. Do you remember Dean's last name?"

"No." He shook his head. "That memory is hazy. To say the very least."

"I guess I also wanted to know another thing. You might know the answer to this question because you were there. But Robert used Eli to find the little boys and girls for him. This was in the papers. Do you know, specifically, if he found all the boys and girls or just some of them?"

Steven looked into the distance and squinted his eyes. "That was so long ago," he said softly. "But I think Robert found most of them himself. He had a van and told me he'd go around and ask kids if they found his lost puppy. The kid would approach his van, and he'd snatch them. He also took them from playgrounds."

I was following a hunch. "But Eli found some of the kids, too. Right?"

He nodded his head. "Right."

"How did he find these kids?"

Steven put his hand on his chin, lost in thought. "Robert would take Eli to different neighborhoods and drop him off. He would make him approach kids playing in the street and tell them the ice cream man was coming. The kids would follow Eli to the van, and then my brother would get out and force them in." He nodded his head. "That was how Robert said he used Eli."

I nodded. That would explain why Eli never ran off. It sounded like he didn't get that chance if Robert was just around the corner.

"Did Robert threaten Eli? Did he threaten him to make him come back to the van? I mean, how did he know Eli wouldn't just go and tell the kids what was going on? How did he know that?"

"Yes." Steven nodded his head. "Robert told Eli that he would kill him if he talked. That's what Eli told me. Eli also told me about the ice cream ruse. I asked him those questions, too. I wanted out of that prison, and I wanted Eli to help. But Eli wouldn't do it because he was terrified of Robert and what he would do. He always told me he didn't want to die." Steven shook his head. "That poor kid. That poor, poor kid."

I took a deep breath. There was one more question that I needed to ask Steven. It was a question that might lead me in a concrete direction on finding Father Kennedy's killer.

"Steven," I began. "I'd like to ask you another question. I hope you can answer it for me."

He nodded. "Sure. I'll answer it if I can. If I can remember, that is."

"Okay. Now, you said Robert was obsessed with Father Kennedy. Do you know if he confessed to him about what he did?"

Steven nodded his head slowly. "Yes. He did."

Steven and Heather made it back to my office two days later, safe and sound, and I gave Heather a check for $3,000, which she gratefully accepted. "Harper," she said, "I found an apartment, too, in the art gallery area. I'll be having a housewarming party, and we'll do it right. Kicking up our heels. Don't worry; there won't be too many freaks there. Just Steven." She nudged him, and he grinned.

"Thank you for bringing Steven here," I said, touching her shoulder. "Now, Steven, let me drive you to your apartment." I hesitated. "I have to say, though, I'm concerned about how well you can assimilate. It's been a long time since you've been in a city."

"Yeah," he said. "But it's almost like riding a bike. I returned to the city with Heather, and it felt like coming home. I'll have to learn everything. Heather was explaining more to me about the internet and cable television. This HBO sounds like a pretty groovy thing. And she told me about VCRs, DVD players, CD players, YouTube, Tik Tok and streaming services." He shook his head. "Wow. It's amazing how much the world moves in a short period."

"Don't I know it? Anyhow, let's go to your apartment. I hope you don't mind, but I furnished it, too. I just wanted you to move in and not worry about much."

Steven nodded. "I really don't know how to thank you, Harper," he said.

"Well, you've been a real help to me. And I think I need to ask you some more questions, too. I have a feeling you might help me crack my uncle's case. So, I know you'll feel you owe me, but I might end up owing you a lot more."

Heather left my office, and Steven and I drove to his new apartment in the Hyde Park area of town. Hyde Park was a stratified area, to say the very least – some parts of Hyde Park were older and a bit run-down, but just down the street a bit, there were veritable mansions. These were mansions built around the turn of the century for the barons of the day - they weren't the "McMansions" that popped up post-1980, but actual mansions.

Steven's studio was in a quiet tree-lined neighborhood and part of a four-plex – two apartments downstairs, two upstairs, all of which had a balcony or a front porch. This building was built in stone and brick and was probably at least 100 years old. The hallway had a musty smell, and as we stood outside the apartment, waiting to get in, a twenty-something guy with a man-bun and a bicycle walked out of the apartment next to us and wheeled his bicycle out the door.

Steven looked at the man-bunned guy and smiled. "Is that the style?" he asked.

"Yeah, unfortunately," I said. "The man-bun style is the worst thing since mullets."

"Mullet?"

"Yeah. Short in the front and side and long in the back. We call it business up front and party in the back." I shook my head. "That was all the rage in the 1980s. Be glad you missed that particular era. The Reagan era."

"Reagan?"

"Ronald Reagan."

He looked confused. "The movie actor? Win one for the Gipper and *Bedtime for Bonzo*? That guy?"

"One and the same. Considering his background, he was a surprisingly serious President, but I don't think he was very good. I didn't like his policies, but I was just a kid when he was in office."

Steven shook his head. "Wow."

"Well, our last President was a reality-TV star."

"Reality TV?"

"Yes." I shook my head. "Don't ask. I'll tell you all about that in a bit, but I need to ask you some more questions. Some things have been nagging me since I saw you in Oregon."

"Okay." He looked around his little apartment. I furnished it with a futon, which I showed him how to work, a flat-screen television, and a coffee table. On the hardwood floor was a colorful throw rug, and on the balcony, I put some flowers in a pot and some tomato plants. There was also a small dining area, and I bought a wooden table and chairs.

Stella, for her part, was sniffing around the place and whining softly.

I showed Steven the microwave oven, and he looked at it with wonder. "You mean you can cook something in there?"

"Yeah, and it doesn't take very long, either. I try to heat stuff up instead of cooking things from scratch, though."

"How much will this apartment going to cost?"

"Well," I said. "It's $1,200 a month," I said. "But don't worry about that for now. I'll help you apply for social security benefits." I was worried about that, though – Steven dropped out of society 50 years ago. I doubted he'd be entitled to many benefits. I knew he'd have to find a job. I'd have to speak with him about that. He had skills – he knew a lot about horticulture and seemed to be a decent carpenter. I'd have to help him find something that would put these skills to use.

But first, though, I needed to ask him some follow-up questions.

We sat down on his futon. "Okay," he said. "Go ahead and ask your questions."

"Thanks." I hesitated. "Did you ever remember the name of that teacher who Robert idolized? You said that his name was Dean. Do you remember Dean's last name?"

"No." He shook his head. "That memory is hazy. To say the very least."

"I guess I also wanted to know another thing. You might know the answer to this question because you were there. But Robert used Eli to find the little boys and girls for him. This was in the papers. Do you know, specifically, if he found all the boys and girls or just some of them?"

Steven looked into the distance and squinted his eyes. "That was so long ago," he said softly. "But I think Robert found most of them himself. He had a van and told me he'd go around and ask kids if they found his lost puppy. The kid would approach his van, and he'd snatch them. He also took them from playgrounds."

I was following a hunch. "But Eli found some of the kids, too. Right?"

He nodded his head. "Right."

"How did he find these kids?"

Steven put his hand on his chin, lost in thought. "Robert would take Eli to different neighborhoods and drop him off. He would make him approach kids playing in the street and tell them the ice cream man was coming. The kids would follow Eli to the van, and then my brother would get out and force them in." He nodded his head. "That was how Robert said he used Eli."

I nodded. That would explain why Eli never ran off. It sounded like he didn't get that chance if Robert was just around the corner.

"Did Robert threaten Eli? Did he threaten him to make him come back to the van? I mean, how did he know Eli wouldn't just go and tell the kids what was going on? How did he know that?"

"Yes." Steven nodded his head. "Robert told Eli that he would kill him if he talked. That's what Eli told me. Eli also told me about the ice cream ruse. I asked him those questions, too. I wanted out of that prison, and I wanted Eli to help. But Eli wouldn't do it because he was terrified of Robert and what he would do. He always told me he didn't want to die." Steven shook his head. "That poor kid. That poor, poor kid."

I took a deep breath. There was one more question that I needed to ask Steven. It was a question that might lead me in a concrete direction on finding Father Kennedy's killer.

"Steven," I began. "I'd like to ask you another question. I hope you can answer it for me."

He nodded. "Sure. I'll answer it if I can. If I can remember, that is."

"Okay. Now, you said Robert was obsessed with Father Kennedy. Do you know if he confessed to him about what he did?"

Steven nodded his head slowly. "Yes. He did."

CHAPTER
THIRTY-ONE

I FELT excited after I asked Steven that question because I suddenly realized there might be a motive for somebody to kill Father Kennedy and implicate Jack in that murder.

"Why do you ask that question?"

"It's something really very simple," I said. "My boyfriend, Axel, is a detective. I told him the facts of the case, and he told me to look for an intersection. I'm supposed to look for somebody who not only had a beef against Father Kennedy but also had a beef against Jack. In other words, the person who killed Father Kennedy was somebody who hated both Father Kennedy and currently hates Jack. And it's somebody who knows Jack suffers from mental illness and blackouts."

"Okay," Steven said. "I'm not quite following your train of thought, but go on. I'll catch up."

I stood up and started to pace around the room. "Here's my theory about who did all this. It was somebody who had a child abducted and killed by Robert Heaney. Maybe this person, whoever it was, found out Robert told Father Kennedy, who knew what Robert was doing and never told anybody. Of course, he didn't tell anybody, right? Robert confessed in the priest's confessional, so Father Kennedy was bound by privilege not to say a word."

Steven nodded along. "Okay. And Jack? Why would this person hate Jack?"

"Well, maybe the kid was abducted because Jack found him. It was in the papers that Jack was responsible for trying to find some of these kids."

Steven pursed his lips. "But this person, whoever he or she is, how would they know about Jack's mental illness? And why would they wait this long to kill Father Kennedy? This happened so many years ago. If it was known then that Father Kennedy knew about Robert and his murders, why wait this long to kill him?"

I sighed. Why indeed?

"Well, I didn't say this was a fool-proof theory. It was just something buzzing around in my head."

Steven looked out his window. A bird had landed on the railing of his balcony and was looking at us curiously, his head moving back and forth as he stared at us. "Harper, don't give up on this theory," he said. "There are holes in it, but fill in the holes. Fill them in, and maybe you can figure it out. I'd hate to see poor Jack serve time in prison after all he went through with my brother. I'd hate to see that."

He hung his head. "He saved my life. He saved Mary's life. He saved the life of countless other boys and girls who might've ended up Robert's victims if he had lived longer. Who knows how many more boys and girls would have been killed if Robert had remained alive? How many more empty spots around dinner tables? How many more grieving families? Jack, or Sam, saved so many lives with his heroism. After all he did for so many, I can't imagine him going to prison."

"I know," I said. "I just wish I could figure it out. I wish I could."

"You can. I have faith in you."

I smiled. "Well, let's change the subject. Now, about those reality TV stars..."

For the rest of the afternoon, I filled Steven in on all the different cultural, political and technical phenomenons he'd missed. He was astounded to know that we had electric cars – "Thank God we do, Harper, because our planet was choking with all those fumes in the air." He laughed and laughed about the concept of reality television – "You mean people actually want to watch ordinary people do stuff on

TV?" And he was in awe of everything I told him about e-mail, YouTube, podcasts, and music streaming. He was from a time before we even had cassette tapes, let alone Walkmen, so he couldn't wrap his brain around the concept that you could listen to music wherever you are and put together different songs on a playlist. And you no longer had to buy CDs to hear your favorite artists because all the big music streaming sites had anything you wanted.

And he was really astounded our current popular genre of music was rap. Rap hadn't even been invented in 1972. He was of the age of Carol King, The Beatles and Crosby, Stills and Nash. I went through all the genres of music that had come up since then, and he couldn't wrap his mind around the concepts of hip-hop, grunge and death metal, all unknown genres of music in the early 1970s.

"I guess I have a lot to learn," he said.

"Well, I'll get cable and the internet hooked up for you," I said. "And you can explore what's on there. It's literally a whole new world."

As I sat with Steven, explaining everything he needed to know to get up to speed, I was struck by something – I'd taken too much for granted. I thought about all the times I cursed because my internet was slow or my computer crashed. I really should've been grateful to have a computer and the internet in the first place. In Steven's world, people still typed everything on typewriters, and if you wanted to research something, you were hoofing it to the library. You couldn't just get on Wikipedia to learn about this or that – you were buying *Encyclopedia Brittanica* for $1,000 a set.

I thought about typewriters, and how, if you left out a single word, you would have to write your entire paper again, and how you tried to erase something, but all it left was a smudge, and I felt grateful and happy we didn't have to go through all that. I never had to use a typewriter, but my mother told me about it, and it sounded like absolute hell.

I realized there was another good thing I got from Steven – I learned not to take anything for granted anymore.

I felt excited after I asked Steven that question because I suddenly realized there might be a motive for somebody to kill Father Kennedy and implicate Jack in that murder.

"Why do you ask that question?"

"It's something really very simple," I said. "My boyfriend, Axel, is a detective. I told him the facts of the case, and he told me to look for an intersection. I'm supposed to look for somebody who not only had a beef against Father Kennedy but also had a beef against Jack. In other words, the person who killed Father Kennedy was somebody who hated both Father Kennedy and currently hates Jack. And it's somebody who knows Jack suffers from mental illness and blackouts."

"Okay," Steven said. "I'm not quite following your train of thought, but go on. I'll catch up."

I stood up and started to pace around the room. "Here's my theory about who did all this. It was somebody who had a child abducted and killed by Robert Heaney. Maybe this person, whoever it was, found out Robert told Father Kennedy, who knew what Robert was doing and never told anybody. Of course, he didn't tell anybody, right? Robert confessed in the priest's confessional, so Father Kennedy was bound by privilege not to say a word."

Steven nodded along. "Okay. And Jack? Why would this person hate Jack?"

"Well, maybe the kid was abducted because Jack found him. It was in the papers that Jack was responsible for trying to find some of these kids."

Steven pursed his lips. "But this person, whoever he or she is, how would they know about Jack's mental illness? And why would they wait this long to kill Father Kennedy? This happened so many years ago. If it was known then that Father Kennedy knew about Robert and his murders, why wait this long to kill him?"

I sighed. Why indeed?

"Well, I didn't say this was a fool-proof theory. It was just something buzzing around in my head."

Steven looked out his window. A bird had landed on the railing of his balcony and was looking at us curiously, his head moving back and forth as he stared at us. "Harper, don't give up on this theory," he said. "There are holes in it, but fill in the holes. Fill them in, and maybe you can figure it out. I'd hate to see poor Jack serve time in prison after all he went through with my brother. I'd hate to see that."

He hung his head. "He saved my life. He saved Mary's life. He saved the life of countless other boys and girls who might've ended up Robert's victims if he had lived longer. Who knows how many more boys and girls would have been killed if Robert had remained alive? How many more empty spots around dinner tables? How many more grieving families? Jack, or Sam, saved so many lives with his heroism. After all he did for so many, I can't imagine him going to prison."

"I know," I said. "I just wish I could figure it out. I wish I could."

"You can. I have faith in you."

I smiled. "Well, let's change the subject. Now, about those reality TV stars..."

For the rest of the afternoon, I filled Steven in on all the different cultural, political and technical phenomenons he'd missed. He was astounded to know that we had electric cars – "Thank God we do, Harper, because our planet was choking with all those fumes in the air." He laughed and laughed about the concept of reality television – "You mean people actually want to watch ordinary people do stuff on TV?" And he was in awe of everything I told him about e-mail, YouTube, podcasts, and music streaming. He was from a time before we even had cassette tapes, let alone Walkmen, so he couldn't wrap his brain around the concept that you could listen to music wherever you are and put together different songs on a playlist. And you no longer had to buy CDs to hear your favorite artists because all the big music streaming sites had anything you wanted.

And he was really astounded our current popular genre of music was rap. Rap hadn't even been invented in 1972. He was of the age of Carol King, The Beatles and Crosby, Stills and Nash. I went through all the genres of music that had come up since then, and he couldn't wrap his mind around the concepts of hip-hop, grunge and death metal, all unknown genres of music in the early 1970s.

"I guess I have a lot to learn," he said.

"Well, I'll get cable and the internet hooked up for you," I said. "And you can explore what's on there. It's literally a whole new world."

As I sat with Steven, explaining everything he needed to know to get up to speed, I was struck by something – I'd taken too much for granted. I thought about all the times I cursed because my internet was slow or my computer crashed. I really should've been grateful to have a computer and the internet in the first place. In Steven's world, people still typed everything on typewriters, and if you wanted to research something, you were hoofing it to the library. You couldn't just get on Wikipedia to learn about this or that – you were buying *Encyclopedia Brittanica* for $1,000 a set.

I thought about typewriters, and how, if you left out a single word, you would have to write your entire paper again, and how you tried to erase something, but all it left was a smudge, and I felt grateful and happy we didn't have to go through all that. I never had to use a typewriter, but my mother told me about it, and it sounded like absolute hell.

I realized there was another good thing I got from Steven – I learned not to take anything for granted anymore.

CHAPTER
THIRTY-TWO

AXEL CAME over that evening and made dinner with me while the girls played video games in the living room. Rina had informed me when she got home that James had, indeed, gone around and told everyone he lied about him and Abby.

"And Abby is more popular than me now, Mom," she said. "Everybody's talking about how brave she was for not pushing James into a locker." She shrugged. "Whatever. She'll be back with the geek squad before the end of next week."

Rina, I gathered, was a queen bee at the school. I hoped and prayed, however, she wouldn't become a full-on "mean girl." I was tormented by mean girls in middle and high school, and I wouldn't put up with her attitude if she became one of them. I'd have to monitor it.

Axel smiled. "All's well that ends well, huh mate?" he asked while he chopped up lettuce, baby carrots, bell peppers, cucumbers and tomatoes for our salad. He opened up a bag of croutons and poured them on top.

"I guess. I'm still astounded, absolutely astounded, that kids are having sex at that age, though." I shook my head. "I assumed I'd get at least a few years leeway before I had to worry about that, but I guess I'm not so lucky."

I was standing over a pot of red sauce I was stirring. I put some on a small spoon, blew on it, and stuck it in Axel's mouth. "What do you think?"

He nodded. "I think it needs some more garlic," he said. "But, then again, I always think everything needs more garlic, so what do I know?"

"What, indeed?" I smiled, took out three more cloves of garlic, and pressed them with the back of a knife, which took off their peels. I put them all through a press and stirred some more. "So," I said. "I think I might be getting closer to finding out who had motive to kill Father Kennedy and hurt Jack simultaneously."

"Oh?" Axel asked me. "Tell me, lass, your theory."

I took the spaghetti I had ready to go and poured it into the boiling water. "Father Kennedy knew Robert was murdering kids but never told anybody about it. He was bound by privilege not to divulge what Robert told him in the confessional booth."

"Ah, I see. I see. Very good. But why wait until now to kill Father Kennedy?"

"That's what I'm wondering. I-" I blinked my eyes. "I wonder if it just became known that Father Kennedy knew all this." I narrowed my eyes. "Maybe…"

"Maybe what?"

"Do you think Father Kennedy might've gone to a confessional of his own? Does a priest confess his sins to other priests? Maybe he held this in all these years, and he couldn't hold it in any longer, so he went to his own confessional and spilled all?"

I could feel my excitement suddenly build. This was something I'd have to figure out.

"Lass," Axel said. "So, he confesses his sins to another priest. And that other priest has the same restriction – he can't very well turn Father Kennedy in because this would have also been in a confessional. Right? And you'll tell me this priest, whoever it was, killed him over this confession? And how does Jack fit into this whole scenario?"

I shook my head. "I didn't say I had it all worked out. I just think there might be something to this. Because you're right – Father Kennedy has known this secret about Robert for all these years and was just now murdered. And whoever it was also had to know Jack was partially responsible for finding the victims for Robert, and Jack was suffering from DID. It all seems far-fetched, but if I could find somebody who found out recently that Father Kennedy was privy to this information and this person also knew Jack, maybe that's our killer."

It was a far-fetched theory, but better than no theory at all, which I previously worked with.

"Well," Axel said. "You can start with the Father Mathews you told me about. The one at that basketball game. It would be him if anybody knew who Father Kennedy might've confessed his sins to. Right?"

"Right."

I stirred the sauce some more. Something was still nagging at me. Something about those tattoos I saw on Father Mathews' arms was significant. And I just couldn't place it.

I went over to chop the mushrooms when I stopped in the middle and looked up.

"Mick said something about Father Mathews' tattoos," I said, squinting. "Oh, God, yes, yes, yes. He did. I was in the car with him, taking him to court, and he mentioned Father Mathews' tattoos and thought Father Mathews was smoking hot."

Axel walked over to me. "Okay, lass, finish your thought here. Why does that matter?"

"Because, Axel, Father Mathews told me he never met Jack. He told me that. How did Mick know Father Mathews had tattoos or if he was hot if they never met? Mick was right on both fronts – that priest is very good-looking and has two arms filled with tattoos. He does. Either Mick is a darned good guesser, and I don't know how that's possible because I wouldn't imagine many priests have a lot of tattoos, or he actually knew Father Mathews and Father Mathews lied about knowing him."

I nodded my head. "Why would he lie about that? Why?"

"Now, lass," Axel said. "Slow down before you try to accuse Father Mathews of killing Father Kennedy. You don't have a motive for him. Even if Father Kennedy confessed to him that he knew Robert was murdering children, I hardly think this would be reason enough for Father Mathews to off Father Kennedy. Think logically."

"No, maybe not, but I'd like to know why he'd lie about not knowing Jack. Not meeting him when he clearly did."

I ground my teeth, a bad habit I had when under a lot of stress. "There's a missing puzzle piece," I said. "And I'll have to figure out just what it is."

Despite what Axel had warned me about not going over and harassing Father Mathews, I decided to do just that. I showed up at the church service on Sunday, and after the service, I asked to speak with him.

"Sure," he said. "I have time to speak with you. If you'd follow me back to my office after I greet my other congregants, I'll be happy to talk to you about anything you need to know. I want to find Kelly's killer as much as you do."

I grimaced, wondering if that were true.

And then immediately felt guilty I was questioning him.

After Father Mathews finished greeting the congregants, I followed him to his office and sat down. "Now," he said. "Ms. Ross, what questions can I answer for you?"

I took a deep breath. "Father Kennedy. Did he do any confessions of his own?"

He nodded. "Yes, of course. Father Kennedy confessed his sins regularly. I do as well, and so does every priest I know. We all do. Why do you ask that question?"

I bit my lower lip. "Okay. Who does he confess to?"

"That's privileged."

"No, actually, it's not. The content of his confessionals is privileged, but it's not privileged to answer the question about who he actually confessed to." I crossed my arms. "Please tell me who Father Kennedy confessed to."

Father Mathews suddenly looked troubled. "Kelly confessed his sins regularly to me." He looked down at the floor. "But I cannot tell you the contents of these confessions, of course."

"Don't worry, I won't ask you about the contents. I think, however, I already know what they are."

He nodded. "You do." That was a statement, as opposed to a question, so I didn't feel the necessity to elaborate further.

"Yes. Now, I need to ask you another question. Why did you say you never met Jack Calhoun, or Mick Calhoun, when you certainly have met him before?"

He shook his head. "Because I never met him. I told you I never met him, and that's the truth."

I narrowed my eyes. "Then why did Mick tell me he thought you were good-looking, and how did he know you had tattoos?"

He shrugged. "How would I know why he'd say those things? Maybe he came to one of our games, and somebody pointed me out. Who knows? I stand out like a sore thumb at our basketball games because I'm a priest with a lot of tats." He was staring at me, and I was trying to assess if he was telling the truth.

It seemed he was.

I nodded slowly. Was my theory crumbling before my very eyes? No, it wasn't. I would just have to find the missing puzzle piece. That was what I always did. Theories rarely come together like a recipe from one of my celebrity cookbooks. There was always a variable I'd overlook, but if I looked hard enough, I'd find it.

It was then that I saw, over Father Mathews' shoulder, a picture. It was three young boys. They all looked about the same age. All good-looking kids with dark hair and dark eyes, and they all looked about five years old. Maybe six. They were standing by the side of a creek, and one of the boys had a fish on a pole in front of him.

I furrowed my brow. "Is that you? When you were a young kid?"

"Yes," he said, handing me the picture. "This is me." He pointed to the kid the furthest to the left. "And this my brother Ryan and my other brother Raymond. You met Raymond. Raymond and Ryan were identical twins."

I nodded my head. "You guys were cuties."

"Yes. Thanks." He smiled. "Well, is there anything else I can help you with? I hope I answered all your questions."

I looked out his window at the birds eating on the little patio outside his office. "Sure," I said uncertainly.

I walked out the door, down the hallway, stopped and turned around.

Dammit. I wanted to ask him another question, but it escaped me.

I uncertainly went back down the hallway, went out the door and found my car.

Did I find out anything more from Father Mathews? Something that would help me solve this case?

Or was that just one more dead-end?

CHAPTER
THIRTY-THREE

A FEW NIGHTS LATER, it hit me. I was right in the middle of watching a movie with the two girls, relieved that, for the time being, everything seemed to be going smoothly. Rina was in the middle of an extended period where she didn't hate me every other day, and Abby was happier than ever. As Rina told me, Abby enjoyed newfound popularity after the rumor stink was revealed to be a big hoax. And, of course, James' status had plummeted. Both of these developments made Abby a happy girl.

"Is it bad that I'm happy that James is unpopular now?" Abby asked me while she helped me put the dishes away in the dishwasher after supper.

I chuckled lightly. "No. The adults have a word for what you're feeling – *schadenfreude*. But you might also learn the word Karma – what goes around, comes around."

Abby laughed. "What was that first word you said? I think I've heard the word Karma, but I've never heard the word shade-"She grasped for the word. "Schaden…"

"*Schadenfreude*. It's when you're happy that somebody else is miserable. Usually, because somebody else, who is miserable, is not such a great person. So go ahead and be happy that James is miserable because, in this case, that misery he's feeling is richly deserved."

She nodded her head. "What language is that?"

"German."

"I'll have to look that up."

I wrote the word down on a piece of paper, and she studied it. "Thanks, Mom," she said. "Now I don't have to feel bad because I feel happy that James is unpopular."

Rina came into the kitchen after hearing our conversation. "James is a tool," she said. "And that, Abby, is all you need to know. Tools aren't popular in our school for long, just because kids don't like liars. And he made himself look like such an idiot by lying about you like that. Just imagine if he'd have put that stuff on Facebook about you." Rina shook her head. "I would have gone ninja on him."

"Do you want to help us clean up the kitchen?" I asked Rina, knowing the answer to that question. It wasn't Rina's turn to help clean up, so she wouldn't help.

"Nah," she said. "It's my turn tomorrow. I just wanted to come in and tell you what I think."

After she left, Abby said, in a low voice, "Rina is actually really mad at James, too. She's part of the reason why everybody hates him. Rina's one of the popular kids; she told all her friends to hate James because of what he did. What she says pretty much goes."

That worried me. I didn't want Rina to be a dominant mean girl, but maybe she was. "What other things does Rina tell her friends to do?"

Abby shrugged. "Not much. I mean, she doesn't want geeks to be picked on because I'm kinda a geek. And she always sticks up for kids with special needs. She never lets those kids get picked on."

"What about gay kids? And trans kids?"

"What about them? Nobody cares if a kid is gay anymore or trans. I told you that before."

"Okay. You did. I was just checking." I cleaned the counter. "Now, if Rina changes, if she starts picking on kids for no reason and gets her friends to do the same, you'll tell me, right?"

She shrugged. "I guess, but she doesn't do that."

"Good." I examined the kitchen. "Well, it looks like it's pretty clean now. The dishes are all done, and the counters are clean. You can go and do whatever you have to do, homework-wise, and get Rina to do the same, then you can both have free time. I, however, have to go upstairs and do some research."

"What kind of research?"

"It's just something I'm following up on. I have another one of my hunches. Or maybe it's not even a hunch. It might be something my brain is trying to piece together from some clues I've come up with."

Abby gave me a look that said she had no clue what I was talking about, and I knew why – I was rambling on like a loon. I knew that.

That was just fine, though. My brain was scrambled like an egg, but I knew I was getting close to showing that somebody else had killed that priest.

I went upstairs to my computer. When I was washing dishes, something struck me. Father Mathews had said something to me that was suddenly flashing like a neon light.

He told me that Ryan and Raymond *were* twins.

Were. Past tense.

I had no idea why I didn't pick up on that right away, but somehow, I didn't. I kicked myself for not picking up on that because I needed to follow up.

Or maybe I didn't.

I accessed the news articles about Steven Heaney, feeling guilty and bad knowing that the actual Steven Heaney had nothing to do with these murders. It was wrong that everybody thought he was a serial killer. I hated that because Steven was not only kind, but he helped me immensely.

I looked through the newspaper articles, looking for the one that recounted the victims of Robert Heaney. Several articles were spread out over seven days, and each of these articles did an in-depth profile of five victims. It made me sick knowing there were 35 different victims known to have been murdered by Robert.

35 young lives who were no longer on this earth just because one crazy guy decided to snuff out their lives. I shuddered as I thought about how they must have suffered. I knew how much Jack had suffered; these kids must've suffered just as much.

I read about them, one by one, my heart breaking with every word.

They were kids typical for the time – an era of relative innocence. Kids walked home from school because their parents didn't worry about them being snatched off the streets. They played kickball in front of their homes. They climbed trees and explored the woods. Kids of today didn't know the joys these kids knew – the joys of having fun and being free. They weren't necessarily going to organized sports like soccer and baseball. Their every minute wasn't tightly scheduled like the kids of today.

But these kids, these 35 children, paid for that freedom with their lives. It was ironic – serial killers weren't a thing back then; at least they weren't called by the word "serial killer," so the parents felt safer letting their kids be kids. These parents couldn't have known a predator like Robert was lurking.

I closed my eyes and tried to get into these parents' heads. What was it like to have your child go missing? What was it like to find out his or her bones were found in an old house? And when the stories hit the paper – the stories about what this monster did to these kids – how would you react? The parents had to have been devastated beyond measure. Their families were probably never the same. There was a hole left in the middle of these families that would never be filled.

I couldn't imagine what these families went through. My mother knew. Her family went through it, but her family was lucky. Uncle Jack made it home whole but not well.

But these other families weren't that lucky.

I went down the hall to see Rina and Abby. I looked in on both of them in their rooms. Rina was talking to somebody on her cell phone. She rolled her eyes when I entered her room, so I walked out and went down to Abby's room and knocked. She opened the door, and I saw her reading a book on her bed.

"What's going on, Mom?" She asked me.

"Nothing, nothing." I shook my head. "I just wanted to tell you I love you."

She smiled. "I love you too."

As I walked away from her room, I realized I wanted to tell Rina and Abby that I loved them because I thought about all those parents who didn't get that chance with their kids. Those parents never dreamed their kids wouldn't make it home that evening from school. They never dreamed they would let their kids out of the house to play kickball, only to be searching for them frantically hours later. That thought must've never crossed their minds.

Did they fight with their kids the day the kids disappeared? Did they say something they never got the chance to take back? I once had a friend who fought with her mother and wasn't on speaking terms with her for months. Her mother died before the two could make amends, which haunted my friend for years. The guilt feelings, the lack of closure…I never wanted to feel that way with my girls.

And I knew one thing – if anybody ever hurt either, I'd hurt that person.

And if anybody ever killed either of them, I'd kill that person.

I returned to my office and looked through the newspaper article until I settled on the profile I was looking for.

Ryan Mathews.

CHAPTER
THIRTY-FOUR

"RYAN MATHEWS," read the article, "was only five years old when he was taken from a playground in Mid-Town. He had an identical twin, Raymond, and a younger brother, Kenneth. Ryan was a precocious child known by others as inquisitive and verbal, with a sunny disposition and a ready smile. His mother, Colleen, said Ryan was what she considered 'easy' due to his mild temperament and readiness to share. The Mathews live on a tree-lined street in Hyde Park, and Colleen stated she wished she could've seen Ryan climb some of those trees and be a kid. His father, Thomas, did not comment on this interview, and it was said that he was no longer living at home. 'You don't know what a tragedy like this can do to a family,' Colleen said. 'It will either tear you apart or bring you together. In our case, it tore us apart. Thomas can't look at our other two boys without thinking about Ryan, and it's especially difficult as they look like triplets.'"

I read about the family and how devastated they were, and I knew.

I didn't think Father Mathews was the culprit. He seemed too genuine in his willingness to help. I didn't see any stonewalling whatsoever from him. He seemed open, honest and eager to give me any information I sought.

No, I'd have to go another way with this.

. . .

I went to see Mick the next day. I wanted to find out what he knew about Raymond and Father Mathews and see what he meant when he talked about Father Mathews' tattoos and how he knew about them.

"Hello, doll," he said as I approached the house. He was, once again, sitting on the front porch, a cocktail on the little table in front of him. "Claire is finally allowing me cocktails," he said. "Hallelujah!"

I had to laugh just a little. "Okay," I said as I sat down. "I need to ask you some questions."

"Shoot," he said. "Go ahead, ask away. Ask away." He took another sip of his martini, which was in a martini glass with three olives. "Dirty martini," he said. "And I like these martinis like I like my men. Dirty, dirty, dirty." He chuckled.

"That's great, Mick," I said. "Listen, you said something to me the other day when I took you to court. I don't know if you remember saying it, and I barely remember it. It didn't register with me at all when I heard it, but then it suddenly hit me that you said it."

"Don't you hate it when that happens?" Mick asked me. "It's right on the tip of your tongue, and you just can't think of it. Then you sit up in bed right before you go to sleep and shout out whatever you were trying to think about earlier." He shook his head. "Happens to me all the time, love."

"Yes, I hate that," I said impatiently. "But you said you thought Father Mathews was hot and loved his tattoos. I don't know why that didn't register with me then. I guess because I was so upset about running late. I must ask you when you saw Father Mathews and how you know about his tattoos."

Mick smiled. "Oh, wouldn't you like to know?"

"Don't play coy with me. I need to know. How did you know about Father Mathews' tattoos?"

"I have seen him playing basketball," he said. "Talk about a silver fox. The man is fifty years old and has the body of somebody half his age. Imma go all Thornbirds on his ass."

"Great, great, great, but since when do you like basketball?"

"Since I saw Father Mathews in shorts, that's when."

I took a deep breath and counted to ten. "Okay, this is circular reasoning at its finest. You had to be initially motivated to attend that basketball game to see Father Mathews play. Right? I'm asking you what initially brought you to that basketball court to see Father Mathews."

Mick took a sip of his martini. "I don't know what you are getting at," he said. "I just went to the Sacred Heart to watch a game, and there he was. Delicious."

"Mick, I'm going to ask you this question. When have you ever gone to a basketball game before?"

"Just the one time. I can't stand that game, love. It's boring to me, believe it or not. But not when there's a hunk of a man like Father Mathews playing. He's beautiful."

I stood up, feeling I was getting exactly nowhere. "Mick, you have to stop arguing with me like this. Okay? You have to stop. Now, you have to tell me, how or why did you go to that game in the first place? Who invited you?"

"Nobody invited me, love."

"Did you know Father Mathews before you went to that game?"

"No, I never saw him before in my life. Why are you getting so agitated?"

"Because, Mick, something brought you to that gym that day. Somebody invited you."

Mick sighed. "Nobody invited me. Or I don't know who invited me. Okay? I was just there. I came out at that game, and another alter went there in the first place. I don't know who."

I blinked my eyes rapidly. I was getting somewhere, but I didn't quite know where. There was still a missing puzzle piece, and I knew one thing.

That missing puzzle piece resided with an alter I hadn't met yet. An alter I haven't heard of yet. I knew this because Mick was generally aware of the movements of Sam, Eli and Jack. He was not aware of the movements of this other alter. He didn't even know this other alter's name.

So close, and yet so far from my answers.

CHAPTER
THIRTY-FIVE
SEPTEMBER 18 (TRIAL DAY)

"COME ON, MICK," I said impatiently as I walked into my mom's house to pick him up. "Why are you dawdling? You're always trying to make us late."

He yawned and stretched. "Listen, girly, this might be one of my last days on the outside. One of my last days. I hate to spend it in court, and I know I have to, but it doesn't mean I have to like it or hurry up and get there."

I rolled my eyes. "No, I guess it doesn't."

I'd decided to roll the dice and try for SODDI. Even though I hadn't yet interviewed or deposed him, I had a pretty good idea about who did this crime. On the contrary, I didn't want him to know what I was up to in calling him as a witness.

My only chance was to break him down on the stand, and there was no way I could do that if I'd interviewed him extensively beforehand.

So, I was flying blind, but I was reasonably confident I could make it happen.

Or so I prayed.

I changed my mind. "Actually, Mick, it does mean you have to hurry up and get there. It does."

"Okay, then," he said. "Let's go."

Mick was dressed in a three-piece suit, and I had to admit he looked effortlessly stylish. His grey hair was newly cut, and I hired a barber to come to my mother's house and cut it. I also hired a personal shopper to go to my mother's home and fit him for suits. Jack had to look his very best if he was going to persuade the jury that he was not a crazed killer who had it in for Father Kennedy.

I could never figure out who was the alter who witnessed the murder of Father Kennedy. I'd considered calling a therapist who could put Jack under hypnosis to figure that out, but I thought better about it. Something could go wrong. Maybe Eli would come out and jump bail. That would be an all-around disaster.

Was I gambling with Uncle Jack's life? There wasn't an easy answer to that question, unfortunately. My trial strategies usually involved at least one risky maneuver. There would have to be a Hail Mary along the way in long-shot cases like this. There simply wasn't any getting around that.

It helped, however, that I knew, with reasonable certainty, who did this crime. I deduced it from the clues I got. The problem was proving it to the jury.

I didn't know how to do that, though – prove it to a jury. I went to the cops with my admittedly circumstantial evidence about who did this, and they almost laughed me out of the station.

"Okay, Harper," Officer Brown said to me. "We have the murder weapon with your uncle's fingerprints on it. We have your uncle at the scene of the crime. He didn't confess, but he didn't exactly say he was innocent. Now you're expecting us to believe some cockamamie story about a man who killed Father Kennedy as revenge for not telling the authorities about a murder that happened 50 years ago?" He shook his head. "You get us some hard evidence, any kind of hard evidence, that this happened, and we'll talk. But until then, please stop wasting my time."

I knew Officer Brown would react like that, so I wasn't terribly upset. I'd have reacted in the same damned way. So even after I thought I figured out who did this, I couldn't prove it in any way, shape or form. I wasn't even sure of my own theory anyhow. Like most of my theories, this one was out there. But that didn't mean it was a bad theory. That didn't mean that at all.

But getting my theory in front of the jury would be extremely tricky. This was made all the more complicated because Mick, who was still out, as he explained that Jack could never take the stress of trial, wouldn't be a lick of help because he had no clue what happened in that rectory.

The good thing was that I decided to have an expert witness at trial. I hired somebody to testify about amnesia, how traumatic events can cause it, and how trauma can cause a person to lose consciousness. I supplied that witness to Vince before the June 1 deadline, who had the chance to depose him. What I hoped this witness could supply was a theory that Uncle Jack passed out at the scene precisely because he was witnessing a murder taking place.

I didn't, however, hire an expert witness who would testify to Jack's mental state at the time of the murder. I could have had a psychologist examine him thoroughly and ascertain the truth, but I didn't want that. I knew that if I hired this psychologist to testify, Judge Greene would more than likely stop the trial and have Jack evaluated further for NGRI, and that would be that. Jack probably would be declared NGRI and be put into a mental institution for the rest of his life. The jury would have never heard my evidence regarding my theory of who did this crime.

The upshot was that I wasn't confident going into this trial. I wasn't confident at all. I had no idea if I could prove my theory of an alternative killer; if I didn't, Jack would go to prison for the rest of his life. In that scenario, I'd be forever second-guessing my strategy of doing things this way. The fact was, a mental institution was infinitely better than prison. I'd forever think I should have just gone for NGRI and not gone for broke.

I wondered if my mother would ever forgive me for my decisions regarding this trial.

I wondered if I would ever forgive myself.

Mick and I got into my SUV and headed to the courthouse. My mother was taking her own car there, and so was Albany, Emma and

Brad. The whole gang would be there to see me either flame out spectacularly or emerge triumphant.

I tapped my fingers on my steering wheel to quell my misgivings about my trial strategy. I couldn't calm my racing heart, and my stomach had a tight knot that wouldn't go away anytime soon. I looked over at Mick, who was looking out the window, and I knew he was terrified, too. I knew that because he was quiet, and Mick was never quiet.

He finally sighed. "Harper, I hope you know what you're doing."

I'd run through the entire trial strategy with Mick, explaining that if we tried to have Jack declared legally insane at the time of the murder, there would be no chance for a full acquittal. I also was honest in that I had a good idea who did this murder, but it would be a long shot to prove it. An extremely long shot.

Mick told me to go for broke. "Doll, I can handle prison. I'll find a strong man to protect me, and I'll be fine. We'll be okay."

I gulped as I tried to focus on the road. "I know what I'm doing," I said weakly. I closed my eyes as the light turned red and bowed my head. "I know what I'm doing."

The courthouse came into view. I parked my SUV, and the two of us walked slowly to the courthouse steps and then walked slowly up them. We were early, for once, as it was 8:45, and we were scheduled to pick a jury at 9. Vince and I had one more pre-trial conference the week before, where we agreed we were going to trial and that neither of us had a pressing motion that needed to be heard.

Vince was surprisingly mellow about this whole thing. He seemed to be sympathetic to my situation. He knew my client was my beloved uncle, so he wasn't doing his usual bullying. He usually tried to psyche me out by telling me how crappy my case was, how I wouldn't win and how I needed to plead. That was his MO.

But not this time. He didn't pressure me in the least to plead Jack out. The only thing he did was gently encourage me to enter a plea of NGRI and ask for a bench trial, where a judge would decide Jack's fate, not a jury.

"I think you know that's the best route for your uncle," Vince had said in one of our meetings.

I knew he was right. I knew doing things that way would be the safest route.

But the way I decided to play it had, by far, the highest risks but also the highest potential rewards. If I played things right, Jack would be a completely free man by the end of the week.

And if I called things completely wrong, he'd be in prison for the rest of his life.

The stakes couldn't be higher.

CHAPTER
THIRTY-SIX

"OKAY, HARPER," Vince said when I came through the door. "We're ready to go. I hope you are too."

"I am," I nodded. "I'm ready to go."

He looked over at Mick, who was sitting quietly at the defense table, his hands clasped in front of him. "It's not too late to avoid this," Vince said. "Judge Greene is a reasonable guy. You can still try for a NGRI plea. Judge Greene would order your client to be evaluated and we can come back here later and make sure your uncle gets the help that he needs."

I stiffened my spine. "We went through this. That's not the direction I'm going." I hoped my voice told him I was more confident than I actually was.

Vince shook his head. "Your move. At any rate, the jury panel will be coming in soon."

Sure enough, 50 men and women made their way into the courtroom and took a seat where the spectators usually sit. They were quiet and solemn. They consisted of men and women from all walks of life. There were doctors in this panel and two lawyers. There were a few construction workers and plumbers and three nurses. There were Asians and Native Americans and Hispanics and blacks and whites. They were all ages - the youngest was 21, the oldest was 80. The jury panel was a perfect cross-section of America, and I'd have to figure out who amongst them would be "right" for my case.

Picking a jury was always a stressful process, made more so in a case like this. I always hoped to pick at least one person sympathetic to my defense, because one juror voting "not guilty" would be enough for the jury to hang, and, if the jury hanged, there would be the potential for the prosecution deciding not to try the case again.

Outright acquittal from a jury was always a long-shot proposition, and it was a *really* a long-shot here. Nevertheless, if I could find a jury that would not be too closed-minded to my theory of the case, I might have a shot.

The prospective jurors sat quietly until the bailiff came out. "All rise," he said, as everyone stood up. "The case of State of Missouri v. Calhoun has now come to order, the Honorable Harold Greene presiding."

Judge Greene took a seat. "You may be seated."

He gave the jury instructions while Vince and I paced around the floor. I was so nervous. I'd never been more nervous. I was gambling with the life of my uncle. I was putting everything I had into a long-shot theory and I was questioning this strategy with every breath I took.

Vince's words rang through my ears. *It's not too late to try for a NGRI plea. Judge Greene is a reasonable judge.* All I had to do was explain to Judge Greene that I made a mistake in not trying for NGRI, and he'd stop the trial so Jack could be evaluated. That's all I had to do.

I took a deep breath and closed my eyes. My insides were roiling and I simply couldn't stop my racing heart. I looked down at my hands, and they were shaking.

I opened my eyes and saw Vince questioning the jurors. It would soon be my turn.

I looked up at Judge Greene, who was smiling placidly at the jurors. He *was* a reasonable, fair-minded judge. Vince was probably right – if I decided to tell him I changed my mind about NGRI, Judge Greene *would* stop the trial. I only needed say the word.

Vince did his *voir dire*, and I stood up to do mine. I asked question after question, trying to get a feel for the jurors before me. This was always a tricky thing, trying to suss everybody out. I did the best I could with my questions, but it was never an exact science. It was more of an art, which meant there would inevitably be variables, mistakes and gut feelings. I had the sense I was too careful with my questioning and I was second-guessing myself.

Calm down, Harper. Calm down. You got this.

I did my questions, the jury was excused, and Vince and I sat down to do our challenges and our strikes for cause. We were entitled to 10 peremptory challenges apiece, and also unlimited strikes for cause, but those were hard to come by. If a juror, for instance, said he or she couldn't put their prejudices and biases aside and judge the case on its merits, that was a strike for cause. Most jurors, however, stated they *could* put aside their biases and prejudices, so that made striking for cause a limited proposition.

As for peremptory challenges, those were typically made with a combination of gut instinct and the facts as they presented themselves. Since the peremptory challenges were limited, unlike strikes for cause, I needed to use them sparingly.

I closed my eyes as I looked at the sheet that listed the jurors on it. I tried hard to calm my heart, but I could feel it. It was almost audible in my ears. I put my hand on my wrist and felt it thumping.

You got this. What's wrong with you? You've done hundreds of trials. This one is no different. It's no different.

But all the little pep talks to myself wasn't doing it this time. I was second-guessing *everything* at that moment. I was second-guessing my jury peremptory challenges and my strikes for cause. I was second-guessing my trial strategy. I was second-guessing my decision not to try for NGRI. I was second-guessing my decision to roll the dice, with my uncle's life on the line.

I looked over at Mick, who was sitting calmly, his hands clasped in front of him. I thought about how Jack would completely disappear if he was sentenced to prison, and how we would lose him forever if that happened. I considered the alternative, that Jack would be sentenced to a mental institution, one that he would never leave, but, perhaps, life would be slightly better than if he went to prison.

But I doubted Jack could handle that fate, either. He was too weak, too vulnerable. He needed the love of his family and a good therapist. I pictured him sitting in front of a window, looking out it, despairing day by day about his fate. I saw the sterile white walls, I smelled the antiseptic scent that always permeated every hospital I had ever been to, and I saw his environment. I had been through tours of those mental institutions, and they weren't fun. People were screaming and cursing through the halls, others were always crying, and still others were wandering the halls aimlessly. Nobody was in touch with reality.

I'd been in a psychiatric facility myself, but that was something different. Where Jack would go would be specifically a facility for the criminally insane, and that was a different beast altogether. It would be a depressing existence, not to mention a dangerous one. These facilities were filled with paranoid schizophrenics who were hearing voices telling them to kill. They were filled with dangerous psychopaths who had not one ounce of remorse. They were filled with people who were in various stages of desperation.

They were filled with people like Robert Dunn, who impaled, stabbed and practically beheaded his daughter because he was convinced she was the Devil. People like John Hinckley, Jr., who shot President Reagan because he wanted to impress the actress Jody Foster. People like Andrea Yates, who drowned her five sons in the bathtub.

These were the people who populated these mental institutions. I feared for Jack's safety if he was committed to such a place.

I shook my head. No, the mental institution wasn't an option for Jack. It wasn't.

I'd have to roll that dice.

Our jury was selected and the trial was set to begin. I looked over my opening statement, closed my eyes and silently spoke to myself. I opened my eyes and looked over at Mick, whose own eyes weren't meeting mine.

He silently put his hand on mine while looking straight ahead.

The bailiff stood at the front of the courtroom. "All rise," he said, as we all stood.

Judge Greene took his seat at the bench. "You may be seated. Counselors, I understand you are ready to proceed to opening statements, is that correct?"

"Yes, your honor," we both said.

"Very good. Mr. Malloy, you may proceed."

At that, Vince stood up and walked over to the jury. "Ladies and gentlemen of the jury. You are here today because a man of God, a man of the cloth, was brutally murdered. Father Kennedy was a good man, a great man, a man that only served God and he served Him faithfully. He was a part of the community – he worked at soup kitchens and animal shelters and he was actively involved in working with high-risk youths. His entire life was devoted to service to others and service to God. If there was a man in this world who did not deserve his fate, it was Father Kennedy."

He paced back and forth in front of the jury, addressing them one by one. "On April 19 of this year, that life was cruelly snuffed out. Cruelly. You will hear evidence that the defendant, Jack Calhoun, was found at the rectory with the Father, who was brutally slain and lying at the defendant's feet. You will hear evidence that the murder weapon, which was a hunting knife, was recovered at the scene. You will hear evidence that this murder weapon was in the hands of the defendant at the time he was arrested. You will hear evidence that this murder weapon had only one set of fingerprints on it, and those fingerprints belonged to the defendant. Thank you very much, ladies and gentlemen."

I was cheered, somewhat, that Vince couldn't really establish motive. Father Mathews had told me Father Kennedy was afraid of Jack, but he couldn't really testify to that, because that would be hearsay – Father Mathews was only aware of Father Kennedy's fear because Father Kennedy had expressed in words that he was afraid.

Still, just with the facts, the prosecutor had enough to convict. That much was clear.

I stood up and cleared my throat. I closed my eyes for three seconds and then straightened my spine. I had to go at that jury with a forceful voice, presence and confidence that told them I knew I had the winning hand. Intangibles like that – tone of voice, posture and body language – were vital. I was always confident, no matter what. Even in those trials where I knew that my case was crap, I could sell it to the jury just by sheer will.

But this was different. This was my Uncle Jack, and I couldn't get out of my head.

I soon got it together.

"Ladies and gentlemen of the jury, you heard the prosecutor's opening statement. I won't argue with the facts. Yes, my client was arrested in Father Kennedy's rectory. Yes, the murder weapon was in his hands and only his fingerprints were on it. All this is true. But I'll tell you what's not true – it's not true that anybody saw my client enter that rectory. Nobody saw my client kill Father Kennedy. But somebody called the police. Somebody did. Why this person called the police is an open question, but I submit to you the person who called the police was the actual perpetrator of this murder."

I did the same thing as Vince – I leaned on the railing and looked every last juror in the eye. "Think about it, ladies and gentlemen. Father Kennedy and my client, Mr. Calhoun, were in that rectory for a counseling session when an anonymous phone call came through stating there should be a welfare check on Father Kennedy. A welfare check. Why would there be a reason for a welfare check? There was no indication Father Kennedy was unwell. Doesn't that sound just a tad suspicious?"

I paced back and forth, turned my back and then turned back around and faced them again. "Just a tad suspicious that somebody would call the police for a welfare check when Father Kennedy was presumably minding his own business and counseling a client. You will hear evidence about this welfare check. You will also hear evidence that a different individual had motive for killing Father Kennedy. That evidence will show Father Kennedy heard the confessions of a serial killer back in 1972, and did not report it due to confessional privilege. You will hear evidence this other individual, whose name is Raymond Mathews, lost his identical twin to this serial killer back in 1972. You will hear evidence that Mr. Mathews blamed Father Kennedy for the death of his identical twin brother because Father Kennedy did not alert authorities to the possibility that a serial killer was in the area. You will hear further evidence that will establish that

Mr. Mathews also blamed my client, Jack Calhoun, because Jack was also a victim of this serial killer and Jack, aged 11, helped find victims for this killer. These two aspects combined in the mind of an unstable individual who was determined that both Father Kennedy and my client would pay for the crime perpetrated on his identical twin."

I nodded, finally feeling my sea legs. I was looking at the faces of the jury, and I realized they were listening to me and didn't look skeptical. I was winning them over, one by one.

I continued on. "You will also hear evidence this man's brother is Father Mathews, the current priest at Guardian Angels, having taken over for Father Kennedy." I took a deep breath. I didn't necessarily know where to go from there. I really had no idea how Raymond Mathews found out from Father Mathews that Father Kennedy confessed to him. I really didn't even know for sure *if* this confession happened. Truth be told, I was telling the jury a story I didn't know would come true. It was a story that would only be told if I could call Raymond Mathews to the stand, treat him as hostile, and break him down.

"So, you see, ladies and gentlemen – my client was framed. I submit to you that Mr. Raymond Mathews went into the rectory, murdered Father Kennedy, did something to make my client lose consciousness, and put that hunting knife in my client's hand. That's why my client was passed out with the murder weapon in his hand. I will further submit to you that Mr. Mathews called the police and asked for a welfare check. Mr. Mathews thought he was committing the perfect crime, one that would exact revenge on the two people he held responsible for the death of his identical twin all those years ago. Please don't let him get away with it. Thank you."

I took a deep breath and sat down.

Mick put his hand on mine. "That was really good," he said. "Now if you can just prove all the things that you told the jury you would prove, we'll be okay."

I smiled wanly. "A tall order."

A tall order, indeed.

"Call your first witness," Judge Greene said to Vince after I was finished with my opening statement.

"The state calls Officer Brown," he said.

Officer Brown was summoned from outside the courtroom and he made his way to the witness stand. He sat down, was sworn in, and waited for Vince to begin his questions.

"Could you please state your name for the record?" Vince asked.

"Officer Larry Brown," he said.

"Officer Brown," Vince said. "What is your relation to this case?"

"I was the first officer at the crime scene and I was also the arresting officer."

"You were the officer who was called to Guardian Angels on the evening of April 19, 2017, correct?"

"Yes."

"Could you please tell the jury why you were called to that scene?"

He cleared his throat. "I was patrolling the area when I got a call about conducting a welfare check at the rectory at Guardian Angels Catholic Church. I was with my partner, Officer Maddox. I arrived at the scene, knocked and announced, and did not get an answer. I could peek through the curtains, as it was still fairly early – it was only 18:20, so it was still light out. I peeked through the curtains and saw Father Kennedy lying on the floor. I also saw the back of somebody's head sitting on the couch. I was unable to identify the person sitting on the couch. Because I could clearly see Father Kennedy lying on the floor, it gave me probable cause to enter the premises, which I did. I kicked in the door and went into the premises along with Officer Maddox."

"And what did you see when you went into the rectory?"

"I saw Father Kennedy lying on the floor, having been stabbed in the heart with a hunting knife. I checked for a pulse and found he was deceased. I also saw the defendant, Mr. Jack Calhoun, sitting on the couch above Father Kennedy. Mr. Calhoun was unconscious and had a hunting knife in his hand. He wasn't gripping the knife, as he was unconscious, but the knife was cradled loosely in his hand."

At that, Vince got out four pictures which were blown up. I didn't object, because the pictures weren't particularly gruesome. Because Father Kennedy was stabbed in the heart, his blood stopped pumping immediately. Therefore, there was very little blood, and what little blood there was didn't show up particularly well against Father Kennedy's black robe.

The pictures showed the Father lying on the ground. His right arm was raised behind him, and his left arm was at his side. His eyes were open, and there was a small amount of visible blood in the chest area of his robe.

Other pictures showed close-ups of Father Kennedy's stunned expression. His blue eyes looked like he had suffered a severe shock and his mouth was open. There was another close up of the chest area of his robe, where the blood had pooled. Still other pictures showed Jack sitting on the couch. His head was bowed, and, in his right hand, which was open loosely, was a knife.

"Do these pictures accurately depict the scene at the rectory of Guardian Angels Catholic Church on the evening of April 19, 2017, at approximately 6:20 PM?"

"Yes."

"Did you arrest the defendant at the scene?"

"Yes."

"Did he regain consciousness?"

"He did."

"When did he regain consciousness?"

"In the squad car on the way to the jail."

"Did he say anything?"

"Yes."

"What did he say?"

"He asked where he was."

"What did you tell him?"

"I told him he was being arrested for the murder of Father Kennedy in the rectory."

"And what did he reply?"

"He said he didn't remember ever being in the rectory. And then he shook his head, as if he was stunned. But he didn't say another word."

"What happened when he was taken to the station?"

"He was processed in. He didn't speak anymore, however, to us. To any of us. At all."

"Thank you," he said. "I have nothing further for this witness."

Judge Greene looked at me. "Ms. Ross, do you have any questions for this witness?"

"Yes, your honor."

I stood up and approached him. "Officer Brown, you indicated you went to the rectory because you received a welfare check. Is that true?"

"Yes."

"What time did that call come in?"

"It was right before I arrived at the scene, so it was between 18:00 and 18:05."

"I see. Do you know who called about this?"

"No. It was an anonymous call."

"Is it unusual to received anonymous calls regarding welfare checks?"

He cleared his throat. "It is unusual, but not unheard of."

"Why do you suppose it is unusual to receive an anonymous call about a welfare check?"

"Objection, calls for speculation." Vince was on his feet.

"Please rephrase the question, Ms. Ross," Judge Greene said.

I nodded and decided to move on. I thought the jury got the point – the call wouldn't be anonymous unless the person was worried about retribution. Of course, that wasn't necessarily true – there was always the chance somebody could make an anonymous call because he or she didn't want to get involved. But I wanted that question out there.

I paced around slightly. "Now, I assume you received the autopsy report. What did that report indicate about the time of death?"

"Father Kennedy expired at 17:30, according to the autopsy report."

"And Mr. Calhoun woke up in the squad car on the way over to the station?"

"Yes."

"Do you have the approximate time Mr. Calhoun woke up?"

"Yes. We arrived at the scene at 18:20, determined that Father Kennedy was deceased, so we then called the coroner to come to the scene and transport Father Kennedy to the morgue. We waited for the coroner, who arrived at 18:35, we cordoned off the scene and then we transported Mr. Calhoun to the station. He woke up in the squad car at approximately 18:50."

I paced around, trying to get the timeline correct for the jury. Vince didn't have anybody lined up to state he or she saw what time Jack went into the rectory, because that was unknown. Jack himself didn't know when he went in there, and there wasn't anybody around to see him go in.

"So, the time of death for Father Kennedy was 5:30 PM and you got the anonymous phone call about a welfare check about a half-hour after Father Kennedy breathed his last. Do I have that correct?"

He nodded.

"Please answer verbally for the record."

"Yes," he said into the microphone. "You have that timeline correct."

I was satisfied with that. I could do something with that in my closing statement – that the anonymous phone call came in just a half hour after the Father was killed. That timing seemed suspicious to me, and I hoped to make it seem equally suspicious to the jury. There was no explanation, that I could see, for why anybody would think Father Kennedy was in danger.

The one thing that nagged at me, though, was I didn't know how long Jack had been in that rectory with the Father before the Father was killed. Maybe he'd been in there for a short time, or maybe it had been hours. Nobody saw him go in there. Plus, Father Mathews had indicated Father Kennedy felt threatened by Jack. This testimony couldn't come in, because it was clear hearsay, but I wondered if Vince could introduce that testimony in the back door somehow. If he could, that might negate my timeline defense, because there might have been a clear concern for Father Kennedy's safety if he'd been in that rectory alone with Jack for a long time.

But I'd present that to the jury as very suspicious timing. I hoped to succeed on that point.

"Nothing further." I sat down and winked at Mick, who smiled and winked back.

"Mr. Malloy, call your next witness," Judge Greene intoned from the bench.

"The state calls Tyrrell Young."

Dr. Young was the go-to forensic expert on DNA and fingerprinting.

He was called when the prosecutor wanted to bring out the big guns. He'd be difficult to shake. I was concerned no other hairs had shown up at the murder scene. Dr. Young was called in to detail the crime scene for hair, saliva and skin that might've been left behind at the murder scene. I got his report and knew he'd indicated that the only hairs he found belonged to Jack and tthe fingerprints on the knife belonged only to Jack.

Not that I thought this was entirely fatal. There was the chance the killer shaved his head before he went to the scene and could also have shaved his forearms. I noticed that Raymond Mathews, like Father Mathews, had hairless arms. This told me they were probably part Asian, because many Asians don't have hair on their arms. I always observed that in my clients from the Pacific Rim.

So, Raymond Mathews, if he did it, might've shaved his head and, since he cannot grow hair on his arms, he most likely wouldn't shed any hair body hair on the crime scene, either. So just because only Jack's hair was found at the scene didn't mean there wasn't anybody else there.

Dr. Young went through his credentials, which were impressive – a master's degree in forensic technology at Berkeley, and he was currently an MD at Menorah Hospital in Leawood. He wasn't a part of the police department, but was brought in on special cases. He testified just like I knew he would about Jack's hair being found and that it was Jack's fingerprints on the knife.

Vince finished his questioning of Dr. Young, and I approached.

"Dr. Young, you testified you found hair you sourced to my client, Mr. Calhoun. And that this was the only hair that found at the scene, except for, of course, the hair of the victim, Father Kennedy. Is that correct?"

"Yes, that is correct."

"And you found this hair on the sofa, where Mr. Calhoun was found unconscious. Is that also correct?"

"Yes, that is correct."

"Do you believe that it's unusual that a rectory would not have other hairs? After all, the Father had counseled many other individuals in this rectory."

"Objection, calls for speculation," Vince said, standing up.

"It goes to how thorough Dr. Young examined the crime scene, your honor."

"I'll allow it," Judge Greene said. "You may answer that question, Dr. Young."

"No," he said. "That would not be unusual. Other individuals might have been in that rectory, but not everyone sheds their hair and, from my understanding, the cleaning lady had been in that rectory that very morning."

I bit my lower lip, not wanting to ask more about the cleaning lady. She was on Vince's witness list, though, so I knew I'd be hearing from her more.

I paced around a little. "Now, if an individual was in that rectory, and this individual had a shaved head and no hair on his arms whatsoever, is it possible this individual could get into that rectory and out of it without leaving behind DNA evidence?"

"It's possible," he said. "If the individual was only in the rectory for a short period of time."

"So, it's possible for an individual to slip into that rectory, kill Father Kennedy and slip out without leaving behind DNA evidence that he or she was in there? Assuming this person shaved his head and did not grow hair on his arms?"

"Yes," he said. "That is possible."

I nodded my head. "Nothing further."

"Mr. Malloy, call your next witness."

"The state calls Kathleen Harbig," he said.

The door of the courtroom opened, and a heavy-set blonde woman walked slowly to the witness stand. This was the cleaning lady who had cleaned up the rectory before the murder. I considered that to be either bad luck on Jack's part, in that the place was cleaned right before he went into that rectory, therefore only his hair would be found in the rectory, or excellent planning on the part of the killer.

I thought it was probably the latter.

Kathleen was sworn in and gave her name for the record, and Vince started to ask her basic questions.

"Ms. Harbig, what is your role at Guardian Angels Catholic Church?"

"I'm the official housekeeper for the priestly rectory."

"What are your general duties?"

"I sweep the hardwood floors, mop them, vacuum the throw rugs and the curtains and the sofas. I also dust and clean the bathrooms by scrubbing the toilets and the bathtub."

"When you clean that rectory, how long does it take you?"

"About three hours."

"Three hours." Vince nodded. "And how big is that rectory?"

"About 1,500 square feet. It consists of a bedroom, a dining room, a living room, a kitchen and two bathrooms. It's not very large."

"So, you take three hours to clean 1,500 square feet. And you're working the entire time."

I knew what he was getting at – this housekeeper does a very thorough cleaning job when she cleans up. Assuming Jack was the only person in that rectory after Kathleen cleaned up, it wasn't a stretch that his hair was the only hair found at the scene, besides Father Kennedy. Kathleen's testimony therefore negated my argument that there really should've been other hairs and DNA evidence found at a place where Father Kennedy conducted most of his personal counseling sessions, therefore Dr. Young didn't do such a good job of sweeping the scene.

"Yes," she said. "I do a very thorough job. I'm there once a week."

"And did you clean that rectory on the afternoon of April 19?"

"Yes."

"What time were you there that day?"

"From 1 PM to 4 PM."

"Nothing further."

I figured it would be pointless to cross-examine her, so I let it go.

"Ms. Ross, do you have any questions for this witness?"

I stood up. "No, your honor."

"You may step down," Judge Greene informed Kathleen.

"Call your next witness," Judge Greene said to Vince.

"The state calls Father Kenneth Mathews."

I screwed up my face, knowing Father Mathews had the possibility of doing some real damage.

Father Mathews took the stand and raised his right hand.

"Do you swear to tell the truth, the whole truth and nothing but the truth, so help you God?" the bailiff asked.

"I do."

Vince approached. "Please state your name for the record."

"Kenneth John Mathews."

"And what is your current occupation?"

"I'm a pastor at Guardian Angels Catholic Church in Westport."

"Father Mathews, before you became the pastor at Guardian Angels Catholic Church, what was your prior position?"

"I was an associate pastor," he said. "To Father Kennedy."

"And as an associate pastor, what were some of your duties?"

"I helped Father Kennedy write sermons, I counseled some of the parishioners, I helped administer the sacrament to the parishioners and I also helped with outreach. Another duty I had was to schedule the counseling sessions for Father Kennedy."

I knew where this was going.

"You helped schedule the counseling sessions for Father Kennedy." Vince paced over to the bench and then paced back in front of the witness stand and made his way over to the jury box, where he put his hands on the railing. He then walked back over to the witness stand.

He was doing his dance. It was his signal that something important was about to be said, so the jury should pay attention. I knew this dance so well I sometimes saw it in my sleep.

"Did you schedule counseling sessions for Jack Calhoun?" Vince asked.

"Yes, I did."

"How many counseling sessions did you schedule for Jack Calhoun?"

"Two counseling sessions a week for about three months, and, in the week before Kel, I mean Father Kennedy was killed, I was scheduling in a counseling session for Mr. Calhoun every day."

I bit my lower lip. It sounded like Jack might've been obsessed with Father Kennedy, but, then again, it sounded like Jack was going through something trying and needed a lot of guidance.

I actually knew the truth, however – Jack was Mick during this period of time, and Mick was in love with Father Kennedy. This explained, more than anything, why he constantly wanted to be "counseled" by Father Kennedy. He wasn't being counseled. He was going in there and mooning over Father Kennedy. That was my impression, anyhow.

"A counseling session every day for Mr. Calhoun in the week before Father Kennedy was killed." Vince nodded his head knowingly. "Was this unusual? Were there other parishioners scheduling so many counseling sessions with Father Kennedy?"

"No," Father Mathews said. "For all the other parishioners, I only scheduled them in once a week at the most." Father Mathews shook his head. "Father Kennedy was a patient and giving man. If somebody needed his help and guidance, he was there for them, no questions asked. But, no, no other parishioner demanded as much time from him as did Mr. Calhoun."

I sighed. This was looking bad. Everything was adding up so nicely for the prosecution. In the meantime, my side of the case would consist of one lousy expert whose only job was to try to persuade the jury that Jack's fainting spell in the church was possibly due to severe trauma, such as the trauma of seeing somebody murdered. I had to hope the jury didn't take that testimony the wrong way and decide Jack's traumatic incident, that caused his fainting spell, was the fact that he, himself, murdered Father Kennedy.

In other words, that testimony would surely backfire. I hoped it wouldn't, but I thought it probably would.

"I have nothing further for this witness."

I stood up to cross-examine him, and I'd have to do it delicately. I had knowledge that Father Mathews knew Father Kennedy was afraid of Jack. He couldn't express that on the stand, though, because the way he learned about this fear was through Father Kennedy's own words, and that was hearsay. The last thing I wanted was to somehow open the door for Father Mathews to get that testimony in.

That would sink our case for sure.

I hesitated, knowing it was far too risky to cross-examine Father Mathews. There wasn't much I could ask that wouldn't lead to Father Mathews blurting out that Father Kennedy was afraid of Jack. If I cross-examined him to ask if he saw anything inappropriate about the counseling sessions, he could volunteer that he knew Father Kennedy was afraid of Jack – even though it would be hearsay, he wouldn't necessarily know that, and it was too much of a risk that he might blurt it out. I could move to strike the answer if he said that, but the damage would be done. The horse would be out of the barn and wouldn't go back in.

I decided the risk that Father Mathews might blurt out something about Father Kennedy being afraid of Jack was just too great. I decided it was better to rest.

"Ms. Ross," Judge Greene said. "Your witness."

I hesitated some more, hating to leave his testimony hanging out there, but knowing there was the real potential for his testimony to get much, much worse. I closed my eyes.

"I have no questions for this witness."

I sighed as Father Mathews was excused.

This wasn't going well.

To say the least.

CHAPTER
THIRTY-SEVEN

"DON'T WORRY ABOUT IT, DOLL," Mick said that evening after Vince put up the rest of his witnesses on this case. "You'll slay it tomorrow, and if you don't, you don't. I'm telling you, we'll be okay."

I shook my head. "No, don't say that. Just don't say that, Mick. We have to be 100% positive we'll overcome this."

"Well, after today's testimony, it doesn't look so good." He shrugged. "I'll just have to find a big burly boyfriend behind bars, one the other inmates won't mess with, and I'll get along fine. Really. By the way, did you notice that amazing alliteration I just did – big burly boyfriend behind bars." He nodded his head. "That's pure gold right there."

I bit my lower lip. I had a plan. It was a risky plan, but what else was new? This entire case hinged upon one risky plan after another. The centerpiece of my trial strategy Raymond Mathews – I planned on treating him as hostile and breaking him down with cross-examination questions. He'd either break or he wouldn't. I was depending on him breaking. If he didn't, we were toast.

The only other thing I could think of was something that could either work or could go horribly, horribly, horribly wrong. I was struggling with it, but when your back is against the wall, sometimes you have to do something drastic to bring yourself back. And this plan was certainly drastic.

High risk, high reward.

The problem was, this plan was so high-risk it was borderline suicidal.

And I couldn't say a word about it to Mick.

If things went right, I could speak with the alter in that rectory and could get decent testimony out of Jack on the stand.

If things went wrong, I could either lose the case completely or have the judge order the trial halted so Jack could be evaluated for a NGRI plea. I probably would have no choice but to go that route if this were the case.

It was my Hail Mary pass, and I had to hope and pray it worked.

I went home and saw the girls, who were playing a board game on the living room floor. They looked up at me and both knew to step lightly. The girls now knew my rhythms and moods, and, while Rina still loved to test me, even she steered clear if I had a certain look in my eye.

I must've had that look in my eye, because both of them came up to me and were as nice as pie.

"Hey, Mom," Rina said. "We knew you'd be tired, so we put a frozen pizza in the oven for dinner tonight."

I nodded, feeling terrible I couldn't engage with them. But, right at that moment, I was so in my head I couldn't possibly be a decent conversationalist. "Thanks, Ladybug," I said. "You guys play your game. I'll be in my office, okay?" I nodded. "I'm so sorry, but I..." I shook my head. The stress of this trial was getting to me. It was weighing on me like a heavy metal vest. I couldn't breathe.

"We know," Abby offered. "Just go on upstairs to your office. We'll bring the pizza up to you."

I smiled. My girls were the best. "Thanks," I said. "For that."

I went into my office and just stared at my computer screen.

What was I doing? What could I do? I was risking Jack's permanent sanity and the case, all with one move. But yet, I knew this move would be my only option.

My plan was to bring Steven Heaney into that courtroom and hope his presence in the courtroom triggered a different alter to come out on the witness stand. This was such a razor-thin gambit, too. I had to hope a different alter came out, but, more than that, I'd have to hope this different alter was the *right* alter – the one in that rectory who knew what happened.

I'd kept Steven away from Jack ever since he got into town. He was doing remarkably well – I helped him get re-established with a state ID and helped him get his social security straightened out so he was receiving benefits. He found a position with a nursery who, because of Steven's amazing knowledge of botany, overlooked that he had no work history whatsoever. He was thriving in this nursery and was telling me every day how grateful he was to be getting a second chance.

Yet, I couldn't overlook that he was Robert Heaney's identical twin. Granted, he was 45 years older than when Jack knew Robert, but I had a hunch there was a part of Jack that would never forget Robert Heaney and this part of him would recognize Steven Heaney as being the man he helped out of that house.

In short, Steven Heaney was the one link Jack had to that house. The one link. Jack had forgotten completely about that house, but would seeing Steven trip him back?

I'd spoken with Jack's therapist again, and he thought this gambit would work. Seeing Steven, especially if I sprang Steven on Jack without warning, might cause a break and cause a different alter to come out. Probably the alter that would come out would be Eli, or it might be Sam, because Sam saved Steven.

You're playing with fire, Harper. You're gambling with the life of a man you love very much. Part of me wanted to stop. Tell Judge Greene the truth, ask forgiveness for the fact that I took up his time and the taxpayer's money, and ask for Jack to be evaluated for a NGRI plea. That would result in Jack disappearing forever, probably, but at least he wouldn't be in prison.

There was another part of me that wanted to throw that Hail Mary pass. If it worked, Jack would be acquitted. The stars had to align just-so for that to happen, but, with my current trial strategy, Jack would at least have a chance.

But what if the price was too high? What if Eli came out on the stand and just never left? What if Jack had a permanent psychotic break when he sees Steven so he gets completely lost? What then? I was risking permanent damage to his psyche. I was also putting Jack at risk of going to prison for the rest of his life.

There were no easy answers.

The next day, I was ready. I was going into battle. Into a war.

Vince had wrapped up his witnesses on the first day, which meant the second day would be all me. It would be my side of the story.

I decided to get Jack's testimony out of the way first.

I went to pick him up, and Mick was waiting for me on the front porch as usual. "Are you ready for this, doll?" he asked me. "It's do or die time today, you know."

"I know."

"Do you think you can break down that Raymond Mathews guy on the stand? You promised the moon to the jury, you know."

"I know. And the answer to that is maybe. With the right approach, maybe. If I don't, I don't, huh?"

"Right. If you don't, you don't. You'll put me on the stand and I'll be no help at all. I don't remember that rectory anymore than Jack does. Just stick to the questions about my relationship with Father Kennedy, why don't you?"

"No, that's not a good idea. I don't want the jury to know how obsessed you were with Father Kennedy. They don't need to know you were in love with him. So far, the prosecutor hasn't established a motive for your killing Father Kennedy. I suggest we don't give them that motive wrapped in a silver bow."

"So, what will you ask me?" Mick demanded. "Seriously, girly, what will you ask me on that stand?"

I had to lie to him. He couldn't know what I'd planned. If he got wind of it, it might not work. I had to have the element of surprise working in my favor. "I'm simply going to ask you questions about your life. I want the jury to get a look at you. I want them to see you as being a calm, kind, nice fellow that would never hurt anyone. Personality and body language go a long way towards convincing the jury that you'd never murder somebody, let alone in cold blood."

Mick looked skeptical. "You have to be kidding me. Listen, you better prepare me better than this. I'm flying blind here."

"Just relax. I got this."

We got to the courthouse and went in, finding the elevator and getting to the courtroom at a quarter of nine. We sat down at our table. Vince was already there, pacing the floor and chatting with his second chair, Suzanne Ortega. He nodded when I walked in.

"I guess you have Jack as your first witness," he said. "And then Raymond Mathews as your second witness. And then your expert on amnesia, trauma and fainting. After that, you're wrapping, right?"

"Correct," I said.

He nodded and looked at me. "It's not too late to stop this," he said. "It's your call, but I'd seriously think about it."

I sighed. "You've been in those facilities," I said. "Those mental institutions. Believe me, this has been the hardest thing I've ever done, but I think my Uncle Jack needs to stay out of those places. I have a chance for a full acquittal, and I'm going for it."

"Okay. Go big or go home, huh?"

"Right."

Fifteen minutes later, the jury filed in, the bailiff announced the judge, everybody stood and Judge Greene took the bench.

"You may be seated," he said. "Ms. Ross, call your first witness."

My heart started to pound as I looked to the door. I had arranged for Steven to dramatically walk through the courtroom door right at 9:10. That would give me time to get Jack on the stand and situated.

I gulped, praying Steven could make it. He said he would. I hoped and prayed for his appearance.

"The defense calls Jack Calhoun."

Mick got up and uncertainly went to the stand. "Please raise your right hand," the bailiff said.

Mick raised it.

"Do you swear to tell the truth, the whole truth and nothing but the truth, so help you God?"

"I do."

"Please be seated."

Jack sat down. I approached.

"Please state your name for the record."

"Jack Richard Calhoun."

I closed my eyes, seeing the clock read exactly 9:10.

When I opened them, Jack was staring into the audience. Just staring intently.

I didn't even have to turn around. I knew what he was staring at.

And, before my eyes, Mick's expression changed.

I would finally meet Eli.

CHAPTER
THIRTY-EIGHT

JACK NARROWED HIS EYES AND, all at once, his posture changed completely. He leaned back in his chair, looking, for all the world, like he wanted to light up a cigarette right then and there. He put his right arm casually on the railing that bounded the witness stand. He nodded and raised an eyebrow.

I took a deep breath as the man in front of me, who might've been Eli or Sam or alter-to-be-named-later, sized me up. I prayed he didn't start babbling about something. I prayed he didn't state his name. But I had a feeling he knew the score. He knew to play along. Especially if he was Eli, who was Jack's protector. I hoped his instinct was still that – to protect Jack at all costs. That would mean not saying anything that would give Judge Greene reason to suspect the man looking at me from the witness stand wasn't Jack.

"Mr. Calhoun," I said. "Take me back the afternoon of April 19 of this year. What were you doing?"

"Well," he said, his cadence tough, his voice sounding like he was talking with a mouth full of marbles. Like Marlon Brando in *The Godfather*. "I was talking with Father Kennedy, like, you know, minding my own damned business." His head started to jut to and fro and his posture got even more casual. He leaned back further in his chair and he reached for a pencil on the desk in front of him and put it in his mouth like a cigarette. It dangled from his lips, then put it down.

I felt a sense of relief. This was the alter who knew what happened! This was him!

"You were talking with Father Kennedy," I said. "What were you talking about?"

"You know, life, whatnot. I won't go into all that, 'cause, you know, that's secret and all, but, yeah, I was talking to him. There's this dude named Mick who had the hots for him, and I knew that. Mick's a good friend of mine and all and I just wanted to, you know, tell Father Kennedy he needed to tell Mick to chill out." He nodded. "That's what I was talking to him about."

He winked at me, smiled and I started to relax. If this was Eli, he wasn't so bad. He had the affect of a fifties hood with a heart of gold – like one of the T-Birds in *Grease*. Danny Zuko and Kenickie came to my mind. I wondered if that was how Jack formed this personality – he based him upon the movies he knew. But, maybe not – *Grease* didn't come on the screen until four years after Jack was sprung from that house.

"So, you were talking to Father Kennedy about a friend named Mick, right?"

"Right. So, yeah, we were in that house, shooting the breeze and shit, I mean stuff, when this man came in." He shook his head. "This dude came in. He looked just like that other priest, that Father Mathews guy, but he wasn't him. It looked like him, though."

I furrowed my brow. "A guy came in. What guy? Did he say who he was?"

"Nah. He just came right on in and said he knew me." Eli – I was assuming this was Eli – shrugged. "He told me he knew I was crazy, loony tunes. I have no idea how he came up with that. I didn't know this guy from Adam." Eli shook his head.

"He told you he knew you were crazy and-"

"Yeah. He accused me of murdering his little brother. Man, this dude was one crazy..." He looked over at the jury and shrugged. "He was one crazy cat, put it that way."

This was gold, and it wasn't hearsay, because Raymond Mathews could testify on cross-examine about this. I turned around and saw Vince. He was watching me warily and then stood up. "Your honor, I would like to object to this testimony. Unless Ms. Ross can show me this mystery man who came into this rectory will be available to cross-examine, I'd like this entire testimony to be stricken as inadmissible hearsay."

Judge Greene nodded and called both of us to the bench. "Ms. Ross," Judge Greene whispered. "Is this man your witness is referring to going to be made available?"

"He is, your honor. My client is talking about Raymond Mathews, who's on my witness list."

"Okay, then. Have him establish this man he's talking about is Raymond Mathews and I'll allow it. Otherwise, I have to agree your client's testimony about this man should be stricken."

"Thank you, your honor."

I went back to questioning Eli. "Now, did you get this guy's name?"

"Nah," he said. "He didn't tell me his name, but I recognized him anyhow. He's the brother of that other dude, that penguin, Father Mathews. I seen him around after that day, and I figured out he was named Raymond Mathews."

I let out a sigh of relief. I had no idea if Eli was telling the truth about how he figured out this guy was Raymond Mathews, but it was out there and he gave a positive ID, so that was all good.

"Raymond Mathews," I said. "And what happened next? He burst into the rectory, said you were crazy, accused you of murdering his little brother, and then what happened?"

"Well, he started saying some crazy stuff to that Father Kennedy. He accused the Father of covering up for his brother's killer, which made me kind of go 'I thought I was your brother's killer,' you know?'" He shrugged. "He couldn't make up his mind about who to kill first, me or Father Kennedy. He said we both would go down for the death of his brother, but then said something about making me suffer by going into the nut house, because I was crazy."

"So, Raymond Mathews appeared in the rectory and threatened the life of both you and Father Kennedy. Is that what you're telling the jury?"

"That's what I'm saying, yo. That's how it went down." He nodded his head to and fro. "And then this dude got out this hunting knife. Oh, and yeah, he was completely bald too, man. Not a damned hair on his head. But he had this hunting knife, he was wearing latex gloves and he plunged that knife right into that poor penguin's heart."

I looked at the jury and wondered if Eli was believable. He was being so callous about all of this. I knew why he was being callous, too – after what he'd seen at Robert Heaney's house, nothing probably fazed him. I hoped the jury didn't think he was unbelievable, though, because of his demeanor.

I nodded my head. "And what happened next?"

Eli shrugged. "Man, he did some kind of hypnosis shit on me." He put his hand over his mouth and looked over at the judge. "Oops, sorry. Didn't mean to say that." Then he turned to me. "He did some hypnosis spell on me, and, next thing I know, I'm in the squad car." He shook his head. "That was some trifling nonsense right there, man."

Hypnosis! That was what happened! I wondered if Raymond was trained for that. I really should've looked into his background better. I'd have to ask him about that.

I was also happy that Eli relayed that he woke up in the squad car. I knew he didn't; Jack woke up in the squad car. But Eli put that in there to make the whole thing more believable.

Good going, Eli!

I didn't want to go further. I didn't know how much Eli knew about what came next, and I didn't want him to testify about things he didn't know about. Vince could exploit that for sure.

"I have nothing further," I said.

"Mr. Malloy," Judge Greene said. "Your witness."

Vince looked annoyed and I knew why. I basically had sprung an 11th hour witness on him. He wasn't prepared to cross Eli. He was prepared to cross Mick, who Vince knew had no knowledge of the killing. But Eli was somebody new and his testimony apparently put Vince off balance.

"Um," Vince said, looking at his notes. "How did you find out this mystery man, who came into the rectory, was Father Mathews' brother Raymond?"

Eli thought on his feet. "My lawyer showed me a picture of Raymond Mathews, after I told her what happened. I said 'that's him. That's him. Looks just like Father Mathews.'"

"Have you ever seen him before this happened?"

"Nah. I mean, I kinda knew Father Mathews. I'd seen him around, but he never knew me. I just saw him around, you know. But that new dude, that dude that came in like that and started with that crazy talk, looked just like Father Mathews."

"And this Raymond Mathews hypnotized you? That's your testimony?"

"Yeah. After he just stuck that hunting knife into poor Father Kennedy like that, well, I wasn't ready to see something like that. I just looked at him and wanted to tackle him. I'm figuring I'm next, you know. But he put his hands on my shoulders and started to talk to me about becoming somebody else and forgetting what had happened to Father Kennedy, and, I don't know, I guess it worked because the next thing I know, I'm being taken downtown in the back of a cop car."

Vince shook his head. I knew he was off-balance and I felt sorry for him. He usually did a decent job of cross-examining, but, today, with Jack, it was like he didn't quite know what to say.

"I have nothing further." He shot me a look like *what the hell just happened?*

I smiled. I had one more witness, besides the expert witness. Raymond.

And it would have to be really, really good.

CHAPTER
THIRTY-NINE

MY HEART POUNDED and my hands were shaking as I asked Eli to step down from the witness stand. I was so nervous because I knew Raymond Matthews was next. I had no idea what he would say. I couldn't know, as I'd treat him as hostile and had to have the element of surprise, so I didn't depose him.

Never ask a question you don't know the answer to. That was Rule 101 for trial attorneys. When you ask a question you don't know the answer to, AND you're not certain the witness will answer the way you want, things go sideways and upside down. Suddenly, you find yourself behind the eight-ball.

In this case, I was certain Raymond Mathews killed Father Kennedy. I was certain he'd never admit to it. I wanted see how he reacted to my questions. The jury needed to hear his tone of voice and see his body language. That was key – if he lied, unless he's a pathological liar or a sociopath, he would give tell-tale signs of not being truthful. Hopefully, the jury could pick up these cues.

I felt a bit more comfortable with this case, though, because Eli came out and told the truth. At least, I thought it might be Eli. I still didn't know. I'd have to ask him after this trial was finished.

"Ms. Ross," Judge Greene said. "Call your next witness."

I nodded. "The defense calls Raymond Mathews." My plan was to ask him questions, and then, if he proceeded to lie, treat him as hostile. If I treated him as hostile, I could ask leading questions and could impeach him if need be.

At that, the bailiff went out into the hallway, where Raymond Mathews was sitting. He had no preparation for what I would ask him. He probably had no clue why I called him. He couldn't possibly know Jack had finally accessed the alter who had seen everything. I didn't know how Raymond knew Jack had different personalities. I imagined Father Mathews also told Raymond that Father Kennedy knew about Robert Heaney and failed to do anything about it. It was good to know he used a hypnosis technique to make Jack lose consciousness and forget about everything. He *thought* he was clever.

He was wrong.

His plan, in the end, was probably that he relied upon me pleading Jack NGRI, or, barring that, showing Jack was crazy, so he couldn't be a reliable witness against him. Raymond knew Jack was clinically insane and would use that as his defense. *Don't rely on a word he says. That guy is crazy.*

He couldn't have imagined I'd be one step ahead of his thinking. An ordinary attorney *would* have had Jack evaluated, and probably *would* have tried for a NGRI plea, after looking into Jack's background and discovering he had DID. Raymond was counting on an ordinary attorney trying this case.

He wasn't counting on me.

I was crazier than he was.

Raymond finally made it to the stand.

"Please raise your right hand," the bailiff ordered.

Raymond raised his right hand.

"Do you swear to tell the truth, the whole truth, and nothing but the truth, so help you God?" the bailiff asked.

"I do."

The bailiff took his seat, and I strode purposely over to the witness stand and stood right in front of Raymond. I didn't say anything at first, but just stared at him for a full minute. I stared right into those brown eyes and didn't look away.

And then I turned my back, walked over to my table, where Eli was sitting and staring right at Raymond as well. I looked at Eli's eyes and I saw him giving Raymond the death glare.

No doubt about it. Raymond knew we knew. We were psyching him out, or, at least, that was my purpose.

It was quiet in the courtroom, so quiet you could hear a pin drop. I looked at the jury and every member of that jury had their eyes fixated on Raymond. They heard what Eli just said. They knew Eli's testimony. Now they were waiting to see what Raymond would say or do.

I smiled. I was happy the jury was paying so close attention to Raymond. That way, when he lied, they could pick up on it.

I finally spoke. "Could you please state your name for the record?"

"Raymond James Mathews."

"Mr. Mathews, are you the brother of Father Mathews?"

"Yes. He is my brother."

"Do you know why I called you to testify in court today?"

He shook his head. "No. I don't know why I was called to testify. I don't know what I have to do with this case except that my brother was the Associate Pastor serving Father Kennedy. That is the only reason why I believe I was called to testify today."

I got right to it. "Did you once have an identical twin brother by the name of Ryan?"

Raymond shifted uncomfortable in his seat and loosened his collar and tie. "Yes," he said softly.

"What happened to your little brother?"

"He was murdered 50 years ago." He looked down at the witness stand. "Abducted and murdered."

I took a deep breath and pressed on. "Who abducted and murdered him?"

"A guy by the name of Steven Heaney."

"Steven Heaney." I looked over at the stands, where Steven was sitting. However, Raymond appeared not to recognize him. That didn't surprise me – Steven was an old man, and, unlike Jack, Raymond didn't spend a lot of time with him.

"Yes, Steven Heaney. Why is this important?"

I ignored that question and went on. "Were you angry with Father

Kennedy for any reason?" I wanted him to lie and say no to this question, so I could treat him as hostile.

"No."

"Permission to treat the witness as hostile," I said to the judge.

Judge Greene nodded. "Proceed, counselor."

"Mr. Mathews, isn't it true Father Kennedy was Steven Heaney's spiritual counselor?"

Raymond looked bewildered and knew he'd have to answer that question truthfully. Yet, he didn't. "I don't know."

"Isn't it true Father Kennedy heard the confessions of Steven Heaney, and he therefore knew Steven was killing children, yet he did nothing to stop it?"

Raymond got quiet and crossed his arms in front of him. "You'll have to ask him," he said defiantly.

"He's not here to ask. That's why I'm asking you." I paused. "Now, isn't it true that you were recently made aware that Father Kennedy, back in 1972, knew Steven Heaney was killing children and did nothing about it?"

Raymond looked away. "That's a goddamned horrible law," he said. "If a priest knows killing is going on he should go to the authorities. If Father Kennedy had gone to the authorities when he first found out about Steven Heaney, my twin brother would be alive today." He crossed his arms again and glared at me.

"Is it fair to say you were angry with Father Kennedy for not going to the authorities when he first found out about Steven Heaney?"

"Listen, Father Kennedy knew about Steven Heaney right from the start. From the start. Steven Heaney confessed everything to him, and he confessed everything to him from the first murder. Steven Heaney kept abducting children and kept murdering them, and, every time he did that, he told Father Kennedy about it." Raymond shook his head. "That was on his head. On his head. All those murdered kids were on his head. Every last one of them. If he would've called the police the first time Steven Heaney told him he abducted and killed a kid, there would be at least 34 kids who wouldn't have suffered and wouldn't have been murdered. Thirty-four families wouldn't have been torn apart."

He shook his head, tears in his eyes. "When I think about how Ryan suffered at the hands of that monster...how my father just up and left our family, leaving our mother to handle everything on her own...how my brother went to prison for manslaughter because he was so messed up by Ryan's death and our family disintegrating that he turned to drugs..." He crossed his arms again. "And Father Kennedy could've stopped that. He could've stopped that. He could've ended it right away."

He looked away and I had sympathy for him. I could see his point of view – confessionals are strictly confidential, and breaking confidentiality would result in ex-communication for the priest who breaks it. If not for that, Father Kennedy could've gone to the police and turned Steven in.

But Father Kennedy *couldn't* have gone to the authorities. Confessional privilege was that inviolate. That was difficult for most people to understand, and, in this case, it had tragic, tragic consequences.

I decided to back off just a bit. I didn't want to have the jury see me hammering away at a clearly broken man.

I didn't know how Raymond found out about Father Kennedy – I could only assume Father Mathews told him about it, probably recently. Father Mathews wasn't supposed to divulge this information, either. He'd risk ex-communication for telling his brother about this.

Not that I would go to the church authorities and reveal to them what had happened. Better leave well enough alone there.

"Mr. Mathews," I said softly. I leaned down on the railing in front of him and looked him in the eye. "Isn't it true you were very angry with Father Kennedy?"

"Yes," he said, biting his lower lip. "But I didn't kill him. I would never do that."

I stood up and walked over to the jury and looked at them. They were looking at Raymond with a mixture of skepticism and sympathy. I hoped the skepticism would win out in the jury room.

I walked back over to Raymond. "Isn't it true you were also made aware that my client, Jack Calhoun, was also involved in the murder of your twin brother?"

Raymond shifted uncomfortably and looked away.

"Yes," he said, and then glared at Jack. "I found out about that."

"Isn't it true you were very angry at my client, too?"

"Listen, your client is legally insane. Legally insane. I don't even know how this case has gotten this far." He crossed his arms in front of him and glared at Mick. "My brother knew him as Mick. But that day, that day…" He shook his head. "I met him one day at this basketball game and he said his name was Sam. But I knew the truth about him, because I had him investigated. I knew he was really Jack Calhoun. Ever since my brother was murdered, I needed to know who Jack Calhoun was, and I found out. So, yeah, my brother knew him as Mick, I met him one day and he said his name was Sam, but I really knew he was Jack - the guy who responsible for my brother being killed." He shook his head. "He's going by three different names. He's nuttier than a damned fruitcake."

That cleared up the mystery on how Mick found himself at that basketball game - Sam went there and ran into Raymond. Apparently Sam was also attracted to Father Mathews. Mick came out later at that game, apparently after Raymond had left to coach the game.

I got my answer to a nagging mystery. Nevertheless, that answer was non-responsive. "That didn't answer my question," I said. "Isn't it true you were angry with my client?"

He crossed his arms again and looked away. "What kind of a person would do what he did? He was a kid and started playing kick-ball with my brother and some other kids. And then he told my brother he wanted to take him to see the ice cream man, but it wasn't the ice cream man, it was Steven Heaney. What kind of a person would do something like that? I don't care if he was a kid at the time. That's seriously messed up, and my brother would be alive today if it weren't for your client."

I wanted to know something else. I wanted to know *how* he knew about Jack's multiple personalities. He met all of them? He met Eli in the rectory, but how did he meet the others?

I looked back at Jack and saw a change in him. I closed my eyes, wondering who'd taken over. I smiled, though, when I saw the familiar bored expression, the one leg crossed femininely over the other and saw him pick his glasses up off the table and put them on. When he doodled with his left hand, I knew.

Mick was back.

I bit my lower lip. "Isn't it true that, on the afternoon of April 19, you went into Father Kennedy's rectory, where you knew my client was speaking with Father Kennedy, and you stabbed Father Kennedy in the heart, and then hypnotized my client so he'd lose consciousness and wouldn't remember anything?"

Raymond screwed up his face. "No."

I pressed on. "Isn't it true you knew my client has severe mental illness, therefore you assumed you could get away with framing him for the murder of Father Kennedy? After all, nobody would believe my client's story because he's insane, right?"

He furrowed his brow and crossed his arms in front of him. "No," he said, looking me right in the eye. "I wouldn't take advantage of a disabled person like that. That's not my nature."

I looked over at the jury, saw their faces and saw the doubt that had crept up on every single one of their expressions. I did my job. I put doubt into their heads.

Hopefully it was reasonable doubt.

I then asked an unusual question. He probably wondered why I'd ask it, but I had my reasons. "I notice your forearms do not have hair on them. Is that a genetic trait?"

He furrowed his brows. His expression said *what the hell?* He shook his head. "Yes, that is. My grandfather was from the Philippines and we inherited our hairless arms from him."

"I have nothing further."

I sat down and Mick smiled at me. "I'm back, doll," he whispered. "Eli had to get out. Something about seeing Steven Heaney in the audience." He then looked over at the on-lookers, saw Steven and waved. "Oh, yes, there he is." He waved again. "Why didn't you tell me he was back in town?"

"I'll tell you later," I whispered.

"Mr. Malloy, do you have any questions for this witness?"

"No, your honor," Vince said, standing up.

He probably figured the damage was done. Which it was.

"Ms. Ross, call your next witness."

"Your honor, the defense rests." I was going to call an expert on amnesia, but decided against it. I didn't need it, and the expert could've backfired anyhow.

"Very well then." The judge then addressed Vince.

"Mr. Malloy, do you have any rebuttal evidence for the jury?"

"No, your honor."

Judge Greene nodded. "We will take a short recess of 15 minutes, after which Ms. Ross and Mr. Malloy shall present the jury with their closing arguments." He banged the gavel and then stood up and went back into his chambers.

The jury filed out of the courtroom and I sat down next to Mick. "So, you're back," I said. "How did you come back so soon?"

He shrugged. "I decided to let Eli out for a limited time," he said. "So you could get your testimony on the stand. I didn't want Jack to go to prison, doll."

"I don't understand. Why now? Why didn't you do this a long time ago?"

"Because, well..." He shook his head. "Actually, I lied. Eli came out when Steven showed up. That brought him out. I..." He shook his head. "I became weak when I saw him. Something happened. I just wasn't ready to see him again. I guess I went into shock, doll, and that was enough for Eli to come on out. He's been dying to tell his story."

"And how did you get back so quickly?"

He shrugged. "Eli felt his purpose was finished. He told his story and that was that. At any rate, I took over again. I'm here now." He whispered. "But if this jury comes back with a not guilty verdict, I have a feeling you'll get Jack back. He's here. He doesn't know what's going on, but I might just step aside and let him live his life if the jury comes back with an acquittal."

I looked over at Vince, who was staring at his files and shaking his head. I wondered what went through his head. Did he believe Eli's story? Did he see how Raymond reacted to my questions and started to believe it then? Or was he simply off his game?

I might never know.

CHAPTER
FORTY

THE JUDGE SHOWED BACK UP in 15 minutes as did the jury. They filed back into their seats, one by one. When they all were seated, the judge addressed Vince and me.

"Mr. Malloy, please present your closing argument," he said.

"Thank you, your honor," Vince said.

He walked over to the jury. "Ladies and gentlemen of the jury," he began. "Father Kennedy was brutally murdered on April 19 of this year by the man sitting in front of you." He pointed at Jack. "Mr. Jack Calhoun. The evidence is overwhelmingly incontrovertible. He was found at the scene of the murder with his hand on the murder weapon, a hunting knife. His fingerprints, and only his fingerprints, was on the murder weapon. His hair, and only his hair, with the exception of the hair of Father Kennedy, was found in the rectory. You heard evidence that Mr. Calhoun was stalking Father Kennedy."

I stood up. "I object to that characterization. That assumes facts not in evidence."

"Sustained," Judge Greene said. "Be careful, Mr. Malloy."

Vince nodded and pressed on. "You heard evidence that Mr. Calhoun was seeing Father Kennedy every single day. You can draw your own conclusions about that. In short, ladies and gentlemen, this case is open and shut. You have the crime scene, you have the victim at the crime scene and you have the defendant sitting there holding the murder weapon. What more do you need? That wild story about Raymond Mathews killing Father Kennedy is nothing but a tall tale. A red herring. Don't fall for that, ladies and gentlemen. Mr. Jack Calhoun is guilty of murder in the first degree, and, for that, I ask you to find him guilty of this crime. Thank you."

He sat down and I stood up. "Ladies and gentlemen," I said. "I admit, it looks bad for my client. He was at the murder scene with the murder weapon in his hand and the body of the victim at his feet. Yes, that looks bad. But don't you think it all looks too perfect? Like somebody staged it? Who would do something like that? Go in there, kill Father Kennedy and pass out? And why didn't that knife fall out of his hand if he went unconscious after the murder? Does that make any sense to you?" I shook my head. "It doesn't make sense to me, either. It doesn't make sense at all. There are just too many holes in this story, holes big enough to drive a truck through."

I paced from one end of the jury box to the other, looking every juror in the eye. "Holes big enough to drive a truck through. Enter Raymond Mathews. You heard he was angry Father Kennedy was aware that Steven Heaney was murdering children. Yet Father Kennedy did nothing about that. He couldn't do anything about that, because he was a priest and priests are bound by their oath not to divulge anything said in confession. You heard Raymond Mathews blamed Father Kennedy for the death of his identical twin brother. You heard he was also angry at Mr. Calhoun because Mr. Calhoun, when he was a young boy he found young victims for Mr. Heaney. Raymond Mathews blamed Father Kennedy for the death of his twin brother, but he also blamed Mr. Calhoun. You heard that testimony."

"Finally, you heard the testimony of Mr. Calhoun himself. You heard him state he was in the rectory with Father Kennedy, speaking with him about an issue, when Raymond Mathews came through the door unexpectedly. You heard him testify that Raymond Mathews stabbed Father Kennedy in the heart while he watched. Raymond Mathews wore latex gloves, which was why his fingerprints didn't show on the murder weapon. He's bald and has no body hair, which is why his hair wasn't found at the murder site. You heard him testify that Raymond Mathews then hypnotized him and that was why Mr. Calhoun lost consciousness."

I decided to use Jack's background to make him sympathetic. "Raymond Mathews also alluded to what Jack did when he was a small child – he helped the serial killer, Steven Heaney, find victims. He did that. He was 11 years old and was abducted by a monster. He had one thought, one prayer – to stay alive. He had the instinct of self-preservation. Raymond Mathews doesn't understand that. He testified that he was angry with my client. His anger is understandable, of course. Any one of us might feel the same as Raymond did in this case – rage and anger at the two people who were partially responsible for our loved ones being murdered. Any one of us might let that rage and anger overtake us, consume us, and cause us to murder the source of our rage and anger. In this way, Raymond Mathews alleged action in killing Father Kennedy and framing my client seem almost understandable."

I continued on. "Nevertheless, my client's testimony, coupled with Raymond Mathews' testimony, adds up to one thing – reasonable doubt that my client had anything to do with Father Kennedy's murder. You might not completely believe my client's testimony. You might not completely believe that Raymond Mathews was responsible for the murder of Father Kennedy. But under the law, you don't have to completely believe my client's testimony. You don't have to completely believe that Raymond Mathews was responsible for the murder of Father Kennedy. That's not required."

I paced back and forth, looking every juror in the eye. "No, you don't have to believe my client 100% in order to acquit. You simply need to have reasonable doubt my client did it. Reasonable doubt – consider it like this. If you are 60% sure my client is telling the truth, that's reasonable doubt. If you're thinking in your mind 'Mr. Calhoun might have done it, but, then again, he might not have.' That's reasonable doubt."

I walked back to my table and put my hands on Jack's shoulders. "My client's testimony was partially corroborated by Raymond Mathews' testimony – Mr. Mathews, after all, admitted he was extremely angry with Father Kennedy and my client. When you combine what you heard from my client, combined with what you heard from Raymond Mathews...that adds up to reasonable doubt."

I walked back to the jury box. "I ask you to acquit my client. I ask for a verdict of not guilty. The evidence in this case demands such a verdict."

"Thank you very much for your thoughtful deliberation on this matter. Thank you very much for your service. And thank you in advance for finding my client not guilty."

I sat down and Mick held out his hand. "You did good," he said. "I think we might have this."

"We'll see."

Judge Greene gave the jury instructions about what they must find in order to find Jack guilty and then he excused them to deliberate.

After the jury left the jury box to go back and deliberate, I breathed a sigh of relief. I was relieved because the trial was over. I was nervous, though. I had no idea what the verdict would be. But it was liberating to leave nothing on the field. Come what may I'd know I did all I could to have Jack acquitted.

I just hoped it would be enough.

Three hours later, the jury foreman came back and said they'd reached a verdict.

My heart pounded. I didn't think the verdict would come in so soon. I had no idea what that meant – I never knew what a short deliberation meant.

I prayed this was good news.

The jury filed back into their seats.

"I understand you've reached a verdict," Judge Greene said.

"We have your honor."

"And your verdict is unanimous?"

"Yes, your honor."

Judge Greene nodded. "Will the defendant please rise."

I stood up with Jack and held his hand tightly. This moment, right before the verdict, was always the scariest moment of my life.

"On the count of murder in the first degree, how does the jury find?"

"Not guilty, your honor," the jury foreman said.

"On the count of assault with a deadly weapon, how does the jury find?"

"Not guilty, your honor."

I felt Jack's hand squeeze mine and I bowed my head. I felt breaking down and sobbing in relief. Every bit of emotion, every second of worry, every second of doubt...I felt every emotion so acutely right at that moment that I had to hold it in.

More than anything, I felt a profound sense of relief.

"Thank you ladies and gentlemen for your service," Judge Greene said. "I understand that every one of you have obligations to your work and family, and you have to set these obligations aside to do your civic duty. Without you, we wouldn't have a judicial system. Your service is really at the heart of justice and makes justice possible. You may be excused."

The jury filed back out. I looked over at Mick, and I saw the change. He was blinking his eyes, and he took off his glasses and hung his head. "June Bug," he said softly. "Where am I?"

"In court. The jury just acquitted you."

He smiled. "You did it. You did it."

I gave him a hug, relieved to have Jack back. I hoped and prayed he was back for good. "We did it," I said. "You're free, Uncle Jack. You won't be locked up anywhere."

Jack nodded and we went back to the audience, where my mother was standing up, bawling her eyes out. Mom hugged Jack tightly, both of them crying. Albany was standing by, as was Emma and Brad. They were all waiting to hug Jack, too, but would have to wait awhile, because mom would seemingly never let go.

Mom finally let Jack go, and everybody hugged Jack one by one. Mom hugged me. "I love you," she said. "And I'll never criticize your occupation again."

I smiled. "Oh, I think you will. I think you will. But I love you too, Mom." I looked over at Jack. "He needs serious help," I said. "Jack is back, and, hopefully, he'll stay out, but I don't know, Mom. He needs an expert on DID to help him integrate."

"I found just the person," she said. "In New York. I already spoke with your brother Jason, and Jason said Jack can stay with him while getting treatment. Dr. Lowell is considered the top expert on DID in the nation. I think he can help Jack. I think he can."

I smiled. "Let's hope so. At any rate, Jack is back with us. I think we should savor that."

"We will. We will. In the meantime, let's celebrate! I made reservations at *Piropo's.*"

I was excited about that – *Piropo's* was an Argentinian restaurant in Parkville, a bedroom community up North. The restaurant was situated high on a cliff and was one of the most highly rated and popular restaurants in the city.

I looked forward to that evening. It was time to eat and be with my family without stress.

Everything was right in the world.

Of course, things didn't go smoothly for long. My stress couldn't stay low for too long. I had an amazing time with my family at the restaurant after Jack's trial, and Jack was shortly shipped off to New York to stay with my brother, Jason, and would see the most respected DID specialist in the country. Jason, who was a Goldman Sachs executive and was making the big, big bucks, was footing the bill.

But I came into my office one Monday and found I'd been assigned a death case. Darnell Williams, an African-American underprivileged youth, was accused of killing a cop.

And Steven was arrested by the KCPD for the murders committed by Robert. After Steven emerged from being in the woods, and got back into society, he was once again on the police force's radar. They went back into Robert's house, found Steven's fingerprints in various places in the house and arrested him.

I was expecting that, to be honest. I was heartened that Steven's bond was only $25,000, which told me the arrest was nothing more than a formality. The police force had to cross its t's and dot its i's. Nevertheless, I told him I'd help him, *pro bono,* and I'd do that.

But the upshot was that I'd be working, simultaneously, two murder cases.

My life was about to get crazy again.

The story continues with *Injustice for All,* available now!

For information about upcoming titles in the *Harper Ross Legal Thriller* series, sign up for my mailing list! You'll be the first to know about new releases and you'll be the first to know about any promotions!!!! http://eepurl.com/hBqhtr

Chapter One of *Injustice for All*

Darnell Williams was a quiet child. A studious child. He was one of six children living in a two-bedroom apartment in a run-down house East of Troost. At age 18, he was the oldest child. He was presently working two part-time jobs, in addition to going to school full-time, because he had to save money for college and for his math tutor. Anything he earned, over and above his savings goals and tutor money, went to his mother, Anita, who worked two jobs herself – one job was full-time as a hospital orderly and the other was part-time working as a housekeeper for a local motel. The motel where she worked sometimes charged by the hour and made a Motel 6 look like the Hilton. She never complained, though, and she never took a dollar from the government. Darnell sometimes wished that she would – it would take some of the burden off of him.

That night, that fateful night, he was working one of his jobs. He was a fry cook at a Church's Chicken, and he was assigned clean-up duty. Basically, he was tasked with closing the place, which meant that he had to stay after everybody else had already gone home. He didn't really mind it that much – it gave him some rare alone time. Every other minute of his life was filled with people – he shared a bedroom with his four brothers and sisters, so he never got a moment's peace at his place. The rest of the time, he was at school and his two jobs. He never got the chance just to sit in the quiet and hear himself think, so he really enjoyed those nights when he was assigned final clean-up.

"Darnell, now, you know the drill," his night manager, Sally Monroe said to him. She trusted him, more than she trusted any of his co-workers, because Sally knew that Darnell would never take an extra dollar from the cash register. She couldn't necessarily say the same about the other kids who worked there. Not that she blamed any of them for wanting to take an extra dollar here or there - she knew these kids' situations. The best that she could do for any of them was to allow them to take home the chicken that was made but not bought – at least that way she knew that these kids would have something to eat at home. She wanted to give them all a pay raise, but that wasn't her call. "Make sure the floor is mopped, clean the bathrooms spotless, take out the trash, clean out the fryer and make sure all the food is put away."

Sally had, in a leather blue pouch, the day's earnings from the cash register. She was the one who made sure this money found its way to the bank every night. She wanted to have Darnell do the drop some-times, but she knew that he rode the bus to the restaurant every day, so that would never do. He might get rolled on the bus and then where would she be?

"I know, Ms. Monroe," Darnell said to her. She always asked him to call her "Sally," but he never would. His mama always instructed him to treat his elders with respect. Sally was at least 27 years old, so that made her his elder. He always addressed her as "Ms. Monroe" and "ma'am." No matter how many times Sally chided him, telling him that "Ms. Monroe isn't my name. That's my mama's name. My name is Sally," Darnell persisted in calling her "Ms. Monroe." His own mama drilled that kind of respect into him.

Sally nodded and smiled. She was a chubby woman, with big blonde hair and too much eye shadow. She probably ate too much fried chicken from Church's, as that was her favorite thing to eat. Darnell liked that she was chubby, because she reminded him of his own mama. His mama was only 33 years old herself, giving birth to Darnell when she was only 15 years old and a sophomore in high school. In her high school, this wasn't exactly an unusual occurrence. A lot of girls in her class were having babies at the same time.

Even so, his mama always told him that he wouldn't be having babies in his teenage years. She dragged him, when he was only 13 years old, to the local birth control clinic and had the doctor there show him all about condoms and how to use them. He stilled cringed with embarrassment when he thought about all the times that his mama gave him a condom and had him slip it on a banana while she watched.

No matter, Darnell had no use for condoms yet. He was way too busy with his two jobs and his schoolwork to even notice girls. His math tutor was a girl, a pretty girl named Chantal, who wasn't much older than him. But he never even really thought about her that way – she was simply somebody who would help him conquer calculus. He had applied to MIT and he was determined that he would go there on a scholarship and go on to study nuclear engineering. That was his dream, anyhow, but he knew that he might have to settle for state university and a degree in electrical engineering. Either way, he knew that he would go on to get a master's degree in some type of engineering. And he was never going to have to share a bedroom again.

Plus, he would take care of his mama, once he got out into the world and started making six figures. He hated that she had to work so many hours just to keep a roof over everybody's head and food on the table. He wanted her to, someday, be able to relax once in awhile. As far as he knew, she had never, ever, had a vacation. She never even had the chance to go and get a massage or get her nails done or any of that. Every penny that she earned was put into groceries, utilities and rent.

All he wanted was for her to be able to slow down. Maybe only have one job, and maybe find a job where she had a paid vacation once a year. Maybe Darnell might be able to give her enough money so that she could actually do something on that paid vacation – maybe something simple, like take a trip to *The Elms*, which was a tiny resort just north of town. He had seen the website and this looked like just the place for his mama – it offered a full spa and a hot tub and pool and indoor baths that promised a relaxation haven.

Maybe he might even be able to send her to Vegas once in awhile.

Not that his mama gambled, but he often caught her watching Cirque de Soleil on television, and he had never seen her face light up so much as when she was watching one of those shows. She also spent her time watching house remodeling shows, and other shows that featured gorgeous high-dollar houses that were for the taking. One such show featured a couple who would look at three different houses and had to pick just one. His mama got mad sometimes that those people on the shows found such faults in such beautiful surroundings – house number one isn't good enough because it doesn't have a pool, and house number three only has four bedrooms, not five, and where are the granite countertops?

"Lordy, Darnell," mama would say while she watched a couple pick apart a seaside mansion that was situated high on a cliff. "Could you imagine if they came and saw this place?" She would shake her head. "They'd run screaming from the room, that's what they would do." Then she would chuckle and speak under her breath.

Darnell always knew that most people in the world had it better than he did. Better than his family. But not anybody he knew. Everyone he knew was in the same boat, some even worse – Darnell always had a lunch to bring to school and his mama always took him clothes shopping before the school year began. Sometimes they went shopping at Goodwill, but, on occasion, his mama could afford to take him clothes shopping at Wal-Mart. A lot of his friends didn't have a mama like his. Some had mamas who were strung out on drugs or were into prostitution. Others had mamas who beat them. Hardly any of his friends had a baby daddy hanging around – most of them had gone to prison or were absent and on the streets.

That was the case with Darnell's mama. He never knew his baby daddy. He wasn't ever around, not even when Darnell was a baby. But that didn't really matter to him – his friends were much the same, so nobody ever felt that they were missing out.

He took his iPhone out, put it on Apple Music, and blasted Drake in his headphones. While he listened to the music, he carefully mopped the floor, taking his time. He enjoyed getting the floor squeaky clean. There was something about seeing a grimy, greasy, oily floor go from being almost black to being sparkling white that fascinated him. He always took his time closing up. Sally had explained that he had to have his work done in one hour, because her general manager would never let him work past that, but Darnell usually took two hours cleaning up. He clocked out after an hour, and then spent another hour, all on his own time, making sure that all the crevices were clean. He would dust and scrub and get lost in knowing that he was doing the best job that he could do.

It was all worth it when Sally would come in the next day, or Chloe, who was the morning manager, and they would marvel about how spotless the restaurant was. Not that he cared about getting gold stars and pats on the back or any of that, but he did like it when they noticed that he did a good job. Anybody would, even though too much praise sometimes embarrassed him.

And, truth be told, he was never in a hurry to get home. He reveled in knowing that he was the only person around. He liked that this restaurant, at this time, was his little bit of space in the world. He never had much control around his own house – with six people living there, it was tough to keep up with the dishes in the sink and the spills on the carpet. There was always spoiled milk on the couch, or bits of cereal ground into the rug. One time, his little sister, Alisha, ate a runny egg on the floor, in front of the TV, and that egg yolk hardened into that spot. The place didn't have a dishwasher, and it didn't even have a dining room. Everybody ate on TV trays or on the floor, and there was simply no keeping up with any of it. There also wasn't a washer and dryer in the apartment, nor was there one in the building, so clothes were constantly piling up in both of the bedrooms. Darnell long since forgot what his bedroom's carpet looked like, as it was always covered with clothes, shoes, books and toys.

But, here at the restaurant, he could make the place look just how he wanted it. He could make sure that everything was put back in its place, that there wasn't a crumb of food anywhere and that the floor was so clean that he could eat off of it. There wasn't the chaos in this restaurant, the chaos that he constantly experienced in his home.

He took off his head phones, gathered up the trash and opened the door into the alleyway.

Humming a tune that was in occupying his headspace, he threw the trash into the bin and turned around.

And stopped.

At his feet was a body.

And a gun was right next to it.

Pick up _Injustice for All_ right now - only $4.99!

ALSO BY RACHEL SINCLAIR

For information about upcoming titles in the *Harper Ross Legal Thriller*
series, sign up for my mailing list! You'll be the first to know about new
releases and you'll be the first to know about any promotions!!!! http://eepurl.
com/hBqhtr

Johnson County Legal Thrillers (Kansas City, Missouri)

Bad Faith

Justice Denied

Hidden Defendant

Injustice for All

LA Defense

The Associate

The Alibi

Reasonable Doubt

The Accused

Secrets and Lies

Until Proven Guilty

Emerson Justice Legal Thrillers (Los Angeles)

Dark Justice

Blind Justice

Southern California Legal Thrillers (San Diego)

Presumption of Guilt

Justice Delayed

By Reason of Insanity

Wrongful Conviction

The Trial

Milton Keynes UK
Ingram Content Group UK Ltd.
UKHW010242221123
432980UK00002B/206